WHAT I'M DOING is walking past tables of strangers, climbing up the steps, and accepting the mic from a very surprised Larry.

Larry is gone before I can reconsider, and I am standing onstage.

It smells like old beer, industrial cleaning solution, and my own animal panic.

It looks like an endless haze of red light and the vague outline of human-shaped shadows just beyond the hot, bright glare.

It sounds like silence.

Not my own silence, though I haven't said anything yet. Their silence. The waiting, watching quiet of strangers who don't know what to expect from me, because—

I realize it then, with equal terror and boundless relief: they don't know me.

I'm not their classmate, or girlfriend, or sister, or daughter.

I'm not Isabel, who is so chill, so easy, the calm in the storm.

I'm not anyone to them. So I can be anything I want.

ALSO BY KATIE HENRY

Heretics Anonymous
Let's Call It a Doomsday
Gideon Green in Black and White

THIS
WILL
BE
FUNNY
SOMEDAY

KATIE HENRY

KATHERINE TEGEN BOOKS
An Imprint of HarperCollinsPublishers

Katherine Tegen Books is an imprint of HarperCollins Publishers.

ISBN 978-0-06-295571-5

Typography by David Curtis
22 23 24 25 26   SB   10 9 8 7 6 5 4 3 2 1
❖
First paperback edition, 2022

For Rob, who makes me laugh so much,

all the time, and every day

CHAPTER 1

HIGH SCHOOL MIGHT be a total joke, but that doesn't mean every-thing is.

Some stuff just isn't funny. Like plane crashes. Or the Black Death. Or William Shakespeare's *Hamlet*—not that Jack Brawer, varsity lacrosse captain and officially the world's worst scene partner, isn't doing his best to turn it into a comedy routine.

"'My lord,'" I say, staring down at my script so I don't have to look at Jack. "'I have remembrances of yours, that I have longed long to re-deliver; I pray you, now receive them.'"

I reach into my cardigan pocket for the—oh, *shit*. The prop letters are still on my desk. I mime handing something toward him, still not looking up, just willing him to *do the damn scene, Hamlet.*

"Wait, whaaaaaat?" Jack says, high-pitched and mock-surprised. I close my eyes. "I didn't give you shit, Ophelia. Have you been getting into the meth again?"

Laughter, then Ms. Waldman's voice: "Jack, that's not the line."

"You're always telling us about the intent, that's the *intent* of the line."

"William Shakespeare did not intend to say anything about meth."

"It's a modern twist."

"'My honor'd lord, you know right well you did,'" I say, louder than both of them, because it's bad enough being up here in front of everyone, it's bad enough Jack is messing up the scene on purpose. "'And, with them, words of so sweet breath composed—'"

Jack snatches the script out of my hands.

I think: *How can a person be this big of a dick?*

I think: *Alas, poor Jack. I knew him well, Horatio, until I had him assassinated for pulling this shit.*

I say: Nothing.

But I do grab it back.

"So are you honest?" Jack asks, vaguely close to his real line this time. "And by 'honest,' Hamlet means, 'Are you a total whore?'"

More laughter, mostly from the corner of the room where Jack's friends sit, their arms sprawled over the backs of their chairs, their pelvises spread so wide it looks like they're about ready to give birth.

I don't understand why Ms. Waldman makes us do these

scenes. The class is called Shakespeare Seminar, not Shakespeare Performance. If I'd known I'd have to talk this much, I would have just taken American Lit with all the other juniors, instead of petitioning my way into a senior class.

More importantly, I don't understand why Jack couldn't have warned me he was going to do this, the half-dozen times we practiced the scene in the hallway. At least then I'd have been prepared, at least I'd be in on the joke—

And then I do understand. I *am* the joke.

"Jack, if you can't respect Isabel as your scene partner, you're going to fail this assignment," Ms. Waldman warns. That's an empty threat. Jack doesn't care about failing this assignment. He's already been accepted to Cornell, early decision, a legacy kid. Come September, he'll be hundreds of miles from here, probably being hazed by his equally terrible frat brothers. The thought comforts me.

I make the executive decision to skip ahead in the scene. "'Could beauty, my lord, have better commerce than with honesty?'"

Jack makes the executive decision to go straight for the kill. "Get thee to a nunnery! And by 'nunnery,' I mean brothel or something, even though they aren't the same thing at all. Except I guess in porn."

"Okay, you're done." Ms. Waldman waves her hand.

"Remember that for the final, everybody, Shakespeare was into nun porn."

Ms. Waldman gets up from her seat in the back, heels scraping against the floor. Jack nudges me. "What about you? You into that?"

I think: *Well, I'm* not *into ruining someone's day for fun.*

I think: *I'm* not *into so obviously peaking in high school. How about you?*

I say: Nothing.

But I feel my face burn.

"Oh, she's blushing!" Jack says. "Confirmed, Shakespeare *and* Isabel—"

"That's *enough.*" Ms. Waldman gets in between us just as the bell rings. She and Jack immediately start talking over each other. Jack with words like "just a joke" and "lighten up" and her with words like "unacceptable," "ridiculous," and "textually unsupported."

Ducking out of both their conversation and their space, I hurry to my desk in the second-to-last row. Jack and Ms. Waldman have moved on to arguing over whether the behavior referral she's giving him is "fair." I think "fair" would be letting me follow him around his next lacrosse game screaming out-of-context Shakespeare quotes, but no one's asking me.

Jack leaves in a cloud of Axe body spray and unjustified ego, but before I can escape out the door, too, Ms. Waldman's voice jerks me back.

"Isabel, hold on a second, okay?"

I stop, reluctantly. She returns the referral pad back to her desk drawer and motions me over. I go, even more reluctantly. She's the kind of teacher who starts the school year by making a big deal about how she's "always around" if anyone "ever needs to talk." The kind of person who thinks you should automatically trust her because she's young, and wears blouses with cats on them, and rolls her eyes at the school song.

"I'm really sorry that happened," she says.

I shrug. Smile.

"I just want you to know, it's not going to affect your grade. I can tell you'd practiced."

Then she waits, expectantly.

"Oh. Um. Thank you," I say.

She waits some more, but I'm out of ideas. She tilts her head. "Are you worried about your grade, at all?"

I shrug again. Smile again.

"You haven't participated in the class discussion at all this week," she says, and it's almost apologetic. As if it's her fault, not mine. "Or last week."

I haven't read the Geneva Code, but if the concept of participation points isn't listed as a war crime, then it's bullshit.

"It's only January," she continues. "There's lots of time to turn it around. Your first essay was fantastic."

"Thank you," I say.

"You know, some people just have a harder time talking in

public. I totally get that." Ms. Waldman leans a bit closer. "But . . . sometimes people are quiet because something's going on. You know?"

Something grips my stomach and twists. "Not really."

"I'm not saying there is," she adds quickly. "But if there were, my door is always—"

"Open," I say, edging my way toward that exact door. "I know."

She sighs. "Just make an effort, please. Say something once a week. Okay?"

I'd rather feed my fingers to a Venus flytrap, I think.

"Okay," I say.

Jack is waiting for me outside. Though I do my best to avoid his eyes and make a break for Alex's physics classroom, Jack plants himself right in my path.

"Hey, about that . . ." He jerks his head back to the classroom. "We're cool, right?"

What does he expect me to say? If we weren't, if I said we weren't, it wouldn't mean *he* wasn't funny. It would mean *I* was a joyless bitch. Either way, he wins, and I lose.

"I didn't know you were going to do that," I say, as if stating the obvious will cause him to spontaneously grow empathy.

Jack runs his hand through his hair. "Yeah, I meant to give you a heads-up, but then I was late, so."

A rock-solid defense. First Cornell, then Yale Law, then

representing oil companies that suffocate baby ducks. It's written in the stars.

"The guys on the team dared me," he says. "So, you know, I had to do it."

I think: *A dare?*

I think: *What are you,* five*?*

I say: Nothing.

He punches me in the arm, softly, but harder than he thinks. Then he grins, toothy and secure. "I knew you'd be chill."

And that's when I do the worst thing. Or maybe the third worst thing, after murder and arson. I smile back.

It can't look like a real smile, I think as Jack turns to go. It doesn't *feel* like a real smile. It feels forced and vaguely sinister, like the antique porcelain doll in my grandmother's parlor. And though I suspect that doll is the veteran of several Satanic rituals, at least she has an excuse. At least she didn't paint that smile on herself.

I slump against the lockers, close my eyes, and resist the urge to brain myself on the cool metal behind me.

"Isabel." Five fingers are curling into my shoulder. "Hey."

When I open my eyes, there's Alex, standing in front of me, looking concerned. He also looks like he just stepped off a photo-shoot for a Ralph Lauren ad, but he always does. I didn't start dating him because his hair is shiny and artfully disheveled and you can see his upper arm muscles under his uniform button-down shirt. I started dating him because he shared new things with me, like all the black-and-white movies he loves, and he remembered the things I loved, too.

It isn't anything like the three-day not-dating I did at sleepaway camp in middle school, where a boy would say he liked you, maybe grab your hand with his clammy fish palm, but then mostly ignore you. Alex asked me to be his girlfriend before the first date was even over. "From now on, it's just you and me." And I thought that was just a line, but whenever we're alone together, that's how it feels. Like there's nothing else in the universe but the two of us.

I'm not going to pretend like the whole Kennedy-cousin look isn't a bonus, though.

"Are you okay?" he asks. "What happened?"

"Nothing." I push myself off the lockers. "I'm fine."

He nods and interlocks his hand in mine. I'm not a huge fan of public displays of affection, not to mention they aren't allowed at school. But even though we've been dating for four months, Alex still always wants to hold my hand in the hallway. Which is sweet. And kind of performative. But still sweet.

"You weren't waiting for me outside physics," Alex says as we walk toward the cafeteria. He's almost pouting, as I'm his mom, late to pick him up from preschool. Though I doubt she's ever picked him up from anything. His parents are a little weird— he has a seventy-year-old dad with the equivalent net worth of a small developing nation, and a fortysomething mom with the personality of a wolverine that only flies first class.

In the end, Alex was raised by a series of nannies, a no-limits credit card, and an internet router with zero parental controls. So I understand why he's clingy sometimes, and I try to be nice about it. Even when he isn't.

"Sorry," I say, squeezing his hand. "Ms. Waldman needed to talk to me."

"God, she's such a bitch," he mutters under his breath, and I prickle, because that's not fair. He wouldn't call her that if he knew she was just trying to help me. But before I can tell him, he's reaching over to smooth down a loose strand of my braid. "I like your hair this way. You should do it that way all the time."

Only if I didn't value my sleep. The chipper vlogger with effortless pastel beach waves might have 130K subscribers, but she's kidding herself to call this look "quick and easy."

"Not all the time," I laugh. "It takes forever."

He frowns. "But I like it."

Alex's phone vibrates in his pocket, and he lets go of my hand to fish it out.

"Something really weird happened in Shakespeare Seminar today," I say, then pause for him to ask what. He doesn't look up from his phone. "Remember how I was telling you I had to do a scene? From *Hamlet*. In front of the class." I wait again.

"Uh-huh," he says, texting someone.

"And my scene partner was Jack Brawer—"

9

"Oh, cool," Alex says.

"Yeah, he's . . . so cool," I say, and my performance as Girl Who Thinks Jack Brawer Is Cool is even worse than my performance as Ophelia. "We'd practiced the scene a bunch, but then when we got up to do it—"

Alex sticks his phone under my nose. "Check out what Kyle sent me."

It's a GIF of a small child being chased by a pack of aggressive-looking geese. One eventually tackles him. "Wow. That is . . . disturbing."

"What?" He sticks his phone in his pocket. "It's funny."

"So anyway, when I got up to do the scene with Jack—"

Alex points at me. "See, *he's* funny."

"Yeah, actually, he—"

Alex cups his hands around his mouth. "Kyle!"

Just outside the cafeteria doors, Kyle and his girlfriend, Chloe, turn around. Alex picks up the pace, and I jog to keep up with him. It's fine. I'll tell him about Shakespeare Seminar later.

As always, we sit at the table closest to the lemonade dispenser, in the same seats, with the same group of Alex's friends. They're all on junior varsity lacrosse, and I've never been able to figure out whether they're all friends because of lacrosse, or they all play lacrosse because they're friends. I think I was supposed to befriend their girlfriends—Margot and Chloe and whoever is on Luke's rotating schedule as he strives to have sex with the entire junior class—but it never quite worked out.

Margot catches my eye across the table. "I—your—"

Four words, or maybe five. Definitely about me. But I can never understand people in places this loud.

"Sorry," I say, leaning closer. "What?"

She repeats it. I mean, I assume she repeats it. I can *hear* she's speaking, but I have no idea what she's saying.

"I, um." I smile, tight, hoping she'll get it. "Sorry."

Her forehead wrinkles, but she tries again, and I try to focus on watching her lips. I can't ask a third time.

There's a tap on my shoulder, and when I turn, Alex is holding out his phone, which is open to the notes section.

She likes your necklace.

"Oh!" I swing back around to Margot. "Thanks, it's new. My mom gave it to me for Christmas."

"It's pretty," she says. I'm 70 percent sure that's what she says, but Chloe nudges her to ask something, and I'm saved.

"Thank you," I whisper to Alex.

"Sure," he says.

Alex isn't the most sensitive person—there are about 618 adjectives I'd pick before that—but he's always been great about my hearing. It's not really my hearing, since my ears are fine. It's the way sound travels from my ears to my brain. I know when people are talking, I can *hear* them speaking, but sometimes—especially if the room is loud, or they mumble, or have a different accent than me—my brain can't process *what* they're saying.

It's annoying for me and probably everyone else, too. Alex never acted like it was.

I start to dig back into my salad, but I have the prickly, unsettling feeling like someone's watching me. I twist around in my seat, looking across the cafeteria, to the corner by the bulletin board. Sure enough, Naomi Weiss is staring back at me. It's so weird—knowing a person so well for almost ten years, and then not at all for the last four months.

Naomi and I became friends in second grade, more out of convenience than real compatibility, at first. She was quiet; I was quiet. She didn't have anyone to partner up with in PE; neither did I. But the longer you stick with someone, the more they become a part of how you see the world, even if you both spend most of your time in easy, uncomplicated silence. We spent hours at her dad's house, Naomi with her herds of pastel ponies, me with legions of plastic dinosaurs. Weekends and winter breaks and hot summer days at my apartment, Naomi on her computer, fixing bugs in her code, me on my bed, thumbing through my dog-eared, broken-spine copy of *Encyclopedia of Plants and Flowers*.

It worked. Until it didn't.

Without even realizing it, I'm standing up from the lunch bench, starting to disentangle from Alex's foot, wrapped around mine.

"Where are you going?" Alex asks, craning his head to follow where I'm looking.

"I—" The truth is, I don't really know. "I was going to get a cookie."

Alex keeps his eyes toward Naomi's table, but puts a hand on my shoulder and gently presses down. "I'll get it. You don't have to get up."

I don't have to sit, either. But I do.

As Alex saunters over to the food line, Margot and Chloe watch him go. They share a look with each other, then turn in unison to me. "He is *so sweet*," Chloe says. Or mouths.

She's right, of course. They can all see it, and if I told them otherwise, they wouldn't believe it. Not that I would, because it *is* true, of course it is. He is sweet.

When I look to Naomi's table again, she's turned back around.

For the rest of lunch, I nibble at the chocolate chip cookie Alex bought me and listen to conversations I can't quite hear. I've got it down to a science, nodding when everyone else does, laughing at the right moments. Maybe it's not a science; maybe it's really an art. Like woodworking. Or taxidermy.

When the rest of them get up to bus their trays, Alex puts his hand around my waist, pulling me close. "Come over to my house for dinner tonight."

There's an itch in my chest, like I can't quite breathe deep enough. "I can't tonight."

"What?" His hand drops to his side. "Why not?"

"It's Charlotte and Peter's last night before they go back to college."

"You'll see them again in, like, March."

"My mom said to come home."

"You don't have to do whatever she says."

I think: *Yeah*.

I think: *Just whatever* you *say*.

I say: Nothing.

"God," Alex huffs. "Fine, I had this whole nice night planned, but whatever. Not like I care."

"I didn't know that. If you'd told me, I could have—"

"It was a surprise, Isabel," he snaps. "Do you know what a 'surprise' is?"

I shrink back. "I'm sorry."

"You don't have to be— That's not what I—" He crosses his arms. "All I wanted was to spend time with you, do something nice for you. And now you think I'm so mean."

His shoulders are still stiff and his arms are crossed, but the only thing on his face is hurt.

"No," I say as a hot wash of shame floods me, because I didn't mean to do that, make him look like that. "I just—"

"I'm sorry," he says, "I'm sorry, I don't want you to—"

"I don't, and everyone's mean sometimes. It's—" I fumble around for something to end this conversation, something to make this less awkward and easier to forget. I laugh a little. "It's like we learned in statistics class, right? Mean is the average, so . . . maybe the average person is mean."

He stares at me blankly.

"You know," I explain, "because the mean and the average are . . ." His expression doesn't change. I clear my throat. "It's a joke. A math joke."

He shakes his head and grabs the rest of the chocolate chip cookie off my lunch tray. "I wish you wouldn't do that."

"Do what?" I ask.

"Try to be funny." Alex breaks the cookie and hands me half. "You aren't good at it."

CHAPTER 2

MY FAMILY IS made up of five people. Two matched pairs of humans, with one remainder. We rarely eat all together, but on nights like tonight, the pairs sit on either side of the kitchen table, across from each other, and I sit at the foot.

"You want to try this one?" Mom asks Dad, holding out a bottle of red wine. "Arthur Sholtz's assistant sent a whole crate to my office, along with this note where he told me I"—she makes air quotes—"'made him believe in God again.' Seriously."

"Because you got him a fantastic plea bargain and no prison time for all but running a Ponzi scheme?" Dad says, dishing out heaps of pasta with red sauce onto plates. "Shouldn't that prove the absence of God?"

Mom considers this. "He didn't say God was fair."

Pair 1: My parents.

My dad is the eleventh generation of Vances in America. His

side of the family has been terrorizing this continent since 1658, stealing land from the rightful occupants, marrying their second cousins like members of some ancient Egyptian dynasty, and giving their children truly awful names including "Enoch," "Jemima," and "Tribulation." My mom is a second-generation American, raised in the backwoods of Pennsylvania by people who deeply valued both the Second Amendment and the Twenty-First Amendment. My parents met in college, married fast, and couldn't be more perfect for each other.

"You set the table backward," Charlotte says accusingly to Peter, rearranging her place setting. "I don't understand how you can do, like, calculus but not this."

Peter rolls his eyes. "If it's all on the table, why does it matter which side I put the fork on?"

"Because we're not animals."

"Exactly! Animals don't use forks!"

Pair 2: The twins.

When my parents brought me home after a month in the NICU, Charlotte and Peter were almost two. Peter was disappointed I couldn't do any tricks, like our grandmother's spaniel. Charlotte was disappointed they'd brought me home at all. In the sixteen years since then, not a ton has changed. Peter mostly pretends I don't exist. Charlotte actively resents me. Charlotte would resent a potted plant, if it took attention away from her.

"We're eating fast, okay?" Mom slides into her seat. "Peter's flight got moved up."

Charlotte reaches for the Parmesan. "Since when do flights get moved *up*?"

"It happens."

"Yeah, but at O'Hare?"

"Charlotte, do I look like a pilot to you?"

"No," Peter says.

"She asked me," Charlotte says.

"Because you're not a dude," Peter says to Mom. "They're mostly dudes."

"God, you are so sexist," Charlotte says.

"That's not sexist," Peter protests. "They *are* mostly dudes. It would be sexist if I thought they're mostly dudes because women can't drive, so they're probably bad at flying, too."

"Ugh, Peter!"

"*If* I thought that, it would be sexist *if* I thought that."

"How did I share a womb with you?" Charlotte mutters.

"Unhappily," Mom says.

"Lots of kicking," Dad adds.

"Isabel was the complete opposite." Mom smiles across the table at me. "You were so still in there, sometimes we worried. But my doctor said, 'There's nothing wrong, you've just got a happy, easy little girl.'"

"And he was right," Dad says. "To a tee."

I can feel Charlotte's death stare.

"How was your day, sweetheart?" Mom asks me. "Do anything fun?"

I'm not sure being publicly humiliated in English class counts as fun, but I want to tell the story anyway. "So in my Shakespeare class, we had to perform these scenes, and—"

"Hold on," Mom interrupts me. "Peter, save some Parmesan for the rest of us."

"It needs more," Peter says, dumping it on his pasta until it looks like the bottom of a cheesy snow globe.

"Well, I haven't had any yet."

I take a breath and try again. "So I had to do the scene with—"

"We have more in the fridge," Dad tells Mom. "In the green bag."

"That's pre-shredded."

"So?"

"So my mother would turn over in her grave."

Peter swallows a mouthful of pasta. "Wasn't she cremated?"

Mom ignores this. "We should all be thanking Isabel for the pasta sauce."

"Why? It's Grandma's recipe," Peter says.

"But Isabel grew the basil." Mom smiles at me, and I smile back.

"She has a basil plant now, too?" Charlotte asks Mom. Not me. I'm basically a plant myself to her. "They're starting to take over the house."

"That's not true—" I start to say. Yeah, I have a lot of plants, but almost all of them are in my room. Charlotte doesn't even have to see them; she just likes complaining. Mom does wish I'd cut them back more. But I like watching them stretch into new corners, unfurl their tendrils. I can almost feel it in my own shoulders and arms. The yearning, the pull, the relief. Like a cat stretching itself in a sunlit spot.

"You can't take them to college," Charlotte says. "They won't let you."

"They might if she majored in horticulture," Dad says, and then he and Mom are debating whether most colleges even *have* that major, and Peter is saying his friend Ethan did a gap year to do urban farming, and Charlotte's cutting in to say that just means Ethan smoked weed for six months, and I'm not saying a thing. No one would notice if I did.

"Isabel's not even in college, what's it matter?" Charlotte says, conveniently forgetting she brought it up.

"And I don't think I'd even major in—" I start to say, but she's faster and louder.

"Vassar's being totally unreasonable about *my* major," Charlotte cuts in. "Something *actually* happening."

She starts telling a long and uninteresting story about how she's planning to get off the waitlist for one of her classes this semester. Every time Mom or Dad or Peter interrupts her or tries to go off topic, she wrenches back focus. Just a little louder than they are, just a little quicker. And every time she does, I hate myself a little more. Why can't I do that? Why can't I be the kind of person everyone listens to?

Why should I have to be a whole different person just to be listened to?

As soon as dinner's over, everyone splits up.

I stay at the kitchen table for a while, picking at a piece of garlic bread and listening to Mom clicking away at the desktop in her office, which is connected to the kitchen. She doesn't seem quite as busy as she's been the last couple days. I get up and stand in the office doorway.

It takes her a minute to notice me. "Hey there."

She turns her attention back to the screen, so I walk into the office and take my traditional spot: perched on the top of her low, sturdy built-in office cabinets. I used to sit here while she worked on evenings and weekends, waiting until she'd spin her chair around, slap her hands on her knees, and say: "Okay. *Now* we can talk."

I wait for a minute, but Mom keeps typing, clicking, typing, clicking.

I think: *I need to talk to you.*

I think: *I really need to talk to you.*

I say: Nothing.

I know she wouldn't be working right now if she didn't have to. But lately, she *always* has to. She told us all the time when we were kids that's what really counts, the effort you put in. But the way she talks about her job, when she and Dad don't think I'm listening—it's like she has to try twice as hard and still doesn't get recognized for what she does. It would have been different, I know, if she hadn't had three kids in three years. Her whole life would have been different . . . if she hadn't had me.

"Dad's going to take Peter to the airport, if you want to go," Mom says finally.

Only if I wanted to hear Cubs stats until my ears bled. I'll pass.

"You're not going?" I ask.

She shakes her head, checking her watch. "I'm about to head back to the office."

It's almost 8:00 p.m. "You've been staying late all week," I say as she rises from her desk chair.

"Crime doesn't sleep."

"Mom. You're a defense attorney."

She taps my nose. "Exactly."

Down the hall, Peter is dragging his suitcase out of his room. The wheels clatter against the wood floor.

"Don't wait up for me," Mom says as she starts to gather papers off her desk and shove them in her bag. "I might just take a catnap in the office. Dad has an early morning meeting out in Evanston, so you're on your own for breakfast. There's yogurt. Bananas."

"I think they're only good for banana bread at this point."

"Might be a fun thing, for after school." She zips up her bag. "You'll be okay, right?"

I smile. Nod.

"God, that's what I love about you." Mom kisses the top of my head.

"What?"

"You've always been so easy."

We both wince at the sound of a collision by the front door.

"Jesus, could you *watch*?" Charlotte huffs, and it sounds like she's steadying the wobbling entryway table.

"Watch what? Watch you not looking where you're going?" Peter asks. "Is the *New Yorker* really so interesting you've got to bury your whole face in it?"

"This is the *Wall Street Journal*, you illiterate."

Mom sighs and slings her heavy bag over one shoulder. She throws me a smile and a conspiratorial look as she starts toward the entryway. "You're the calm in the storm."

Sometimes, I wish I were the storm instead.

CHAPTER 3

WE'VE HAD A warm winter so far—warm for Chicago, anyway—but as soon as Peter and Charlotte go back to college, we hit a cold snap that lasts for days. And apparently, my brain takes that as a signal to hibernate. When I wake up on Saturday and I grab my phone to check the time, I've slept through the whole morning, two alarms, and three texts from Alex.

Hey

And then, an hour later:

Uhhhh hello?

Fifteen minutes after:

wtf Isabel

I type out a response as fast as I can.

> **Ahhh sorry!!**
>
> **I was asleep**
>
> **What's up?**

He responds so quickly, it almost seems like he's been by the phone this whole time. I picture him cradling the phone in his arms, pacing like some lady on a widow's walk, pining for her husband lost at sea.

God, what's wrong with me? I should be happy he cares this much. All he wants is to talk to me.

Well get dressed, Kyle said to get there at noon

What? We're not hanging out with Kyle today—at least I'm not. My mom isn't working today, and we're going shopping together downtown. We planned it weeks ago.

You didn't say anything about going to Kyle's

Guess I forgot?

I know it's far but his parents are gone the whole weekend so we're going

Obviously

Obviously he's going, because he wants to. And obviously I'm going, because he wants me to go. I won't just go, I'll *want* to go, because *he* wants to go. It's so obvious he didn't even bother to ask. I shake my head, because I should be grateful I'm the most important thing in his life. He tells me that, all the time. And I am grateful.

But I don't want to go.

I can't, I'm sorry

I'm spending the day with my mom

wtf

you never told me that

Didn't I? I was sure I did. But I guess maybe I forgot, too.

                                                    I'm sorry

   Ok

                                              I'm really sorry
                   We can hang out tomorrow, do whatever you want

Hoping that's enough to pacify him, I throw a sweatshirt on over my pajamas and head for the kitchen. I feel bad, because I know he wants me there with him, but Mom has so few days off lately. I have to take advantage of every one.

But the only things waiting for me in the kitchen are a bear claw on a plate and a note written on my mom's office stationery.

Isabel 🖤
Good morning! Or maybe afternoon . . . ;)
The house is yours—I have a client lunch and a partner dinner. I know! Too much. Dad's tennis tournament is today, but he'll be back by 6. You guys can order a pizza. Maybe watch a movie? I'll see you later.
Love,
Mom

I can't believe it. She forgot. She put it on the calendar herself and she still forgot.

Without even meaning to, my hand clenches around the note, balling it up. I stuff it in my pocket. I don't want Mom seeing it all crumpled up when she comes home.

As I pick at the bear claw, I consider my options.

A) Tell Alex I'm free, put on enough makeup to cover up my disappointment, and go with him to Kyle's

B) Call my mom at her client lunch and tell her the apartment is on fire

C) Buy a plane ticket to Canada, start a new life as a woodland hermit, and see how long it takes anyone in my family to notice I'm gone

The right answer is A, of course. I should text Alex. He'd never forget something we planned, like my mom would. I'm the most important thing in his life, even if I'm just a minor player in hers. I should text him.

So why don't I want to?

Outside my bedroom window, the sky is a cloudless cornflower blue, and there's no wind swaying the bare tree branches. If I'm not going to Kyle's house—and I still don't understand why I'm not—I might as well go outside.

The L takes an eternity to come and an additional eternity to get me downtown. I opt out of Grant Park and the bundled tourists waiting to see Seurat at the Art Institute or take selfies with the Bean. I walk north on South Michigan, breathing in crisp air through my nose. Walking in a big city you know is the best kind of anonymity. I could find my way back home with my eyes closed, but I'm in a crowd of people who have never seen me before and won't ever again. I catalog the people I pass and wonder how they'd catalog me.

Girl. Sixteen to nineteen, probably. Not tall, not short. Long hair, light brown. Body type indeterminate, due to giant puffy coat.

But what else could they tell, just from looking? Nothing. Maybe *that's* the best kind of anonymity. When you're no one, so you could be anyone.

I wander farther and farther north, over the bridge, past the Wrigley Building with its ornate clock tower that tells me it's nearly 2:00 p.m. I like this neighborhood, with its sleek hotels and spare art galleries.

I'm standing with my back to the street, studying one particularly odd sculpture, when I hear a laugh, low and loud and very familiar, off to my left.

Shit.

A second ago, I was almost shivering in the cold, but now my whole body is hot and every muscle is tensed. Just up the block, walking toward me but mercifully not looking in my direction, is a group of teenage boys.

And one of them is Alex.

Oh, shit, oh, *shit*, why is he *here*? He said they were going to Kyle's house; that's practically in the suburbs. And he never comes down this way. Why would he start today? I thought I was safe—

Safe, of course I'm safe, I think as I press myself against the brick building behind me. But if he sees me, he's going to know I lied, and when he knows I lied, I'll have to explain why, and I don't know what I'd say. Maybe that's why in movies, when a character says they "can explain," the script never makes them. Someone always cuts them off or leaves before they have to. Maybe no one can explain themselves.

Alex's head starts to turn in my direction. He can't see me. I can't explain. I spin away from the boys and duck into the closest open door without glancing up at the sign. It doesn't matter, I just need to be somewhere else, to be able to take another breath.

I stumble through the doorway, push past a dark curtain, and find myself in a small entryway. Heart still pounding, eyes adjusting from the bright outside to low, artificial light, I realize I have no idea what I walked into. There's a menu on the wall, under glass. A podium stands at the back of the room, next to a slightly open door, with an open ledger on top. A tall, thin man with an unfortunate goatee suddenly appears in the doorway. He startles when he sees me, then goes to stand behind the podium.

It must be a restaurant, and it must still be open for lunch, because I can hear low noise from the adjoining room. The man—or I guess the maître d'—beckons me over.

I hesitate for a second. I can stay at this random restaurant, where I don't know what kind of food is served, how expensive it is, or whether it's secretly a front for money laundering. Alternatively, I can go back outside and risk the chance of seeing my boyfriend.

This should be an easier decision.

With one last glance at the curtain, I walk toward the maître d'. I haven't eaten all day, and by the time I'm done with lunch, Alex and his friends will definitely have moved on.

"Hi," I say, raising my voice over the noise coming from inside the restaurant. It's weird—it's loud, but almost a singular sound, like a buzzing. I can't pick out multiple voices. But then again, I usually can't. "I'm guessing you're open?"

He looks confused, but nods. "Do you—" he says, and then several other words I can't pick out. He's got a low voice, even for a man, and that's always harder.

I smile. "Sorry?"

I hate always having to apologize for not catching something, but saying "What?" sounds rude, and "I can't understand you" sounds like an accusation. So I tell everyone "I'm sorry, please excuse me, so sorry." Over and over.

He frowns. "Do—want a t—"

This time, I catch the "t" sound in the last word. "T" for "table." Duh. It's a restaurant, of course he's asking if I want a table.

"Yes, please," I say, way too eager. "Thank you."

He mumbles something else I can't understand, opening the ledger.

I try not to groan out loud. "Um—"

He looks up, locks eyes with me, and then says a single word, overly slow. *"Name."*

"Oh!" I say. "Isabel."

He looks like he's got a couple follow-up questions, but shakes his head, opens the door, and ushers me through it.

Inside, I notice three things very quickly:

1. This restaurant has no windows.
2. This restaurant has no food on the tables.
3. This restaurant is not a restaurant.

The tall man points me to an empty table right near the door, and I take it without question, sliding down into a plush chair with a plastic back. I clutch my bag on my lap, trying and failing to process what I've just stepped into. My mind is in overdrive, every one of my senses vying to feed information to my brain in the first half second.

It smells like old beer and the cleaning solution they used to clean out the horse stalls at my sleepaway camp, artificially fresh and overpowering.

It looks like if Dracula tried to throw his daughter a sweet sixteen party: a big, dark room lit with red and purple lights. Fake candlestick holders. Black-and-red-patterned wallpaper. But the crowd doesn't match the decor. They're mostly young and mostly guys and mostly in jeans and hoodies. So it looks like if Dracula tried to throw his daughter a sweet sixteen but made her invite all the employees of a local tech start-up.

It sounds like—it sounds like someone's giving a speech. God, maybe it *is* Heather Dracula's sweet sixteen. And here I am without anything to give her. Besides my blood.

I swivel around in my chair in the direction of the voice.

Behind me, against the far wall is a low stage, the kind you might use for bands without much of a fan base. Onstage is a tall, three-legged wooden stool and a tall, two-legged human girl holding a mic. She's got big eyes, a wide smile, and a short, messy mop of dark hair.

"So, I have a confession to make, and I hope you won't think differently of me afterward," she says into the mic. Maybe this is an Alcoholics Anonymous meeting. Though it seems weird to hold an AA meeting in a place with a bar. The girl pauses dramatically.

"I," the girl says, "was a theater kid in high school."

She doesn't get another word out before someone in the back cheers, loudly. I expect her to ignore it, but she grins and points toward them. "Oh, you too? No, you don't have to answer. Only a theater kid would interrupt someone's set for a half second of attention."

A set—she said a "set," not a story or a speech. This isn't a party or an Alcoholics Anonymous meeting. This is a "show." A comedy show.

Everyone laughs. The girl slides right back into her act. "And you know, people always say theater kids are dramatic, but even the most over-the-top fourteen-year-old *Hamilton* fangirl has nothing on sports people. You guys set cars on fire when your team *wins*." She throws her arm wide. "What the fuck! That makes no sense!"

As the audience giggles, I pick up my bag and look for an

exit. I shouldn't be here—I didn't buy a ticket and I don't know anything about stand-up, aside from watching my dad watch *Seinfeld* reruns. I don't belong here. Best-case scenario, I remain as invisible to these people as I am to everyone else. Worst-case scenario, this girl onstage makes fun of me for her set. That's a thing comedians do, right? Pick on people in the audience?

"I'm not saying sports fans are bad people," she continues, almost placating. "But I *am* saying New York City doesn't have to grease all the light poles after the Tony Awards."

Everyone laughs. Including me. I relax my grip on the bag, because whatever, I can stay for a minute. Just to see where she goes with it.

"Can you even imagine what that would look like? A post-Tonys riot?" She takes the mic off the stand and places the stand behind her. "Just like, a mob of upper-middle-class white people marching down Broadway, doing the original choreography from *A Chorus Line*."

I've never seen *A Chorus Line* and don't know if what she does next is the original choreography, but she puts her whole body into it. She's made entirely of limbs, a self-aware cartoon character high-kicking and box-stepping her way through a fictional riot. She looks totally ridiculous, and she must know that. The audience definitely does, and they laugh louder. But she doesn't cringe or break character. It's like she soaks up the laughter, without worrying why it's coming.

"They're blocking traffic, bashing pedestrians in the face with

33

their high kicks. Everyone's chanting"—she crouches down a bit and pumps her fist—"'BRA-VA, BRA-VA, BRA-VA,' until eventually it's just guttural screaming, like—" She pauses, arches her back, makes her hands into claws, and demonstrates this. It's inhuman. And hilarious.

How does she do that? I wonder. How can she be so sure she'll be heard, so confident she'll be liked? Even her clothes are confident; the maroon sweater layered artfully over a half-tucked gray-patterned button-down. Her sleeves rolled up and perfectly cuffed as if she studied a J.Crew mannequin. I can't tell if I want to keep watching her until the sky goes black and the sun explodes, or if I want to *be* her.

She points to her right. "There's a guy in a jersey that says *Sondheim* on the back and he's wrapping his hand in a cashmere sweater so he can punch out the lights on the *Jersey Boys* marquee—"

She takes a beat, then points out to a spot over the audience's heads. "Dame Judi Dench has stolen a police horse—"

I'm too enthralled to laugh, even though everyone else is cracking up. The girl keeps going, but I can barely hear her over this buzzing in my ears, this itching in my skin down to my bones.

And then she's putting the mic back on the stand, saying "Thank you! You were great!" and waving as she clambers off the stage and down the stairs, without grace and without shame. The audience applauds and cheers. It takes me a second to realize I should be clapping, too, and another second to be certain I still have hands.

The maître d'—or I guess the emcee, actually—takes the stage. He leans into the mic. "Let's hear it one more time for Mo Irani!"

We clap more, cheer more. She's settled herself back at a table up front, squeezed in between a couple boys her age.

"All right, all right," the emcee says, and it's amazing how much crisper and clearer he sounds to me when he's got a mic. "We've got one more comedian to see, and then we'll let the Pyramid Lounge get back to being a club, and let all of you get back to your usual Saturday-night plans of, I don't know, eating pizza while masturbating."

"Uh, that seems unhygienic, Larry," someone calls out.

Larry is unmoved. "Don't be such a puritan." He glances down at his ledger. "Last up, please put your hands together for . . . Isabel!"

Wait. What?

"No last name," he adds. "Who knows, maybe it was—what do you call it?—asexual reproduction. Like with nematodes. Anyway, let's hear it for Isabel!"

Wait. No.

"Isabel?" He squints into the crowd. "The girl who just came in? With the gray coat and the long hair? Kind of spacey, no offense?"

No no no no—

"Is she in the bathroom, or—" He shakes his head. "Okay, whatever, let's give a big round of applause to all of today's—"

"No," I blurt out, and for a moment, I can't tell if I've said it out loud. "Wait." That was definitely out loud, because Larry stops short, and the audience turns to stare at me. Then I'm scrambling to my feet and screaming into my own brain, *What are you doing Isabel what the fuck are you doing*

What I'm doing is walking past tables of strangers, climbing up the steps, and accepting the mic from a very surprised Larry.

Larry is gone before I can reconsider, and I am standing onstage.

It smells like old beer, industrial cleaning solution, and my own animal panic.

It looks like an endless haze of red light and the vague outline of human-shaped shadows just beyond the hot, bright glare.

It sounds like silence.

Not my own silence, though I haven't said anything yet. Their silence. The waiting, watching quiet of strangers who don't know what to expect from me, because—

I realize it then, with equal terror and boundless relief: they don't know me.

I'm not their classmate, or girlfriend, or sister, or daughter.

I'm not Isabel, who is so chill, so easy, the calm in the storm.

I'm not anyone to them. So I can be anything I want.

The mic is slipping out of my clammy hands. I adjust my grip, all ten fingers tightly curled around it, refusing to let go.

I think: *I can't do this.*

I think: *I don't know how to do this.*

I say: "Last week, the weirdest thing happened in my Shakespeare Seminar."

CHAPTER 4

CRICKETS. OR, NOT crickets, I don't understand why that's still the universal symbol for a silent audience, like we're all sitting outside on hay bales wondering if this new vaudeville craze is going to take off. The twenty-first-century version is a phone vibrating on silent.

I think: *Keep going.*

I think: *Keep going before they drag you off the stage.*

I say: "We were reading *Hamlet*, because of course we were." I take a breath, disconnect my brain from my vocal cords, and keep talking.

"The man wrote like thirty plays, but the only one anyone ever wants to talk about is the one with a whiny prince who can't figure out whether to kill his uncle who is, like, such a cartoon bad guy he's literally the inspiration for Scar in *The Lion King.*"

A few chuckles, scattered and—it takes me a second to

realize—expectant. They aren't laughing because it was all that funny. They're laughing because they're expecting it to go somewhere. And I have no idea where it's going.

"I mean, *The Lion King* is basically *Hamlet* for kids," I tell them. "Except *Hamlet* has more stabbing."

True. And it gets one laugh, from someone I can't see.

"Did you know Shakespeare had a kid named Hamnet, who died? I mean, died young," I clarify. "Obviously all of Shakespeare's kids are dead now. Death comes for us all."

Also true. But it does not get a laugh.

"Um. Anyway." There's a waver in my voice that wasn't there before, and I know it's because I'm panicking. I have to get to the point of this story, and it's not Hamnet Shakespeare's tragic ice-skating accident.

"So we were reading *Hamlet* and we all had to perform scenes because . . ." My face screws up as I think back to Ms. Waldman handing out the assignment. "I don't know. It was *meant to be performed*. Yeah, okay, and it was meant to be performed by a bunch of dudes in tights who didn't bathe, to an audience of drunk people who also didn't bathe." I take a breath. "It was like Burning Man. But with more stabbing." I take a longer breath. "I assume."

That gets a laugh. A small one. But a laugh.

I think: *You can say whatever you want up here.*

I think: *You can say what you actually think up here.*

I say: "My scene partner was this guy in my class named Jack, and he is just . . . the fucking worst."

The laugh I get there has to be from the sheer earnestness in my voice. Or maybe from the gallon of sweat dripping down my back.

"I'm allowed to say 'fuck,' right?" I ask in a sudden rush of self-consciousness. No one answers. "Yeah, of course I can, this isn't a . . . kid's birthday party. Actually, it's funny, when I walked in, I thought this was a sweet six—"

I think: *Actually no, that isn't funny at all, Isabel.*

I think: *Just talk, just talk before they stop listening like everybody else.*

I say: ". . . Never mind. Anyway, Jack sucks. And I hate him."

On pure impulse, I take a couple steps forward, closer to the audience. I peel one hand out of the death grip I've got on the mic and attempt to set the stage for them.

"So he's Hamlet." I point out a spot they can imagine Jack standing. "I'm Ophelia." I point to another spot where she could be standing. The me from last week, who already feels like a different girl entirely.

"And we're doing that famous 'get thee to a nunnery' scene, only he keeps changing his lines. He keeps changing the lines to make me the joke."

I know I'm just staring at two spots on an empty stage, but it's almost like I'm there, all over again, and so is the humiliation, and the rage, and the powerlessness.

"So I'm standing there, wondering . . ." I pause and tilt my head toward the invisible Jack onstage. "How was this such a hard decision for Hamlet? The whole murder thing. Because *I* want to full-on kill this dude who embarrassed me in a bullshit class, but Hamlet looks at his uncle who assassinated his dad and then married his mom and is like, 'I don't know, maybe we can work it out at the next family reunion.'"

That gets an okay response, so my mouth decides to continue down the Murder Path while my brain fails to stop it.

"Hamlet acts like it's wrong to even think about murder, but that might be my favorite pastime," I say. And then, for no good reason at all, I double down. "Honestly, planning a hypothetical murder is the perfect hobby."

Well, this is officially off the rails.

"No, hear me out," I say, aware I just encouraged a room of strangers to plot death like my grandmother encourages people to take up crocheting. "It costs no money. You can do it from anywhere. Your home, school, when you're stuck on the train— especially when you're stuck on the train. And man," I sigh, "is it *fun*."

Well, this is officially off the rails, in a ditch, and on fire.

"So go ahead," I hear myself telling the audience, as if this can't get worse. "Plan a murder. It's just like they told you in abstinence-only sex ed: it's okay to have murderous thoughts, just don't act on them until after marriage." And then, like a spark, I know my next line. "Because they can't make your spouse testify against you."

41

There's a half-second silence. Crickets and phone vibrations and a train on a ditch on fire and then . . . they laugh. All of them, or it *seems* like all of them, because I still can't see, and I can't feel my legs now, but I can hear. I can hear them laughing. And maybe it's not as loud as it could be, maybe it's only out of surprise or pity, but it's like something warm swells in my soul. I hear them. And they heard me.

It isn't going to get better than this, and I know it. It's time to get off this stage, peel off the shirt I've sweat all the way through, and forget this ever happened. It's time to go.

"Thank you!" I shout, as if they're clapping too loud for me to speak normally, which they aren't because they don't know it's over yet. I struggle the mic back into its stand, then hold both hands up like I'm being robbed in an Old West saloon. "Sorry!"

Larry's beside me onstage now, and I use him for cover as I speed-walk to the stairs. Like that'll work on an elevated stage with lights so bright they could stun small animals.

"Give it up for . . ." Larry double-checks his clipboard. "Isabel. Yeah."

The applause is nowhere as loud or as genuine as it was for the girl who went before me, but it's there. I walk back to my seat half-dazed, and it's not until I sink down into my chair and the familiar puffiness of my coat beneath me that I come back to reality. That wasn't me, onstage. I don't know who it was, but *I* could never do that. I could never stand under a spotlight and tell an audience what I really think.

But I did.

It sounds like Larry the Emcee is wrapping things up—thanking everyone for coming, reminding them when the next open mic night is—so I turn away from the stage to gather my stuff. As the room explodes into noise, audience members talking and laughing with each other as they leave, I fumble around in my bag for my phone, hoping Alex hasn't texted.

Zero calls or texts. None from Alex, and none from my parents. Which is a huge relief. Would it be nice to have *some* indication *someone* gives a shit about where I am and what I'm doing? Yes. But in this case, would I have actually told them the truth? No.

Someone taps on my table, and I look up to see the girl who performed before me—the theater girl, the one in the maroon sweater—sidled up to the far edge. Her smile is warm and easy, but I just stare at her, too surprised to smile back.

"You d—have to—" she says, not quite loud enough to top the noise around us.

"What?" I ask, too surprised she's talking to me at all to use a more polite "Sorry?"

She repeats it. I shake my head and point toward my ear. "I can't . . ."

The girl hesitates, her fingers still on the edge of my table. Her friend—even taller than her, lanky, with a guitar case slung over his shoulder—is a couple steps in front of her now. When she looks over at him, he nods his head toward the door. She turns away from him, pulls out the chair next to mine, and sits down.

"I said," she tells me, "you didn't have to apologize. After your set. Everyone here has seen worse."

That is almost impossible to believe.

"Really?" I ask her.

"*Way* worse," she promises.

I want to believe her.

She throws a question to her friend, over her shoulder. "Do you remember the time that guy threw up twenty seconds into his bit about Tinder?"

"Right into the orchestra pit," he confirms, heading over. "But I think it improved the joke."

"The orchestra pit?" I ask, scanning the room for one.

"Oh, not here," she says. "Another room, across town."

"Was it here the dude with the soul patch ran way over time and threw his water glass when everyone told him to stop?"

The girl considers, then shakes her head. "No, the emcee was Colin so it must have been at the Forest."

He nods. "Right."

"See? You're not even in the top ten." She smiles at me, then sticks out her hand. "I'm Mo."

"Yeah, I know," I say. Then I think about what I just said. "I mean, I don't know, I don't know you, I just heard your, um, set? Your set. It was really funny, and you're really brave to be that negative about sports in Chicago—but then at the end of your set,

44

they said your name at the end, so I did know your name because of that."

Mo bites back a laugh. "You talk a lot, don't you?"

That is the longest string of words I've said to anyone since third grade. I choose not to tell her this.

She misunderstands my silence. "That's a good thing. In this case."

"What case?" I ask.

"Comedy." She leans in. "I'm guessing this was your first time?"

"Huh?"

"At an open mic," she says. "Doing stand-up. Was that your first time?"

I hesitate, because I'm honestly not sure what just happened could be considered anything other than word vomit.

"It's okay," her friend says. "Your first time is always awkward."

"This is Will, by the way," Mo says. He sticks out his hand, and I shake it.

"This is kind of a weird room for someone super green," Mo says. "Just so you know."

"Green," I repeat.

"New," Will clarifies.

"We can show you way better places to start out. With bigger student crowds." Mo tilts her head. "So what are you, a freshman?"

That makes me prickle. Do I really look fourteen to her? People never think I'm younger than I am, only older. "Um, no, I'm a junior."

Mo doesn't look fazed. "Oh, okay. We're seniors. UChicago. Do you go there, too, or—where?"

Oh. *Oh.*

I think: *I go to Davis Preparatory School, which is for high schoolers, which is what I am.*

I think: *No one here knows what I am. I could be something different.*

I say: Nothing, for a very long moment.

I should tell her I'm sixteen. I should tell her I'm not in college. Shouldn't I? Should I?

She wouldn't be inviting me to come out with her friends if she knew I was in high school. She probably wouldn't even be talking to me.

I can tell Mo the truth and risk her not wanting to be friends.

I can lie, and risk getting caught.

I exhale. I inhale. I choose.

"Roosevelt," I blurt out before I can change my mind. "I go to Roosevelt. By the Loop."

"Oh," Mo says. "Cool."

"It's funny, I've never met anyone who goes there," Will says.

Yeah, that was the idea.

"It's pretty small," I say, trying to picture the flyer in my college counselor's office. "Close-knit. You know?" I cautiously pump my fist. "Go . . . Lakers."

Another boy around their age appears by Mo's shoulder, wearing a leather jacket layered over a hoodie and a scowl.

"I don't know what's taking so long, but I'm not sticking around to find out what this shithole is like at night," he says to her.

"What are you picturing?" Mo asks him.

The boy in the jacket spreads his arms wide. "Cannibalism. Animal sacrifice. Twelve-dollar gin and tonics."

"What kind of nightclubs do you go to?" Will asks him.

"Because of the *decor*," the boy in the jacket says. "Look at it. It looks like—like—"

"Like Dracula's daughter's sweet sixteen party?" I blurt out.

Mo cracks up, and the boy in the jacket seems to notice me for the first time.

"Oh, hey," he says. "Murder Girl."

"Isabel," I say, sincerely hoping that nickname doesn't catch on.

"Jonah." He glances around the room. "Yeah, teenage vampire seems about right. Let's *go*."

As if on cue, Larry the Emcee pokes his head through the curtain by the doorway. "Why the fuck are you all still here? I'm locking up. Leave."

Mo puts a hand to her chest. "Larry. What would we do without your chivalry?"

"Your eloquence," Jonah adds. "Your wit."

"Leave faster," Larry says.

They all start for the door, and I scramble to grab my bag and zip up my coat. Larry shuts the door behind us as we exit, Mo and me at the back, the boys ahead of us trading one-liners so fast I can't make them out. I linger for a moment at the front entrance. What if Alex is outside? It's been long enough, I can't imagine why he would be here, but still. I take a breath. It's fine. He's probably gone, and plus, I'm with Mo and everyone else. Alex wouldn't do anything with so many people around.

I shake my head. I'm being ridiculous again. What do I think he would *do*? That was one time, on the train platform, just one time—

When I step outside, the sun is high overhead, and I blink into the blazing light. I wonder if this is how it feels to leave a cocoon. Or for a snow crocus to poke through the dirt at the first sign of spring. I rub at my eyes. Mo already has her sunglasses on.

"We're probably going to go get a drink by campus, if you want to come," she offers.

"I can't." Not a lie. I can't get into a bar. "I have to study." Also not a lie. I have a math test on Monday.

"Maybe next time," she says, and my breath catches. She wants there to be a next time. Do I?

"Do you guys do this, a lot? Open mics?"

She shrugs, pulling on a pair of knit fingerless gloves. "Not every night, but once a week for sure."

I try to picture her life. Days in the library or the dining hall

48

or dusty classrooms arguing about dead men I've never heard of and books I've never read. Nights with her best friends in dark comedy clubs, under a glowing spotlight. It's almost like a movie.

"That's so cool," I say.

"You should come out with us," she says. "I'll text you, the next time we're going."

"Oh, I don't know—"

"It's more fun with friends, trust me. And it would be nice to have another girl." She taps on her phone for a second, then holds it out. "Here, put in your number."

It's not as if I haven't given my number to people I like way less. And it's not like I'm giving her my address. Or my soul. I type it in and hand the phone back.

"Seven-seven-three," she says, glancing at the area code. "Are you from Chicago?"

"Yeah, I grew up here," I tell her. I don't tell her at least legally, I'm *still* growing up here.

"Cool. Maybe you can help us find some new spots."

"Mo—" I take a breath. "I don't think I can actually—you know." She says nothing, so I elaborate. "This wasn't supposed to happen."

"What wasn't?"

"Getting up on stage, the whole thing, none of that was supposed to happen. It was an accident."

Mo deserves to know that, because she's serious about this. Comedy. Stand-up. She knows so much about it, she *must* be serious, and I—I stumbled onstage and stumbled through a murder-fantasy monologue, and I'm stumbling to explain I can't do this. I wait for Mo to figure that out herself, and to walk away. But she doesn't.

"What a wonderful accident," she says, and her whole face breaks into a smile. And I can't help it. Mine does, too.

Mo pops her coat collar against the wind. "See you later, Izzy."

CHAPTER 5

I DIDN'T THINK much of *Hamlet*, but I'm enjoying the sonnets. They're so much nicer to read. No duels, no madness, no absurd piles of dead people by the end of Act 5. Just one man telling the people he loves how much he loves them.

Alex and I are in my bedroom, doing homework. Well. *I'm* doing my Shakespeare analysis for Monday, and Alex is wandering around my room bothering my plants. I decide if he's not going to do his work, he might as well help me with mine.

"Tell me what you think of this one."

He groans. "I didn't take this class for a *reason*."

"I have to analyze the rhythm, so I need to say it out loud."

"It's Friday. You have the whole weekend. Would you relax?"

"'Love is not love,'" I read to him, "'Which alters when it alteration finds, / Or bends with the remover to remove: / O no! it is an ever-fixed mark, / That looks on tempests and is never shaken.'"

I glance up. But Alex isn't even looking at me.

"What do you think?" I ask.

He shrugs. "I think it doesn't mean anything."

"Of course it does." I look back down at the sonnet. "It means if you really love someone, you love them even if they 'alter.' Even if they're different, someday. Or if they aren't there, anymore. He's saying love is constant and unchanging, even if everything else changes around you."

"Sure." Alex slides down next to me on the bed.

"Don't you think that's—" But before I can finish the sentence, he's pulled me closer and is kissing me. It's easy to melt into this, when he kisses me like that. It's like the universe narrows to a pinpoint, and everything that could hurt me, *does* hurt me in the real world—all my frustrations and uncertainties and fears—they're too big to fit inside.

It would be so easy to let the world around me contract and forget what I was thinking or doing before he kissed me. But it's just—I wasn't done. I had more to say.

So I do something I've never done before: I pull away.

"Not all the sonnets are about love," I say. So he didn't like that sonnet. There are 153 others. "Well, they are, but there's more in them than that." I ignore the obvious annoyance in his eyes and turn my head back to the book, flipping through the pages. Alex lets his hand drop. "Like this one—I think this one's my favorite."

He flops down on the bed, as dramatic as the ingenues in the old movies he likes so much. "Isabel—"

"'When I perceive that men as plants increase, / Cheered and check'd even by the selfsame sky—'"

"Men are plants?"

"Men are *like* plants; they grow," I say. "Under the same blue sky. People change, over time, like plants do, and we all have a prime of life that doesn't last long."

"Uh-huh," he says, getting up from the bed for the phone he left sitting on my dresser.

"It's like this whole nature metaphor." I look back down at my book. "Love is a forest, something natural and untamable, or something. And then at the end, he says: 'And all in war with Time for love of you, / As he takes from you' . . ." I pause. "'I engraft you new.'"

I love that final line. *I engraft you new.*

Ms. Waldman told us "engraft" comes from the Greek word for writing. Shakespeare is immortalizing his love through words. But grafting is something gardeners do, too, when they join two plants into one. They take the roots and the stems of one plant and attach the delicate shoot of another. It becomes one plant, a new plant, stronger than it ever could have been before.

I look up, ready to explain to Alex why I love that line so much. But he's bent over his phone, texting. I go back to my book, trying to lose myself in Shakespeare, plants, and the idea of unchangeable, ever-fixed love.

"When did you get this?"

I close the book. My closet door is open, and Alex is holding up one of my dresses. A new one. My mom plucked it out of Bloomingdale's final-sale clearance rack after Christmas, but I haven't worn it yet. I haven't even tried it on. My mom shops sales racks with the fervor of a religious fanatic and the aggression of a five-star general, so the dress is more her style than mine: long sleeves, high neck, and a delicate green floral pattern you might also find on vintage curtains.

I'd have gone for something more neutral, personally. Something that makes it easier to blend in. But a gift is a gift.

"A couple weeks ago," I tell Alex. "My mom bought it for me."

"I can tell."

"You don't like it?"

"It's like a, what do you call it? Pioneer dress."

"Prairie dress?"

"Sure."

Alex is a man of simple taste when it comes to women's fashion. Leggings. Boots. Tops without ruffles or peplums or necklines that cover the collarbone.

"It's like something a nun would wear," he says. "A grandma nun."

"Nuns usually aren't grandmas."

"Huh?"

"They marry Jesus." I pause. "And I don't think he puts out."

"Is that a joke?"

"No. I genuinely don't think he puts out."

He blinks at me, then shakes his head and turns away to hang the dress back up.

"You should give it to Goodwill," he says.

Then he starts texting someone, giving me a prime opportunity to roll my eyes without him seeing.

My phone vibrates. I pick it up. Alex doesn't notice.

Hey Izzy! This is Mo. We're going out tonight. You free?

It's been almost two weeks since I stumbled into the comedy club. I assumed Mo had forgotten about me, or decided the girl who riffs onstage about killing a man is not the girl to add to your team. But here it is. An actual invitation.

I glance over at Alex, who's buried in his own phone. We don't have plans together tonight, but I can't tell him about Mo, or any of this. Not unless I also want to tell him how I managed to end up at a comedy club in the first place, and that story doesn't paint me as a great girlfriend.

My phone vibrates again.

9 PM list, 930 start @ The Forest

This time, Alex does notice. When he sees the phone in my hand, he instantly loses interest in his.

"Who's texting you?" he asks, striding over to look over my shoulder.

"Mo," I say, both hands around my phone now.

"Mo?" Alex repeats. "Who is *he*?"

"She," I say quickly. "I think it's a nickname —"

"Fine, who is *she*?"

"Nobody." He narrows his eyes. I swallow. "I mean, nobody you'd know. She's in college. We just kind of struck up a conversation."

"You," he says, beyond skeptical, "struck up a conversation."

"She was really the one who—" I cross my arms. "She's nice. She wants to hang out."

"What, is she gay?"

I recoil. "Alex."

"Well?"

"We talked for five minutes, I have no idea." I throw up my hands. "Why do you care?"

"I don't *care*." He chews on the inside of his mouth. "I'm just wondering."

"Why?" I press.

"Because maybe she's trying to get with you. Why else is she texting?"

Is that what he thinks? No one would talk to me unless they wanted to have sex with me?

"You know," I say, trying to keep my voice even, "it's possible she wants to be my friend. I've had friends before."

"Friend," he corrects me. "And it was Naomi Weiss."

"She counts."

"Barely."

"What does that mean?"

"I'm the reason people talk to you now. I'm sorry if that

hurts your feelings, but it's true."

I think: *People talked to me.*

I think: *Just because you don't care about them doesn't mean they aren't people.*

I say: Nothing.

It's like he can read my thoughts, even the ones I never put into words. "Don't take that the wrong way."

"How *should* I take it?"

"All I mean is—I can see what other people can't, about you. You know? *I* can see it, but on the surface, you're not all that . . ." He shakes his head. "I don't know the word. Approachable, I guess?"

"If I'm that unapproachable, why did she approach me?"

"That's what I'm saying!" He sighs. "That's why you need to be careful. Who knows what she wants from you?"

I think: *She wants me to be her friend. She wants me to get up on stage and take a risk.*

I think: *And all you want is . . . all of me.*

I say: Nothing.

"So forget this weirdo you met on the bus." He plucks the phone from my hand before I even know it's happening, and gently tosses it behind me on the bed. "Okay?"

I think: *You're not really asking me.*

I think: *It's not a question if there's only one acceptable answer.*

I say: "Okay."

He smiles and kisses me on the forehead. I raise the corners of my mouth just high enough. An approximation of a smile.

He checks his own phone. "Shit, I've got to go," he says, springing up from the bed. "I can call when we're taking a break."

"No, it's okay. Go have fun." Personally, indoor paintball with Kyle and Luke sounds like as much fun as sticking a fork in a toaster, but hey. "I'll see you tomorrow?"

"Yeah." He shrugs on his coat, then grabs his backpack. "Keep your phone on, though. I'll text you."

He leaves without closing the door behind him, and I listen to his footsteps across the living room. A click as the front door opens, then another click as it closes and locks. I sit very still on the bed, counting out the seconds. Sixty for the elevator to come. Thirty for it to travel back down to the lobby. Another thirty for him to walk past the doorman, through the glass revolving doors, and out onto the street.

Five. Four. Three. Two.

I grab for the phone behind me.

Hi Mo! Yes. I'm free.

It's after seven, and practically my entire wardrobe is spread out on my bed. Skirts and pants and literally every single sweater I own. But nothing seems right. The only thing I definitely *can't* wear is my current outfit: a high school uniform.

I throw down yet another pair of jeans and slump onto my bed. This shouldn't be so hard. It's just clothes, necessary only to protect against the Illinois winter and a charge for public indecency. This should be simple. I close my eyes and try to picture the perfect outfit, one that has no downsides.

I can't look like a slut but I can't look like a nun but I can't look like a boy.

I can't look like I'm trying too hard, I can't look like I'm not trying hard enough, and God, what *can* I look like? A genderless void? Maybe I'll make two eyeholes in a bedsheet and cut my losses.

When I open my eyes, my gaze snags on the single item left hanging in my closet. The prairie dress. I strip off my uniform and pull it on.

Alex hates this dress.

It hugs me, loose and warm, like the fleece blanket on my very first bed.

If Alex hates it, everyone else will, too.

It doesn't pinch at my waist, slip off my shoulders, or scratch my skin.

Alex hates it, because it's unflattering and unappealing and unapproachable.

I'm wearing it.

"Hey, Mom?" I peek my head in her office. She's only just put down her bag, but I need to ask now.

"Hey," she says, starting up her computer. "What's up?"

"Is it okay if I sleep over at Naomi's tonight?"

That gets her attention. I haven't spent the night with Naomi this entire school year. It's a little risky, since my parents have her dad's number, but a sleepover is the perfect cover. It means I can stay out as late as I want without suspicion. And when I come home, no matter what time it is, I'll just say I was feeling sick. It wouldn't be the first time. Naomi's dad has low standards when it comes to food safety. And girlfriends.

Mom nods at the coat in my arms, the tote bag at my feet. "Looks like you're already on your way out."

"Um—"

"I'm home tonight, you know," she says, with a twinge of hurt in her voice. "I only have a couple emails to send and I'm done. I thought we were going to have dinner together."

I think: *Well, I thought we were going to have the whole day together, last Saturday.*

I think: *You promised. I didn't.*

I say: "I'm sorry."

Her face softens instantly.

"Oh, honey, no, it's fine," Mom says. "I'm glad. It feels like you and Naomi haven't seen each other much lately."

I nod.

"You aren't taking a lot," she notes.

"I have clothes at her place." That's true. She still has one of my favorite sweaters, and I think at this point it's hers. Friend breakups aren't like regular breakups. You can't demand they bring over a box with all your stuff.

"Have a good time. Call if you need anything."

I kiss her on the cheek. "Thanks. See you in the morning."

The computer screen glows behind me as I sling my bag over my shoulder, and her fingers clack against keys in the office while my boots clack against the hardwood floor to the front door. She's not worried, and why should she be? She's never had to pick me up from a broken-up house party or police station or a black-ops field site. She's never even fielded a call from my principal.

Charlotte always gets my mom scarves for her birthday, and Peter always forgets entirely, but my gift is better, because it's constant. I give my mom peace of mind. Every second. Every day.

I wonder if she knows it's a gift.

Alone in the hallway, I reach for the elevator down button, but then pull my hand back. I could still go back inside. Tell my mom I changed my mind. Tell her what's really going on with me, with Naomi, with . . . everything.

The carpet is soft underneath me as I slide back a step. Just an inch. Just an inch closer to my front door, and my home, where I know who I am. Even if I don't like her.

What if they don't like me, either? What if they ditch me? What if I'm not like they thought I would be?

I'm standing there, hand on the door, heart in my throat, when my phone buzzes in my coat pocket. I fish it out to see another text from Mo, but in a group chat with a bunch of numbers I don't know.

Hey guys I'm starting a new chat with Izzy on it FYI

Huh. She called me Izzy again. I've never gone by that, but I kind of like it.

Another text comes in, I'm guessing from Jonah:

Sup, Murder Girl

As far as nicknames go, I vastly prefer Izzy. I've never had a nickname, but why shouldn't I? People pick new names all the time, when they get married or get famous or get on the Most Wanted list. When people's lives change, their names change, too. So why can't I be Izzy? Why can't I choose her?

I whisper the name in my own head, on a loop, until it's nestled inside of me like it's been mine all along. Izzy.

I engraft you new.

I push open the door.

CHAPTER 6

MY TRAIN IS delayed, so I have to run the last five minutes to the venue. I get there on time but panting and sweating underneath my puffy coat.

There's a sign outside that says the Forest in a Ye Olde English kind of font. And just below that sign stands a bald bouncer approximately the size of a Ye Olde English cottage. Shit. I figured we were going to a bar, but I didn't think about how I'd actually get in.

Before I can truly panic, Mo materializes by my side.

"Hey," she says to me, waving the rest of them over with one hand. "You made it."

I'm so hot I pull off my coat, despite the cold. "No thanks to the L."

Mo looks me up and down. "Nice dress," she says as the boys join us.

"Yeah?" The high collar seems tight, all of a sudden. "My

boyfriend wanted me to throw it out."

Mo scoffs. "Might as well throw out the boyfriend."

That makes me laugh. And then *that* makes me feel horribly guilty.

"So, which fundamentalist cult are you in again?" Jonah jokes.

Before, that would have made me go red, maybe even tear up. I would have put my coat back on. But not now.

I smooth down my skirt. "We call ourselves the Hipster Mennonites."

Will chuckles. "Hipster Mennonite. That's good."

I've never made fun of myself before. At least out loud. It felt like an invitation, like if someone like Jack ever heard it, he'd use it to tear me down. But I don't think they would.

"We already put ourselves on the list," Mo says. "Did you want to go up tonight? Your time might suck, but they have spots open."

"I think I'll just watch tonight. If that's cool."

"For sure."

The boys look like they're itching to get inside, and I know I can't stall this any longer.

"Um, Mo—" I sidle closer to her, stealing a look at the bouncer. "I'm sort of . . . not twenty-one."

She's unfazed. "I didn't think you were. It's fine. Neither is Jonah."

I look over at Jonah, surprised. He's a senior in college, and he's only twenty? He grimaces.

"Skip second grade, they said." He throws his arms out. "It *won't* suck to be the last of your friends legal to drink, they said."

"That's a very inappropriate thing to say to an eight-year-old," I agree.

Mo laughs. "We'll sneak you both in the back. We've done it before." She nods to Will. "You grab the table. I'll go."

IDs in hand, they head for the door, and Jonah leads me around back to an alley that would probably smell like garbage if it wasn't so cold out. Midwestern winters have their occasional perks. We wait by a green door, shivering and generally avoiding looking at each other.

"Why don't you have a fake?" I ask finally, desperate to make conversation, but also genuinely curious. Some kids at my school have them, and they're much less believable as twenty-one-year-olds than Jonah. But my classmates aren't dying to get into dive bars, anyway. If they want to escape reality, kind as it's been to them, their parents' medicine cabinets are much more accessible.

"Well," Jonah replies, "when you're raised by super-nice, super-intense Lutherans, you develop this constant, crushing guilt over spending money and also breaking the law."

I think about this for a moment. "But when you get inside, aren't you still going to break the law? By drinking?"

"Yes. But having a fake ID means it's premeditated."

That doesn't make much sense, but I nod anyway.

"Why don't *you* have a fake?" he asks.

"I . . . don't get out much."

"Yeah." He blows on his hands. "It seems that way."

My phone buzzes in my pocket. I expect it to be Alex, since it almost always is, but when I fish it out, it's Peter.

yo

This is so weird, he never texts me. Why would he? I don't watch TV shows with explosions or dragons, I don't follow the Cubs, and according to him, I didn't "get" *Fight Club*. Our lives have diverged.

Yes?

what's this plant called

He attaches a picture of some leaves, which is profoundly unhelpful.

why

is it toxic

WHY

if you only had like two bites will you die

I REPEAT, PETER

WHY

it was a dare

Oh my God. This is what my brother does with his Friday nights? Consumes unknown plants on a frat house dare?

"You okay?" Jonah asks.

"Yeah," I say as I text Peter, *Send a pic of the whole plant please!!!* "It's my brother. He's in college."

To Peter's credit, the new photo pops up right away, and I sigh with relief. It's just a parlor palm. Common and entirely harmless. They had to sentence Socrates to drink the hemlock tea that killed him, but my brother would probably eat it for twenty bucks and the eternal admiration of all his bros in Kappa Sigma.

it's fine

you're fine

thx

Jonah shifts next to me. "That's kind of a weird way of phrasing it."

"What is?" I ask, still texting.

you're welcome

maybe don't eat plants you don't know??

k

"You said your brother's in college."

I pocket my phone. "He is."

"Weird way of phrasing it," he says, staring me down. "Since you're in college, too."

Shit.

"Right. Yeah, right." I take a breath. "That was context. Um. For the next thing I was going to say, which is that my brother texted me because he ate an unknown plant on a dare so it was important for me"—I gulp air again—"uh, for me for *you* to know he's an adult man and not a . . . toddler."

"Got it," Jonah says, obviously still skeptical.

"If he were a toddler, I would be calling poison control."

"Responsible."

"But if he were a toddler, I guess he wouldn't have texted me."

"Probably not."

"God, you know"—I look to the doorway, trying to sound breezy and/or casual, but instead coming across panicked and/or frantic—"it is taking them a *very long time*. What do you think is taking Mo and Will so—"

But as I'm saying it, the door creaks open, and Mo pokes her head out. "Hey, guys."

Oh, thank God.

"Right in the nick of time," Jonah says, and I can feel his eyes still on me.

Mo frowns as I scramble past her, into the bar. "For what?" she asks Jonah.

"Yeah," he says. "That's my question."

Whoever named this bar the Forest might not have been super creative, but whoever designed it really knew how to commit to an aesthetic.

I've never been in a bar that was just a bar, only restaurants with bars attached, but I'm guessing most of them don't have walls fuzzy with artificial moss, or chairs and tables that look straight out of "Goldilocks and the Three Bears," before she went on that whole destruction-of-property rampage. It's a small room, barely big enough for the stage on one end, the bar on the other, and the tables crowded in between, but that hasn't stopped someone from filling it with plants.

Some might be fake, like the vines snaking up on wooden trellises on the walls and what look like maidenhair ferns cascading down from baskets near the low ceiling. But the spiky little snake plants decorating the bar look real enough.

"Sort of dive-y," Mo acknowledges, pushing an old French fry off the sticky table with the back of her hand. "But it's a good room."

"It's great," I say. "What other bar has bromeliads?"

"Is that a kind of medication?"

I point them out, on the shelves below the back windows. "It's those plants, the pink and the yellow ones. It's a whole plant family. Bromeliads. A pineapple is a bromeliad, but I think the only one you can eat." Then I remember Peter. "Safely."

"Huh." Mo seems to take it in. "So I'm guessing you like plants?"

"I love plants. And flowers, and trees. Really anything that grows." I pause. "Except mold."

"I totally get it," Mo says. "There's nothing like the smell of fresh-cut grass."

"Did you know it's a distress signal?" I ask. "When the grass gets cut, it releases these chemicals. It smells really nice to us, but it's basically the grass . . ." I clear my throat. "Um. You know. Screaming."

Mo looks amused. "That's so weird."

I try not to cringe. Alex says the same thing, whenever I mention something about gardening or flowers or . . . a lot of things I like, actually. *Weird.* He tosses the word over his shoulder, without a second of hesitation. Like he doesn't expect it to hurt. But also like he knows it will.

The phone buzzes on the table with a text. I start to put it in my purse, but before I can, another comes in. And then another. All from Alex, of course.

Hey we're taking a break

Did you finish Shakespeare stuff yet

Send me a pic or something

I hate it when he asks for that. He says he just likes getting to see me when we aren't together, but . . . I don't know. And I definitely can't take a picture of myself *here.*

Just hanging out at home

My camera's being weird though ugh

"You okay?" Mo asks me.

"Yeah." I look up from my phone. "It's just my boyfriend, he wanted me to—um. He likes knowing where I am."

Mo's expression flickers. Just for a second. Then she nudges Will. "Hey, Izzy knows the wildest shit about plants." She turns back to me with a grin. "Go ahead, tell him."

So I turn my phone to silent, stuff it deep inside my purse, and tell them the weirdest things I know.

"Thank you for the warm welcome," Mo says. "Just like my student loans, I don't think I can ever repay you."

The audience laughs.

"I've been in my current relationship for a year now. He's the most amazing guy." She squints into the audience. "Okay, so this is my favorite moment, because I get to watch everyone's brains recalibrating, like, 'Did she just say her partner's a man? Is she not gay, because she *looks* gay, oh my God, am I a bad person for assuming she was gay? Am I a . . . ?" She mimes gasping. "'Republican? Do I have to burn my Whole Foods canvas shopping bag?'" Mo leans down to speak directly to a man in the front row. She nods at him. "Yes."

Then she straightens up with a grin. "No, I'm just fucking with you. I am gay, I have a girlfriend, and the only amazing guy in my life is Jesus Christ." She waits another beat. "I'm still fucking with you! But this is fun, right?"

From the laugh she gets, the audience must agree.

"My girlfriend is the greatest. We are so compatible. She just gets me, you know? Even with all my flaws. We laugh about how competitive I am"—Mo leans into the mic, suddenly intense—"but *I laugh more.*"

Huh. I'd expected to hear Mo doing the same Broadway riot bit as last week, and apparently so did Will.

"Wait, is this *all* new?" he whispers to Jonah.

"You know her," Jonah says. "Can't stick to a set."

"It's so much better than my last relationship," Mo continues. "My ex-girlfriend had all these super-weird quirks. She hated avocados, which is just . . . not human. And it seemed like she started every single conversation by saying"—she puts on a higher, irritated voice—"'Wait, have you even been listening to me?'" She pauses for the laugh. "Right? *So* weird."

And then a voice, loud and demanding and male, cuts her short. "You suck."

We all swivel our heads around, trying to identify just who that came from.

"What's that, now?" Mo says mildly, her eyes searching through the audience.

"I said, you *suck*." It's easy to find him, now that I'm looking. A red-faced, jersey-wearing dude. Older than me but not much older than Mo, and shaped like an upside-down triangle.

If it were me, I'd have run off the stage already, or maybe be frozen and panicking. It *isn't* me, and my mouth is still dry and my heart is beating too fast. But all Mo does is lean down, one hand on her knee, with the expression of a kindergarten teacher about to pluck a glue stick out of a five-year-old's mouth.

"Ooh. Let's meet *you*," she says, almost gleeful. "What's your name, buddy?"

"Braden."

"Of course it is." She looks him up and down. "Your species

is so interesting. The Bradens." She waits a moment, considering. "It's fascinating how you all emerge from the womb wearing cargo shorts."

Everyone giggles. Braden looks down at his cargo shorts. He glares back up at Mo. "Suck my dick."

Mo blinks at him. She takes a beat. "You'll have to mark the spot, Braden, because you look like one giant dick to me."

That gets a bigger laugh, and Mo swiftly turns away from Cargo Shorts Braden.

"So St. Patrick's Day is coming up." She smiles. "The Most Holy Day, for the Braden species." That gets a laugh, too, but Mo doesn't rest on it, just launches right back in. "St. Patrick's Day has the weirdest decorations, right?"

I lean over to Will.

"Does that happen a lot?" I whisper.

"What?"

"That . . . guy."

"Hecklers?" I feel his shoulder shrug against mine. "Sometimes. They're mostly just drunk people. Mo can handle them."

I don't know Mo all that well, but I'm pretty certain she can handle anything.

When it's Will's turn, he takes his guitar up with him. He's the first one all night to sit on the stool, not just use it to hold water or a beer.

"Hello," Will says, leaning into the mic stand. "I'm Will

73

Nichols and this song is called 'Things I Think about Instead of Falling Asleep.'

"I think about:

Earthquakes, shark attacks, calling people on the phone, and dying from an atom bomb

Failing tests, failing college, climate change, the time in third grade I called my teacher 'Mom.'"

"Oh, he changed that," Mo whispers to Jonah.

"About his teacher?"

"Yeah. It used to be something about going alone to prom?"

"Same rhyme scheme, though."

I'd sort of assumed once you wrote a set, that was it, but of course you'd change things. It's writing, I realize, and no one writes a good first draft. Didn't Ms. Waldman say that? No matter how confident or off-the-cuff everyone might seem onstage, they must have spent hours going over and over their jokes, second-guessing their words and trying out new ideas until their throats went raw.

Will strums faster now.

"When that white lady at the grocery store said, 'Hi, David, how've you been?'

Was she being racist, or do I really look like him?"

He pauses for a beat, almost self-conscious, though I can't tell if that's part of the performance or not.

"Or am I racist for assuming she was racist?

Or is David her dead husband and I'm mocking someone with

Alzheimer's disease?

Or could someone just shoot me and end this self-destructive thought spiral, please?"

Jonah's up right after Will.

"So when I'm not doing this," Jonah says, "I'm—"

"Jacking off?" someone calls out from the back.

"Oh, is that what your mom calls it?" Jonah shoots back without missing a beat. "Yeah, so when I'm not doing this or fucking your mom on your race car bed, *Tyler*"—he holds up a middle finger—"I'm a tutor. It's great. Parents pay you all this money to pretend their terminally stupid kid just isn't being *challenged* enough."

Jonah uses the space a lot more than some of the other comics, I notice. Lots of them stay close to the mic, and of course Will has to, with his guitar. But Jonah stalks back and forth across the stage like he's rallying troops before a battle.

"I was tutoring this one girl in math," he says. "Like, third-grade stuff. And all these word problems, they were so stupid. Like, if Johnny has thirty-six apples and Betsy wants twelve of them, how many does he have left. Okay, first off, at this point Johnny has a hoarding problem and I hope Betsy's staging an intervention. TLC would buy that show. *Extreme Apple Hoarders.* But in what universe would any of this actually happen?" He stops pacing. "I think word problems should prepare you for the harsh realities of adult life."

Now he crouches down, as though speaking to a small child.

"Okay, Aiden, so if you want a quarter ounce of meth but you still owe your dealer for a half, how much cash do you need to prevent him from breaking both your kneecaps?"

Jonah pretends to listen to the answer. "That's right, it all depends on the current market price. That's what we call a *variable*."

A comedy show isn't like a regular show, at least not the ones I've been to. When the last performer climbs off the stage, there's no mass exodus for the door. The audience doesn't suddenly pull out their phones and battle for the next Uber.

It takes me a second to realize why: there *isn't* an audience. There are the people who were going to this bar anyway, and there are the people who finished their set and stuck around to support everyone else. And when it's over, those two groups both want the same thing: another drink.

Mo and her friends aren't any different. I sip my Coke through a straw and listen as they hash out the best and worst of their sets.

"The bit about the lady at the grocery store didn't land," Will says. "Right?"

"I heard some laughs," Mo says. "But yeah. I thought it would do better."

"You know if it was part of a special, and they filmed it, that's the moment they'd cut to the one Black person in the audience," Will says. "So all the white people watching knew it was okay to laugh."

"I think you need to go further with it," Jonah says. "Alzheimer's disease isn't much."

"Yeah, no, just the slow deterioration of the brain," Mo says. "Not much of a *closer*, I mean."

Will dutifully types the note on his phone. "Degenerative . . . brain . . . disease . . . bad . . . closer."

Mo gulps down the last of her beer. "Can we go? Or is anyone getting another?"

The boys shake their heads, and Mo starts to grab for her bag under the table. Then, realizing, she turns to me. "Oh. we're all going to go hang out in my room. If you wanted to come."

"Yes," I say, too quickly, too eagerly. I clear my throat. "I mean yeah. Sure. I can stick around."

Mo grins. "Awesome."

"Hey, is your girlfriend coming?" Jonah asks Mo as we all pile our layers of coats, scarves, and mittens back on.

Mo fixes him with a look. "Why?"

"She hates me."

"She does *not*—"

"At your birthday, she glared at me like—"

"Well, to be fair, Jonah, you did ask her if she grew up in a cult."

"Only because she told me she'd never read Harry Potter!"

"Still," Mo says. "But no, she's at the *Maroon* office tonight, working."

"Mo's girlfriend is always working," Will tells me. "You'll never meet her."

"She's a copy editor for our school paper, the hours conflict with, like, every open mic," Mo explains. "Plus, she gets super embarrassed hearing me talk onstage about sex and dating and stuff."

"Another point for the cult theory," Jonah says.

"She was not in a cult!"

As Jonah and Mo bicker, Will nudges me.

"So what did you think?" he asks.

"I love this place," I tell him, turning around to take it in again, a little emptier now. It looks like someone tried to grow a garden in a cave, which absolutely shouldn't be a good thing, but somehow, it is. It's wild. It's weird. It's perfect. "I feel like . . . I could waste my whole life here."

"Watch out," Jonah mumbles through the glove in his mouth. He pulls it onto his hand. "You wouldn't be the first."

CHAPTER 7

"SORRY IT'S MESSY," Mo says when she unlocks the front door. "Throw your stuff wherever."

Mo's room looks like she's taken her own advice. It's like a small tornado went through, if a tornado could somehow be artful. I'm the last one through the door, and I take a long moment to pick out what's underneath the top layer of wool coats and notebooks and lace-up boots strewn everywhere.

A wrinkled buffalo plaid comforter on an unmade twin bed, and resting on the pillow, a half-finished embroidery project with bright red roses and lettering that currently reads:

FUCK GENDER R

There's a scratched white mini fridge with an even more scratched black microwave stacked on top of it. And right beside that, a plastic milk crate filled with single-serving noodle cups and the kind of sugary kids' cereals my mom refuses to buy.

This is the first dorm room I've ever seen. The first *real* one, anyway, not an empty model during a college tour or a fake one on TV. Peter's and Charlotte's move-in days both happened while I was still at sleepaway camp, so I never saw their dorms, either.

Rainbow Christmas lights frame the window. Stacks and stacks of books overflowing from the single desk shelf and colonizing the floor space by the chair, next to the bed, and on the windowsill. A bulletin board over the desk, every inch of it covered with photos and ticket stubs and a big world map dotted with pushpins.

I'm pretty independent. I get myself to school. I do my own laundry. I can make my own dinner, though it's likely to be bagged salad. But this is different. A door you can close and know your mom won't open without knocking. A mini fridge full of whatever you took the time to buy, not what your dad remembered to have delivered. A closet of clothes that's up to you to wash, but up to you to wear as you see fit, without a dress code or a skeptical parent to question it.

A thousand daily decisions squashed into a tiny rectangular room. Real choices. Real life.

"I like your room," I tell Mo.

"Oh, thanks." She throws her coat over the desk chair, already piled with clothes. "Part of me would rather live off campus like everyone else, but you can't top free rent."

"Free?"

"I'm an RA." She shrugs. "So yeah, I guess it's more a trade. They give me room and board, I drag wasted eighteen-year-olds to the hospital, give out free condoms, and host a finals-week pizza party no one goes to."

"Are you in the dorms at Roosevelt?" Will asks me.

"No," I say, before realizing it would have been smarter to say yes. "I . . . live with my parents."

"Oh, so you're a commuter."

That word makes me think of businessmen in cars inching down I-90, but I nod. "Yeah."

Out in the hallway, there's the sound of heels clomping on linoleum. Then someone shrieks. I startle, but no one else even blinks. The shriek dissolves into giggling.

"Hailey," a girl in the hallway whines. "Hailey. Where's my other shoe?"

Her friend hiccups. "Wha?"

"My shoe. My other—I have one on, but where's the other?"

"Maybe you weren't wearing it when we left," her friend suggests.

"What the *fuck*, yes, I *was*."

A door slams shut. Mo rolls her eyes, like this happens every weekend.

"God," Jonah sighs. "I don't miss the dorms."

"Same," Will agrees.

"Where do you live, if you're not in the dorms?" I ask Will.

"Jonah and I are roommates," he answers. "Off campus."

It's not weird for college kids in big cities to have apartments, I know, but thinking about the logistics makes my brain short-circuit. How do they make money for rent? How do you even *pay* rent—can you put it on a credit card? Or do people use checks? My grandma sends checks to me and the twins on our birthdays, but Mom always converts them into regular money for us. Dad talks about "balancing the checkbook" sometimes, but I have no idea what that actually means.

"That must be so cool," I say to them. "Living on your own."

"Yes, so glad I'm going into debt for the privilege of listening to our neighbor's shitty thrash band practice every night," Jonah says.

"They're getting better," Will says.

"They're getting louder. It's not the same thing." Jonah nudges Mo. "You're not on duty tonight, right?"

"Nope." Mo strides over to the bulletin board above her desk. She runs her finger down a pink piece of paper. "Rajiv has the duty phone."

"Rajiv Shah?" Jonah asks. "Didn't he used to sell, like, crappy dime bags to freshmen?"

"He still does," Mo says. She retrieves a brown bottle and a blue one from under the bed. "That's how I know we're safe."

"Sometimes I feel like you're not a good RA," Will says.

"Sometimes I feel like you don't get any whiskey now."

Will holds up his hands. "Let's not jump to extremes."

82

Mo uncorks the brown bottle with a flourish, and Will hands out red cups from a stack on top of her mini fridge. She passes the blue bottle to Jonah and pours from the brown bottle for herself and Will.

"Whiskey or tequila?" she asks me. I hesitate. She notices. "Or are you not a drinker?"

"No, I mean, I do," I say, which is true only in the most technical sense. I've had champagne on New Year's with my parents, though my dad finished my glass, and I've had sips of terrible, watery beer with Alex at parties, but sips were about all I could stand.

"No pressure. I have soda." She digs a can of Coke out of the mini fridge.

"Well—" I hesitate. It's not that I want them to think I'm cool or anything, because no one seems like they care. Why should they? This is college, not Kyle Carson's rec room. Nobody's judging the choice I make, and for some reason, that makes me want to choose something new.

"Maybe," I say slowly, "I could just have a little bit? With the pop?"

Mo grabs a plastic cup off the table and turns back to me. "Do you know the trick with red cups?"

I shake my head. I expect her to place it down lid first and play some kind of shell game, but instead, she holds it closer to me.

"See the first line, closest to the bottom?" She taps on the first indentation on the cup, just about an inch high. "That's one ounce. One drink, if you're drinking liquor." She grabs the brown bottle and pours carefully, stopping when she hits the line. She tops it off with the whole pop can, then hands me the red cup. "As long as you don't, like, chug it, you're going to be okay."

I take a cautious sip. You can barely taste the whiskey.

"You'd fill it up to the next line for wine, and the line after that for beer. It's actually really helpful, if you *care* how much you're *drinking*," she calls over her shoulder at Jonah, who's in the middle of a pretty heavy pour.

"Thanks," I say. Then, with a sudden wave of self-consciousness, "Sorry for being, I don't know—"

"Dude, no, it's fine," Mo says. "You only just met us, it makes total sense."

Right. From her perspective, it's not that I'm sixteen and don't know *how* to drink, it's that I'm twenty and don't want to be drunk around strangers. But it doesn't matter why. What matters is she doesn't want me to feel uncomfortable. My shoulders loosen. I take another small sip.

"Hey, did you see if Sean was filming tonight?" Mo asks Will and Jonah. "I think that was my best heckler moment yet."

"Someone was filming us?" I ask, suddenly seized with panic that footage of me could end up on TV, somewhere my parents could see.

"Not *you*," Jonah says, with a roll of his eyes. "You didn't do a set."

"Sean the Bartender tapes most of the open mics at the Forest," Mo says.

"He tapes them?" I wrinkle my nose. "Why?"

"So comics can buy them," she says, like it's totally obvious. "You can use clips of yourself performing as audition tapes to get into real clubs. Places you have to be invited."

"Places that pay," Jonah mutters.

"Even if you're not looking for that, yet," Will assures me, "you can still upload them on YouTube. Everybody does."

"Oh, um—" I clear my throat. "I . . . don't have a YouTube channel. Or any social media. At all."

"Okay," Jonah says flatly. "Bullshit."

"No, really, it's true." It's not, of course, but I figure this way they won't try to search for me anywhere. But Jonah still looks suspicious, so I keep talking, letting the lie snake out its tendrils like a vine. "My older brother did all this dumb stuff on the internet when he was in high school." True, not that my parents know. "So then my mom and dad were really protective of me—like any parents would be—so I just . . . never got into it."

"And see, here I imagined you with a million-subscriber YouTube account for, I don't know, baking," Mo says.

"Or unexpected animal friendships," Will offers up.

"God, I wish," I tell him. "I love those videos. They're basically my whole family dynamic."

"Huh?" Mo says.

"Oh, I mean—" I hesitate, because this is just something I've thought before, not something I've ever said. "I'm the odd one out, like that. Like my parents and my siblings are a pack of stunning golden retrievers and I'm the, like, teacup pig trotting behind them trying to make this whole dog thing work."

Will laughs. "You're the unlikely animal friend of your own family?"

"If anyone gets to identify with the teacup pig, it should be the adopted kid here," Jonah says, indicating himself.

"Teacup pigs are an inclusive community. Don't be such a gatekeeper," Will says.

Mo reaches across them to get my attention. "That could be a good bit."

"For who?"

"For *you*, duh." She shrugs. "No offense, but your murder fantasy set isn't working."

"It wasn't a set."

"That's the part that isn't working."

I say nothing for a moment. Then: "Do you think I really could?"

"Could what?" Mo asks.

"Do this. Be . . ." I gesture vaguely, at all of them, at the room around us. "This."

"Yeah, well, I wouldn't aspire to this level of clutter," Jonah says. Mo socks him in the arm.

86

"I'm serious," I say. "You guys are so confident, and smart, and brave, and I—" I hesitate. "I know you just met me, and everything, but you should know I'm not. Brave. Like you."

Mo lets the silence linger, like she doesn't know what to say back. Or maybe, like she's trying to think of just the right words. Finally, she replies, "Maybe you're brave like you."

And then it's me who doesn't know what to say.

"It's not brain surgery," Will jumps in. "Doing stand-up."

Mo smiles at him. "Will would know, since he's premed."

"There's a couple basic rules, but then it's just getting up on stage over and over."

"Yeah, and failing, over and over," Jonah adds. "Not everyone's cut out for that."

Will tosses him a look. "Sure. But you get better. It gets easier. You figure out what works for you and what doesn't. You don't have to be a special kind of person to do this," he assures me. "You just have to be willing to try."

I put my cup down. "You said there are rules."

"Not about what you say onstage. But about how you treat the people around you. So it's closer to etiquette."

"Like, be nice to the bar staff," Mo offers up. "That's rule number one of stand-up."

Jonah shakes his head. "The first rule has to be the light."

She considers. "The bar staff usually controls the light. So it's connected."

"What light?" I ask.

"You didn't see it?" Jonah asks. "When you were onstage at the creepy Goth club?"

"Her set was too short," Will says. "She wasn't even close to going over."

"It depends on the venue," Mo explains, "but there's usually a light somewhere in the room. Facing you, not the audience. At a real comedy club, it might be part of the bigger light setup."

"At the places we go, it might be the barback shining a pen light in your eye," Jonah adds.

"But when you see the light go up—and you should notice— that means you've got a minute. And when you see the light flash, that means you're done."

"Doesn't matter where you are in the set, you get offstage," Will says.

"Respect the light," Mo says. "Always, always respect the light."

I wish we had that in the world at large. A red light letting you know you've talked enough and it's someone else's turn. Maybe I'd finally get a word in edgewise at school. And at home.

"What are the other rules?" I ask.

"Buy a drink if you can," Will says. "And tip on every one."

"Keep your phone in your pocket when someone's onstage," Mo says. "Pay attention to everyone who gets up, not just your friends."

"Break the box," Jonah says.

Will shakes his head. "That's not really a *rule*."

"It's just a thing we say," Mo explains to me. "The three of us."

"Have you heard of typecasting?" Jonah asks. "For actors?"

I nod. "Yeah, it's when people play the same kind of role over and over because it fits them."

"Because it *looks* like it fits them," Jonah corrects me. "Not because it *does*."

I feel like I've said the wrong thing, but I don't quite know why. Will glances from Jonah to me and takes the reins.

"There's a similar sort of thing in stand-up," he says, "where you get onstage and people expect you to do a certain kind of set. Talk about certain things."

"Especially if you don't fit the white-straight-comedy-guy prototype," Mo adds. "You get boxed in to only talking about how you're different. Even if you don't want to."

"But screw that," Jonah says. "I introduce myself onstage and you're wondering why I'm Asian, but I've got a Norwegian last name? Fuck you, keep wondering."

"Look, sometimes it can work for people." Will picks at his sweater sleeve. "The things they want to talk about onstage are the same things the audience expects to hear from them, and if that's them . . . well, okay."

"But it sounds like it isn't," I say, "for you."

Will shakes his head. "A white dude goes up with a guitar,

nobody bats an eye. I go up, and you can just *see* people trying to figure it out. They don't think I *look* like I should do that kind of comedy."

"They just want a tight five about the differences between Black people and white people?" Jonah asks.

"I guess. Or they want permission to laugh at Black culture and dialect because I'm telling the jokes, so it must be okay. Or, they want, I don't know, to hear about life on the South Side, even though I—"

"Grew up on a country estate?" Jonah cuts in.

Will looks embarrassed. "It is not an estate."

"Your backyard's the size of my entire hometown."

"That's a huge exaggeration."

"It's a huge backyard."

"Doesn't your sister have a horse?" Mo asks.

Will buries his head in his hands. "Yes, but it doesn't *live* at the *house!*"

"It's the same for me," Jonah says. "Doesn't matter what I put in my set, I know there's someone in the audience hoping I'll make fun of my mom's accent."

"You do make fun of your mom's accent," Will points out.

"Yeah, her Wisconsin accent," Jonah says. "I was raised by two white people in a tiny, white cow town. I can't give the audience what they're expecting. Even if I wanted to."

"But that's such an interesting perspective to have," I say. "To be able to talk about."

"Interesting," Jonah agrees. "And complicated. You've got five minutes before the light, Murder Girl. Not a lot of room for nuance."

"I don't have a box," Mo says. "I have a whole Jenga tower. I'm a girl, I'm pretty visibly not a *straight* girl, and then on top of all that, I'm"—she waves her arm like she's painting a rainbow with her hand—"ethnically ambiguous."

"What a phrase," Will says.

"I know, right? It sounds like a rare disease."

"People really can't guess you're Iranian?" Jonah asks.

"No, they guess I'm Iranian," Mo says. "But they also guess I'm Mexican, Indian, Moroccan, Spanish, and . . . Sicilian."

"You can go anywhere in the world," Will says.

"Yeah, sure," Mo deadpans. "Full passport. Just have to get through that 'random' TSA screening first."

They all laugh, but I'm not sure if I'm supposed to. I don't know what that's like, at all. To be seen as different or, God, *dangerous* for no reason. If anything, people assume I'm no possible danger at all. Like a fluffy little kitten. One that's been declawed.

It seems like such a painful thing to be laughing about, or even talking about as openly and casually as they are. But . . . I can see how there's power in that. Taking something so unfair and hurtful and constant and still finding the humor in it. When Mo makes it into a joke, she's not diminishing what she goes through. She's showing a shitty situation to be exactly what it really is: ridiculous.

"One time, I was in a medieval history class and my professor asked me for the Muslim perspective on the Crusades." Mo takes a gulp of her drink. "And I told him he would have to ask an actual Muslim person, not just a brown one, because my Zoroastrian ancestors were not involved."

"And that's really it, isn't it?" Will says. "It's the same thing with stand-up. The audience sees you get up and they expect you to—not teach them, they don't want to be *taught*—but—"

"Explain yourself," Mo says. "Justify your existence."

"Stand in for a whole identity," Jonah adds. "As if one person could ever fucking do that."

"That's what we mean by break the box," Mo says to me. "Say what you want to say. Not just what the audience expects you to."

"But it doesn't apply to me, right?" I point out. "The . . . box."

"Oh?" Mo raises an eyebrow. "You don't think so?"

"Well, no," I say, surprised. "Because I'm . . . white."

"You don't say," Jonah deadpans.

"And straight," I add, quickly, feeling like I've missed something important that everyone else knows. "And I've got money. I mean, *I* don't have money, my parents have money—and not that I have money like Will has money, apparently—"

"Oh my God," Will says to Jonah. "This is why you have to stop saying it's an estate."

"Yeah," Mo agrees with me, "you're white and straight and not on scholarship. I get it." She pauses. "You're also a girl."

"What does that have to do with—"

"Did you notice the lineup tonight?" Mo asks. "How many girls went up?"

I think about it. "You."

"And?"

I think about it longer. "Just . . . you."

"You'll get your own box, hate to tell you. It'll look a little different than mine, but"—she shrugs—"it's still a box."

I've never thought of myself as having a box. I just thought . . . this is the way the world is.

"You're a very pretty, very young girl on a stage. There are dudes in that audience who will never see you as anything but a body to look at. And there are dudes in that audience who think you are biologically incapable of being funny."

"What?" I shake my head. "Biologically? No way."

"Yes," she says. "They might even write a think piece for *Vanity Fair* about it."

"You read *Vanity Fair*?" Jonah asks. Mo swats him away and focuses back on me.

"Even the ones who *do* listen, who *do* think you can have a vagina and a sense of humor at the same time—well, they'd prefer it if you talked about sex. A lot about sex, and all the sex you're having, so they can better imagine you without clothes on."

I know men do that, sometimes imagine girls naked. Sometimes, if they're extra gross, they'll even *tell* you they're doing it, as you walk past them. But how messed up that you become a part of someone's sex life before you even have one yourself.

"I'm not saying you don't have it good," Mo says. "Or that you aren't enormously privileged, because you are, and you know it. There are a lot of shitty things about this industry you'll never see. But there are some you will. And you should know that, going in."

"Especially if you ever want a bigger stage than the Forest," Will adds.

That seems to spark something in Mo, who hits me on the arm lightly. "I almost forgot! We haven't told you yet, about the All-College Showcase."

"Wait, Mo—" Jonah interrupts, but she brushes him off.

"What? It's an open call. Don't be weird."

It's pretty clear Jonah isn't thrilled Mo brought me along, but I'm not sure if it's because he can tell I'm lying about everything, or because he doesn't think I'm serious, or because he thinks I'm some kind of threat.

"You're not scared of a little more competition," Will teases him.

Jonah rolls his eyes in a way that distinctly says, *As if.*

Oh, he doesn't think I *can* be a threat? Okay. We'll see.

"It's this showcase," Mo explains. "I think Loyola sponsors

it, but it's for any college kid in Chicago. You audition with like three minutes and they choose ten folks to go on and do their set for a bunch of industry people."

"And an audience filled with the losers," Jonah says.

"It's a really cool opportunity," Will says. "You get to be front of people who make decisions. And they aren't judging you against older people with way more experience or anything, because everyone's in the same place."

"The auditions are in March, I think, and then the showcase is maybe a few days after," Mo says. "So, not a ton of time."

"Oh, yeah." I nod, and try not to look disappointed. "Maybe I can try next year."

Mo snorts. "What are you talking about? You'll do it this year."

"But you said March, I won't be ready to perform by March—"

"Of course you will."

"We'll get you there," Will agrees. "Between the three of us."

Mo nudges Jonah, who looks just as skeptical as I feel. "Yeah. Won't we?"

Jonah takes another sip of his drink, but he doesn't say no. Mo turns back to me.

"So, what do you say?"

I think: *Getting up on stage was an accident, and I don't think I'm cut out for this.*

I think: *By the way, I'm sixteen and you just gave me whiskey.*

I say: "Okay." And then I say it again. Not because I feel like I have to. Because I want to. "Okay."

"You'll try it?" Mo asks. "Will's right. We'll all help, the first set is the hardest."

"Yeah," I say, louder this time. More certain. "I'll do it."

Mo holds up her drink. "Cheers to that."

I tap my red cup against hers and take another sip.

"Hey. Izzy."

Someone's pushing on my shoulder, and I startle awake. "Huh?"

"Sorry," Mo whispers, though I don't know why. Everyone else is already up. "Didn't mean to scare you."

"What time is it?" I ask, pushing myself up on my hands.

"Six. You fell asleep for a little bit."

I rub at my eyes. After a while, everyone moved on to a no-holds-barred rehashing of the open mic and who sucked the most (obvious winner: Cargo Shorts Braden). The last thing I remember is all of us crowding on Mo's bed to watch *Airplane!*, which I'd never seen and couldn't understand without the subtitles on. And since I'm still in the same spot, I guess that's where I fell asleep. It's pretty embarrassing, but in my defense, I don't think any of *them* had a 7:00 a.m. AP Bio lab this morning.

"I only woke you because we're going to the roof," she says. "If you want to come."

The roof? "But it's still dark."

"Not for long," Mo says.

The only reason we haven't frozen to death in this concrete stairwell is because we're so closely packed together. When Mo said we were going up to the roof, I assumed she meant the top floor. Or an observation deck. Instead, she shepherded us all up to the twenty-first floor, through an unmarked door, under another set of stairs, and to another door. This one is marked, though it's with the words "Staff Only" in red letters.

"This can't be allowed," Will mumbles.

"It says 'Staff,'" Mo reasons. "I'm staff."

"RA does not stand for 'Roof Access.'"

Mo turns the handle, and the door creaks open. She stops for a moment, like she's waiting for an alarm, but it's quiet. She turns back to Will. "See? Not a problem."

"Not a problem unless we get caught."

"Yes," she hisses. "So be quieter."

Mo pokes her head out into the darkness, scans left and right, then waves us all through the doorway. I feel wobbly, standing on something so high up, but with no guardrails at the building's edge, no benches or gates to crowd the view. Like we're floating in the sky. Jonah fiddles with his phone for a moment, then points to the left.

"That way," he says. Mo plops down first, facing the same

direction as Jonah's finger. We all crowd around beside her and wait.

I'm past the point of tired, past the point of exhausted. My eyes are heavy, but my head is light, and the world around me seems airy and boundless. Staring out at the city in front of me, I almost want to reach out and touch them, all those buildings, that fit together like interlocking puzzle pieces. Like a garden of glass and brick and steel, untended and unending.

It's so strange. You can live in a place your whole life and never really see it. A whole life, and still everything can change in a second. All it takes is a shift in perspective, and all of a sudden, you might as well be on Mars. All it takes is a new vantage point, and all of a sudden, you're home.

It happens like a painting played backward, flecks of nothing giving way to color, one by one. It happens like a curtain being lifted inch by inch. It happens so slowly you can barely see it at all, not until the light is already warm on your face. The world cracks open like an eggshell, easy and satisfying, like it was always meant to be broken. And I watch it spill out, the sudden sun and the warmth, red and orange and bursting. It's almost as if I can breathe it in, fill up my lungs with the sky.

Mo's arm brushes mine as she turns to Jonah, cutting into a story he's telling Will. Jonah throws an arm across her chest, talking over her, refusing to be outdone, and then they're all laughing, and I am, too, though I couldn't hear anything over the sunrise.

There's a jolt of recognition deep in my stomach, an almost-disorienting feeling. Like déjà vu, but not quite. Like déjà vu, only turned around. The flicker in my soul doesn't say, *You have been here before.* It whispers—maybe it promises—*You will be here again.*

"Happy you came?" Mo asks.

"Yes," I whisper. "I'm happy."

CHAPTER 8

THE BOUNCER AT the Forest is only there on Friday and Saturday nights, Mo explains. Any other day, you can walk right in and not be bothered, especially if the owner knows you. So today, Sunday, I meet her and Jonah at the bar, and she introduces me to the owner, Colin, an older and *extremely* Chicago guy with a bushy gray mustache and a faded, holey '85 Bears sweatshirt.

Mo buys herself and Jonah a beer to share, and I go for a Coke. When we sit down at the least sticky table we can find, Mo takes a thin binder out of her bag, and presents it to me.

"What is it?" I ask, staring at the blank cover.

"A gift," she says. "To start your brand-new life."

"Like the wise men gave to baby Jesus," Jonah says.

"Don't get too excited," Mo warns me. "It's not that good."

"Anything's better than myrrh."

I flip it open to read the title at the top of the first page.

HOW TO WRITE A JOKE
THAT MIGHT NOT SUCK

A Non-Comprehensive Guide by Mozhgan "Mo" Irani

Mo leans across the table. "I didn't make up the method. It's from this comedy book I have. I tailored it for you, though."

"This is amazing," I tell her. "Does it really work?"

"It's a guideline. It won't write the jokes for you, but it's the building blocks of comedy," she says. "Target, Hostility, Realism, Emotion, Exaggeration, and Surprise."

"The biggest surprise is how hard it is," Jonah says. "Everyone's sure they're funny until they actually try to write a joke, and then—"

Mo glares at him. He shuts up.

As I'm skimming through the pages, Mo drops the bomb: she wants me to go up with my new set at the Forest next Monday. Just six days from today.

"*Next* Monday?" I say. "I'm not going to be ready by then."

"You'll never really be ready," Mo says with a toss of her head. "You have to try it anyway. It's the only way you're going to learn."

"Mo. That's not enough time."

"We'll all work with you," she assures me. "We'll help you come up with something."

Mo flips me back to the first page of the guide. "But before we even get to a joke, let's figure out how you're going to start."

"I won't start with a joke?"

"You want to introduce yourself," Mo says. "Well, the emcee will say your name—"

"Does he have to?" I interrupt. "I mean, say my real name."

Jonah leans forward, his chin in his hand. "What's wrong with your real name?"

"Nothing," I say, avoiding his eyes. "I just thought people picked new ones."

"Maybe if they're hiding something."

I hold my breath for a moment, still keeping my eyes on the blank page in front of me, but Mo shakes off his comment like it's nothing.

"Would you stop?" she says to Jonah. "I go by Mo, it doesn't mean I'm *on the lam*."

Jonah doesn't say anything, but also doesn't look convinced. Mo turns back to me.

"You start by welcoming the audience. Getting them comfortable." She taps on my notebook. "Maybe you say—"

"Thank you. It's so good to be here tonight."

I wonder if I'll say this every time, not just this first time. Even if I'm in places it's not *as good to be.*

Keep going, I have to keep going, Mo said pace is important right up front.

102

"I was born here." I rest for a half-second pause. "I mean, not in this bar, that would be . . . unfortunate." I lean forward, as if I'm having a conversation with someone in the audience, but I forget to make eye contact, like I'm supposed to. "'Oh, you were born at Northwestern?'" I nod. "'Cool. I was born on the floor at the Forest.'" I nod again. "'Yeah, thanks, I did immediately contract hep C.'"

And there it is, the first laugh. Low and short, but there. A laugh. I straighten up and call out to the bar area, a little sheepishly: "Sorry, Colin."

"The first thing you've got to do is pick a victim," Mo says. "A target."

"Shouldn't be tough for you, Murder Girl."

"Jonah, if you're not going to be helpful, you can go."

"Helpful is in the eye of the beholder."

"I'm going to behold you over the train tracks pretty soon."

"See, in that instance," Jonah says to me, "I'm the target."

"There are a lot of common comedy targets," Mo says. "Girlfriends, sex, airplane food—"

"Politicians, public transportation—" Jonah adds.

"But the important thing is to punch up, not down," Mo says.

"What if I just don't punch anyone?" I suggest. "I don't really know how."

"When I say punch up, I mean choose the right target. Look, comedy is just like being in kindergarten—"

"Yes," Jonah agrees. "Eat lots of glue, take lots of naps, and cry when anything goes wrong."

"You have to pick on someone your own size," Mo says to me, ignoring him. "Someone who can take it, not the weird kid in the corner who still wets the bed."

"This metaphor is losing me," I tell her.

"Don't make fun of people the world is already beating down. Save your jokes for the people and the groups that have power. Punch up."

"Is making fun of my family punching up?" I ask.

"You're really making fun of yourself, not your family."

"So what's that?"

"Masochism?" Jonah suggests.

"So, anyway——" I shift on my feet. Whoops. I can't see Mo, but I can almost hear her, reminding me to plant myself. I try to imagine my legs like roots, tethering and steady. "I was raised here," I continue, "in Chicago, as an only child." I pause. "My siblings were super uncool about it."

A longer pause, here, giving people time to get it. It takes a split second before I get the second laugh. But I don't rest on it. Mo told me I'm not allowed to rest on the laugh. I have to keep going. "No, actually, my brother and sister are way closer to my parents than I am," I tell the audience. "Or at least, they're way more similar to my parents than I am." I use my hands to show the distance between us, weigh the differences.

"They're all really athletic." A beat. "The strongest thing about

me is my password." A laugh.

"They're super sociable." A beat. "My Wi-Fi goes out more than I do." Another laugh. "Basically, they're all extroverted. As I'm sure you know, that just means they have a hard outer shell protecting their internal organs."

No laughs there. Not even one. Mo said it wouldn't land. I cringe, and die, and then breathe, and keep going.

We're all together after a Wednesday open mic. The three of them critiqued each other's performances first, but then the topic of conversation turned to me, and my half-written bit about me and my extrovert family.

"The internal organs thing isn't going to land," Mo says, and reaches to cross it out.

I frown. "But you get it, right? It's an exoskeleton."

"We all get it," Will says. "Doesn't mean people are going to laugh."

Mo pulls her pencil back, holding her hand up in surrender. "Try it and see. That's the only way you'll know."

"I think you need an anecdote now," Will decides, and the other two nod.

"An anecdote?" I ask.

"Like a story," Jonah says.

"Like a representative story," Mo adds. "About you and your family."

"I'm worried this is getting too . . . real." I put down my pen.

"If I tell a story, does it have to be a true one?"

Everyone looks at each other.

"Good comedy is real," Mo says. "Even if it's exaggerated, it sounds real, it feels real, that's what makes it funny. Otherwise it's just . . . fantasy."

"People like fantasy. Haven't you ever seen pictures of Comic Con?"

"Please," Will says. "I have *been* to Comic Con."

I turn back to Mo. "See?"

She shakes her head, not buying it. "You're braver than you're acting. So what's going on? What's stopping you?"

I hesitate. "I'm not sure I should tell them this."

"Who's them?"

"The audience."

"And why?"

"Because it *is* real," I say. "This is my actual family, and my actual life, and I don't know, it just seems so . . . personal."

"That's why it'll work," Will says gently.

Mo puts her hand on top of mine. "It took me a long time to figure this out but trust me: you can tell them anything." I open my mouth to object, because *anything*? But she stops me. "Anything. All you have to do is make it funny."

I shake my head. "I don't even want to tell them my *name*."

"Why not?" She wrinkles her forehead. "What's your last name?"

106

I can't tell her my real one. What if she looks me up? Thanks to my complete lack of extracurriculars, there aren't any track and field scores or debate wins floating around on the internet, but still.

"Um. Van . . . Tassel."

"Like in 'Sleepy Hollow'?" Jonah asks slowly.

My heart skips a beat. "What?"

"Van Tassel," he says, even more slowly. "Isn't that the name of the lady in 'Sleepy Hollow'?"

I gulp, because yes, that *is* the name of the girl in 'The Legend of Sleepy Hollow.' I really *did* just name myself after the lady who wouldn't fuck Ichabod Crane.

"Uh . . . yeah," I say, trying to play off my terror as vague embarrassment. "Um. The story's fiction—I mean, obviously, but—it's a real last name." Which is true. Some of the Van Tassels still live in the Hudson Valley. My grandma even knows them. "My family's been in America a really long time," I add, which is also true, though not technically relevant. "But it doesn't seem like a stand-up's name, you know?"

"Isabel Van Tassel." Mo thinks this over. "It does sound like you're an heiress with a closet full of mink coats and three husbands who died under mysterious circumstances."

"It sounds like you're the villain in an eighties workplace drama," Will says.

"It sounds like you're a passenger on the *Mayflower* who later gets accused of witchcraft for cursing the neighborhood cows," Jonah says.

I point at Mo. "Winner."

Jonah is unwilling to accept this. "*Mayflower* was better."

"What about Izzy?" Mo suggests. "Just Izzy?"

"I was kind of thinking . . ." I take a breath. "Izzy V. So it's me, but it's not . . . *all* of me."

"Izzy V." Mo smiles. "I love it."

"No, obviously, my family are not insects," I say, aware of the nervousness creeping into my voice. I'm trying to recover, but I'm just sounding panicked. "They're more like a pack of very beautiful, very lovable golden retrievers. Except they have more than four brain cells between them."

A small laugh. More a chuckle. But it's not nothing, and I cling on to it.

"Like golden retrievers, they're energetic and outgoing and they always want to be your friend." I wait a beat, letting them know a story is coming. "My mom met her best friend on a nonstop flight from New York to San Francisco." I wait another, letting them know they should find this as ridiculous as I do. "That's right. A woman talked to my mom on an airplane for six straight hours, *and that lady became her best friend." I lean in, conspiratorially. "If someone tried to talk to* me on a plane for six hours, *that person would become my next murder victim."*

A bigger laugh, a better laugh. I don't crack a smile, though I want to. I just nod. "Yes. I said my next murder victim." *I shrug, step back. "So, you know. Watch out."*

◆◆◆

"When you're performing," Mo tells me. "Try to count those laughs, if you can."

"*Count* them?"

"Not if it distracts you too much, but a five-minute set goes by like a blur. You're aiming for about five laughs a minute, so twenty-five laughs total."

"A laugh per minute rate," I say. "Very scientific."

"It's just one metric. But try for five. Five is great."

"Honestly, Mo, it's all personal preference, but—" Jonah holds his hands about five inches apart. "Five is *extremely* average."

"I swear to God, Jonah," Mo says. "The only reason you do stand-up is because you get to say shit up there no one would *ever* tolerate if you said it on the street."

"Oh, okay." Jonah holds his palms up as if he's offended, but his grin gives it away. "You want to go there?"

"Bring it," she says.

"*You* only do stand-up because you're a theater kid who couldn't dance well enough to be on Broadway."

"Glass houses, you dick," she says. "I've seen you try to dance."

"And Will only does it because he wants to make people happy, just like he did as the golden boy of Dental Floss, Illinois."

"Flossmoor," Will corrects him wearily. "You know it's called Flossmoor."

"I like Dental Floss better."

"So I like to make people happy," Will concedes. "So what?

It's nice. You should try it occasionally."

"What about me?" I ask. All four of them turn in my direction, but no one gives an answer.

"I mean, I know I haven't really done it a lot," I add, feeling embarrassed for even asking. Of course no one has an answer, they've been friends for years and I just got here, but I wanted to feel like I was part of the group. Not an intruder, not a project, but a friend.

"You do it for the audience," Mo says. And then leaves it there, like that tells me all it needs to.

"Doesn't everyone?"

"Yeah, but for you . . ." She goes quiet for a moment, as if she's trying to find just the right words.

"For me . . . ," I prompt her.

"I think you do stand-up"—when Mo smiles, there's a little bit of sadness in it—"because you just want to be loved."

"I was not born a golden retriever," I admit. "It's kind of like—do you ever watch those videos, on the internet with unlikely animal friends?"

It's a rhetorical question, but I act like I can see them nod, hear them say yes. "Yeah, right? Like a kitten and penguin, or a bunny and a frog, or a sloth and a . . . I don't know, marmoset."

I put the mic back on its stand, because I need both my hands for the next bit. "But then there's this other subtype," I explain, "which is animals raised by unlikely parents. You'll see them give, like, a dog mom one miniature piglet to raise, in her litter. And then the pig grows up surrounded by dogs, so they think that's how they're supposed to act, too."

I point at myself, with both thumbs. "That's me. I'm the miniature pig." They laugh, and so do I, because this part has to be upbeat. I have to laugh at myself so they'll be comfortable doing it, too.

"Just like, trotting behind my majestic golden retriever family on my stubby little hooves." I make my hand into approximate hooves and mime the stubby walk. "Just trying super hard to be a dog, even though it's obviously not in the cards. Like—" I put on a higher-pitched, faux-enthusiastic voice. "'Yeah, this is fun, you guys. So much fun! I love barking and fetching and running and dog stuff.'"

I pause there and, still in character as the miniature pig, hold one stubby hoof up. "'Hey, wild thought, though: what if we just lay down in this mud for like eight hours and didn't move at all?'" I pause, for the laugh. "'You know, just for a change of pace?'"

"I think this is working," Mo says as we sit on the bed in her dorm together on a rainy Saturday afternoon, and she looks over what I've written between Wednesday and now. "But you should practice, before Monday."

"I have been practicing," I promise her. "And watching all those comedy clips you sent me."

"That's great. But I meant more." She reaches into her bag and pulls out a beaten-up mic. "With this."

"Did you steal it from the Forest?" I ask, but accept it when she holds it out to me.

"I borrowed it from Will so you can practice holding it."

I grip it with both hands. "I think I'm okay."

"See, you say that, but"—she reaches over and removes my left hand—"one-handed. Not so tight. It's an extension of you."

But it feels cold and heavy and not like me at all. *None* of this is like me at all. And everyone's going to be able to tell.

"What if I look weird?" I say. "What if I don't do it right? What if—" I hesitate, because Mo's going to think I'm ridiculous. Performing is as natural as breathing to her. "What if I *can't* do it?"

She frowns. "What do you mean?"

I think about all the times I've been called on in class and froze. All the times I tried to speak at the dinner table and was talked over. All the times I've wanted to disagree with Alex but swallowed the words.

What if I go onstage, and I'm the same as I've always been?

"Sometimes I . . . clam up," I tell Mo. "When I'm nervous. Or, I don't know, sometimes it's just hard to talk, and what if that happens during my set, what if I get the mic in my hand and can't do it?"

"Breathe," she says.

"I am."

"No," she says. "I mean, if that happens, onstage. *Breathe.* In through your nose." Mo's shoulder's hitch as she takes in the air, slowly holding up one, two, then three fingers. She releases it just as gradually, removing one finger each second. "And then out, just like that. Try."

I try. Three seconds of oxygen in, three seconds of dioxide out. My mind feels steadier. Calmer.

"If you focus on the count, you can't worry about anything else. And then you dive right in, while you're still feeling that release."

"And everyone watching is perfectly aware this pig is not a dog, and so it's that fun mixture of sweet and super pathetic. Everyone's like"—I go for a condescending, singsong voice here—"'Aw, look how hard she's trying. Do you think she knows how much she doesn't belong with them? So cute. She is going to make the most adorable sausage links.'"

That gets a groan, not a laugh, but Mo said it would. We planned for it.

"What?" I say, as if I don't understand the reaction. "We eat pigs! I understand where I am in this food chain."

"Last thing," Mo says, turning to the final page in the guide, "is the twist ending."

"It says 'surprise,'" I say, reading over her shoulder. "Twist ending sounds like I'm in a horror movie."

"I did see a pretty bad nosebleed onstage once," she says. "Call it a twist, call it a button, call it a surprise—whatever you want. It's the last little moment you get. When your audience thinks you're out of moves, but you've got one more rabbit to pull out of the hat."

"I think that's a mixed metaphor."

"I think you're kind of pedantic," she replies. "If you want to get academic about it, that's the biggest reason people laugh at anything. Surprise. Unpredictability. We love being wrong about things."

I don't know if that's universal. "Do we?"

"Yeah," she says. "Even if we don't always admit it—" She smiles. "The surprise is the best part."

I take the mic off the stand again. "Movies have taught me what to expect out of life, as a miniature pig raised by golden retrievers. No, seriously, think about any movie with a pig. Even children's movies."

I plant myself dead center stage and make each word crisp and clear and like they matter.

"Every movie with a pig is about that pig desperately trying to escape its violent, impending slaughter." I take a beat. "Every movie with a golden retriever is about it being a jock."

I lose track of the laughs at some point, but I lose track of my fear and uncertainty, too. And then in a flash—it's over. Before I can even blink, I'm thanking them, and waving, and trying to remember whether the stairs are to the right or the left. It isn't until I've stumbled all the way down them and my heels hit solid ground I even hear it—the applause.

I did it. I can barely believe it happened, but it did, because I did it. It wasn't as perfect as in my dreams, or as traumatizing as in my nightmares. I failed a little, succeeded a little more, and survived all the way to the end. I didn't die, or cry, or surrender. I made it to the applause.

It isn't thunderous. It only lasts a few moments. But it rings in my ears long after it dies, as if my body knows my soul still needs it.

Mo was right. The surprise is the best part.

CHAPTER 9

"**I HAVE A** surprise for you," Alex tells me on Friday at lunch. "When can I bring it by?"

"You could come tonight," I offer. My dad's visiting his parents for my grandma's birthday, and Mom already told me to count her out this weekend. Her big case—Greg Shea, creator of a Ponzi scheme *and* owner of a giant clown figurine collection—is getting closer to trial, so she's been staying close to the office, too.

"Can't tonight." He rolls his eyes. "My dad has this stupid dinner at his club, and he wants me to go. What about Sunday?"

"SAT prep," I sigh, trying not to sound like the liar I am.

I *was* supposed to be signed up for SAT prep, but my mom's been so swamped on the Creepy Clown Guy case she obviously forgot, and it's not like my dad was going to remember. My mom was always our scheduler, always the one to get us into swim classes and summer camp and tutoring.

"That sucks," he says.

"Yeah." I nod and focus on not looking—not even for a second—at Naomi's table.

Because that's really where I'm going on Sunday. To see her.

It isn't even my fault. When Mr. Sosa paired everyone up in our history class for oral presentations, he did it by last name. It's not the first time we've been paired up because Vance and Weiss are so close together, but it's the first time neither of us were happy about it.

But it wouldn't matter that I didn't choose this. Alex would still be mad. So to keep the peace, I've kept quiet.

Alex and I eventually decide on hanging out Saturday afternoon. When he arrives at my apartment, he's got two giant bags with him, one on each arm.

"Surprise," he says.

"Are they heavy?" I reach out. "Here, let me—"

"I got it." He slides in the door past me. "You don't need to carry anything. They're your gifts."

Alex likes getting me gifts. I don't consider myself the most materialistic person, but I like getting them, too. Even when there's something a little off about them. Like the necklace he got me for my birthday—very pretty, but made of nickel. I thought I'd told him I was allergic, before, but when he asked me to wear it that night, I did. The rash on my neck didn't last long, anyway.

He sets both bags on the table and pushes the larger brown

one toward me. I reach inside and pull out a big wooden box with a hand-stamped label that reads—

"The Homestead Farm?" I gasp, and when I look up at him, he's grinning. "Like the one out by St. Charles—"

He nods, grinning bigger now. "Where you went every fall with your family—"

I only told him that once. How my parents would take all of us out to this little tourist farm where everything was like the nineteenth century. You could milk a cow, and go on hayrides, and the fall leaves blanketed the apple orchards. "I loved it there," I whisper.

"And you especially loved . . ." He slides the box lid off. "Their honey."

Then I gasp again, at the box filled to the brim with honey sticks, all different colors and flavors.

"How did you get this?" I riffle through them. "The farm doesn't sell them online. I've checked."

"People will sell anything if you pay them enough."

Dating Alex is like a seesaw. Every time he snaps at me for no reason or checks in on me three times in an hour, I feel hurt and suffocated and unsure I should be dating him at all. I think: *Why am I even here?* But then he does something like this, and the seesaw flips. And I beat myself up, wondering: How can I even think those things, when he spent so much on me? When he went to so much effort to get me something I loved?

"It's amazing. You didn't have to do this," I tell him.

"I'd do anything for you," he says. "You know that."

He didn't have to sit down next to me in art class last fall, or ask me out again after I turned him down the first time, or bring me to his lunch table and tell all his friends I was the best thing to ever happen to him. He did those things because he wanted to. He wanted me. Not just someone, anyone, but *me*.

I haven't had one of these honey sticks in years, and maybe my taste buds have changed, because it's sweeter than I remember. Almost cloying. But I do my best not to let that show, because how sweet was it for Alex to remember this, and then go to the trouble of finding it? He really *would* do anything for me.

Except let me be friends with Naomi. Or Mo. Or anyone else.

Except wait ten minutes after texting me before sending another, asking where I am, asking why I haven't responded.

Except trust me.

I swallow the honey, swallow down the thoughts. Why should he trust me? It's not like I'm telling the truth. And yeah, I'm only hiding things from him because I know it wouldn't go well. He'd get upset. I've seen him upset, and I don't want that, I don't want a repeat of the train—

"Last and best," Alex says, snapping me back to reality. He hands me the big white paper bag. "Open it."

Cautiously, I peer into the bag.

"Oh," I breathe out. "It's—"

119

"An orchid," he says, clearly delighted with himself.

I pull it out of the bag as gently as I can and look it over. An orchid, though I can't tell which kind. Young, but not a seedling. Green and closed and out of bloom.

"Don't you like it?" he asks. I've been quiet for too long, my mind already whirling with what I need to care for it, what I have already and what I don't, where we are in the typical bloom cycle and what planting mix would work best—all the details that go into keeping this tiny thing alive.

"Of course," I rush to say. "I love it. I don't have any orchids."

There's a reason for that. Orchids are tricky. Fragile. They need patience and tons of care to grow indoors, and honestly, I might not have the sunlight or the skill to ever see it blossom. But that doesn't mean I won't try.

"It's going to be beautiful when it blooms." I smile and kiss him.

"It'll be white," he says as I pick it up to look closer. "The lady told me when I bought it."

I wonder where he got it—not a real garden center, for sure, or they would have packaged it better. I can already see little white roots growing out of the plastic container, which means it needs a new home.

I get up from the bed abruptly, and Alex trails behind me, like a shadow. If a shadow had a lot of questions.

"Where are you going?" he asks as I lead him from my bedroom to the entryway closet. "Don't you like it? The ones they had up front didn't look good enough, so I made her go in the back—"

I turn around and place both hands on his chest. "Alex, it's great." Crouching down on the floor, I fish a slightly bigger ceramic pot out of the back of the closet and hold it up for him to see. "It just needs some room to grow."

"So how was the fancy charity thing last night?" I ask Alex, snapping on clean gloves as a pot of water boils on the stove next to me.

"It sucked," he mutters, kicking lightly at the dishwasher door. His phone rings in his pocket, and he swears as he takes it out of his pocket to silence it. I turn back to my task.

It gets messy, sometimes, taking care of plants. But the gloves aren't for me. They're for the orchid, to keep it safe from whatever germs I might carry. That's why I'm making Alex stand here, at the kitchen sink, while I carefully sterilize everything.

"I'm sorry," I tell him.

"I wish you could've come." He reaches over and tucks a strand of hair behind my ear. "Kept me company."

"Me too," I agree, though I'm not sure it's true. I gently pull the orchid out of the plastic pot and inspect the roots. It could be worse. Some of the roots are healthy, green and white, but some are dark brown and slimy. Rotted. That doesn't mean the plant is doomed, though. You just have to cut off what's killing it from the inside out.

I grab my shears and go to work. As I snip away at the dying roots, Alex keeps looking down at his phone. But not like he's reading something or getting a text. Quick glances. I think it would be ringing, if he'd left the sound on.

"Is someone calling you?"

He grips the phone tighter. "It's my dad."

"Oh, go ahead, answer it." I set down the clippers and turn on the water. "You can use my room, if you want."

But Alex just tosses the phone on the counter. "No."

"Really, it's—"

"I said *no.*"

The phone lights up with another call. He ignores it.

"What's going on?" I ask.

"I don't want to talk about it."

I let it go, for a moment. Return to the orchid in the sink and the planting mixture I need to prepare for it. Before I started trying to grow things, I assumed it was simple: you watered a plant and gave it food and it bloomed and was beautiful. But it isn't that easy.

"Are you sure you're okay?" I ask him.

He folds his arms and shakes his head. "It's not a big deal."

"It seems like it's a big deal to you."

It's a delicate balance. The right amount of water, the right kind of soil, to get flower petals to open up, just like a person might need the right combination of words.

"So." Alex huffs. "You know how much this whole college process has sucked for me."

122

I nod. "Yeah, of course."

"And you know my parents dragged me to this stupid whatever fundraiser at the University Club last week? And I'm just trying to get some cocktail shrimp out of this whole shitshow, when my dad's friend comes up and he's like, oh, I heard you're going to Penn next year, congrats, which—I haven't even gotten in yet! Then I see my dad standing there looking all smug, and it's so clear *he* told his friend that, because he's so certain his *other* friend on the board is going to get me in. That's like the only thing we've talked about this whole year. Him getting me into his stupid alma mater. Otherwise, he's not interested. You come over all the time. How much do you see him? He doesn't even remember your name. He thinks it's *Imogen*."

Pretty sure the last person to name their child Imogen died in World War I, but whatever, Mr. Akavian.

"And then I realize—I'm just, like, a prop for him. Not even a person. Just something to show off at parties."

I get why Alex is hurt, but then I wonder—does he realize he does that to me, too? Brings me places I don't really want to be because he likes people seeing me with him?

"So I don't know," Alex continues. I shake my head and focus back. "I kind of snapped. I said to his friend, 'Actually, I'm thinking of taking a gap year and protesting oil drilling in Alaska.'"

I wince, because I'm pretty sure his great-grandfather *made* his money in oil. "Was that a joke?"

"No, it was a fuck-you. For my dad. Don't worry, he got it. Flipped out right back at me, and for the whole night after that, because I embarrassed him."

This part is tricky. I can't make it seem like I'm blaming Alex, though I know he probably made the situation worse. I know he isn't . . . perfect. Naomi acted like I was just too stupid to see it, back when she and Alex were battling it out over me. Like I couldn't see he was intense or couldn't tell he had a temper. I'm not stupid.

So he's not perfect. Who is? I'm definitely not. If he can see past all the things that make me imperfect, then shouldn't I be able to see past his imperfections, and the person he could be? *Will* be, if I help him?

"What did you say next?" I ask him.

"I didn't say anything. I haven't said anything to him since."

"You're giving him the silent treatment?" I snatch a look at his phone. The missed calls are in the double digits.

Alex shrugs. "Works when my mom does it to him."

"I know it's really hard, but you're not going to feel any better just ignoring his calls. That's what he does, right? Ignore you. And how does that make you feel?"

"I don't know. Bad."

"You don't like it when he shuts you out. It just makes you *less* likely to listen to him. Or take him seriously."

"I shouldn't take him seriously! He did it to me first!"

"I know, I know," I say, trying to sound soothing. "I'm not

124

saying it's your fault. I'm just saying, unless you get to the root of it, it's just going to rot and fester."

"He made me so fucking mad."

"I get it," I say. "But he might not." I pause. "Unless you tell him."

"Why should I care?"

"Because if you talk to him, you show him you're the bigger person. Which you are."

There's a still, tense moment, when I'm not sure whether he's going to hug me or completely explode. And then he sighs, and it's like all the anger's gone out of him.

"Thanks." His shoulders relax. "You always make me feel better."

My heart swells. Alex's life is complicated, so it only makes sense he's complicated, too. Without me, I don't know who he'd talk to. He could vent to Kyle and Luke, I guess, but they're about as empathetic as potatoes. I can see the whole conversation now:

ALEX: Yeah, I just feel deeply abandoned by the people who are supposed to love me unconditionally and it fills me with rage.

KYLE: That sucks.

LUKE: Yeah. Bruh. Sucks.

ALEX: Sometimes I feel like I should light my whole fucking penthouse on fire. What do you think?

KYLE: Sounds cool.

LUKE: Yeah. Bruh. Fire.

But I can help him, I can talk him through tough things in a way nobody else in his life can. Or will. As long as I'm here, I can see what's eating at his soul, I can keep him from exploding, I can make him feel better. I can make *him* better.

He isn't good for you. That's what Naomi said to me, over and over, before she stopped saying anything at all. But even if he isn't, even if deep down, I *know* he isn't, the fact remains—I'm good for him.

He's better because of me. He'd never say so, and I'd never ask him to, but . . . he needs me. And there is no one else in the world—not my parents, not the twins, not anybody—who needs me, *really* needs me. I start to reach out and wrap him in my arms, but then I remember I'm wearing filthy gardening gloves.

"Call your dad," I say, nodding toward my bedroom. "I'll be here when you're ready."

He kisses me on the top of my head, takes his phone from the counter, and leaves the kitchen. When I hear the bedroom door creak shut, I turn my attention back to the orchid. Now that it's clean, I can lift it out of the plastic pot and replant it in my newly sterile ceramic pot. It resists, a little bit, when I pull, but with careful tugging, it leaves its too-small world for something just a little bigger and much better. I pack the potting mix around the plant, carefully and tightly.

My hands are clammy when I peel off my dirt-covered gloves, and my hair's gone frizzy from standing over the water I boiled. But the orchid looks perfect. And when the green leaves give way to beautiful white flowers, I'll know it was because of me.

I wipe my forehead on my shirt sleeve as the sound of Alex's voice floats in from the bedroom, too low to be heard, and too soft. He can't be yelling, if it's that soft. He's talking, instead of lashing out. He's calmer, gentler, *better* than he was fifteen minutes ago, and that's because of me, too.

Mo told me I do comedy because I want to be loved, but I'm not sure she was right. What I really want is to matter to someone. Anyone.

And right here, and right now, I do.

I matter.

CHAPTER 10

ON SUNDAY, I meet Naomi so we can work on our history project. The café she picked is way too cool for me. Naomi discovered coffee last winter, when she stayed up for two nights straight working on her entry into the National Robotics Challenge, and she quickly became insufferable about it. Personally, I'm still not there. When I ask the barista at the register for a hot chocolate, she looks at me like I've asked her for literal dirt in a mug.

"We don't *do* that," she said flatly. Then, though she clearly wasn't, added: "Sorry."

So now I'm sitting at a table with Naomi, as she waits for her complicated coffee order, and I wait for whatever tea the barista listed first. Naomi looks toward the kitchen, clearly more interested in her drink than me. Which is fair, because this is awkward. So awkward. Worse than that guy's set on Thursday, where he just read all the rejection messages he's gotten while online dating.

"Let's just pick somebody, and get this over with," Naomi says.

"Okay." I pull a notebook out of my bag. The assignment is to present on someone who changed American culture and show the impact they made.

"Did you have an idea?" Naomi asks. "You were always better at history than me."

I do have an idea, but I don't know if Naomi will go for it. "Well—"

"Why's it have to be a cultural impact, anyway?" she complains. "Why couldn't it be scientific? That makes an impact, too."

"I was thinking Fanny Brice," I blurt out before she can say anything else.

Naomi frowns. But she doesn't say no. She says: "Who?"

"Fanny Brice. She was a performer. She did vaudeville, and burlesque, and . . ." I pick up the creamer jug off the table, to give me something to do with my hands. "She was a comedian. A really great one. You know *Funny Girl* the musical? That's her."

"That's Barbra Streisand."

"It's *about* her."

Naomi's frown deepens. But she still doesn't say no. She says: "Why her?"

"She was super popular, and she brought all this knowledge of Yiddish and Jewish culture to all of America, which is

129

obviously important. And I thought you could talk about that part."

"And you could talk about what?" she asks. "The comedy part?"

I shrug, trying to seem casual. "Yeah."

"What do you know about comedy?"

I fiddle with the creamer jug, trying to think of how to explain it—or not explain it. Do I try to make her believe I liked comedy all along? No way, she's seen every book in my room and knows all my favorite movies. Do I say I've just gotten really into it—that if she saw my room now, there would be how-to comedy books and journals filled with ideas and a browser history filled with stand-up clips? Or do I tell her I'm—

"Izzy?" a voice from behind me says.

I spill the creamer all over the table.

"Whoa," Naomi says, rushing to save her notebook and phone.

"Oh, shit, here—" Someone is shoving a stack of napkins at me. I look up to see a guy—young, in a half apron—with our tray of drinks in one hand and a bunch of napkins in the other. He helps me mop up the creamer and then sets the drinks on the table. Then he straightens up, still beaming at me.

"I knew it was you," he says to me. "What's up?"

My heart rate, for one thing, because he called me Izzy. No one does that, except for Mo, Will, and Jonah, but he is *not* Mo or Will or Jonah. He looks vaguely familiar, but I can't place him, let alone remember his name.

But if he called me Izzy, that means he knows *Izzy*. Not Isabel, the person sitting at this table with her high school ex–best friend and covered in milk.

"Um," I say as cold cream seeps through the napkins onto my fingers. "No."

He tilts his head. "I mean, yes, though?"

"I don't—" I go back to the spill. "You must be thinking of someone else—"

"Yeah, no," he says, clearly not buying it. "I'm terrible at, like, numbers and shit, but I'm so good with faces, you have no idea."

I look up, smile back, and desperately try to will him out of existence. "I'm really sorry, I don't—"

"I'm Dave," he says. "You're Izzy, you're friends with Mo and those guys." He pauses. "Feels weird to tell you who you are, but you seem kind of unsure."

Forget tsunamis or serial killers or all your teeth falling out. This is my nightmare.

"I go to the Forest a lot, too," he continues.

"What forest?" Naomi asks.

"No, *the* Forest, it's a—"

"Arboretum," I say.

"Dive bar," he says simultaneously. From the way Naomi's eyebrows go up, I can tell which answer she heard.

"How did you get into a bar?" Naomi asks me.

"Um. The door," I reply. Dave laughs. Naomi does not.

"You've got to have seen me," Dave insists. "My set is the one about demonic squirrels?"

"Squirrels," Naomi repeats.

"Oh, not live ones," he clarifies, as if that was the source of her confusion. "Taxidermy."

"Right! Dave!" I cut in, because maybe if I admit I know him, he'll finally shut up. "Yeah, of course. Sorry, it took me a second. Just so weird, to see you here, in the daylight. Not that you're a vampire, or, um, a raccoon—"

"Shit, I wish I was a raccoon," Dave says.

"Isabel," Naomi says. "What's going on?"

"Nothing," I say, too quickly. "I mean, not nothing, this is—Dave and I, um. We have friends in common." I gesture to Naomi, then back to Dave. "Dave, Naomi. Naomi, Dave."

"Oh, hey." He holds out a sticky hand to Naomi. She does not take it. "Have you ever come out to see Izzy?"

"I'm . . . seeing her right now," Naomi replies. She flicks her eyes to me. "Or some parallel-universe version of her. I guess."

Oh my God, when will death come?

"That's funny," Dave says. "Are you in comedy, too?"

"Am I—" Naomi whirls around to me, then back to him. "Do I look like I'm in comedy?"

Dave takes a swaggering step forward. "I mean, from where I'm standing . . ."

I pull my notebook and cup closer. "Yeah, extremely close to the table—"

Dave ignores me. ". . . you actually look like you could use a drink."

"Yes," I interrupt again, "she does, so it's great you brought us this coffee. Maybe we'll drink it now?"

"I meant like a *drink* drink," he says, still looking at Naomi. Then he winks. Then I die inside. "You down?"

"Um, *no*," Naomi says. "Because I'm *sixteen*?"

"Oh." Dave nods. "Okay. No worries." Then waves his hand between me and Naomi. "So is this like a Big Sister–Little Sister thing, or—"

Naomi's eyebrows have now fully disappeared under her bangs. "A Big Sister–Little—"

"THANK YOU FOR THE COFFEE, DAVE," I shout. "SEE YOU LATER, DAVE."

"Cool, yeah," he says, infuriatingly unfazed. "I'm stopping by the Forest tonight. Maybe I'll catch you."

I shove the creamer back into his hands. "CAN'T WAIT."

He smiles, salutes me with two fingers, and finally, *finally* leaves our table. Naomi stares at me. I pull out my notebook and strenuously avoid her eyes.

"So, I think we should do Fanny Brice."

"Really."

"Yeah, because she's awesome."

"Great."

"And it's not like a typical choice—not that it's *atypical*, but—there aren't going to be like five presentations on Fanny Brice—"

"Isabel," Naomi says, louder.

I stop. "Yes?"

"What was all that?"

I almost go for the creamer, to fling it across the table again. Just as a distraction.

"We had a weird barista," I say.

"Who knew you."

"He knows friends of mine."

"Who you go to bars with, apparently."

Ugh. This is so like her. Anything I do is subject to judgment. I shrug. "Don't worry about it."

"That doesn't answer my question."

Why does she feel entitled to an answer? We're not friends anymore; we're just partners on a stupid project. She gave up the right to answers when she made me choose between her and Alex.

"It's not a big deal, okay?" I snap. "Would you just drop it?"

"God, I can't—I can't do this," Naomi mutters, grabbing for her phone and notebook.

Oh, shit, I didn't mean to do that. All I did was ask her to drop it, I didn't ask her to leave.

I lean across the table, trying to stop her. "Wait, where are you—"

"You're lying to me."

"I'm not *lying.*"

"You're not telling me the truth, that's the same." She stops. Swallows. "We used to tell each other everything. And now you're this whole different person I don't know anything about."

"That's not true."

"It is." She shoulders her bag. "I'll email Mr. Sosa and convince him we have to change partners."

"Naomi."

"No." She shakes her head. "Something weird is going on with you, and you don't want to tell me? Whatever. Fine. I don't know how exactly you're sabotaging yourself *this* time, but I'm not going to sit here and pretend I'm cool with it."

She stands to go, but I grab for her sweater sleeve and hold on tight.

"Fine," I tell her through gritted teeth.

"It's not fine."

"I mean *fine*, I will *tell* you if you'll sit *down*."

She lowers herself into the chair slowly.

"I do go to bars," I say. "But not to drink. I go because that's where all the open mics are."

"Like . . . for music?"

"Like for comedy."

"You sneak into bars to watch comedy shows?" Naomi asks, incredulous. I don't know if she's going to think the truth is better, or worse.

"Not to watch. Well, I do watch, but—" I take a breath in. "I'm also sort of . . . in them."

"What do you mean *in* them?"

"I perform. As a performer. Onstage with a mic and a set and—" I don't know what to say. So I make jazz hands. Naomi just stares. "It's stand-up comedy. And I am the comedy."

Her mouth drops. No wonder. *I am the comedy.* Jesus. I sound like a bitter children's birthday party clown turned doomsday prophet.

"You," she says slowly, "are a stand-up comic?"

"Comedian," I clarify.

"What's the difference?"

"I can't remember."

"Since when?"

"January."

"How did *that* happen?"

I definitely can't tell her I stumbled into a club trying to hide from Alex. Even if I explained it was *my* fault, *I'm* the one who lied to *him*, she'd still find a way to make it his fault. Better to just avoid it.

"It's a long story."

"Do your parents know?"

"Obviously not, since I'm here and not at some maximum-security boarding school."

"That's not a thing."

"It is in Utah."

She snorts, but that's not a joke. After Peter almost lit our building storage's room on fire when he was twelve, my mom tried to scare him with a brochure to one of those places. It was called Crossroads, but I think only because Your Kid Sucks and We Hope They'll Suck Less with Jesus wouldn't fit on the sign.

"Wow. I can't believe Alex lets you . . ." Naomi hesitates. "Never mind."

But it's too late, I can tell what she was about to ask. "Just say it."

"I'm glad he does, I guess. It just seems like he wouldn't be cool with you doing that. At all."

"Alex doesn't exactly . . ." I fold my hands in my lap. "Um. Know."

Naomi shakes her head, slowly. "I don't get you."

No shit. That's why we aren't still friends. "He wouldn't want to come. It's not like I'm holding out on him."

"That's not why you didn't tell him."

"You don't know that," I say. So what if she's right? She doesn't *know*.

"Yeah? Does he know where you are right now?"

"No."

"And I bet he doesn't know you're with me, either."

I shake my head.

"What do you think would happen," she asks, softer this time, "if he found out?"

Nothing. That's what I should tell her. Nothing would happen, of course nothing would happen. I mean, he'd be upset, of course he would. I've lied to him, I've hidden things from him. Look at how upset *you* got, I should tell her, when I hid things from you just now. He'd have a right to be angry. If he were. Like he's been before.

It wasn't that bad, I remind myself. It could have been worse.

It could happen again.

When I open my mouth, none of that comes out. What comes out is the truth, in the simplest way I can say it.

"I don't know."

Naomi stares at me, and I stare right back. Neither of us knowing what to say, or how to fix something that feels so broken. Then she lets out a world-weary sigh.

I glare at her. "Stop it."

"What, I can't *sigh* now?"

"You make me feel so awful, every time I talk about him."

"I don't know, Isabel." She folds her arms. "Maybe that should tell you something."

It tells me she's judging me. Just like she always does. It tells me she thinks I'm stupid and weak, and that's only based on the parts she knows about. How much would she judge me—how much would *everyone*—if they knew everything?

"It's more complicated than—" I chew on my lip. "You've never been in a relationship."

"Yeah, because I'm not interested in one," she says. "That doesn't mean I can't tell this is messed up."

I stare at the tabletop and don't say a word. Neither does she, for a long, uncomfortable moment.

"I'm sorry," she says. "I told myself I wasn't going to bring this up. We've got a project. Let's just . . . do the project."

I nod. Look back to my notebook. "Yeah."

"It's not like we don't have practice."

That's true. Naomi and I always paired off together. We've done more projects than I could count probably.

"Remember the time we had to make a volcano together in fourth grade?" I ask her.

She laughs, I think without meaning to. "Yeah, I do, because you mixed up the baking soda with the powdered sugar and it didn't work."

"They looked similar!" I say, feeling a smile start to creep up.

"My dad's fault for not labeling, I guess."

We're quiet for a while before I can gather up the courage to ask.

"Do you think—" I almost swallow the words. But I need to get them out. "Do you think we'll ever do that again?"

"Do what?"

"Hang out together."

I don't say "be friends again." I don't say "be like we used

139

to." But I know she can hear me, all the same.

"Well," she says, flipping her own notebook open, "if we don't finish this stupid assignment today, I guess we'll have to."

And I see it, just for a second, before she ducks her head. A ghost of a smile.

That night, after we all do our sets, everyone decides to stick around for a drink. One single beer in my case. More than that, in theirs. It's late by the time we walk out of the Forest into the freezing night air.

"We have to stop somewhere," Mo says, who had at least three drinks of her own, plus whatever she stole of Will's.

"No," Jonah moans. "Come on, I'm tired."

"I have to pee."

"Well"—Jonah gestures at a side street to our left—"I don't know, find an alley!"

"She can't do that!" Will says, looking appalled.

"Why not?"

"Because it's a sex offense," Will says.

"Because I'm wearing skinny jeans," Mo says at the same time.

"Okay, everybody calm their tits." Jonah holds his phone aloft. "I'll find a McDonald's."

"Yessss," Mo says, drawing the word out. "Shamrock Shakes for everyone!"

"Mo. It's February."

Suddenly, Mo grabs my arm with one hand and points in the distance with the other. "Look!"

When I finally realize what she's pointing at, I nearly pee myself.

"That's a Roosevelt building," she says, shaking my arm harder than necessary. "Izzy, isn't that a—"

I'd deny it if I thought it would do any good, but the building in front of us reads *Roosevelt University* in big, lighted letters. It might as well read *Screw you, Isabel.*

"Uh," I stumble, first with my words, then with my foot, because Mo is holding on too tight. "Yeah?" I clear my throat. If it's my school, which it isn't, I shouldn't sound surprised. Or horrified. Which I am. "Yes."

"Oh, cool." Jonah pockets his phone. "Never mind on McDonald's, then."

"What? No!" Mo protests. "You promised me a Shamrock Shake."

"First off, I definitely didn't," Jonah says. "Second—and I can't stress this enough—*it's still February.*"

Will steadies a now-pouting Mo. "You take her in," he says to me. "We'll wait outside."

"That's the dorm," I lie. "I'm a commuter. I can't take her in a dorm."

Jonah tilts his head up, studying the building. "It can't all be dorms. It's like twenty stories high. What, do you all get penthouses?"

"Penthouses are only on the top floor," Will says. "By definition."

"Jeez, sorry." Jonah rolls his eyes. "We don't all *summer* on *Martha's Vineyard*."

"I really have to pee," Mo interrupts, grabbing for my arm again. "And maybe throw up, but first pee."

"This is your twenty-first birthday all over again," Jonah mutters.

"What happened on her twenty-first birthday?" I ask.

"She drank three Long Island iced teas like they were regular iced tea," Will says, counting on his fingers, "tried to leave the bar with one of the tablecloths tied around her neck like a cape, threw up in a trash can, said we should go ice skating even though it was midnight and *August*, and finally fell asleep in a Carvel ice cream cake."

"It was great," Mo says to me. "You should've been there."

"*You* were barely there," Will says.

"I don't get the issue, Murder Girl," Jonah says to me. "Just take her in. I mean, you have a school ID."

"Well—"

Jonah tilts his head. "Do you *not* have a school ID?"

I swallow. Jonah hasn't used that tone—half-accusatory, half-suspicious—all week. Maybe he figured, if I wanted to steal Mo's identity or recruit them all to a cult compound, I would have done it already. He was starting to warm up to me, and now I'm dangerously close to square one.

"Um," I say, trying not to look as trapped as I feel. "I—"

"All she can do is try," Will says. "You'll try, right?"

I could pile lie on top of lie on top of lie. Or I could tell the truth and disappoint people who haven't disappointed me yet.

Or I could try.

"Yeah," I say. "I'll figure it out."

Will smiles at me, and for a brief second of giddy idiocy, I feel like I actually will.

"Okay." I sling Mo's arm around my shoulder and start across the street. "Let's go." She's a lot taller than me, so her elbow digs into my shoulder blade with every step. I'm basically a human crutch.

"I really want that milkshake."

"I know, Mo," I say, trying to sound both comforting and firm, like when I babysit our upstairs neighbor's toddler. He also slurs his words and demands ice cream at random times. "But you can't. Remember? Because it's too early."

"The Shamrock Shake is a Pisces!" she declares, flinging her arm out. "Empathetic and visionary but elusive!"

"Okay."

"We understand everyone, but no one understands us. This is our great curse."

"Okay." But then— "Wait. If your birthday's in August, aren't you a Leo?"

"Yeah." She hiccups. "But my *soul* is a Pisces."

When we push open the door, central heating blasts us in the face. Several feet away, a man built like a refrigerator watches us silently from the security desk.

"You sit here for a second." I coax Mo down onto the linoleum by the big floor-to-ceiling windows. "I need to, I don't know, sign you in."

"Lemme get you my—" Mo digs around in her coat pockets, but unless she's got a Get-One-Free-Miracle next to her Chap-Stick and Ventra Card, it's not much use.

"It's cool, just . . . don't move. Okay?"

"I am not moving a muscle," she says, using several of them to tap me on the nose.

"Great."

"Especially my bladder muscles."

"Good plan."

Walking toward the security desk feels like I'm a third grader about to try out brain surgery. Like I'm not sure how it's all going to go down, but there's no way it isn't a disaster. I started sweating through my green prairie dress hours ago, before I even got onstage, and between my nerves and the heat in here, it can't be better now. My boots are dripping from the sleet, my coat smells like the beer Mo spilled on me at the bar, and my hair smells like smoke from Jonah's cigarette.

Who wouldn't want to let me in, right?

"Hey," I say, trying to sound casual and mature and not like I'm trying to sneak a drunk girl into a school neither of us attend. "Hi. So I'm a Roosevelt student, but I don't have my ID—"

"What's your ID number?" he asks.

Well. Shit.

"So I'm not a Roosevelt student," I say. "Actually, I'm going to be very real with you here"—I glance down at his name tag—"Patrick. You see, Patrick, I kind of boxed myself into an unfortunate situation where I've been pretending to be a student at Roosevelt when, as I said, I am not, but all my friends outside think I am."

Silence.

"And you might be thinking, 'What a weird thing to lie about for no reason,' but the thing is, Patrick, I'm sixteen years old and in completely over my head—not in like a dangerous way. I haven't been kidnapped, my friends couldn't kidnap a wet paper bag—not that you can kidnap a—" I take a breath. "Basically, I needed them to think I was in college because I wanted to go to bars with them."

Silence.

"I'm not an alcoholic! That sounded like something an alcoholic would say, like a child alcoholic, but I barely drink at all. I promise. My friends do, because . . . college, am I right? I don't know if I'm right, because again, I am sixteen, but my friend over there has had a lot of beer and really needs to use the closest bathroom literally now because otherwise I think she might literally pee on your floor."

I look over at Mo, still propped against the window. She gives me a thumbs-up.

"So even though I'm sure I sound like a complete basket case right now—what a funny word, basket case. Right?" I laugh, a little. He doesn't. "Okay." I put both hands on the desk and go for broke. "Patrick, you seem like a great guy, and it would be so great if we could use the nearest restroom real quick for a second."

Silence.

And then without taking his eyes off me—actually, without moving a single facial muscle—Patrick pushes a button.

My head whips around at the sound of the accessibility gate to my left buzzing. I whirl back around to Patrick. With raised eyebrows, he indicates his head at the gate.

"Patrick," I say, with more sincere appreciation than I've ever felt for another human soul. "Thank you. You're too good for this earth."

He snorts and goes back to his magazine. I rush to hold the accessibility gate open.

"Mo!" I call over to her. She gives me another thumbs-up. "Come on, let's go."

"Tonight was really fun," she says, clutching the shoulder of my coat as we walk through the gate and toward the women's room sign.

Minus the last couple of minutes, sure. "Yeah, it was."

"I'm so glad you came out with us."

"I'm so glad you didn't get arrested for peeing in that lobby."

She blinks at me. "What?"

"Nothing." I push open the bathroom door for her. "I'm glad I came, too."

CHAPTER 11

I'M LESS THAN a minute into my set when it happens.

Maybe it's because I went first, which I never do, except I was late to sign up for a slot this time. Alex called right before I was supposed to get on the bus, and there wasn't anything I could do except duck into a quiet little café and pretend that I was home, just *super* swamped with Shakespeare homework, and yes, it *sucked* that I couldn't come over.

By the time I got to the venue—the same one I stumbled into two months ago, with its vampire sweet sixteen vibes—this was the only time slot left.

I must have jinxed myself. Because right before I'm about to set up my bit about the unlikely animal friendships . . . it happens.

Someone in the back yells out, something deep and slurred and three- or four-syllabled. He sounds like a dude and pretty wasted, but other than that I've got nothing.

"Uh—" I look around to the front row, trying to gauge their

reaction and make an educated guess, like I always do.

". . . If someone tried to talk to me on a plane for six hours, they'd become my next murder victim," I say, but it's unsteady this time, not at all like it should sound. Half my brain is on my set, and half is still trying to figure out what the guy shouted. But then he yells it again. And that's when I see two guys in the front row, guys I've seen before at open mics and who I'm half sure are *both* named Aidan—that's when I see them smirk.

At me.

That guy in the back isn't yelling for a waitress, he isn't yelling for his friend, he's yelling *at me*. But I can't see him, which means I can't understand him. I can't hear him over the lights in my face and the ringing in my ears.

I don't know what to do. Ignore it. You're supposed to ignore it when men yell at you, so that's what I'll do. I'll—

When he yells it a *third* time, one of the Aidans leans over and whispers to the other. I can't remember my next line. I can't remember anything.

"I'm sorry," I call out into the darkness. "I can't—" I swallow. "I can't really hear—"

Then I stop, because where the hell am I going with this? *Hey, I know you're already mad at me for some reason, but I have a complex auditory condition I'd like to explain in depth.*

Chair legs scrape. Blinking into the dark pit of humans in front of me, I can just about see a vague blob in the shape of a person, elbows spread all out like a chicken flapping its wings, or—like a man cupping his hands around his mouth.

The fourth time he yells it, in that voice like a giant, drunk bullfrog somehow mastered English, every word is crystal clear.

"SHOW US YOUR TITS."

Jesus Christ, I think, as if he's going to be of any help in this situation. *Jesus fucking Christ*, I think, as if swearing in the middle of his name would make him want to help me more.

The guy must think I'm ignoring him instead of having a minor theological crisis. So he raises his voice.

"I *said*—"

"Yeah, I heard you!" I yell back. "It's—not really that kind of dress."

Oh my God. Why would I say that? What am I trying to do, convince this asshole all that's stopping me from stripping onstage for his amusement is a high neckline and a finicky back zipper?

Not that kind of dress. Jesus. At this point, it's a shroud. And this is my funeral.

I envy squirrels. Hamsters. Particularly inbred golden retrievers. Any creature with a walnut brain tiny enough it can only feel one emotion at once. Because as I stand there, it feels like I'm cycling through them all in the space of each breath. Shock and humiliation and rage, rage, fucking *rage*, and I can't tell whether I'm more likely to burst into tears or jump behind the bar for a makeshift Molotov cocktail. But when my psychological roulette wheel finally slows, it skips right past Homicidal Thoughts and lands, improbably, on Curiosity.

"Do you actually think I might?" I ask the stranger in the darkness. "Like, do you really think I'm going to do it?"

I've wondered this so many times with creepy men, though I've never said it out loud. Did that boy on the L last year really think I'd be flattered by his play-by-play description of my body? Did the guy yelling at me from a car by Dearborn and Erie really expect me to swoon at the sound of his wolf whistle? "At long last!" I imagined myself calling back to him, like a maiden from a fairy tale. "For six long years, I have waited at this accursed intersection, pining for the day a brave knight with a vape pen would ask to motorboat me from the back of his friend's Kia Sorento!"

There's a moment of silence as I stand under the hot, relentless light. Then:

"NAH," comes the voice from the darkness.

"So, why?" I try to sound firm, demanding, but it just comes out a whine. "Why would you ask me to show my tits?"

"BECAUSE THEY'RE BETTER THAN YOUR JOKES."

He collapses into laughter, along with what sounds like half the audience. My face burns, and I know everyone can see it.

"Do you ever watch those videos, on the internet," I say, trying desperately to recover, "with—um, unlikely animal friends?"

My voice cracks, and I know everyone can hear it.

I'm repeating the rest of my set by rote now, the same way I mumble through church when we visit my grandparents. Without feeling, without energy, without being sure I'm even saying it right and not really giving a shit if I don't. Like it's compulsory.

Something tiny and bright flashes in the front row. A phone. Someone is checking their phone, right in front of me, and I don't even blame them. *I'm* tired of this set, and it's *mine*.

Even as I'm saying my own words, things I came up with and was proud of before Bullfrog Bob, King of the Assholes, decided to share with the class, all I can think about is him. This guy I can't even see.

Because they're better than your jokes. Ugh. That was actually a decent tag. You know, aside from being sexist and gross and mean. When I poison this man's seventeenth beer of the evening, I hope his gravestone reads:

SON, BROTHER, CAME UP WITH A SINGLE GOOD LINE THAT RUINED A STRANGER'S DAY.

I could say that. I don't say that. I slam the mic back down onto the stand and walk off the stage.

If I had to make a list of the last places on Earth I'd rather be, it would read as follows:

1. The floating mass of garbage in the Pacific Ocean
2. Wherever Bullfrog Bob lives, which I'm assuming is a windowless room filled with empty pizza boxes, unimaginative porn, and a small army of cockroaches he's named and trained to do his bidding. Like Cinderella, if she were destined to die alone.

3. This bathroom

The door creaks open just an inch. Mo slides her left foot in first, cautiously, as if there's a possibility being humiliated onstage has turned me feral, and I might try for a chunk of her leg.

"Hey," she says.

"Hey," I mumble back.

"You ready to talk about it?"

"I'm fine," I snap, and then instantly cringe. Maybe Mo was right to protect her vital organs. She plops down next to me anyway.

"So." I can feel her looking at me, but I keep my eyes focused on the tile. "That was . . . pretty rough."

God. If she thinks it was "pretty rough," after all the shows she's been to and all the things she's seen onstage, then it must have been brutal. "Yeah."

"This is my fault," Mo says.

I sigh. "It isn't."

"It's important you get up in a bunch of different places with totally different vibes," she explains. "I figured that's the best preparation for the All-College Showcase for you."

That makes my throat close up. "Will there be hecklers *there*?"

"No," she assures me. "Sort of the opposite problem, the judges barely react to anything. But here—I knew this can be a heckler room. You weren't ready."

I'm not mad at her. I'm mad at myself, because I *want* to be ready. But most of all, I'm mad at the man who thought his opinion on my body was more important than anything I had to say.

"It's not your fault," I say. "It's his fault."

"He really was the worst."

"Yeah. And so are they."

She frowns. "They?"

"Everyone else. The audience."

"Don't blame the audience."

"Why not? They laughed."

"The audience isn't your enemy. And if you start to think about them that way, you'll never get another laugh."

"But they *laughed with him*." I fold my arms across my chest. "He said I wasn't funny and it's like . . . the rest of them just believed him! He ruined my whole set."

She shakes her head. "No. You ruined your set."

My jaw drops. I didn't ruin my set. How could I possibly ruin my set when I never *got to say it*?

"What?" I splutter at her.

"You lost the audience."

"*Lost* them?"

"People start out on your side. They want you to be funny. They're happy if you're funny. But you let that guy shut you down, and then the audience couldn't root for you. They saw you'd lost your confidence, so they lost *their* confidence in you, too. *That* is why you bombed."

"So what was I supposed to do? Get off the stage and punch him out?"

She looks skeptical. "Have you ever punched anyone?"

"No."

"Then I wouldn't start with that guy." She leans against the sink. "But yeah. You were supposed to fight back."

"With what?"

"Words," she says, like it's the most obvious thing in the world. "Most people have a couple lines in their back pocket."

"Huh?"

"Dress pocket, in your case."

"This dress doesn't have pockets."

"Really?" She glances at the side seams. "The patriarchy is cruel."

"What do you mean by 'lines'?"

"Oh, you know, a few quippy comebacks you can use against almost anyone," Mo says.

"Like what?"

"One classic is . . ." She puts on her stand-up voice. "'Hey, man, let me do my job. I don't come to where you work and knock the dicks out of your mouth.'"

"Wow. I'm not saying that."

She wrinkles her nose. "Yeah, it's pretty homophobic, so I wouldn't suggest it. But you've got to say something."

"I can't just ignore them?" That's what my mom says to do. *Just act like you don't hear them,* she told me.

No one does that when Alex is around. I didn't understand why, at first. He's not very tall or big, and he looks exactly like the heir to a mid-range-hotel fortune he is. Not exactly intimidating. But then I realized—men didn't suddenly leave me alone because they were *scared* of Alex. They'd just decided he *owned* me.

"You can ignore them," Mo concedes. "It's your set and your stage time. But I don't think you should."

"Why?"

"The longer you let a heckler talk, the more confident they get. A heckler is the kindergarten bully grown up, just with more sexual frustration and a graveyard of Coors Light bottles on his table."

"Good detail work there, Mo."

She sighs. "Look. I know how embarrassed you are. I know it hurts to bomb. But this is going to happen again. I'm sorry, but it's not the last time, not by a long shot, and I'm *trying* to tell you how to deal with it."

"But I can't do that!"

"Fight back? Why not?"

"Because . . ." I look down at my shoes. "They'll get mad at me."

Mo is quiet for a moment. "Izzy," she says. When I look up, her eyes are fixed on me. "Why do you need everyone to like you?"

156

"I don't—"

"You do," she insists, "because if you need *that* brainless potato to like you, then you need everyone on this planet to like you."

"Isn't that the point? Isn't the point to make people laugh and like you and come back and see you?"

"People," she says. "Not every single person. Of course you want people to like your set. But you aren't your set. And not everyone is going to like it. Or you."

"So I'm not supposed to take criticism?"

"From that guy? No."

"He's an audience member."

"Everyone's entitled to their opinion. Doesn't mean their opinion is worth anything. That guy—"

"Yeah, he's a jerk, I get it." I sigh, ready for this conversation to be over, ready to get off this bathroom floor.

"No," she says firmly. "Let me tell you about that guy. He sits in his chair, pounds Jäger shots, and thinks, 'Oh, I could do that. I could get up on stage and be funny. I could do it better than *her*.' But he never will. All he can do is tear down something you were brave enough to put out there and *wish* he had your figurative balls." She runs her hand through her hair. "And besides that, so what if he doesn't like you? So what that some dick with a mouth doesn't think you're the greatest? Who cares?"

"I care."

"That's not your job."

"What isn't?"

Mo looks me straight in the eyes. "It is not your job to make everyone happy. Especially not if it makes you miserable."

Is she right? I don't know. Even if it's not my job, I want it. I want to make people happy. What's so terrible about that?

"This is good for you," she declares. I resist rolling my eyes at the idea she *knows* what's good for me. "Getting onstage. Even when it stings." She pauses. "If you really think about it, stand-up is the ultimate fuck-you to the patriarchy."

That time, I can't help rolling my eyes.

Mo purses her lips. "I'm serious."

"The *ultimate* fuck-you, Mo? More than, like, the first female president?"

She holds up a hand. "Okay."

"More than closing the wage gap?" I ask. "More than the Eighteenth Amendment?"

"Izzy, honey, that one was for Prohibition."

Shit. Well, I'll try to remember that for the AP US History test in May.

"I'm saying for *you*, the individual human girl you are, stand-up comedy is *your* ultimate fuck-you."

I shrug. She frowns.

"What?" she says. "You don't buy that?"

"It seems kind of dramatic."

She leans forward. "What does the world want from girls?"

"Oh, God, I don't know."

"Yes, you do," she presses me. "Of course you know."

I huff. "Fine. Prettiness, I guess. Girls are supposed to be pretty."

"Decorative," Mo agrees. "We're supposed to be decorations, something to make the place look nice. Like a painting. Or a lamp."

"Who looks at a *lamp*?"

Mo keeps going. "When you're onstage, are you a decoration? Does it matter what you're wearing?"

"It mattered to him."

"Because he's a *dick*, Izzy. He would've made fun of my bow tie if I'd gone up." She takes a beat. "I'll put it to you this way. If you got up, as pretty as you are, if you got onstage and just smiled and said nothing, would the audience be happy?"

"No."

"Because?"

"Because the point is what I say." I pause with the weight of that. It's so simple. But it's so rare. "They want to hear what I have to say."

"How often does that happen for you? A lot?"

I shake my head. "It's not fair."

"It's not. And it's hard, to unlearn all the terrible, unfair stuff the world has worked so hard to teach you. But comedy makes you do it. To do stand-up, you have to demand attention for yourself."

"You have to be loud," I add.

She nods. "You have to take risks."

"You have to not give a shit what anyone thinks of you."

"The world wants girls to be pretty and polite," Mo says. "And careful and deferential and selfless. You can't be any of those things onstage. The world is a better place when you're onstage."

"When any of us are."

"Yes. So let's make a pact. What do we say, all of us, to that guy tonight, or the guy tomorrow night—because there will be other guys just like him—what do we say to all of them?"

There's only one answer.

"Fuck you," I say.

"Fuck you," she agrees.

CHAPTER 12

"I'M NOT JUST an introvert," I say to the audience. "I'm also a pessimist."

But not so introverted it's stopped me from doing this set a dozen times now. And not so pessimistic I worry I'll fail every time now. I won't say it gets better each time, because it doesn't. Some nights are good and some are bad, and you can't guess which. It's a roller coaster, not a steadily upward slope.

"People are always saying to me, you know, 'Be positive.' And I find that really frustrating, because I just"—I take a split-second breath—"*can't* figure out how they know my blood type."

But it does gets more familiar, each time. And the more familiar it gets, the more risks I take. Tonight, I decide I'll try to use the space during this next bit, the way I've seen Jonah do. It gives everything more energy.

"That really is my blood type, by the way," I tell the audience, then shake my head. "It's so funny, there are so many personal details you would never tell a group of strangers, but that's not one of them." I lock eyes with a man in the front row. "Because what are you going to do, ask me for a kidney?" Then, to the whole audience, conceding: "I mean, I know I have two. But that's only because I harvested one from that man I lured into my car." I take a beat. "No, I'm totally kidding." I take another. "I don't have a driver's license."

As they laugh, I see the red light go on—right on time.

"So I can tell you my blood type, but like, I wouldn't tell you my birthday. Or my address, or my phone number, or even the name of my childhood pet because that's what everybody uses as their password, right?"

There's a murmur of agreement, and I nod along.

"Which is kind of weird, that this is how we choose to honor our deceased pets." I look to the ceiling, as if really seeing something up there. "Sometimes I think about them, looking down at us from pet heaven." My voice gets slower, more serene. "Mr. Muffins on his cloud, just already pissed, because he's a cat, but then also like: 'Oh, goddamnit, Kyle! I've been dead for five fucking years and my ashes are still in that paw-shaped urn you got from the vet, you dick.'"

It took me forever to come up with a voice for dead Mr. Muffins, but I like this one I've settled on. It's nasally and grumpy, like everyone's least favorite grandpa. "'You said you were going to plant a tree in my honor, but sure, go ahead and use my name to register for that Pornhub account.'" I spread my arms wide. "What a legacy!"

I grin, and then put my hands out in mock apology. "I'm sorry. I should not have implied your dead pets are watching you masturbate. They're definitely not." I pause. "But your dead grandparents are."

Through the last laugh, I start my goodbyes.

"That's my time, thanks so much, everybody!" I wave to an audience I can't see, but I can hear them all clapping and one person—almost definitely Mo—gives a piercing whistle. "You've been great, and I've been Izzy V."

After my set, I go back to the bar and flag down Colin.

"Can I get a Coke?" I ask him.

"You like the ones with the real sugar?"

"Yeah, I'm not a monster." I pause. "Or a diabetic."

"We just got the ones in the glass from Mexico." Colin pushes himself off the bar. "Let me get one for you."

"Thank you!" I call down the bar as he goes.

Someone taps me on the shoulder. A man, tall and dressed much better than anyone else in this bar.

"Hard to get your attention," he says. Oh. He must've said something I didn't hear.

"Sorry," I say. "I've got a—" I gesture vaguely toward my ear. That's usually enough for people to understand. A vague "thing" that means whatever I did to annoy them isn't my fault.

"This seat taken?" he asks. I shake my head and smile back, just for a moment. Just long enough not to seem rude. Then I turn my head back to the door, where Colin should be coming through again.

"You were very funny," he says.

"Oh," I reply, startled. I guess I assumed he was going to hit on me. Which isn't fair. "Thank you."

"I've seen you before. Haven't I?"

"Probably not."

"I think I have," he says. "You've got one of those faces."

Oh no, is he one of my dad's friends, or something? Does he know me from real life?

"I'm pretty new," I say quickly. "To this whole . . ." I wave in the direction of the stage. "Thing."

Colin returns with my Coke. The man nods at him.

"How's it hanging, Colin?"

"You tell me," Colin replies, wiping down the bar. "Then we'll both know."

"Ha. You should get up on stage," the man says.

"Can't," Colin says. "Bad knees." He walks away.

"So, what's your name again?" the man asks me.

"Izzy," I say. "Izzy V."

"Mitch." He holds out his hand and I shake it.

"It's very nice to meet you," I say, more out of habit than truth. Mom was always big on manners.

"Good grip," he says. Mom was always big on strong

handshakes, too. Everything she taught us—me and Charlotte, anyway—seemed to swing back and forth. Be nice, but don't be a doormat. Be sweet, but don't seem stupid. She made it look easy, but it's not. It's hard work, that delicate seesaw of politeness and power.

"Can I buy you some whiskey to go in that, Izzy V.?"

"Oh, no thank you," I say. "I'm good."

"You are good," he agrees. "Have you ever heard of Stage 312?"

I shake my head.

"It's a club. I do booking for them." He holds out a business card. I hesitate. He laughs. "I'm not scamming you. Go ahead, you can google it."

I accept the card and type the information into my phone. Stage 312. Wells Street. It pops right up—a comedy club in Old Town.

"Sorry," I say, feeling bad I doubted him. "I don't know all the clubs. My friends pick the open mics."

He chuckles. "That explains it. We don't do open mics. Invited shows only."

"Invited shows," I repeat.

"Yeah, you know. *Actual* comedy shows, not this bush-league stuff. No offense to Colin."

I don't think Colin would take offense, but *I* do. This is the place that made me feel safe, and welcome, and . . . *good* at something.

"You're too pretty to play a dive bar," he continues. "You're wasted on this crowd."

"The light isn't very flattering," I concede.

"How'd you like a better stage?"

"What do you mean?"

"I mean, I'd like to book you for a show. At my club."

The eyebrows go up. "Really?"

"Really," he says. "You've got a tight five, right?"

"I have a tight . . . three a half."

"Look, as long as you've got a tight something." He winks. I must look horrified, because he holds up both hands. "Oh, come on, I'm just kidding. You're a comedian, you know how it is."

I do not know how it is. I do not know how anything is.

"So what do you say?"

I think: *This feels cool, but this also feels . . . weird.*

I think: *But I don't know if this only feels weird because it's never happened to me before, and I don't know what questions I'm supposed to ask, and I don't know if I'm supposed to ask questions in the first place, and I don't know anything at all.*

I say: "Yeah. Of course."

"Great. Let me get your contact info and we'll set it up." He holds out his phone.

I take it but then hesitate. "Um. Is email okay?"

"As long as you check it."

I set up a fake email weeks ago, right after the night at Mo's dorm. I figured I might need it, in case any of them asked for one, but I haven't used it until now. I type what I hope is the right address into Mitch's phone.

"It's a bringer show, of course," he says, sliding his phone back into his jacket. "Five people but no drink minimum, so that should make it easier."

"Okay," I say.

"You won't get your time until day of, so block off the whole night."

"Okay."

"Well, there we go, doll," he says. I wonder if he forgot my name so quickly. "I'll be in touch with more details."

This is weird. I don't know what exactly I signed up for, but I do know there's no way I'm going by myself.

"Wait," I call after him. He turns. "Do you think my friend could come?"

"Like I said, it's a bringer show," he says. "Bring anyone you want."

"No, I mean, as a—she performed tonight, too. She's really good. A lot better than me. Not that I'm not—I just—"

He looks amused. "Oh, you're *very* new, aren't you?"

I nod.

"Which one was she?" He scans the crowd of people.

"The girl with dark hair who went third. She was wearing suspenders."

"Ah," he says. Then shrugs. "Takes all kinds. I guess."

167

I have no idea what that means, but I just smile and nod. He swirls the ice in his drink around, like he's considering.

"Sure," Mitch says, almost tossing the word away. "Why not? She brings ten, though."

I have no idea what *that* means. "Okay."

He puts his hand on my back, right below the middle seam of my dress. "Why don't you introduce us?"

CHAPTER 13

IT'S THE WEIRDEST thing.

Mo shakes the booker's hand. She says all the right things, laughs at all the right moments, is as effortlessly charming as a human being can be. But I know Mo. So I know when she's faking.

Will and Jonah smile, too, flanking Mo like bodyguards she doesn't need. But there's something so off. Even when Mo enthusiastically agrees to do the show, even when the boys congratulate her as the booker walks away—it's like they're performing happiness. Not feeling it.

Jonah waits a full five seconds before making his opinions known.

"What bullshit," he says, sharp and hot, looking around at everyone. Except me. "What fucking bullshit."

"Look, it's . . ." Will stumbles for words. "It is what it is."

"It's fine," Mo says to them. But not me. "Let's not make a thing about it."

"Don't do that," Jonah snaps at Mo. "Don't lie to her."

"Jonah . . . ," she sighs.

"We *all* know it. You aren't doing her any favors."

Mo shakes her head at him. Jonah glares at her. I wonder whether everyone's forgotten I'm still standing here.

"What are you talking about?" I ask.

"Don't worry about it—" Mo starts, but Jonah is louder and quicker.

"That guy didn't pick you because he liked your set," Jonah tells me in bitten-off words. "He didn't pick you because he saw your potential. He picked you because he enjoys looking at you."

Oh.

Ugh.

I stare straight ahead, through Jonah's chest. I need a second before I can look him in the eye. I need a moment to shove all the pain I don't want him to see. Honestly, he might as well have stomped on my foot. It would have hurt less, and then I'd have an excuse to kick him back. I breathe in through my nose and tilt my chin up.

"The audience is supposed to want to look at the people onstage." I blink at him with doe eyes and baby-bunny innocence. "I'm sorry. Do you feel like no one wants to look at you?"

Mo discreetly coughs into her hand. And maybe Jonah just

wants to twist the knife, because he says: "You aren't as good as the rest of us, and you know it. He only invited you because you're a pretty little white girl who gives him a great big hard-on. And I bet you know that, too."

"Screw." I take a deep breath in. "You."

"Do you know how hard it is for a person of color to get booked?" Jonah says. "They'll take *one*, for a show. Maybe. But not two, never two! Will knows."

"Please leave me out of this," Will mumbles. But he doesn't say Jonah's wrong.

"But you just waltz in with your big blue eyes and your"—he puts on a Shirley Temple kind of voice, high and innocent—" 'Aw shucks, mister, what's a joke?' The rest of us have been working for almost a year at this, and what, you skip the line? Because you've got tits?"

"Stop," Will says.

"I also have tits," Mo points out.

"At least you cover yours up," Jonah says.

"Jonah, seriously, *stop*," Will says.

This is basically a turtleneck, I think. *What do you want me to wear, a bedsheet?* But the words stick in my throat. It burns.

"You're being really shitty," Mo tells him. "I know why you're mad. But that doesn't give you the right to be a dick."

Jonah glares right back at her, and I feel like I'm holding my breath. But then he just turns on his heel and storms out the door.

"It's okay," Will says, laying a hand on my shoulder. "Jonah's disappointed. He doesn't . . . It's going to be okay."

"Is he right?"

"About bookers passing over people of color?" Mo says. "Yes. It happens all the time. Remember what we told you about boxes?"

I do, of course I do, but Will jumps in before I can say so. "What Jonah was saying—we might not have told you there's another type of box. The"—he makes air quotes—"'diversity slot.'"

"They'll book one person of color, they'll book one queer person, and it's like . . ." Mo mimes dusting off her hands. "All done. Good enough."

That's awful, and it makes me feel even more awful, to think about taking someone's spot, when there are so few spots in the first place. But that isn't what I was asking.

"I mean about . . ." I hesitate. "Is that really why the booker picked me? Is that what you all think, but Jonah's the only one who'll say it?"

Will and Mo share a look.

"Stop staring at each other and just tell me."

"So, um, I'm gonna . . ." Will's already edging away. "Find Jonah."

I turn back to Mo. "Well?"

"I'm not going to pretend like it's not a factor," Mo says, "that you're conventionally attractive."

I hate that phrase. "Conventionally attractive." I never know what anybody means by it. *You're pretty in the most boring kind of way?*

Being pretty is such a mind screw sometimes. But I would never say so out loud, because it's like people expect me not to *know* I'm pretty. Everyone seems to want to be the first person who's pointed it out. Like the only way for me not to be a conceited bitch is to be delighted by this brand-new information they've bestowed upon me. I'm not a feral child brought out of the wilderness last week who's just learning fire is hot, forks help you eat, and having shiny hair and big blue eyes is valuable social currency. Please.

I know I'm lucky. I know being pretty is a privilege I didn't earn, and I know I get put on a pedestal because of it. But if it's a pedestal, then I'm chained down to it.

"But is that the only reason?" My eyes are getting hot. "That I'm pretty? Is that the only thing I have to offer?"

I won't be pretty forever. There's an expiration date on this piece of me, the only piece anyone cares about. What if this is all I'll ever have, and then it just . . . disappears?

"No," Mo says firmly. "You're funny. And smart. And a million other things that matter more."

"You're funnier," I say. "And smarter. That's why I made him take you, too."

She sighs. "Yeah—I know you thought you were doing me a favor."

"What do you mean?"

"Well, first off, I don't need *charity* to get a slot somewhere—"

"Oh my God, why are *you* mad at me?"

"I am not mad at you," she says, decidedly calm. "I am . . . annoyed."

"But . . . what did I do?" I'm suddenly, embarrassingly close to tears. "I got you a gig, didn't you want—"

"It is not a gig," she says, and it's the third time she hasn't used a contraction. It's like she needs each extra syllable to collect her thoughts. "It is a bringer show."

"I don't know what that means."

"Yes," she says through gritted teeth. "And yet you agreed to be in one."

"It's a real club, isn't it? He showed me his business card."

"It's real," she confirms. "And they don't do open mics, it's true. But he didn't offer you a guest spot, or an audition, he offered you a show where *you* have to bring people so *they* will drink alcohol and *he* will make money."

Oh.

"Fine," I say, feeling incredibly stupid and even more naive. "So we'll tell him we aren't doing it."

She runs her hand through her hair. "We're doing it."

"But—"

"It's not my favorite kind of show to be invited to, but then again, it's the *only* show I've been invited to. And he seems like a douche, but it is a real club. Who knows, someone who matters could be watching."

"So you're saying I got scammed?"

"I'm saying you got played a little," Mo says. "Chalk it up to experience. Plus, the showcase at Loyola is in a month, and you've barely gone up anywhere except the Forest. So, honestly? You could use the experience."

Three days later, I'm sitting in the cafeteria, realizing I don't actually have any friends. If a friend is a person who will pay a cover charge for a bar they aren't allowed in at all to come see you tell stupid jokes, then I definitely don't have any friends. Not at school, anyway.

I could ask Alex. Your boyfriend is supposed to be your friend, right? It's in the name. When my older cousin got married last year, she stood at the altar and sobbed, "I just can't believe I'm marrying my best friend." And I was happy for her and all, but I also thought: Wouldn't it be kind of weird to have sex with your best friend?

I thought I'd get by on borrowing Mo's friends, but that didn't fully pan out.

"Izzy, I can give you the guys, and I guess my girlfriend, maybe someone else, too, but—" And then she frowned. "You're from here. You don't have *one person* who would go?"

The truth is, not really. But for more reasons than one, the truth wasn't an option. So we agreed: I'd find one person.

There's a flash of red hair in the corner of my vision. I turn just in time to see Naomi, backpack half-open, walking past our table toward the doors. She's always done that, forget to close her bag all the way. In elementary school, you could track her through the halls by the Hansel and Gretel trail of colored pencils and animal-shaped erasers she left behind. For a moment, I'm tempted to reach out and zip her backpack all the way up. The way I used to.

But I don't. I sit at the table in silence, listening without hearing, Alex's and Margot's and Kyle's voices buzzing in my ears like mosquitoes in the summer. I get up, suddenly, and my knee bangs into Alex. He looks over, surprised.

"Be right back," I tell him. "Bathroom."

But when I push open the cafeteria doors, I don't turn left, toward the girls' bathroom. I turn right, into the locker bays.

I don't know why I'm doing this. She's not going to say yes. Just because our history presentation went well—she ended up liking Fanny Brice, I ended up feeling way more comfortable at the front of a classroom than I ever had before—that doesn't mean we're friends again.

But she's the only one who knows about Izzy. So she's Isabel's only real option.

"Hey," I say tentatively.

Naomi, standing by her locker, jumps. When she turns, her eyes widen. "Isabel?"

"I wanted to invite to you a comedy show," I blurt out as quickly as I can, hoping it'll stop her in her tracks. Which it does.

"You—what?"

"There's this comedy show. That—uh—I need someone to go with me. Well, not with me, exactly, but to watch me—"

"You're performing?" she asks.

I nod. "It's a bringer show, though—which means I have to bring people, so I thought—"

"Are you bringing Alex?"

I shake my head. "No."

"Because he still doesn't know?"

I think: *Because he wouldn't like it, and you might.*

I think: *Because he'd tell me to stop, and you never would.*

I say: Nothing.

She sighs. "What day is the show?"

"Thursday."

Naomi chews on her lip. But before she can choose either way, I hear it: the sound of someone walking down the hallway perpendicular to the locker bays, someone with heavy footsteps walking in our direction, about four seconds away from us seeing him and him seeing us.

I have trouble hearing people when they talk, but weirdly, I can hear other sounds so much better than most people. The upstairs neighbor's cell phone ringing. Peter when he'd sneak in way past his curfew. And this person walking the hall, closer and closer to us, and oh, God, what if Alex followed me? What if he could tell I was lying and he's coming to find me but he's only going to find me with—I grab Naomi by the arm and yank her around the corner. Whoever was coming down the hallway—Alex or not—walks straight on, and out of hearing. I let go of Naomi and breathe out my relief.

"Ow, what the hell?" she says, rubbing her arm.

"I'm sorry," I say as my heart rate goes back to normal. "I thought it was—"

"I know who you thought it was." The way she says it, so bitterly and so resigned at the same time.

"It's just not the right time," I say, trying to explain. "He's stressed about college stuff, so I was going to wait to tell him about how we—"

"How we did *what*?" she asks, but it isn't a question. "Talked? That you dared to hang out with a non-approved person?"

She makes it sound so evil. "You guys never gave each other a chance."

"Because I knew what he was," she says, turning away from me. She shakes her head, then spins back around on me with such pure fury it almost knocks me over. "I *told* you. That's the worst part, I knew what was going to happen and you didn't listen to me. I told you not to go out with him."

I think: *Yeah, and he told me not to see you.*

I think: *Why does everyone think they can tell me what to do?*

I say: Nothing. Because just then, my phone vibrates in my pocket.

Forget lacrosse. Forget film. Alex's true talent is his impossibly bad timing.

where are you??

you're taking a really long time

I knew what I'd find before I even pulled out my phone. And so did Naomi.

"Have you ever considered he might be doing this on purpose, Isabel?" she asks, sounding just on the verge of tears now. "Have you considered there's a reason he only wants you talking to *his* friends, not yours—"

"So he wants me to be friends with his friends!"

"Why he only wants you to hang out with *him* after school—"

"People in relationships spend time together, okay?"

She steps in closer. "That he doesn't send you all those text messages hour after hour because oh my *God*, he just *loves* you so much, it's because he wants control over you even when he's not around!"

"You don't understand," I say, and it's like six months ago all over again. "Nobody in his life is there for him. His parents are never around, they act like he barely exists, and—yeah, so he's clingy. But I'm good for him. At least with me he knows some-body cares about him."

"Does he care about you?" she shoots back.

"Of course he does."

"He doesn't," she says, and God, it stings, the dismissiveness in her voice. She wants to tell me what I can't believe? *She* can't believe someone might actually be able to love me.

"I tried, so hard!" she throws at me. "I tried to make you understand—all I did was try to help you—"

"You judged me!" I say. "*That's* all you did. The second I didn't make the choice you wanted me to, you started treating me like I was too stupid and weak to choose at all!"

"Well, if you can't see what he's doing to you, maybe—" She stops short, but we both know what she was going to say.

After a long moment of silence, I take a step closer. "I'm trying, okay? I want us to be friends again."

"I know," she says softly.

"I never wanted us *not* to be friends."

"I know."

"So then—"

"I can't do it, Isabel," she says, her eyes wet and her jaw tight. "I can't, I can't let you drag me around corners because you're terrified of your boyfriend."

"That's not true. That's—"

"I miss you so much," she says, jabbing at the air with her

180

hand with each word. "But I just can't do this."

"Do what?" I ask, throwing my own hands up. "I don't understand—*do what?*"

"Watch you destroy yourself."

Destroy myself?

"He's my boyfriend," I say.

"He's your *jailer*."

The word hits me so square in the chest, I nearly double over. *Jailer.* I know why she thinks that, I get that's what she's sees, but . . . Alex loves me. I'm the most important person in his life. That's why he's always texting, that's why he wants to see me whenever he's free, because I matter to him. Not because he thinks he owns me. If it was only that, like Naomi thinks it is, if it was only control—then—that would mean I didn't matter. To anyone.

But it isn't true. So it doesn't matter. I straighten my shoulders.

"That's a really shitty thing to say."

"It's not shitty. It's true."

It can be both. The thought seizes me without warning or wanting. I close my eyes, take a breath, and remind myself it isn't true, of course it isn't true.

Naomi is just jealous.

Naomi is vindictive.

Naomi is a crazy weirdo stalker, Isabel. Ignore her before she goes full psycho and boils your pet bunny, Isabel. Just delete her number from

181

your contacts—here, I'll do it for you.

"Forget I asked," I snap at her, already turning around, already storming off. "Forget I even tried."

"God," she says. "Isabel—"

"Don't worry." I toss over my shoulder as I go. "I won't make that mistake again."

CHAPTER 14

CHARLOTTE'S HOME FOR spring break this week. Peter's was last week, but he opted to go stay with his roommate. I would, too, if my roommate had a house in Palm Beach.

The closest thing I've got to roommates are my plants, which, on the upside, are much quieter.

The second closest thing I've got is Charlotte, who's found some reason to barge into my room every day this week. Today, it's to borrow a scarf that, to be fair, I borrowed from Naomi last year and never gave back.

"Just don't lose it, okay?" I ask her. Naomi and I probably won't be friends ever again, but on the off chance we do, I don't want to re-destroy everything over a scarf.

"Please." Charlotte wraps it around her neck. "Even if I did, it would be payback for my green coat."

One time. One time I took a coat from her closet without asking and she acts like I'm a seasoned shoplifter.

"Do you need anything else, Charlotte?" I ask.

"Touchy," she says, holding up her hands in surrender. "You know, some sisters actually hang out together. Talk, even."

"Yes," I deadpan. "I've heard tell of such things. In the ancient tomes."

She tilts her head at me. "Huh."

"What?"

"I don't think I've ever heard you tell a joke."

That wasn't really a joke. Just a line. But I'm not going to correct her, so I shrug.

"My roommate, Lily, and her sisters talk like, all the time, but they're weird, anyway," Charlotte says, brushing it off. "So."

I pick at my bedspread and say nothing. Which only proves her point.

"I don't take it personally," she says. "I want you to know that."

How benevolent. "Thanks."

"Yeah," she says, with the same kind of easy confidence my mom has in the courtroom. "You don't like talking at all. Why would it be different with me?"

I can't help it. I start laughing.

"What?" she says. "I mean, you don't."

"I do, actually," I tell her. "It turns out I do like talking, and I want to talk, and have things to say, but only when I feel like someone's actually going to listen."

"Oh my God." She rolls her eyes. "This is what happens when you're the baby of the family, I guess. You think everything is about you."

That makes me laugh even harder. "How could I think *that*?"

"Yeah, beats me."

"How could I possibly think everything's about me when all you guys do is shut me down. You especially."

Charlotte drops the plant leaf she was holding like it's suddenly hot. "Me?"

"You're always interrupting me. Talking over me. Like if I got a single word in during dinner you'd . . . I don't know, spontaneously combust."

Now it's her turn to laugh. "What?"

"Or I guess just that you'd lose, if I got to talk. If anyone paid attention to me for one second, instead of you, you'd die. Like it was you or me, every dinner, every family trip . . . ," I huff. "Always."

"Wait." She plops herself down on my bed. "Is that what you think? That I'm always cutting you off or interrupting you because I, what—see you as a *threat*?"

When she puts it that way, it does sound kind of dramatic. "Yes," I mumble, and then am instantly embarrassed by how defensive I sound.

Charlotte buries her head in her hands. "Jesus Christ." She straightens up and looks me in the eye. "That's so not true."

185

"What do you mean, of course it's true. You're always interrupt—"

She cuts in then. Which only proves my point.

"Not to *mess* with you, Isabel." She pauses, and seems to realize it, too. "Sorry."

"You see what I mean?"

"I said sorry!" Charlotte grimaces. "Yeah, I guess I cut people off, a lot. You think it's not my best quality, fine. You and my Sociology 101 TA can have lunch and commiserate."

"I don't know what that means."

"It means it's *bullshit* to drop my recitation grade ten percent because I talked over Noah White maybe *twice*. He sucks. It was a public service."

"Charlotte." I snap my fingers. "Focus."

"It's not about you, okay? It's a 'me' thing. I just—I don't know, I feel like . . ." She shakes her head. "This is going to sound stupid."

Charlotte has said things that were dismissive, or flippant, or even mean, but she's never once said anything stupid. "What?"

"I feel like the only way people pay any attention to me at all," she says, "is if I make them."

Even though I don't want to admit I understand, I do. Deep down in my bones, I do. Charlotte doesn't just want to be seen. She's fighting to be heard, too. Just like I am.

"You always got attention because you were so cute, you know?" she says. "From birth, which is weird, because most babies look like angry aliens. And then when we got older, all anyone at parties, at school ever said to me was 'Your little sister's *so adorable.*'" She shrugs. "And what was I going to say? You were."

"But who cares, Charlotte?" I roll my eyes. She was editor in chief of the paper, senior-class vice president, the goddamn salutatorian—next to that, who cares if I was a cute kid?

"I cared," she says. "How could I not? I was always standing next to you. I was always being judged *against* you, and I was never, ever going to measure up."

"What do you think it was like for me?" I ask her. "Being two years behind you, having every teacher already know you? 'Oh, you're *Charlotte's* sister.' So excited. So hoping for another Charlotte."

"Peter's older than you, too," she points out.

"Yeah," I say. "They were *not* hoping for another Peter."

We both laugh. And then I keep going.

"But then I wasn't you. I wasn't as smart, and didn't work as hard, and needed extra help all the time and—" I swallow. "I was never going to measure up to you, either."

We were judged against each other from the time we were kids. Both of us, not just me. And we both feel so shitty because of that judgment, not just me. Charlotte never felt pretty enough, just like I never felt smart or charming or *approachable* enough, and it wasn't because of anything we did to each other. We didn't do anything except exist.

"It's weird, going to college," Charlotte says abruptly. "You'll see when you go."

I already feel like I'm there, half the time. High school feels like a doctor's waiting room, beige and boring. Or maybe it feels like purgatory. A vast nothingness, with only the promise of something beautiful ahead. The more hours I spend with Mo and Will and Jonah, the more I forget I'm sixteen. The more I lie to them—to myself—the less it seems like a lie at all.

"Don't you like Vassar?" I ask Charlotte, not sure where she's going with this. "It seemed like you did."

"No, it's great," she says. "But it's weird. Because you spend eighteen years being part of a family. You go to school, yeah, but you come back to the same place every night, and . . ." She trails off, searching. "Even if it's not perfect, it's simple. It's—"

"Familiar," I say. It's like I finally realize what that word is supposed to mean.

"Right." She turns and stares out the window. "But when you go to college, you're totally disconnected from that. You're not part of a family, not like you were, anyway. You move around this totally new world as one person, this . . . singular unit."

"Yourself," I say softly.

She looks back to me. "And that's the weird part. When you're all on your own, you suddenly have to figure out what it even *means*. To be yourself. Not somebody's daughter or sister or some part of a family but *you*. Just . . ." She shakes her head. ". . . you."

I hesitate for a moment. "Why are you telling me this?"

She puts her hands up in mock surrender. "Jeez, sorry I—"

"I don't mind," I interrupt her. And I can admit—it feels good. Getting control of the conversation. Making sure I get to finish my thought, instead of waiting for someone to give me permission. "But you don't do something without a reason. You're . . . intentional like that."

"You know me so well."

She's being sarcastic, but I'm not. "You're my sister," I say. "Of course I do."

Charlotte chews on the inside of her mouth for a moment before she speaks again.

"Another thing that's weird about college," she says. "It makes you want things. New things."

"Like a fake ID?"

Charlotte blinks in surprise at the second joke she's ever heard me tell but recovers fast. "Yes, but I took care of that during orientation."

She's pretty quick. She'd probably be good at improv.

"So, then—" I prompt her.

"You get a new perspective is what I'm saying." She looks down at my bedspread. "You watch your weird roommate with her weird sisters, and even though they're all so annoying you could kill them . . ." She looks back at me. "You sort of wish you had that, too."

I've spent my whole life thinking Charlotte despised me. Or, at the very least, resented me. But it was more complicated than that, and neither of us knew how to talk about it. So we just never talked at all.

"Maybe we could," I offer. "Maybe it could—"

"I don't mean right away or anything," she jumps in, and instead of seeing her wresting away the conversation, all I hear is the nervousness in her voice. "I'm not expecting, like, miracles—"

"Will you come to a bar with me tonight?" I blurt out.

"Uh," she says. "What?"

"Like not just any bar, a specific bar. It's on Wells Street."

"Did you hit your head and forget you're sixteen?"

"It's an eighteen-and-over event."

"Yeah, again, you're sixteen."

"They're not going to card me."

"Why?"

"I was sort of . . . invited."

"Invited?" She pauses. "What *is* this?"

"It's not bad. It's—"

"Because if some guy told you he's a model scout, that's a scam."

I roll my eyes. "It's not a—"

"And if he told you he needs you to help him with a wire transfer, *that's* a scam—"

"Duh, Charlotte."

"And if he told you he knows this great little hole-in-the-wall restaurant that doesn't show up on Google—"

"Let me guess, it's a scam?"

"No. You're going to wake up in a bathtub in Englewood minus a kidney."

"It's a comedy show," I tell her. "Stand-up. No model scouts or missing kidneys, just jokes. And probably a gross bathroom. But mostly jokes."

She makes an impatient sound and starts to rise. "It's nice of you to invite me, but I'm not really into stand-up."

I close my eyes, swallow my doubt, and tell her the truth. "Not even if I'm the one . . . standing up?"

It's a miracle. After all these years, I've finally found a way to make my sister quiet. The secret ingredient is . . . sheer shock.

"No," she says finally. "No way."

"Yes."

"But—you're not even funny!"

"You'd make a great heckler, Charlotte."

She's silent again. For a long time. A couple more seconds and I might have to call 911.

"Do Mom and Dad know?" she asks.

It's easy to forget, sometimes, that even if Izzy doesn't actually have parents, Isabel does. And if they found out what I've been doing since January, my very real parents would flip their very real shit.

"What do you think?" I ask.

"I think my mousy little sister was replaced by a lizard person."

"Pod person."

"What?"

"*Invasion of the Body Snatchers*," I say, thinking back to the rainy day I watched the movie with Alex. "That's what you're thinking of, but it's pod people, not *lizard*—" I shake my head. "Please come. I really need you to come."

"You *want* me to come watch you?"

"I have to bring people, or they won't let me go up."

"Oh," she says, and it's curt. Almost disappointed. Almost like Charlotte *wants* to be there. Or maybe it's more than that. She wants me to want her there.

"Why are you asking me, anyway?" she continues. "Why not one of your friends? Your boyfriend?"

"You're my sister."

"Thank you, I'm aware."

"You're my family," I say. "I can't tell Mom or Dad, but . . . I can tell you."

Another long silence. I'm going to have to remember this trick.

"Okay."

Now it's my turn to be shocked. "What—okay, what does 'okay' mean—"

"It means text me the address."

"So you'll come?"

"No, I just want the address for when I have to report you

missing—*yes*, obviously, I'm coming."

"Thank you thank you thank you," I say, flinging my arms around her and ignoring her attempts to shove me off. "You are the greatest sister in the entire world. The known universe. I'm sorry for every bad thought I've ever had about you."

She peels herself out of the hug. "Oh my God."

"And that time I peed on your teddy bear when I was three."

"I'm leaving now."

The problem with being a chronically late person is everyone assumes it's your fault, even if you got on the exact right bus at the exact right time, and then that bus ran into the exact wrong traffic.

"Ridiculous," the lady in the seat next to me mumbles.

Everyone on the bus looks like they're about ten seconds from a French Revolution–style riot. Minus the beheading.

"Damn, man, what's going on?" a young guy at the back yells up to the driver. "Jesus, let's *move*."

Maybe I spoke too soon.

I check my phone for the third time in two minutes, watching the seconds tick down. If I got off right here and ran, I could still make it mostly on time. I get up from my seat and walk to the front.

"Hi," I say. The driver ignores me. "Um—"

"Traffic," he says curtly. "I've got no more information than you do."

I scan the long line of unmoved cars in front of us. "Can I get off here?"

"This isn't a stop."

Well, we haven't moved in forever, I want to say. *So this isn't a bus; it's a prison on wheels.*

"I know, but can I please just get off?" I beg.

"Can we *all* get off?" a man in one of the front seats agrees.

"This isn't a stop!" the driver repeats.

"We've been stopped for ten minutes," another woman yells. "It's a stop now."

The driver swears under his breath and opens the back doors. "Get off if you want to get off, god*damn.*"

"Thank you," I whisper to him.

If you get hit by a car, I'm telling my supervisors you incited a riot, his eyes seem to say.

I jump off the bus almost giddy it worked, and I'm not stuck, and I might actually make it on time. I take exactly one step before I realize I'm going in the wrong direction, spin around to correct myself—and crash right into a light pole.

"Ow," I yell, clutching at my cheekbone. "Fucking *shit.*"

An old woman walking past me glares. "You don't have to swear."

"Yeah, well—you don't have to talk!" I shout after her.

I gingerly pull my hand away. No blood. And no broken bones, I don't think. But the whole left side of my face is throbbing, and when I check myself out in my phone camera, it's bright red, too. If I know my own body after sixteen years, there's going to be a giant bruise in about two hours.

And I'm totally out of time to fix it.

This place looks like a TV show set. Or more accurately, it looks like every comedy club I've ever seen in a movie. A real stage, smooth floorboards with nails that aren't trying to escape this mortal coil. Tables on multiple levels, and judging by the girl by the bar tying on her half apron, waitress service. An honest-to-God redbrick wall, in a building that isn't otherwise made of red brick.

"Oh, damn," Mo says when I walk in the door, ten minutes later than we planned to meet here. "Who did you fight?"

"A light pole."

"I think it won."

"Is it really bad?"

"No," she lies. "It's fine."

"Oh my God," I say, digging around in my bag for a mirror. "Oh my God."

"You can joke about it," she suggests. "Maybe you could open with that."

"That's not my opener!"

"I'm suggesting you improvise."

"You said everyone hates improv!"

"I said everyone hates improv *shows*." She sighs and grabs my hand. "Come on. I'll fix it."

Mo drags me backstage and into a little alcove with a single chair, a streaky mirror, and a vanity table covered in drug store makeup of every kind and every color, most of them half-used and a bit dusty-looking.

"We don't know where any of that's been," I protest. "I'll get scabies."

"Look, you can go out as you are, or you can risk scabies."

I sigh and plop down in the chair. "Scabies."

Mo snorts and selects a foundation.

"Kind of fucked up," she muses as she pats it on my face with surprising gentleness and ease. "Actively choosing skin disease. I've seen guys go on looking like absolute shit. Way worse than this."

"I don't want people judging me."

She stops. "For what?"

"I don't know." I bite my lip. "Maybe I just don't want them noticing me."

"Izzy. You're onstage. That's the point."

"Noticing me for the wrong things."

"There are worse things than being seen," Mo says. "Even if it's scary."

She steps away from me and surveys my face.

"How is it?" I ask.

"Not as bad." She grabs a different bottle from the table and leans in again. "But I think this one might work better."

It's cool on my skin, whatever it is. Scabies or not. This feels almost like when I was younger, and my mom helped me put on her borrowed makeup, before something special.

"How do you know how to do this?" I ask Mo.

"Do what?"

"Makeup."

"So just because I own a bow tie means I can't do makeup?"

"A bow tie? You own like *twenty* bow ties—"

"My consumerism aside," she says with an eye roll.

"You don't wear any, do you?"

"Nothing but sunscreen and ChapStick."

"Then why'd you learn how—"

"My mom." She snaps the foundation shut. "I did it for my mom."

"You wore it for her?"

"No. I did it for her." Mo leans against the table. "When I was in my senior year of high school, she got diagnosed with Parkinson's."

Oh. Oh, no.

"Mo," I breathe out. "Oh my God."

"You're not supposed to get it that young, but she did."

"I'm so sorry. I'm so—"

"Basically what happens is all the cells making dopamine—the stuff that makes you happy, you know?—they die," Mo continues, as if she hasn't heard me at all. "And when that happens, it damages your nervous system, which messes with the way you walk and talk and think. And it's degenerative, so—" Mo swallows. "You stop being able to do the things you used to. Slowly, not all at once. She had trouble walking, she had trouble swallowing, and eventually she had trouble putting on her makeup. Her hands spasmed too much. And that made her feel so awful, she never wanted to leave the house. And at first I was like, that's so messed up. That she feels like she's not worth anything if she's not pretty. She's sick! Who cares about mascara?

"But then I realized I was being unfair. Who cares? She cares. However *I* might feel about it, putting on lipstick and having her eyeliner on point makes her feel good. It makes her normal. So . . . I learned how to do it. Her entire *ten-step* morning routine, I learned how and did it for her every morning before school. And she fell a lot, so I learned how to cover up bruises, too." She tilts her head and scans my face. "I did get pretty good at it, I've got to say."

"Who does it now that you're gone?"

"My dad. He's not as good. She says so all the time, on the phone. Though the phone is getting harder."

"You must miss them."

"Yeah, I do. Way more than I thought I would. I mean, I always wanted to go away for school. When I was like eight, I asked if I could go to boarding school."

"Wow. You wanted *out*."

"No," she laughs. "I was just always independent like that.

Ready for life to start. I figured, why wait? Anyway, they didn't even let me go to sleepovers. I don't know why I tried." She sighs. "I never thought I'd be homesick. I wasn't at all, my first year. I'd wake up in the morning, in my dorm, and I'd be so happy I was there. And then I'd feel so guilty, for feeling happy."

"Why?"

"Because I abandoned her. And my dad."

"You went to college."

"I could have gone closer. I didn't."

"But it's not like you *wanted* to leave her."

"What if I did?" she asks. Then pauses. "I mean, I'm not saying that's *why* I chose Chicago. I chose it because it was the best school I got into. But what if a part of me was . . . relieved? To know I'd be so far, I wouldn't have to think about it every second of every day. I'd be almost normal again. Do you think—would that make me a horrible person?"

"No," I tell her, because I don't. Even if I don't understand what that feels like, I know she could never be a horrible person. "I don't think so."

"Well." She rubs at her nose. "Sometimes I do."

Just then, there's a knock on the door. Mo clears her throat.

"Who is it?" she calls out.

There's a pause. "Candygram."

"What?" I say, turning to Mo. She only laughs.

Another pause. "Flower delivery."

Mo smirks. "Okay, come on in, Land Shark."

"Wait. Why would a shark have flowers?" I ask, knowing there must be a joke I'm missing here.

"Exactly," she says as the door opens and Jonah steps through.

He and I stare at each other, then quickly look away. This couldn't be more awkward if we tried. Maybe he is trying. Maybe this is his final revenge.

"I'm going to go ask for the set list," Mo says. "Nobody kill each other. That rug looks bad enough already."

Then she disappears through the doorway, leaving me and Jonah alone.

"I just wanted to say—" Jonah heaves a sigh. "I was really shitty to you. I'm sorry about that."

"It's okay," I say.

"I think I just felt like—"

"You don't have to explain," I say. "It's fine, not a big deal."

"Yeah, it is," he says. "It is a big deal that Will and I don't get asked for things like this. It's a big deal that you had to get Mo in yourself. That is a big deal, Izzy."

"I know," I say. "That's so unfair. I'm sorry. And I'm sorry I didn't realize that until Mo talked to me about it."

"It's also a big deal that I made *you* responsible for it," Jonah says, dropping his eyes to the carpet. "And you're not. All you did was say yes to something. We all would have. I was frustrated, and mad, and made it about you and it isn't, and it's even worse that I made it about you being a girl. That's not the kind of person I am—want to be. Not to my friends."

200

"We're still friends," I say. "Aren't we?"

"Yeah," he says. "Yeah, of course."

There's a knock at the door, and Will pokes his head in the room.

"Izzy, there's someone here asking for you."

"The booker guy?" I ask.

"She didn't tell me her name, but she's tall and blond and terrifying."

Ah. I stand up and gesture to the door. "Who wants to meet my sister?"

CHAPTER 15

CHARLOTTE IS POLITE enough as she meets everyone, though it's clear she's still wary of the whole situation, and not psyched about spending an hour in this bar before we start.

"You didn't need to come to this early," I tell her as we settle into one of two tables Will has saved.

She peels off her coat. "Would have been nice of you to mention that in your text."

With all this time she's going to be hanging out, I realize we have a more pressing problem. "Um. Charlotte."

"Yeah?"

"There's something you should know."

"What, do you have another secret hobby?" she asks. "Model airplanes? Necromancy?"

"Well—"

"Drinks first. Then dark secrets." She swivels around, looking for a waiter.

"I want you to know now: people might say weird stuff," I tell her, aware this is probably too cryptic and also that she's definitely stopped listening, "Or things that don't seem true. About me. But it's complicated and I'll explain everything after so just . . . be cool, okay? Just—"

"Izzy!" Mo snags my arm. "I want you to meet my girlfriend."

She's nearly as tall as Mo, but that's about the end of the similarities. Her hair is long and wavy under her beanie, her winter coat puffy and practical in contrast to Mo's flashy coat that can't possibly be warm enough. She's a little younger and much quieter than Mo and doesn't fight for attention as Mo and the boys banter back and forth. She's got a soft voice, so I don't quite catch her name when she introduces herself. Something with an L. I'll ask Mo later.

But the way they look at each other—that's exactly the same. Total comfort. Real affection. I wonder what that would be like. Having someone you can relax into. Someone who balances you out.

"Are you drinking tonight?" Will asks me. "I'm heading to the bar."

I shake my head. "My sister is, though. She has an ID," I add, but don't add that it's fake. "I bribed her to come with the promise of a drink. Like a real drink." I reach for my purse. "How much would it—"

Will stops me with a hand on my arm. "No worries, I got you."

"You're always buying."

"It's no big deal."

"I know your parents are wealthy, but you shouldn't feel like you have to cover us all the time."

Will stops. He turns back to me, and I can almost see him debating inside his own head what to tell me. We stand there in silence, for a moment.

"My dad owns a vintage Shelby Mustang," he says finally. And then pauses, like it means something.

"I don't really know cars," I say apologetically.

"Well, it's beautiful. And very expensive. And he has never driven it off our property."

"Because . . . he wants to keep it nice?"

"Because he's worried if a cop sees him driving it, they'll assume he stole it."

"Oh," I say, feeling horrible and stupid and out of better words to convey how horrible and stupid I feel.

"Yeah. My family's got money," Will concedes. "A whole ton of inherited wealth, if we're being real here. But we're also Black, and you can't buy your way out of people's racist assumptions." He sighs. "That's the default, you know? Suspicion. From everyone. But especially from wealthy white people, who don't understand why someone who looks like you is in their space, because so few people who look like you are ever there."

I want to say: *it isn't their space, of course it's your space, too.* But would that really make him feel better? Or would it just make me feel better?

"Jonah gives me a lot of shit about summering on Martha's Vineyard, and I get how bougie it sounds, but . . . my family's been going there, to Oak Bluffs, for nearly a hundred years because it's a place without that kind of suspicion. They made this place where everyone understands where you're coming from. It's the same reason my mom signed me and my sister up for Jack and Jill, and my dad joined Sigma Pi Phi, and—" He pauses. "You have no idea what I'm talking about."

"No," I say, "I'm sorry."

"It's okay," he says. "Basically, Izzy, there's a lot I feel like I can't do with the money I have—that I'm very lucky to have—because of all that constant suspicion." He looks back over to our table. "But I can cover most of Jonah's rent so he doesn't have to take out as much in loans. And I can get the next round at a bar, because it feels good to be able to do nice things for my friends." He shrugs. "So I do. You know?"

I don't know exactly. I don't think I can ever really understand, being the person I am, and Will knows that, too. But I can listen.

"Yeah." I nod. "I hear you."

Will smiles, claps me on the shoulder, and heads to the bar.

Mo helps Will bring over the first round, then goes back for two glasses of Coke. One for me, and one for her girlfriend, which makes me feel better. It's always a little weird to be the only one not drinking.

"Fancy," Jonah says, nodding at Charlotte's drink—clear and iced, with a sprig of something green as a garnish.

"Figured they couldn't mess up a gin and tonic." Charlotte takes a sip. "It's like eggs."

"High in cholesterol?" Jonah jokes.

Charlotte looks back at him coolly. "So easy a toddler could make it."

"'Gin' is a funny word," Mo's girlfriend cuts in. "It doesn't sound like it at all, but it's Dutch. I mean, it's English, but it comes from the Dutch word for juniper. Like, the berries, because they used the berries to flavor it, I guess? Maybe they don't still." She looks to Jonah. "Does it taste like juniper berries?"

"Ellis, how would I know that?" he asks.

"You were a Boy Scout," Will points out.

"I got one merit badge in three years. And it was for traffic safety."

Mo's girlfriend—Ellis, I guess, I knew there was an L somewhere—turns to me. "So, what's your major?" she asks.

I cough into my hand to buy a second to think, but Charlotte gets there first. "Isabel? She doesn't have one. She's—"

"Undeclared," I interrupt. Charlotte swivels her head to stare at me, but I don't look over. "But I like Shakespeare. That's my favorite class."

"Oh, high five," Ellis says, brightening. "I'm an English major."

"And linguistics," Mo adds. "Double major, which is *hard* at our school. Trust me." Ellis blushes.

"And linguistics," she says, nudging Mo. "Don't brag for me."

"It's not bragging if it's true."

"I'm not sure you're right."

I can't imagine Alex bragging about me like that. Being proud of the things I do, not just the way I look. Something warm but painful swells in my chest, and it takes me a moment to find the word for it. Not jealously, exactly but . . . longing.

"Where do you go to school?" Will asks Charlotte. "With Izzy?"

Oh, shit.

Charlotte frowns, then jabs her thumb in my direction. "With her? No, I'm in—"

"Junior year," I interrupt again. "At Vassar."

I can feel Charlotte death-staring at me. "Um. What?"

Oh my God, why did I say junior year? So she seemed legal to drink? She has a fake! I guess it's because I'm pretending to be older, so she should be older, too.

"Wait, so you're twins?" Jonah asks. "If you're both in junior year."

Give up, the reasonable part of my brain says. *Keep digging that hole*, the louder and much stupider part of my brain says.

"It's funny you say that," I tell him, though it isn't funny at all. "So we're really close in age. Right?"

"Right—" Charlotte confirms.

"So when Charlotte skipped second grade, we ended up in the same, you know, class."

"Oh," Mo's girlfriend says politely. "Cool."

"Extremely cool," Charlotte agrees, between gritted teeth. "Isabel, can I can talk to you for a second?"

"Yes," I say brightly. "You're doing it right now."

"Hysterical." She grabs my elbow. "You're a delight. Let's go."

"Who are you?" Charlotte demands once we're standing by the bar, too far away for everyone left at the table to hear us.

"I don't really know how to answer—"

"Not in a Descartes way," Charlotte says. I have no idea what that means. She motions toward my friends. "Who do these people think you are?"

"Me," I say. "Mostly."

"Bullshit."

"Minor details were changed."

"They think you're in college!"

I throw a look back to the table. "Charlotte, not so *loud*—"

"Where?" she asks. "Where do they think you go?"

"Roosevelt," I admit.

"No one goes to Roosevelt."

"That's what made it a good choice."

"Okay, so—" She counts off on her fingers. "They think you're like twenty, a junior in college, and apparently, *older than me!*"

"I forgot what I told them before. I had to make up something—"

"You made me your little sister!"

"I had you skip a grade!" I say. "It makes you seem smarter!"

"I could kill you right now. Do you know that?"

"Charlotte—"

"A crime of passion. That's not even premeditated. Mom could get me off."

"Please don't tell them," I beg her. "Or Mom. Please let me keep this."

"Ugh." She takes a giant gulp of her drink. Then sighs. "Fine."

"Thank you, thank you—"

"You owe me."

"I know."

"Like, monetarily. Whatever you're making from this performance."

"I'm not getting paid."

She takes another gulp. "Jesus Christ."

But when we sit back down with everyone else, Charlotte doesn't say a word.

"Izzy's really good," Will tells her. "You're going to love her set."

"Oh, yes," Charlotte replies with only the barest hint of

exasperation in her voice. "I've always looked up to her."

I squeeze her hand into the table. She kicks my ankle. I let go, but I can tell she's trying not to smile, too.

As it gets closer to the show's start time, I feel my nerves begin to bubble up. My chest is tight, my heart is beating faster, and my leg is jiggling so much Charlotte kicks me in the ankle again, to make me stop. I've got to focus on something, so I pull out my notebook from my bag and read my set, over and over, letting the noise of the others' conversation wash over me like a wave. This is one of the nicer things about the weird way I hear—it's easy to tune things out when I want to.

I wonder if there's something else I'm supposed to be doing. Do Mo and I need to do a mic check, or clear our set with the booker, or anything? But when I look up from my notes to ask—Mo is nowhere to be found.

I lean across to table and get her girlfriend's attention. "Hey, have you seen Mo?"

"She went to the bathroom." But then she frowns. "Kind of a while ago."

"Oh." I swivel my head around, searching the room for where the bathroom might be.

"Is everything okay?" She starts to get up from her chair. "I can go look for—"

"No, no worries," I tell her. But truth be told, I *am* a little worried. It's weird for Mo to disappear like this, especially so close to start time. She's always right in the middle of the group, pitching a last-minute new joke or getting our thoughts on a callback that didn't land the last time. "I'll get her."

When I find her, she's sitting against the wall by the sink in the women's room, eyes closed. Breathing in sharply through her nose, then out through her mouth. Just liked she taught me to do. But I don't think it's working.

"Mo?" I ask, taking a cautious step forward. "It's almost call time. What are you doing in here?"

She opens her eyes then, and the look she gives me is pure panic. "I can't do this."

"Do what?"

"Perform."

"Of course you can."

This is kind of a strange reversal. Her having a crisis on a bathroom floor, me trying to pump her up. She's better at comforting someone, and honestly, she's better at having a crisis, too. I perch myself on the edge of the sink ledge. This bathroom's cleaner than the one at the Forest by a long shot, but I'd still prefer to avoid touching the floor.

"I can't." Mo closes her eyes again. "Tell the booker that I have, I don't know . . . homework."

"Mo."

"Surgery."

"What?"

"Rabies."

"I don't get it," I say. "You've gone up a million times before. What's different?"

"This isn't an open mic," Mo says. "People paid to be here."

"They paid to get *in* here. I don't know if that's—"

"This is the next step," she continues. "Shows like these, this is where people figure out if they're actually going to make it. If they're good enough to go anywhere."

"You are good. Everyone thinks so."

"Good."

"Yes."

"But not great."

"I don't—"

"*Good* isn't good enough," she says. "Not if you really want to make it. You have to be great. You have to be something special, and I'm not."

"Maybe not yet," I say. "You've only been doing it, what, a year?"

"A little less."

"No one's great right away, are they? So what if it takes time?" I might not be great at stand-up, or even good yet, but I'm a good gardener, and that took time. The first plant I ever had died. It was a succulent and it died. That's barely even possible.

"I need something to show for it," Mo says. "All the time I've spent—when I could have been studying, or doing an internship, or . . ." She shakes her head. "My mom thinks it's a hobby. Like her book club, or something. And my dad's always like, 'Where exactly is this *going*, Mozhgan?' They don't see what it could be. How it could be my life, not just a . . . distraction."

"Well, who cares what they think?" I shrug.

She blinks at me. "I do."

"But you don't care what anybody thinks."

"They're my parents, Izzy. Not *anybody*." She sighs. "They sacrificed a lot for me to be where I am, my grandparents sacrificed absolutely everything for them, so it's like, what am I doing with that sacrifice? How am I paying them back?"

"You don't owe them that."

"What?"

"Your . . . whole life."

"That's very American of you," she says.

"Are you not American?"

"Yeah, I'm American. What's more American than the pursuit of happiness? Your own happiness, at the expense of everything else. But I'm Persian, too, and I respect all the sacrifices my family made for me. I have to."

Iran and Italy are far apart, but that tracks with my family, too. At least on my mom's side. Her parents were first-generation Americans who worked minimum-wage jobs they never retired from, never got out of their little town, but pushed my mom to leave them behind the second she could. She pushed herself, too, through college and law school with full academic scholarships and sheer force of will. And what am I doing, with this easy life she built for me out of her own sweat and grit? Sneaking into bars and telling jokes for free.

"I know—" I start to say, but then stop. This is important. Mo needs to feel like I'm here, really here, the way she's always been for me. I sit down on the floor nex o her, close enough our knees are touching.

"I know you want to be great," I say. "I know you need to be successful. But . . . even if you aren't great—and I think you are. Even if you aren't successful—and if there's any justice in the world you will be . . . that doesn't mean this is a mistake. Doing this has made me braver. And happier. And just way more . . . myself." I shrug. "Maybe you were born this brave and happy and sure of what you want, I don't know."

She laughs through a sniffle. "Definitely not."

"Then the point isn't greatness, or success. The point is you. All the joy it gives you. And the person it makes you into."

"I get what you're saying. It's a net benefit, no matter what."

"I'm saying a lot more than that." I put my hand on my shoulder. "Mo. This thing we do—it's magic."

She stands, rolls her shoulders back, cracks her neck. Then she sticks out her hand the same way she did the first day we met, all confidence and certainty. This time, I take it without a moment's hesitation.

"Well, come on, then." She pulls me up with her. "We've got magic to do."

For all her worrying, Mo did great. Not just good, but great. Though she'd told me beforehand she was just going to do her Broadway riot bit, she ended up mixing and matching from her various sets. I think she might have been doing it on the fly, which is even more impressive.

Luckily, I went first and didn't have to follow her excellent performance. It went well, better than I expected. Fourteen laughs for a three-and-a-half-minute set, which is almost at the marker. It was fun, and I was good, and that's all that matters to me. None of this means to me what it means to Mo, and I'd be her warm-up act over and over, if it would make her believe she could be great.

When I get off the stage, it's not Mo or any of the boys who find me first. It's Charlotte. She's got a drink in her hand—I wonder who bought it for her—and a look that can't be summed up in a single word. She looks baffled. And amused. And maybe even proud.

"I was right." She shakes her head. "You're a pod person."

"Was it weird?" I ask. "Seeing me do that?"

"Yeah. But a good kind of weird."

I think back to my first night at the Forest. Weird isn't weird, I'd thought. But maybe Charlotte's closer to the mark. Letting people into your life, letting them see who you really are *is* weird—but it's a good kind of weird.

"Where did you tell Mom and Dad you were going tonight?" I ask.

"They didn't ask." She sips her drink. "The benefits of adulthood. You?"

I can feel my mouth tightening. My shoulders, too. "They didn't ask me, either."

Charlotte is quiet. She probably thinks I'm being ridiculous. She was always skipping out early on family dinners and evading Mom's questions. Peter was always showing up hours past his curfew with terrible excuses. I've never done any of that, but I could have, a lot more easily than either of them. She probably thinks it's unfair, that I can go anywhere—even a bar, at sixteen, on a Thursday—with no interference.

And yeah, I wouldn't be in this club if my parents kept tabs on me like other kids' parents do. I should be grateful I made it here, that my parents didn't stop me at the door and interrogate me about my plans.

But they didn't even ask.

"Is that really how you feel?" Charlotte blurts out.

"About what?"

"Our family. What you said onstage. That you don't really belong with us?"

"Oh. It's just a bit."

"Yeah, okay. But is it true?"

"Some of it," I admit. "Some of it has to be true, or it's not funny."

"Is this because I used to tell you that you were adopted and your real parents were carnival clowns?"

I laugh. "No."

"That's a relief." She sets her drink down on the bar. "I couldn't live with the guilt."

"It's just—" I hesitate. "You and Mom and Dad and Peter are all so—I don't know. Confident. Outgoing. Loud."

"But you were all those things." Charlotte tosses her head toward the stage. "There. Right now."

"I was?"

"Yeah."

"It's just a character," I explain. "Or a persona, or—it's acting. It's not really me."

"I don't know. It sure looked like you." She shrugs. "Maybe you just needed a different stage."

Huh. As I turn that around in my head, I realize . . . Charlotte's right. Our kitchen table isn't the only place I'll ever eat. I'll have other classrooms outside my high school, other homes outside this city, other families besides the one I was born into. And if I'm different, somehow, in any of those places, it doesn't mean I'm faking it. It doesn't mean I'm pretending or acting.

It's just a brand-new stage.

Mitch the Booker sidles up alongside us. "Didn't she do great?" he says to Charlotte, without bothering to ask who she is. Which is weird. He puts his hand on my shoulder. Which is weird, too.

"She did amazing," Charlotte agrees, and my heart swells.

"I just need to borrow her for a moment," he says, almost apologetically. Then turns to me. "Let's go to my office real quick."

Mitch's office is smaller than I expected, with enough room for a desk, a file cabinet, and a couple chairs. He's got a couch, lumpy and a horrible mauve color, shoved to one wall, but it still seems in the way. The door knocks against one of its armrests as he ushers me in. The room would be way less crowded if he got rid of it. Maybe he has to sleep here, a lot.

"So. Did you have a good time?" he asks. "Did you like the room?"

I nod. "It was a good crowd."

"They always are."

"It was really nice of you," I add, feeling bad for focusing on the audience and the room before I even thanked him. "To invite me."

He smiles. "It was nice. Wasn't it?"

Well . . . yes? I just said it was nice. He didn't have to say it again. You're not *supposed* to say it about yourself.

"Yeah," I say, but slowly, like I'm not so sure anymore. And maybe I'm not.

His smile doesn't break. "I bet you're nice, too. You seem like a nice girl."

"Um—"

"Though I've got to say, you're not dressed like it."

My face goes hot and my shoulders go rigid. I look down at myself—I didn't wear my green dress today. It didn't seem professional enough. So what I'm looking down at are my tallest heels, sheerest tights, and the slimmest sweater dress I own, the one I bought with my own money. When I looked in the mirror before I left, I felt pretty. Grown-up. Maybe even elegant. And now I feel . . . naked.

I stare back at him, and some of the shame must show on my face. He laughs. "It's only a joke. Of course you're a nice girl."

I don't understand. I don't understand what makes this dress *not nice*, as if it's got a middle finger painted on it or it holds small children for ransom. I don't understand what I'm dressed like, if it's not like a *nice girl*. I don't understand why he keeps talking about what kind of a girl I am at all.

"You are, aren't you?"

"What?" I ask, feeling stupid, and small, and a little scared.

"Nice."

"Yes."

He gets up from his chair. And though he doesn't move any

closer, I can feel it. The shift. The shift in his weight from the chair. The shift of the mood in the room.

"And you had fun, didn't you?" he asks. "Tonight."

"Yes," I say, quieter this time.

"I did, too." He leans on the edge of his desk. "I think we could get a good thing going here. You and me."

I know I'm supposed to be getting this. I can tell from the way he's looking at me, I'm supposed to understand what's happening.

"I'd love to perform again," I say, trying to sound calm. Like a professional. Like the girl who would wear this dress and these heels, whoever she is. "If you'll have me."

"Well, now you're getting it," he says. But I'm not. I'm not at all. I frown. He takes a step forward, cautiously, without sudden movements, like I'm a large and potentially dangerous bird of prey. "I want to have you any way I can get you."

Or maybe I'm the prey.

"I don't—" My mouth is dry, my throat is tight, the words are jumbled letters in my frozen brain. "I don't know what you—"

"You do something nice for me," he says. "I'll do something nice for you."

And with the sickening thud of my heart into my stomach, it clicks. I know. I know why he closed the door, why he said that about my clothes, why he's walking toward me now, like a hunter who's wounded his target and is ready to deliver the kill shot.

I think: *I shouldn't be here. He shouldn't be doing this.*

I think: *Do something, do something, before he does something.*

I say: "My sister is waiting for me."

He laughs, like he's heard that one before. "She can wait five minutes."

Then he reaches in with a big, eager hand and pushes a loose lock of my hair behind my ear. Just the way Alex does.

I don't think. I don't say. I only react, like a fox in a trap, and lash out, knocking his hand away with one of mine, shoving his heavy, broad chest away from me with the other.

"Jesus!" he says, stumbling back a step. He looks at me half-wounded and half-stunned, like I just shot an arrow into his foot for no reason. "What the fuck is your problem?"

I wish I had an arrow. I wish I had an army. I wish I had words instead of jumbled letters in my brain. "Don't—"

"Jesus *Christ*," he says. "All I did was *offer*, you crazy bitch. All you had to say was no."

I didn't have the word, I try to explain helplessly, silently, in my own head. *I don't have words for anything anymore.*

"Don't play this game with me," he says. Nearly snarls. "You shoved your tits in that little dress, came up here alone, and now you want to act offended? You knew what this was. You just wanted another gig out of it."

"I'm—" I swallow. I grab my bag on the floor, without taking my eyes off him. I don't want to see him and his stupid face, his terrible hat covering his thinning hair, his bleached teeth gritted in his angry mouth. But I can't let him out of my sight. "I'm going."

"So go!" he yells, flinging an arm at the door. "I'm not stopping you. Fuck, you try to be nice to somebody and they try to take your goddamn arm off—go ahead and go!"

I open the door and flee, like the dumb, helpless animal I am.

CHAPTER 16

I DON'T TELL Mo about it. I don't tell my parents, or Alex, or even a diary, not that I have one. I don't tell anybody.

It's just one moment, and I can bury one moment down deep inside my brain. It's not that big of a deal, anyway. A shitty, gross guy saying a shitty, gross thing. It's not the first time. The first time, it was a college kid in a Northwestern sweatshirt who yelled at me to impress his friends and told me I was so fucking hot. I was so fucking *twelve*.

It's not the first time. It's not the worst thing I've heard. But we were in such a small room, and I didn't expect it, and I'd been so happy. He said I was good onstage. And then he showed me all he really thought I was good for.

I hate him. I hate myself. I never want to get onstage again.

Charlotte went back to college two days later, so the only other people who know about that night are my friends. If I just stay at home, in my room, surrounded by plants and plays and no people, I'm safe.

I know that's stupid. I do. No one is ever really safe.

But I can't imagine how bad I would feel if I saw Mo again. If I went back to that club he brought me to, or the Forest, where he found me, or . . . anywhere. Anywhere like that. If I can stay away, maybe it'll help keep this feeling away. It's hard to describe it. Put it into words. I'll be fine, I'll be thinking of something good, and then I'll hear something, or see something that reminds me of what happened, and—it feels like a stitch in my side, the kind you get from running. Sharp and unexpected and searing. It feels like a splinter under my fingernail. So small. So painful. And impossible to ignore.

After a week of this, though, Mo loses her patience.

"We're getting lunch," she says to me on video chat. "I'm free Saturday."

"I don't know, I'm kind of—"

"Izzy, you've been super weird since the bringer show."

I grimace. "I haven't."

"Can you see your face right now?" She points toward the corner of the screen, where she knows I can see myself. "That is a weird face."

"Are you calling me ugly?" I say, trying for a joke.

She's having none of it. "I'm calling you full of shit. We're getting lunch."

◆ ◆ ◆

"Wow," she says, her eyes traveling from my hair, half-brushed and up in a bun, to the oversized flannel shirt poking out of my coat sleeves, down to my oldest boots, caked with mud. "You look, um—"

"I woke up late," I mumble, dropping down next to her on the bench at Millennium Park.

"Okay."

"I know I look terrible."

"You don't," Mo assures me. "You just look . . . not like you."

I shrug. "I mean, these are my clothes, so."

She looks taken aback, and I feel bad. I know I'm being rude, and it's not her fault. I'm just mad at everything and everyone and she's the person who's here.

"Okay," she says again. "But . . . I've never seen you wear pants, let alone sweatpants."

She's always seen me in a dress, the green dress and the black one. The one I wore in the club. My throat tightens.

"Or sneakers . . ."

I almost tripped in my heels, going up the stairs to his office. My stomach clenches.

That's what he saw, he saw the heels and the dress and thought that meant I wanted things I didn't. My heart pounds, my chest caves in.

"What if nothing I do is actually for me?"

Mo wrinkles her brow. "Huh?"

"What if all the things I thought I chose for myself were really

225

for everyone else? What if I only wear skirts all the time because people treat me nicer when I do? Or I put on makeup because I like it, but also because I feel like I have to, just to look *normal*. Or I have long hair because my mom's been telling me how pretty it is, that other girls would kill for hair like mine, since I was *three* and hacked off a hunk of it with scissors."

I'm getting louder, without meaning to, but I can't seem to bring it down. I don't want people to stare, but I can't be quieter. And Mo doesn't ask me to.

"You said I don't look like me, but I don't even know what that *means*. How much of it *is* me, and how much of it is the makeover kit I got on my seventh birthday, all those dolls I never played with—God, the pink onesie I wore out of the fucking hospital!"

"You can ditch it," Mo says. "All of it, the dresses and the makeup and the pink, if you want to. You're allowed to. I did."

But that's not me, either, I want to say. *It would just be a different box.* But I don't want Mo to take it the wrong way, so I just shake my head. Then, after a moment: "Mo," I ask. "Do you . . . feel like a girl?"

"Yeah." She blinks at me. "Do you?"

"I guess. Maybe. I don't know," I say helplessly. "What does it *feel* like, to feel like a girl?"

"Well—" Mo runs her hands through her hair. "It just does. I don't think it goes into words like that."

226

"Then how do I know if I do, or I don't, if there aren't any words?"

"You don't have to identify as a girl," she says gently. "If it doesn't fit."

"But it's not that I feel like a boy."

"There's more than just 'girl' or 'boy,' you know."

I do know that. And it's good that it's true, but what I can't figure out is whether it's true for *me*. Do I really not feel like a girl, or is it just that I don't want to deal with all the baggage that comes with it? It's like turning thirteen—and suddenly going up four inches in height and three cup sizes—came with all these terms and conditions I never agreed to.

You can't wear that. It's too short now.

You can't say that. Someone will think you're flirting with them now.

Don't bend over like that, sit like that, stretch like that—

Mom always talked about womanhood like it was this great gift, but it wasn't ever on my wish list, and sometimes I think I'd like to make a return.

"If you could wake up tomorrow," Mo asks me, "and everything was perfect. What would that look like?"

"I don't know." When I try to think about who I am—*really am*—it feels like looking at myself in a photo someone else took. It's me, of course it's me, but the person behind the camera is there, too. Choosing the angle. Picking the shot. It all gets tangled up together, the parts of me that are real and the parts that

227

got filtered through outside eyes. How much of me is only a reflection of how people have treated me, instead of what I wanted? What would it look like if I could tell the universe who I was before it could decide that for me? What would *I* look like?

"I want to wear clothes and have them not *mean* anything," I say. "I want to take up just as much space as I need, I want to stop smiling when I don't feel like it, I want to walk down the street and not be a target because men want to fuck me, or be invisible if they don't. I just want to be a person." My voice cracks. "Am I ever going to get to be a person?"

"Of course you are," Mo rushes to say. "You already are. And I know it sucks, believe me, but it'll get better—"

"No it won't!" I say, suddenly furious. "It *won't* get better, because I won't get better, because I'm weak and stupid, so *stupid*—"

Mo, suddenly looking alarmed, reaches for me. "Izzy, holy shit, you're not stupid—"

"I am." Even my hands are weak. They're shaking. I fold my arms across my chest to stop them. "I'm not good enough to get invited to a show, Jonah knew it and you knew it, too, but I did it anyway and of *course* he wanted something, of course he just thought I was some stupid—" I blink away tears. "It's my fault."

"What happened?"

"I can't."

"You can." She rests her hand on my knee. "Izzy. Please."

So I take a breath, wrap my arms around my stomach, and

228

tell her. More accurately, I tell her shoes, because I can't look Mo in the eyes as I do it. No matter what her expression is—pity or disgust or anger—I can't see it and speak at the same time. I start from the moment he approached at me the bar, and by the time I get to the end, the legs of my jeans are covered in little wet spots. This is so stupid. I didn't cry then. Why am I doing it now, when it's over and I'm safe? What's *wrong* with me?

Mo only lets the silence linger for a half second after I'm done, just a cursory moment to be sure there's nothing else. Then she explodes.

"That creep. That total fucking creep. I'll kill him."

"Mo—"

She's already digging her phone out of her coat pocket. "I'll tell everyone I know. And tell them to text everyone they know. Good luck booking anyone in your shitty little club after that."

"Mo—"

"We'll blacklist him."

"He'll blacklist *me*." I put my hand on hers, the one holding the phone, and ease it down. "I just found my way into this world, you know? You and the guys have been so nice to me, but no one else knows who I am. No one else has any reason to believe me."

"Then they're assholes."

"Okay," I say. "So they're assholes. That doesn't change anything. That won't make anyone decide to book me."

"But—"

"I don't want to be the girl who got propositioned on her first gig."

"It was just a bringer show—" Mo tries to say, but I talk over her. Because that's not the point.

"I don't want to be that guy's victim, okay?" I say. "I don't want my name to be attached to his name every time I get up on stage. That isn't how I want people to know who I am. I want my own name."

Mo looks off into the distance for a moment. Then back at me. "Is that really why you don't want to say anything?" I look away, but she moves closer. "Or because you think it's your fault?"

We sit in silence for a moment.

"It's not your fault," she says. "I know it might feel that way, but what Mitch did, none of it is your fault." I nod, but I don't believe her, and I think she can tell. "Whatever he did, for whatever reason he thought he was entitled to do it—or could get away with it—It. Is. Not. Your. Fault."

"But if I had . . ." I trail off, because I can't even pick what to say next. If I had believed I wasn't good enough for an invited show. If I had worn something different. If I had seemed less young, less naive, less like myself.

Mo shakes her head. "Stop. There's no 'I' in 'He's a dickless predator.'"

I think about that for a moment. "Yes, there is."

"Fine," she concedes. "'He's a . . . sleazy predator.' Okay?"

"Okay. But—"

"No. Full stop. You are not responsible for that man's terrible behavior."

I start to nod but then feel my phone, deep in my jacket pocket, vibrating. When I dig it out, I see not only that Alex is calling, but—*oh, shit*—I've missed a whole string of texts from him. Twelve, over the last hour, showing the full range of human emotion, from *Hey* (#1) to *Isabel if you don't text me the fuck back soon I swear to god* (#12).

"Fuck," I breathe out.

"Are you okay?" Mo asks.

"It's my boyfriend. He—" I stare at the phone, not knowing quite what to do. "He texted asking where I was, but I didn't respond, because we were talking, so now he's calling—" The vibrating stops. I text him back as quickly as my thumbs will go:

Sorry!!! Phone was on silent I'll call in 1 min

When I look back up, Mo glances away so quickly I can tell she was reading over my shoulder. I put the phone in my pocket.

"It seems like he texts you a lot," she says, working to keep her tone even.

"He likes to know where I am." And then feeling defensive: "But it's because he wants to know I'm safe."

"That's one reason," she says in the same forced tone, "he could be doing it."

My phone rings again. I don't know whether Alex didn't see my text or didn't think it was an acceptable response.

"I have to talk to him," I tell Mo, getting up. "I'm already in trouble."

Mo's face contorts into something unreadable. Surprise. Pity. And maybe some of her own anger, too. She shakes her head and clears the expression.

"Izzy," she says gently. "You shouldn't be in *trouble* with your own boyfriend."

She's right. I know she's right. So why do I still feel like I've done something wrong?

"I really have to go."

"Don't forget what I said."

"Mo," I plead. "I don't want you to tell anyone about Mitch."

"I heard you. We'll handle Mitch however you want. I'm not talking about that part."

"Then what?"

"You are not responsible for *any* man's terrible behavior." She leans closer. "No matter who he is."

CHAPTER 17

MO INVITES ME out to two open mics that week, but I turn her down both times. The thought of getting back onstage makes my stomach clench. What if Mitch told people? There's nothing to tell, but what if he lied? What if this whole time, the audience has seen me exactly the way he did? A stupid airhead with nothing to give the world except her looks and a blow job?

I can't do it. I tell Mo I just can't. She says she understands.

So my entire Spring Break is a week of days with Alex and stomach cramps and black-and-white movies. But on Thursday night, Mom announces she's taking me out to lunch on Friday.

She has a hearing in federal court first, so I meet her at our usual spot, a little Italian place close to her office. The owner's mom makes all the pasta by hand, and whenever Mom sees her, they'll have a short back-and-forth that always ends with them both laughing at my mom's terrible Italian.

But she's not up front today, so my meal with Mom is quiet.

She gets a salad to start. I go for the minestrone soup.

"So. How's school?" Mom asks.

It takes me a second to realize I have absolutely no idea. I don't think I'm failing anything. But ever since I started doing shows, none of my classes have seemed super relevant. Chemistry isn't going to make it into my tight five. How helpful is US history, really, unless I'm going to do a bit about the time Ben Franklin tried to cook a turkey by electrocuting it, as a party trick.

I grab a piece of bread. "Fine."

Mom looks skeptical. "When we get your mid-semester report, there aren't going to be any surprises?"

Aren't surprises just supposed to be for good things? Otherwise, it's shock or horror, or something. No one comes into the house and yells, "Surprise! I backed over the dog with my ATV!"

But I smile at Mom and shake my head.

"Well, good." She smiles back. "How are things going with you and Alex?"

"Fine," I say again, but it comes out weird, like I have a piece of bread stuck in my throat, even though I don't.

"Almost six months, right?" she says, all eager, like I'm about to let her in on a secret. A good secret. A surprise. "That's pretty serious."

"Yeah. I mean, not that serious. Not that he *isn't* serious about me, but six months is long for high school. Not long in real life, right?" I don't even notice I'm tearing the bread to bits until the crumbs start gathering in my skirt. I brush them off. "We're great. We're, you know, it's—" I search for the right word. They all suck. I give up. "We're great."

Just then, Mom's phone buzzes, and she picks it up without a moment of hesitation.

"Shit," she whispers when she sees the caller ID. Her chair squeaks against the floor as she pushes it back, phone in hand, mind already on the case. "I'll just be a minute."

I watch Mom through the big front windows as she paces, one hand clutching her phone to her ear, the other clutching around her waist. She forgot to take her coat. It must be a real crisis, if she had to run outside without her coat.

I'm nearly done with my soup before Mom returns to the table, cheeks flushed from the cold. She sighs, and it lasts a full three seconds. "God." She picks up her fork but doesn't move to eat anything. "The incompetence of some people with seven-figure salaries would astound you, Isabel."

It wouldn't. I nod anyway.

"What were we talking about?" she asks.

I think: *Alex.*

I think: *We were talking about Alex and I said everything was great, but I don't know if it is. I want it to be great but that doesn't make it true.*

I say: Nothing.

She uses the silence as an opportunity to type out a quick message to someone.

I can't throw my problems at her when she's got so much to handle already. What's happening with Alex is fine, and what happened with Mitch . . . is over. It's fine. I'm fine.

"How was court?" I ask.

"Well." She sets her fork down, then sets the stage. "Matt and I get to the courtroom—you remember Matt?"

I nod again, because I know he's my mom's cocounsel for this case, but truthfully, all the young dude lawyers they seem to pair Mom with blend together.

"So he and I are appearing before Judge Riley, in the Greg Shea case. You remember which one that is?"

She knows we live in the same apartment, right? Not only has she been working nonstop on this case for months and talking to Dad about it nearly every night she's home, but Greg Shea is way too weird to forget. "The guy with the clown collection."

"Unfortunately, yes." Mom grimaces. "I've never argued in front of Judge Riley, and neither has Matt. My opposing counsel has, though. So we get to the courtroom, and this judge—a dinosaur, seriously—starts talking to Matt. *Only* to Matt. And it takes Matt five tries to explain to Judge Riley *I'm* the lead counsel."

"Why would he assume Matt was in charge? He's so young," I say. Then, quickly, "Not that you're old."

She laughs. "Thank you. Yes, Matt is young. Matt is also male."

Oh.

Ugh.

"That's awful," I say. "That's so—"

"The judge is an old guy." Mom shrugs. "It's not typical."

My mom can do anything. I've always known that, so it seemed impossible anyone would ever doubt her. I guess I knew it hasn't been easy, her getting where she is, but I didn't think it was because she's a girl. I thought it was because she was a *mom*.

She only planned on two kids. Charlotte made sure I knew that, and the older I got, the more sense it made. None of the guys at her level ever had to show up to court eight months pregnant. She must have been thrilled to find out about the twins. Two babies, one maternity leave! But then she was pregnant again, less than a year later. And that's when all her plans got messed up.

She hasn't ever *said* that to me. But I overheard her once. She was talking to one of her friends at a party, a stay-at-home mom. "It definitely threw a wrench in things. A giant wrench." That's what she said. "Isabel put me on the mommy path. And it's been hell trying to get off it."

Those are the words she said. I would get on a witness stand and testify to every single one.

"So," Mom continues, "we finally establish I'm the one in charge, and I present my evidentiary motions, the things I want excluded from the trial, all of that. And then the prosecutor, my opposing counsel, he takes his turn. And do you know what he asks for?"

I shake my head.

"He moves to exclude 'emotional displays.'"

Emotional displays? "He doesn't want your client freaking out on the stand, or something?"

Mom starts laughing. "Honey, that man is not taking the stand."

"Then—?"

"He was asking to preclude emotional displays from *me*."

I'm not a lawyer, but I am the daughter of one and have also seen every episode of *Law & Order: SVU*. And I've never heard of something like this. "What does that even mean?"

"He said it was to, uh"—she makes scare quotes—"'limit displays of emotion that could sway the jury.' Specifically . . . tears."

Wait. Crying? He filed a motion to keep *my mom* from crying? My mom doesn't cry. I've lived with her for sixteen years and only seen it happen once, when my uncle called and told her their mom had died.

"He thought you'd . . . cry?" I ask. She nods. "But why?"

"Like I said, I've never argued before that judge. My opposing counsel made that motion to make it seem like that's my MO. I'm an overly emotional woman who cries to sway the jury."

"*Why*, though?"

"That's how he wants the judge to see me. Every time I file

a motion, or make an objection, he wants the judge to think about how I cry in court."

"But you don't!"

"Perception isn't the same thing as truth."

"That's so—" I stumble, searching for one word that sums it all up. Backward. Horrible. Infuriating.

Mom reaches over and pats my hand. "I'm fine. It's just part of the deal."

"It shouldn't be."

"I know."

"They shouldn't have treated you like that."

"Preaching to the choir, honey."

"But it's not *fair*," I say.

"It's not," Mom agrees.

"Aren't you mad?"

"I definitely was, when I was younger. Like you. But once I accepted it wasn't fair . . ." She pauses for a moment. "Once I realized it wasn't going to *be* fair, that I would have to work harder and be better to go half as far . . . it was a kind of weight off my shoulders, you know? Okay. So it isn't fair. I didn't ask for this, it shouldn't be happening, but it is. And I'm going to fight like hell anyway."

That prosecutor and judge didn't treat my mom like that because she's weak or stupid. They couldn't, because she isn't. And if that can happen to my mom . . . then maybe—maybe

Mitch didn't pick me out because he saw me as weak or stupid, either. Maybe he wasn't even looking for what kind of person I was, because he never saw me as a person in the first place.

What happened to my mom was awful and unfair. And what happened to my mom wasn't her fault.

Mo could have told me over and over, and no matter how right she was, I needed to hear it from my mom before I could really believe it.

What happened to me wasn't my fault, either.

We sit in silence for a long time before I gather up some words. "I'm sorry that's the judge you got."

"He's not so bad, all considered," Mom says. "I could tell you real horror stories."

"Was he mean to the other lawyer, or just you?"

"Oh, the judge knows John." She stabs a spinach leaf. "They probably have drinks together at the Harvard Club. Play squash."

"How do you know they both went to Harvard?"

Mom smiles. "It's like with vegans, sweetheart. They tell you."

CHAPTER 18

THERE ARE SOME times when kissing Alex feels like making out with a carnivorous plant.

Not that I'd tell him that, because he'd definitely take it the wrong way. This isn't *Little Bedroom of Horrors*. It's not like a Venus flytrap at all, which is the only predator plant anyone seems to know about. As if the only way something can kill you is with a hair-trigger set of teeth.

It's more like a cobra lily, which you'd never know were carnivorous, if you saw them in the wild, though the tops do curve in, like little snake heads. A cobra lily doesn't claim its prey by biting down the second it feels pressure, like a flytrap does. All it does is look inviting. Safe and warm. It's easy to walk right in. But once the prey steps inside, the exit disappears.

I have homework to do. I said I'd be home fifteen minutes ago. I need to work on my set. I know there's a world outside this room, outside Alex's warm body pressed up against mine and his hands in my hair, I *know*. It's just that I don't care.

It's so easy to get lost in it, sink into it. It swallows me up before I can catch my breath. So maybe it's more like quicksand, and if you struggle against quicksand, it only drowns you faster. I don't want to struggle, though the feeling I should itches at my skin.

Something sharp stabs at my elbow.

"Ow!"

"I didn't hurt you," he says, almost defensively.

"I know." I reach behind me and grab the real culprit, my copy of *Titus Andronicus*. "Ugh. This is the play that would stab me."

Alex looks confused.

"It's violent," I explain. "Like you wouldn't believe how violent."

He doesn't seem impressed. "How violent could it be without guns or grenades?"

Titus and his pals might not have AK-47s at their disposal, but one character's already been stabbed and another one executed by having his limbs hacked off and his entrails fed to a sacrificial fire. And that's just in the first act.

"You'd be surprised," I tell Alex. "It was popular entertainment. People always seem to go for blood and guts, don't they?"

He nods at the book. "Why don't you put it on the floor where it won't hurt you."

I lean over to set it down, but I can't help trying to convince him *Titus* can hold its own against any modern horror.

"Ms. Waldman says most productions need buckets of blood. It's basically *Game of Thrones*. Except in the sixteenth century. Actually, it's set in ancient Rome, but—"

When I straighten back up, Alex has a phone in his hand, but it isn't his. It's mine.

"What are you doing?"

He doesn't respond. Just frowns at it.

"Alex," I say, louder. "What are you doing with my phone?"

"What are *you* doing?" he shoots back, turning it around to show me the lock screen. My stomach drops when I see the text from Mo.

Hey when are you leaving your bf's?

"It's just a text from my friend."

"Your friend," he repeats.

"Yes," I say, barely above a whisper.

"Mo."

"She's nice. You'd like her." I reach out like I'm going to pat him on the arm. "If you met her you'd—"

He's quicker than me, though, so he jerks his hand up before I can grab the phone. "The girl I told you to leave alone, right?" Alex stands up, still with my phone in his tightly clenched hand, and starts pacing the floor. He's getting louder now, and I can feel myself getting smaller. "The one who stalked you on a bus—"

"What?" I throw up my hands. "I never said a bus."

"So where did you meet her?" he demands. "Where was it?"

I stand up too, then, and just as I get close enough to Alex to see my phone screen, it lights up with another message.

We're doing the Forest at 7 if you're free

"The *Forest*?" he asks. "What the fuck is the Forest?"

It comes out before I can stop myself. "It's a place with lots of trees, Alex."

Maybe it's the deadpan delivery, or maybe he really is unclear on the concept, because that distracts him enough to lower the phone. I swipe it out of his hand and rush back toward the bed.

"What the hell is going on?" he demands as he follows a half step behind me. I sit down on his bed, my back to the wall. I'm holding the phone close to my chest now, both hands over it, like I'm a corpse in a coffin.

"Nothing," I say, and I hate that it comes out a whine. "My friend texted me and—"

"That is such bullshit."

It is, I think, as I stare up at him, but it isn't. Why can't I have a friend without him flipping out? "Why did you pick up my phone?"

"It buzzed," he says. "You didn't hear it."

It couldn't have. I always keep it on silent when I'm with him, *always.*

"You shouldn't have looked at my phone," I tell him.

"I'm glad I did!" he explodes, and I wish the wall behind me was a portal. To the Forest, to the gates of hell, anywhere but here. "At least a phone can't fucking lie to me!"

244

"I didn't lie—"

"I told you not to talk to her," he fumes. "I told you and you did. I said I didn't want you hanging out with her."

"You don't want me to hang out with anyone!" I say, and even though I'm trying so hard to keep it in, a tear drips down my cheek.

"Oh, now you're going to cry?" he says, and it's almost mocking. "Do you think that's going to work?"

"I'm crying because you're—"

Scaring me.

Humiliating me.

Hurting me.

"Because—" I breathe in. "Because you're being such an unbelievable jerk!"

His mouth drops. He clearly can't believe I said that, and honestly, neither can I. But I keep going, keep talking, letting all the things I've tried to push away or keep inside come spilling out. "You're always checking up on me, you never want me going anywhere without you, you don't want me to have any friends at all."

"When have I ever stopped you from talking to Chloe, or Margot—"

"They aren't my friends! They're just dating *your* friends. Naomi was my friend."

"Again? Really? We're doing *this*?"

"You don't trust me. Why don't you trust me?" I ask softly.

"Why should I trust you?" Alex demands. "Why should I trust you, Isabel, when you're obviously lying to me?"

This isn't like all the lies I've told to Mo and everyone else, not even like the ones I've told to my parents. And I can't quite figure out why.

I lied about being older because I wanted Mo to be my friend, because I wanted to get into bars, because I wanted to get out of my house. I lied because I wanted things.

But with Alex—when I lie to Alex, or don't tell him everything, all I want is—

It isn't until I look up at him again and see the way he's bristling that I figure it out.

All I want is to be safe.

"Relationships are about choices," Alex tells me. "That's what my dad says. You either choose them, or you don't."

The man has been married three times, and I'm 99 percent sure he's banging his personal assistant. I do not consider him a font of knowledge.

"You either choose someone, or you choose *stuff*, like my mom does. You choose what's important to you."

"You're important to me," I promise him.

He folds his arms. "So, choose."

I recoil, because I know what he means. Of course I do. We're in his room instead of mine, the trees outside are bare and frozen instead of orange and brown, but this is last fall all over again. He wants me to lose Mo just like I lost Naomi.

And he wants me to choose it.

But I can't do it. And I can't say it. And what comes out instead, before I can think better of it, is:

"No."

He stares down at me. "What do you mean, 'no'?"

"You shouldn't ask me to choose," I say, "and I'm not doing it."

"You're not *doing it*."

Why does he keep repeating everything I'm saying? "No."

Suddenly, Alex wheels around, grabs *Titus Andronicus* from off the floor, and flings it across the room.

"Alex, *Jesus*," I gasp, "would you calm down?"

"I'm not going to calm down," he rages at me, pacing the floor by the bed. "You know why I'm not going to calm down? You did all this shit, Isabel. You hid stuff from me and you're going places I've never fucking heard of with people I told you not to see, and you haven't even apologized."

"I can explain what happened, if you'd just calm—"

"Not until you apologize." He wheels to a stop, right in front of me. "So. Do it."

"I'm—"

And it's on the tip of my tongue. *Sorry.* But it's caught inside of me like a pill I can't quite swallow. Like a lead ball in my stomach. I'm not sorry. I'm not sorry, and I can't say it.

No. I can say it. I possess language and vocal cords and, up until recently, a decent sense of self-preservation.

I can say it. But I won't.

He and I stare at each other for a long and silent moment. He towers and clenches his hands and waits for me to say it. I hold the bedpost and lock my knees and know that I won't.

Downstairs, there's a metal clatter, like one of the household staff has dropped a pan. I flinch. Alex blinks. And maybe he remembers then—we aren't alone.

"Fine. You know what? Fine." He tosses my backpack across the room, overhand, and I have to raise my hands all the way up to my face to catch it. "Take your stuff"—he lobs my coat at me the same way—"and get out."

All this because of a text? Half a year just gone, because I made a single friend? "I can't believe you."

"Go."

My copy of *Titus Andronicus* is still on the floor. I raise my hand to point it out. "But—"

"You better go," he says, another decibel softer, another step closer to me. And he doesn't say the second part, but I hear it all the same. *Before I make you.*

A cobra lily does its damage slowly, inch by inch. But that doesn't make it any less horrible, if you're the thing it's hurting.

I swallow my heart into my stomach, unstick my feet from the mahogany floor beneath them, and go, leaving Alex and *Titus* behind.

In high school comedies, people with no friends eat at a table by themselves, but I guess we've upped enrollment this year, because there *are* no empty tables. I really should have considered this before I got a tray full of food.

I can't sit with Alex. Obviously. I can feel him watching me from across the cafeteria. He took a different seat than he usually does, one facing the door. I wonder if he did it on purpose. To watch me better. Make sure I don't come too close.

He doesn't need to worry. I don't want to be anywhere near his table. White-knuckling my tray of food, I take an absurdly circuitous trip around the room, hugging the wall. It's almost like a math problem. *If Izzy's boyfriend just broke up with her and she is pathologically afraid of confrontation, what route will keep the greatest distance between them at all times? Also, he's the jerk in this scenario, right? Explain your answer.*

I turn to look at the table in the center of the room, a spot both familiar and completely alien. Naomi is looking right back at me, and a part of me thinks maybe she'll wave me over. Maybe she'll even get up, cross the room, and lead me back to the place on the bench that used to be mine.

But she doesn't.

When she turns away, it's like a punch in the stomach. How could I expect anything different, after what happened the last time I talked to her? I want to grab her shoulder, force my way in next to her, beg her to understand why I did what I did. But I don't understand, either. So how could she? I can feel eyes on my back, and not just from Alex's table. Everyone is watching me, just to see if I'll burst into tears, or flip a table, or lie down on the linoleum in silent protest.

It's so strange. Half my time is spent pleading with a skeptical audience to like me, listen to me, pay attention to me. And the other half, I'm trying my best to be invisible.

I guess I got what I wanted, because I'm invisible now. At least to the two people I ever cared about.

I dump my entire lunch into the trash and leave the tray on top. I'm not hungry anymore.

Ms. Waldman is the newest teacher at my school, so I guess it makes sense she has the worst classroom. It's all the way at the end of the third-floor hall, by the lockers that never get assigned, and the hinges on its door creak louder than the floorboards at my grandparents' house, so her eyes are already on me when I step through the doorway.

"Isabel," she says, putting her red pen down on a stack of papers. "Hey."

"Hi," I reply, but then don't know what else to say. *Sorry to bother you? Can I hang out for a while? Or possibly build a fort out of Dostoevsky novels and live there permanently?*

Ms. Waldman watches me flounder for a moment, then pushes her rolling chair away from her desk. She leans forward. "What's up?"

I think: *Depends on how far we're going back.*

I think: *Six months ago I lost my best friend, two weeks ago a grown man propositioned me, and yesterday, my boyfriend broke up with me.*

I say: "Do you have another copy of *Titus Andronicus* I could use?"

She raises an eyebrow. "What happened to yours?"

"I . . . left it somewhere."

"No chance of getting it back?"

Whenever Ms. Waldman looks at me, it's like she can cut through my skin, break my ribs, and see right through me. I drop my eyes to the floor and shake my head.

She scoots the chair back to her desk and opens the bottom drawer. After rummaging through it, she retrieves a battered book and holds it out toward me. I walk forward and take it.

"Thanks," I say, trying and failing to smooth down its peeling spine and cracked paperback cover.

"It's a different edition than the one we're using in class," she says. "It doesn't have the vocabulary guides on every page."

"That's okay."

"I know," she says. "You don't need that kind of hand-holding."

It's such a small thing, but it's ridiculous how good it makes me feel. I was never *that* girl in class, the one all the teachers liked and trusted and talked to like a mini adult. I never felt like my teachers saw me at all, and if they did, they saw the girl who missed every instruction and quietly lagged behind. Ms. Waldman sees something else.

But then she asks, "Are you enjoying *Titus* so far?" and the moment breaks. All my sadness and rage and pain come flooding back.

"I finished it already." It comes out nearly a snarl, and I don't know why. It isn't Ms. Waldman's fault I stayed up too late reading it last night, curled into the couch corner with my laptop open to a free online edition.

"Oh," she says lightly. "And what did you think?"

"I *hated* it," I blurt out before I can think twice, and the vehemence catches us both by surprise.

If Ms. Waldman was a normal person, she'd say: *Okay, let's not talk about it, then.*

If Ms. Waldman was a self-preserving kind of person, she'd say: *Maybe you and the guidance counselor can explore this inexplicable rage toward a play. In her office. Far away from me.*

But since she is not normal, self-preserving, or apparently all that committed to grading papers, she gestures at a desk in the front row. "Do you want to talk about it?"

Yes. I do. I want to talk about *Titus Andronicus.* I want to talk about Shakespeare and his stupid plays and how his stupid haircut looks like if the ring of Saturn experienced humidity. I sit down. Ms. Waldman slides into the desk next to me.

"So what struck you?" she asks.

Nothing struck *me.* In order, my laptop screen struck the keyboard as I slammed it shut, my computer struck the couch when I threw it down, and my slippered feet struck the hardwood floor as I stalked out of the room.

I shrug.

"You're not the first person to dislike *Titus*," she assures me. "The cannibalism is obviously . . . gross. And I had a student once who thought Tamora, Queen of the Goths, was a very problematic representation of his chosen subculture."

She smiles. I can't.

"Lavinia," I mumble.

"What?"

"I hated it——" I take a breath. "Because of what they did to Lavinia."

Her sigh sounds knowing. "Ah."

Suddenly, it's spilling out of me, and I can't stop. "She starts off the play with Titus basically trading her from one guy to another, which I guess he's allowed to do because he's her dad, and then both of those awful men fight over her like she's a *toy*. Then a *third* awful man decides to have her abducted for his own, like, political revenge shit, and so she gets taken to the woods and raped."

I take a breath. Ms. Waldman cuts in. "It is a very violent play, I can understand why——"

"We're not even done with act two!" I say. "They don't just rape her. I guess that would be too garden-variety for William Shakespeare. Better have them cut out her tongue and chop off her hands, too."

Ms. Waldman is quiet for a moment, and so am I. "Keep going," she says. "It's okay."

"So there she is. Handless. Tongueless. Fucking *traumatized*, because how could you not be?" I pause, because I didn't mean to put it quite like that, but Ms. Waldman says nothing about the swearing. "And still, she does what she's supposed to. When her dad demands the names of her attackers, she obeys. She uses her bleeding *stumps* to write their names in the dirt. And what does he do? What does he do, after he's killed her rapists and made Lavinia help him do it? He *murders her*. He stabs his own daughter to death because she's . . . what does he say? Stained. He thinks she's better off dead."

"An unfortunately common sentiment, for the Romans."

"No one asked Lavinia. Pretty convenient, taking away her tongue. You don't have to care what she might have said, if you take away her ability to say anything at all."

"I can tell how much this upset you," she says. "I'm sorry. I thought I covered all the potential triggers at the start of the unit, but clearly I didn't do a good enough job."

"No, I remember, you said it, but—"

But that was before Mitch. Before Alex broke up with me. I didn't think it mattered then. And now it does.

"I didn't . . ." I swallow. "I didn't think it would be like that. She *trusted* him, and he *hurt* her."

And there it is. The sudden stitch in my side, the splinter under my nail, pain that sears and gnaws and won't be ignored. I don't want it. It doesn't care.

"I like Shakespeare," I tell Ms. Waldman. "I do. But I'm sorry,

I'm sick of all these plays where girls just get hurt, and called whores, and kill themselves and get murdered because of all these awful, awful men Shakespeare thinks are the heroes."

"You know, there are some people who think a woman really wrote all these plays."

Yeah, whatever. The more I read about Shakespeare, the more it seems like everyone wants it to be some big conspiracy, plays written by dukes or queens or a secret cabal of influencers. What does it matter who wrote them? The play's the thing, as Hamlet would say. It's the words that matter. Not the author.

But I do know one thing: no woman would write Lavinia.

"I get it, Isabel. I promise I do." Ms. Waldman shrugs. "I mean, do you think I enjoy reading *The Merchant of Venice*?" she asks. "The pages and pages of anti-Semitic abuse heaped on Shylock and his daughter? Terrible stereotypes, the forced conversion at the end? It hurts."

"But you love Shakespeare."

"I do. It still hurts me."

"You said, on the first day, he was progressive. For his time. That when his friends wrote about women and Jewish people, they were so much worse."

"That's true. And I can believe William Shakespeare loved his daughters and thought women were actual people. I can believe he thought Jews were actual people, too. He wrote them that way." She leans in. "But here's another thing that's true: not long after they torched synagogues and destroyed Jewish homes on Kristallnacht, the Nazis broadcast *The Merchant of Venice* on the radio."

That's so horrible. To make art into a weapon.

"We're going to be talking about *Titus* for the next couple weeks," Ms. Waldman says. "If it ever gets to be too much and you need to leave the room, just take the hall pass and do it. You don't need to raise your hand and ask me."

I nod.

"And by the end of the month, we'll be on to our next play, which I hope you'll like better."

"Please tell me it's a comedy."

"It is."

Thank God. "Why do we have to read all this depressing stuff, anyway?"

"The tragedies are easier to start with," Ms. Waldman explains. "Comedies have a lot of jokes, and wordplay, and that takes more effort to understand."

"I mean, there's *bits* of funny stuff in the tragedies, right?" I say. "Like with the Gravediggers in *Hamlet*, and I know you said how the Porter in *Macbeth* might have been the first person to tell a knock-knock joke. But even those little bits are important, because life can be so—" I struggle for a word to sum it up, and fail. "Hard. Scary. Unfair."

"Even more so, in Shakespeare's time."

"Yeah," I agree. "And with comedy, when you get to laugh

in the middle of something so difficult, you feel—" I struggle for a word, again, and fail, again. "I don't know. Release. Connection." I swallow. "Hope. It feels like hope."

We sit there together, and it's like we're holding that spark of hope between us. Quiet and small and bright.

"Do you like comedy?" she asks.

"I love comedy." I say this with a level of seriousness more common at war councils.

"Really." She doesn't ask, this time. It isn't a question.

"Yeah."

"Our next read is *Much Ado About Nothing*," she says. "But in the meantime . . ."

She turns her head toward the overflowing cabinet of books in the back corner. Jack and his friends like to open it and flick paperbacks at each other when she isn't looking. Ms. Waldman stands and strides toward the cabinet with purpose.

"I have one for you," she declares, holding up a red-nailed finger. She pulls a thin, battered paperback from the bottom shelf. She returns and holds it out, but I don't take it just yet.

I lean in and read the cover aloud. *"As You Like It."*

"A comedy. With a true happy ending."

"Is it about love?"

"Yes. But also . . ." She searches for the word. "Transformation."

Transformation. I like that. It's the kind of word that blooms.

"I think Rosalind is a girl after your own heart," Ms. Waldman says.

"When are we reading this one?"

"We aren't." Ms. Waldman presses the play into my hand. "She's just for you."

CHAPTER 19

IT'S SATURDAY, AND the sky is a brilliant blue speckled with perfect, fluffy clouds. It's hotter than any March day should be, but none of us are complaining. Millennium Park is more crowded than it should be, which we might be complaining about if Will and Jonah hadn't gotten here early and snagged us space in the shade of a big oak tree.

Looking at Mo lying on the ground beneath the tree, staring up through the branches, I think of this one moment in *As You Like It*. A song, actually, sung by the exiled duke's happy band of followers as they camp out in the Forest of Arden.

> *Under the greenwood tree*
> *Who loves to lie with me*
> *And tune his merry note*
> *Unto the sweet bird's throat,*
> *Come hither, come hither, come hither.*

Here shall he see
No enemy
But winter and rough weather.

I loved it the minute I read it, but I wondered—a greenwood tree? I'd never heard of that before, and I wondered if they only existed in the Forest of Arden. Either *As You Like It*'s Arden—a mystical utopian land of runaway girls and shepherds—or Shakespeare's Arden. The real one, nestled up against the Avon river, not far from the little cottage where he was born. But when I looked it up, the answer was simpler and sweeter than I could have guessed.

There is no greenwood tree.

It's not a name, like I assumed. It isn't even one tree, though it sounds like it should be. What it actually means is a forest in full leaf, green and wet and new.

Any tree can be a greenwood tree.

I lie myself down next to Mo. The grass tickles the back of my neck. Sunlight and sky poke through the tree branches, leaving dappled shadows on my face.

It pricks at my brain again, that weird sort of foresight. The reverse déjà vu from the first night I spent at Mo's dorm. *You will be here again.* And more than that. *You will feel this way again, and again, and again.*

It's like I can see all the days I'll have, all these long moments in the light, spread out before me. I would grab them all now, if I could. Or maybe I wouldn't. Maybe it's better to take them as they come, knowing they're just on the horizon.

"Come on, Izzy." When Mo shakes my shoulder, she shakes me out of my thoughts, too. "We've got to go."

"Can't we stay?" I sigh, raising myself up on my elbows. "Just a little longer?"

"It's supposed to start at six," Will says. He's the one who suggested this new open mic, downtown at some cocktail bar. I looked it up and it seems way too fancy for us, but Mo agreed we should go.

Jonah checks his phone. "We're going to get terrible times."

"They don't have a list. They're pulling names from a hat."

"Why are we going to this place?" I whisper to Mo. The sun is so bright and the grass is so soft, I'm not thrilled about trading it in for dim lights and bar stools.

"The All-College Showcase auditions are right around the corner. If we want to have a chance at making it there, we need the prep." She doesn't say "you especially," but I think it's implied.

"So let's go to the Forest, then," I suggest. I start to lean back down on the grass. "Tomorrow."

Mo puts her hand on my back and gently pushes me upright again. "I know you like the Forest. But the showcase won't be there."

"It's not going to be at this bar Will found, either."

"But it'll be new, like this place is. You won't know what to expect. And you've got to practice that."

"I do practice," I protest. "I practice my set all the time—"

"You have to practice *adapting*, Izzy. We all do."

I pick at a blade of grass and say nothing. Mo turns to Will and Jonah, who are already getting to their feet.

"You guys go ahead." She waves them off. "We'll catch up."

When they're out of earshot, Mo turns back to me. "Look, I know this has been a really tough time, with the breakup and everything—"

Mo doesn't even *know* everything. I told her about Alex, that he broke up with me because he didn't like me spending so much time away from him. But I didn't say he broke up with me because I wouldn't choose him over her. I didn't want to make her feel bad.

"And I get how vulnerable you must be feeling—"

"It's a nice day," I say, cutting her off, "it just feels like we should spend it outside, in nature."

Mo stares at me, unblinking and searching. "Is that really it, Izzy?" I look away. "Or is it that you're scared?"

I haven't gone up much since the thing with Mitch. Mo promised me I'd never see him again at the Forest, and I didn't ask how she knew that or what she'd told Colin to make it happen, but I trusted her. That's the only place I'm sure is safe.

"It's a lot," Mo tells me, trying so hard to sound reassuring.

Like she's trying to coax a neurotic cat into its carrier without getting bit. "It's a shit ton to deal with, I promise I know that, and I've tried not to pressure you. But please—"

"Please *what*?" I ask, trying not to snap but doing it anyway. Whatever she's going to ask—for me to be braver, like her, or to go public with what Mitch did to me, like she would—I can't do it. And maybe Mo can sense that, or at least my annoyance, because she hesitates for a second. She breathes in through her nose, locks her gaze on mine, and says:

"Don't let them do it. Please don't let them take this from you."

And then I'm just confused. "Take what?"

Her eyes are sad. "Your voice."

They're only jokes, I want to say. *They don't really matter.* But the longer I think about it, the less true it seems. Yeah, people act like only the serious stuff matters. History class focuses on wars and tragedies and the news does, too, but that isn't life. Not all of it. Not the best parts of it, anyway, the parts that make all the tragedy worth it. When people laugh, they open up. And when you're the one to make them do it . . . you open up, too. Not all at once, but slowly, so slowly you don't know it's happening until it's there in full view. Like flowers blooming on a greenwood tree.

The funniest things can free you.

I stand up, so quickly it startles her, and put out my hand.

"Let's go."

She grabs it. "Yeah?"

"Yeah." I pull her up. "Before the guys leave us behind."

It's clear from the second we arrive and throw down our coats at a corner booth that this place was *never* meant to have an open mic. For one thing, it's way too expensive for anyone on an aspiring comic's budget. For another, we're the youngest people here by twenty years.

But at least we fit in better than Dave, who I bump into as I'm leaving the bathroom. For one thing, he's wearing sandals.

"Hey, Izzy!" Dave holds up a hand for a high five.

I keep my hands in my pockets. "Hey, Dave."

He plays it off like he was stretching. "So, how's your friend?"

"Still sixteen."

"Right." He nods at the mic and stool set up by the back wall. "You going up tonight?"

"I don't know," I say. "It's always weird going up at new places."

"Totally." He rummages around in his pocket for a minute, then pulls out a little tin. "Here, you want something?"

"Huh?"

"You know. Something to help." He flips it open, and I peer inside.

"What are they, like, gummy bears?"

He considers this. "*Like* gummy bears, yeah."

I look closer. They're not really bears, just blobs, and they don't look particularly appetizing, but I haven't eaten today. Might as well have a little sugar. I take one and pop it in my mouth.

He grins. "Have a good set, Izzy."

It's a half hour past when the open mic was supposed to start, and still, no one's gone up.

"Totally typical," Mo grouses. "Everybody thinks they can do an open mic, but they have no clue how to deal with logistics."

"I'm sorry, okay?" Will says. "You said we needed to branch out."

Jonah pushes the menu away. "This place is weird. All their beers are made by, like, German monks who, I don't know, mash the beans with their feet."

Will doesn't laugh. "That's not how you make beer."

"It is at the Monastery of St. Pretentiousness."

I don't know what Jonah's problem is. I like this place. The lights are soft, the booth is comfortable, and the music is really nice, whatever it is. Plus, we're right near the doors to the kitchen, and whatever they're making in there is making me drool.

All of a sudden, Mo's leaning in close to look at my face. I blink and pull back.

"Are you okay?" she asks me, brow furrowed.

Actually, now that she says it, I am feeling a little weird, but

I don't know how to place it. I'm not sick to my stomach, I don't have a headache, I just feel . . . off. Like everything around me is happening, but I'm separate from it. And also, very hungry.

"Yeah, I just feel kind of weird."

"Oh no, really?"

"Maybe I should I order something." I reach for the menu. "The only thing I ate today was this, like, gummy bear from Dave."

They all turn to look at each other. Then turn back to stare at me.

"Dave gave you what, now?" Mo's voice sounds much higher than usual.

"A piece of candy," I say. "When I came in."

"And you *ate* it?" Jonah asks.

"No, I saved it in my cheek like a chipmunk, Jonah."

"Motherf—" Mo buries her head in her hands. "That wasn't a regular gummy bear."

"Yeah, no kidding," I say. "It tasted super weird."

"IT IS DRUGS," Mo whisper-screams at me. "YOU ATE DRUGS."

"Say it louder," Will hisses at her. "Let's make sure the whole bar knows."

Oh, shit.

"That was an edible, Izzy," Jonah says. "It's weed."

Oh, holy fucking *shit*.

"It was just a gummy bear!"

"Smokey the Bear, maybe," Jonah replies. Mo jabs him in the ribs. "Ow!"

"Didn't your mother ever tell you not to take candy from strangers?" she asks me.

"Dave's not a stranger," I point out.

"Yeah, if she knew Dave she would have mentioned him specifically."

God, I feel stupid for having trusted Dave, and embarrassed that all my friends now know how stupid I am, and suddenly desperate to seem less stupid than I clearly am.

"I was trying to be polite!" I whine, as if somehow that's a justification. "Like when Jonah forced us all to eat those cheese curds his mom sent!"

"Hey, there is nothing wrong with cheese curds," Jonah says.

"Have you ever been high before?" Mo asks me.

"Not really," I say, though the truth is "not ever." I've never really wanted to, especially since my only opportunities have been with Alex, at one of his terrible friends' houses. If I was going to try it, it wasn't going to be around them.

"Okay," Mo says, launching straight into damage-control mode. "So, you know, you might feel sleepy, or you might get hungry, but it's going to be fine. Okay? Don't freak out. And if you start feeling bad, we'll go."

"Maybe we should go now," Will says to Mo.

"I'll be fine," I say. Nobody should have to leave because of me. "It's not my first time," I lie, because I don't want to seem as stupid and unexperienced as I really am. "No big deal."

So I sit there as they all talk, light-headed and starving and trying to convince myself I'm fine. Of course I'm fine. It's just a gummy bear. Why gummy bears, anyway? How did they decide that bears were the best animal shape for gummies? Why not go for the whole menagerie, like with animal crackers? The zoos in the gummy universe must suck, with only bears to look at, and I guess also an exhibit of worms just flopping around.

I think I need to lie down. But just as I'm about to rest my head on the tabletop, something—someone—sitting by the bar catches my attention.

Huh. I'm definitely high now. I have to be high, because one of the middle guys at the table by the bar, looks like—it almost looks like—

My dad.

"Oh, shit." I scramble under the booth. "Oh, shit, oh, shit, oh, *shit*."

"What the hell?" Jonah says. Or something along those lines, I can't hear exactly, because, as I mentioned, I am now under the booth.

"It's my dad," I whisper back.

"What?" Mo says, ducking under so she can see my face.

"It's my dad. My dad's at the table closest to the bar, with the glasses and the sweater and the face."

Mo searches him out, then ducks back down to me. "It's not."

"It is. It is my dad and I am dead."

"You're just paranoid, okay? That can happen. It's not your dad."

I swipe through the photos on my phone until I find one with him in it—our Christmas card from three years ago. We haven't done one since the twins went to college. I shove the phone in Mo's hand. "Look."

She straightens up so I can't see her anymore. It's quiet for a moment. Then she says, loud enough for me to hear: "Oh, fuck."

"I told you!"

"Chill," she says, ducking back down. "You're out with your friends. That's not a crime."

It is when you're sixteen and in a bar and high, I want to say, but obviously can't.

"He would not be cool with this," I tell her, grabbing my phone back. "He would be the opposite of cool with this. Volcano with this?"

"He probably won't even notice you," she reasons. "Just come out and we'll all leave, really quietly, okay?"

But I'm already texting Charlotte. In all caps.

CHARLOTTE

The moments between my text and when her typing speech bubble pops up are the longest of my life.

what

CALL DAD

wtf?!

Okay, I'm now realizing out of context, that text is very ominous.

SORRY NO ONE IS DEAD

?????????????

Okay, I'm now realizing *that* text makes it sound like I'm apologizing for the lack of death.

My phone rings.

"Is everyone okay?" she blurts out the second I pick up.

"Yes," I whisper, doing my best to block out the noise of the bar with my free hand. "Everyone's fine."

"Jesus, Isabel, you scared me—"

"I need you to call Dad and tell him you can't hear him."

"What? Why?"

"We're in the same bar."

"What do you mean—"

"I mean I am in a bar and he is also in a bar and they are the same bar."

There's a moment of silence. Then she groans. "Oh my *God*."

"You have to make him leave so then I can leave."

"Give it up. You're caught."

"Nope," I say. "Nope nope nope."

"It's just *Dad*. It's not like he's going to actually *parent* you."

"This is a situation where he would, I think, maybe. He would parent. As a verb. He would do the parenting. Or maybe just take me to a hospital maybe?"

"Izzy." I hear Mo clap her hand to her forehead. "Calm down. You're fine."

"I don't remember his policy on this," I babble to Charlotte. "Maybe he'd be cool with it. Maybe he did it, in college. Maybe he even did it on purpose, not because of Dave. Do you remember if Dad went to Woodstock?"

"Exactly how old do you think he is?"

"Izzy, honey, maybe let's end the call." Mo leans down and tries to pry the phone out of my hands. I resist.

"Isabel, what the *fuck*," Charlotte says, "You sound like you're on *drugs*."

"Do you consider weed a drug?"

She's silent for a beat. "Yes!"

"But what about Fred, that public defender friend of Mom's? He says it isn't a drug, it's just an herb, but I ate it, so maybe it doesn't still count as an herb."

"Hi, focus, please," Charlotte says. "What do you want me to do here?"

"Call Dad about . . . something, I don't know, anything, but then tell him it's too loud, you can't hear him, so then he goes outside."

She sighs, loudly and long-suffering. "You owe me."

271

"I'll get you a pony."

"Oh my God."

"I'll get you Will's sister's pony."

"What?"

"Just call thank you love you!" I hang up the phone, then pop my head back over the table. "My sister's going to call him and get him to go outside. You have to tell me what's happening, though."

I lower myself down just an inch below the tabletop so I won't be seen but can still mostly hear them.

"Okay," Mo narrates. "I think it's ringing. He's reaching in his pocket . . . looking at the caller ID . . ."

"He's letting it ring," Jonah says, sounding appalled. "Is he screening a call from his own *kid*?"

"You screen calls from your parents daily," Will says.

"That's not the same."

"Has he picked up yet?" I ask.

"Hold on," Will says.

"There he goes," Mo whispers to me. "He's talking . . . talking . . . Okay, now he's getting up."

I shoot back under the booth. I can't see my dad, but he must be walking out, because all three of their necks turn in unison from his table to the door.

"Come on." Mo beckons me out from under the booth. "We've got to go. Now."

I hesitate. "What if he's right outside the door?"

"Doesn't matter, we're going out the back."

"Is there a back door?" Will asks.

"There's always a back door," Jonah says.

"Because of Prohibition, right?" I ask as Mo hauls me up by the arm. "It was in my AP US History textbook."

"Uh-huh," she says, dragging me past the bar, and the stage, and the crowds of people so quickly everything blurs.

"The drinks were illegal so they built lots of secret doors and rooms and buildings and things."

"Yep."

"And they made the gin in bathtubs but I don't think the bathtubs were secret."

"Cool." She cranes her neck around the corner, but there's only a bathroom there. No back door.

"I read it a long time ago, though," I say, suddenly aware of how much I've been talking about an AP class for someone who's supposed to be in college. "The textbook. Not recently. Because it was in high school and I'm not in high school anymore, so—"

"Shit," Mo says, and for a second, I think she's figured it out. But then she says: "We have to go through the kitchen."

"No way," Jonah says.

"That's got to be a health code violation," Will says.

Mo rolls her eyes. "Fine, go out the front, then. I'll take her myself."

The kitchen staff death-stares at us from their stations as Mo drags me through the kitchen by one arm.

"Sorry," Mo says to each person we pass, "very sorry, just passing through, emergency."

"We don't have hairnets but we're still very clean!" Mo's still dragging me, but I call back over my shoulder: "Also the food smells so good. I wish you could eat it!"

CHAPTER 20

IN 1895, A man named John Medley Wood was wandering through the Ngoya Forest in South Africa. He found a cluster of cycad trees, tall and topped with a crown of green leaves. Almost like a palm tree, but with a sturdier trunk. He'd never seen anything quite like them before, and neither had anyone else, outside this forest.

He could have left this living thing the way he found it, untouched and wild. But he didn't. He cut off a main stem, replanted it in a box, and shipped it halfway across the world. That's where it sat, alone in a box, for decade after decade. Cut off from anything familiar, isolated from all its kind. They named it after him, which seems like a mean joke. Wood's cycad. The loneliest plant in the world.

That's how I feel at school. Like a cycad in a box.

It's not so bad during class, because I never talked to anyone in my classes, even when I had a boyfriend. During lunch, I avoid the cafeteria entirely. Ms. Waldman doesn't mind if I eat my sandwich and fruit in her room. She grades papers and makes lesson plans; I read and text Mo, if she's not in class.

But I can't stay in her room forever. At some point, I'm going to have to brave the cafeteria again. I can sit with strangers; what does it matter? This isn't my real life anyway. So after Shakespeare class, I hang back for a moment, so I can return Ms. Waldman her book. Jack hangs back, too, but only to complain to her—*again*—about his grade on our last test.

"This one should have gotten half credit, at least," he says. "We both know it."

If he wants an argument, Ms. Waldman refuses to give him one. "As I said yesterday and the day before, the grade is final." She motions to me. "Isabel?"

Jack, looking annoyed at being denied a fight, stalks past me and positions himself in the doorway. I wait for a moment, but it becomes clear he has no intention of leaving, so I walk to Ms. Waldman and hand her back the copy of *As You Like It*.

"I finished it," I tell her. "If you wanted it back."

She waves me off with a smile. "Keep it. I've got another copy at home. Or three."

I stick it back in my bag. "Thanks."

"So, did you enjoy it?"

"Yeah, a lot," I say. "It was great. Way better than all the sad, gory ones."

"What do you like about it?"

"You were right, when you said it's about transformation. I liked seeing it happen. Rosalind starts out as this scared girl. But then you watch her, and she . . . changes. She gets all this confidence; she talks to people—especially men—in a totally different way. She's bold and brave and so, so funny." I pause then, because there's something I've been wondering. "Do you think that can really happen?"

"A girl dressing up as a boy named Ganymede to flee her evil uncle and live in the forest with her exiled father, who doesn't recognize her, and then tutor her crush, who also doesn't recognize her?" She shrugs. "I would say it's a stretch."

Not *that* part. "I mean do you think people can change like that?" I ask. "Become a totally different person than the one they've always been?"

"I think we're always changing. It's just bit by bit, and we might not see it." She turns it back to me. "What do you think?"

I open my mouth to answer that I don't know. But I hope so. Then I think—maybe we're both looking at this wrong. "What if she didn't change?"

"What do you mean?" Ms. Waldman asks.

"What if—" I take a breath. "What if she was *always* that person? Deep down, that's who she was all along. She just finally got a chance to show it."

Ms. Waldman nods, but before she can say anything back, Jack interrupts. "Hey, should I leave?" he calls to us. "Don't want to get in the way of anything *intimate*."

"Would you fuck off already?" I snap at him. Ms. Waldman makes a small, surprised noise, and I can almost hear Jack's jaw hit the floor. But nobody's more shocked than me. I hadn't thought about it; I'd just . . . responded. Like I would have onstage.

Jack, suddenly aggrieved, looks to Ms. Waldman and gestures to me. "Aren't you going to give her a referral?"

"No," Ms. Waldman replies. "Would you like one?"

He scoffs at that, but finally leaves.

I talk for another minute with Ms. Waldman, wanting for Jack to be long gone before I make my escape, but one step into the hallway and I'm face-to-face with him.

And not just him. Alex, too.

When they see me, Alex keeps his expression neutral. Natural. Like this is any other day, like nothing's changed. Jack, on the other hand, grins.

"Watch out, man," Jack says to Alex. "Your girl's feisty today."

He punches Alex in the shoulder and then swaggers down the hall, leaving us alone.

"You should probably tell him," I say to Alex. "Because I'm not going to."

Alex tilts his head like a confused cocker spaniel. "Tell him what?"

"That I'm not 'your girl.'"

"Oh." He slips an arm around my waist. "Don't get all offended.

278

He doesn't mean it like that."

"Wait." I try to take a step back but can't, because of the hand looping me in. "I don't—"

"What took you so long, anyway? Did Ms. Waldman try to have another heart-to-heart with you?"

"Alex—"

"She needs to get a life, seriously. Or maybe a cat."

"Alex," I say, louder. "What are you doing?"

"Standing in this hallway talking to you instead of eating lunch, apparently."

"Why are you being nice to me?"

"Uh." He stares at me like I've lost my mind, and I'm starting to feel like I have. "You *are* my girlfriend."

That catches me so off guard I recoil. "Since when?"

He thinks about it for a moment. "October."

Early September, but that's not really the point. "You broke up with me."

"No, I didn't."

Does he—does he really not remember? He has to remember. How could he not remember? It was awful, it was very recent, it was *in his house.*

"But—" I flounder. "In your room. We were talking about . . ." I don't want to say Mo; I don't want to remind him. Wait, why do I care if I make him upset? We're not even dating anymore. I *thought* we weren't dating anymore—

279

"Shakespeare," I throw out. "We were talking about Shake-speare when you took my phone and you got so mad and then you broke up w—"

"What, that?" He sounds a second away from laughing. "That's what this is about? Isabel. So we had a fight. It happens."

"You told me to get out. You told me it was over—"

"I never said that."

"Yeah, you did," I say, bristling. "I was there, you know."

"So was I."

"You told me over and over to leave—"

"The house, not the *relationship*."

"And then the next day at lunch—this whole *week* at lunch—"

"You could have sat down. No one stopped you," he points out. "I figured you wanted some space."

"But the way you *looked* at me—you told me you were done! You told me!"

"Can you hear yourself right now?"

"Yes," I say. "Can you?"

He pulls me over to one of the locker banks. When he speaks again, it's softer. Deliberately gentle, the way my mom would talk to my grandma at the end, when she was confused all the time and seeing dead relatives by her bedside.

"Look." He leans down so our eyes can meet. "I know, okay? I get it. You were really upset."

I was upset? *He* was the one yelling, throwing books and

backpacks around, backing me into a corner.

"When people are really upset, they don't remember everything the right way, you know? I think that's what's happening."

Is he talking about me, or him? We can't both be right. I remember what happened. Not every second of it, now that I try to—but it doesn't mean Alex didn't *say* those things. I still know what happened. Don't I?

"This same thing happened with my mom one time when we were in Venice. She *swore* we both promised her we'd go to this one island in the canals where they make, like, *lace*, and my dad and I were looking at each other like, 'What the hell?' Because that never happened." He sighs. "It's probably good we don't do family trips anymore."

I guess I can believe the part about his mom, because that's just kind of her deal. Maybe all the keratin from her weekly Brazilian blowouts seeped into her brain and damaged the memory center.

"I love you, Isabel, but you always do this."

"When have I—"

"It's just like after that thing on the train platform," he says, with a world-weary sigh. "We have a fight, you get upset, and then you come up with the wildest idea of what happened."

The train platform—God, it *is* just like the—I shake my head. I'm not doing this. I'm not remembering that.

"What train?" I ask Alex, trying to match the way he tilts

his head. The breeze in his voice.

He opens his mouth, then closes it. "When—never mind. I guess."

"So I'm still your . . ." I trail off. "I didn't think I was still . . ."

"Of course you're still my girlfriend," he says. I'm not sure that was even the word I was planning on saying next. I'm not sure of anything. "One little fight isn't going to change that."

I could change it. I could. I should. I know I should.

"Don't you want to be my girlfriend again?" he asks.

I think: *Yes. No. I don't know.*

I think: *Again. You said "again," why would you say "again" if you'd never broken up with me?*

I say: Nothing.

It's not as simple as Alex thinks it is, and it's not as obvious as Naomi thought it was, either. There are parts I want and parts I don't. I want him to hold me tight against his chest while we watch movies again. I want him to brush the hair out of my eyes and tell me I'm the prettiest girl in the room again. But I don't want to be called names, I don't want to be backed up against a wall, I don't want to replay conversations in my mind and wonder if I truly made them up.

This is the part of the movie where the girl leaves. Where she walks away strong and tall, and never once looks back. There's never a movie about a girl who goes back, and back, knowing she shouldn't but not knowing what else to do. It's no mystery why those movies don't exist. No one wants to root for someone weak.

If I stay, I'm only proving how weak I am.

But if I leave, everyone will find out why.

If I leave, everyone will know just how weak I've been.

I stare up at Alex, scrape out my doubt, and mold it into a smile.

"I was always your girlfriend," I say. "Wasn't I?"

When I hold out my hand, he takes it and squeezes tight.

It's horrible, what people do to flowers, when you think about it. They plant them by design, grow them in rigid rows. If one stalk dares to bend a little, people bind them to stakes. *Be straighter, be taller, be prettier and easier to manage*, we tell them.

And when they finally bloom, we cut them off at the legs. The moment they're beautiful is the moment they finally have worth, and that's the moment we kill them. We snip them at the root and prune away the thorns so they can't even fight back. Pretty and harmless and fucking dying. That's how we like them best.

I haven't been taking the best care of my orchid lately. It's not that I don't care; it's just that I've found other things to grow. Instead of watering and checking soil, I'm spending my afternoon with an open notebook, writing and editing and rewriting my set for the All-College Showcase.

The Showcase has a three-minute limit, shorter than my regular tight five, so I've got every draft I've ever written spread out on my bed, trying to choose the best bits. The changes never seem so big from draft to draft—a line added here, a failed call-back cut there—but when I compare the first version to the last, they're worlds apart. But there's something good in all of them, and together, they might even be great.

When I finally get up on the Showcase stage, that's what I want the judges to see. The very best version I can give them.

There's a knock on my door. Before I can say "Come in," Mom does anyway. I'm not sure what the point of knocking is if you don't give your kid enough time to hide their weed, or their porn, or, in my case, a handwritten guide to stand-up comedy. But I doubt she'll even notice it.

"Hi there," she says, one hand on the door, other hand carrying a laundry basket. "I'm doing a load of whites. Do you have anything?"

Doesn't she know I've been doing my own laundry for years? I'm too lazy to separate by colors, so I just wash everything on cold. "I did mine a couple days ago."

"Oh, okay." She sets the basket down, and I can see it's empty. Was she just looking for a way into my room? She didn't need one. I'd have let her in.

I've been waiting weeks for her to come in, give me some signal I could talk to her.

"I can do them," I offer. "The whites. If you want."

"That's nice of you," Mom says. "I might take you up on it. I've got this brief due by midnight and you wouldn't believe the nonsense John Tomlinson is pulling. . . ."

I want to talk to her. But how can I, when she's already talking? How can I, when she's got so much on her plate already? I don't want to make her life harder. She's got a million problems to deal with, but she doesn't think I'm one of them. And—if I'm being honest—I *like* not being a problem for her. I used to be one, before I could help it. I don't want to be one again.

"That's a new one," Mom says, inspecting the orchid.

It's not. "Yeah."

"When's it supposed to bloom?"

Weeks ago. "Soon."

"You know, you haven't been home for dinner a lot lately."

Neither has she. "I guess."

"Poor Dad," Mom says. "He says he's eaten alone this whole week. What have you been up to?"

"Just . . . hanging with Alex," I say.

"Not Naomi?" Mom asks. "I haven't seen her at the house in so long." I hesitate for a second too long, and Mom zeroes in on it, like a beagle with a rabbit. "Is she doing all right?"

Maybe this is a way to tell my mom the truth without risking anything. Every time I thought about it before, I'd stop myself, remembering that I didn't know how she'd react. She wouldn't be happy, for sure, but *how* unhappy? All I could imagine was her losing her shit, calling up Alex's parents, filing a restraining order. All I could imagine was her staring at me like I was a stranger. It seemed so much safer to say nothing at all.

But if it's Naomi, Mom won't do any of those things. She

likes Naomi, though; she cares about her. She'll know what to do, and she'll tell me so I can pass it on. I'll get the advice I need, but without all the questions and dramatics that might follow.

"Actually . . ." I pause for dramatic effect. "No. I don't think so."

Nothing in the world catches my mom's attention like a problem she can solve. She all but flings herself on my bed.

"What happened?" she asks, and I can practically see the gears turning in her head, calculating the probabilities before I can even respond. Family illness? Failing grades? Eating disorder?

"She has this boyfriend—"

"Naomi?" Mom's forehead wrinkles. "Since when?"

"Um. A few months."

"And you don't like him?"

"No, I—" God, even in my fake story I can't bring myself to be mean about him. "He isn't all bad. That's the thing, if he were all bad and I didn't like him at all it would be so simple. But it's not like that. Half the time, he seems so nice. He's always telling her how pretty she is, and bringing her presents, and acting like she's his whole world."

"And then . . . what about the rest of the time?"

"I don't know," I say. "She's kind of quiet about it, but . . ."

"But?" Mom prods.

"Sometimes it seems like he's a totally different person. Like he'll yell at her for no reason, and she'll apologize even though she didn't do anything wrong, and then he'll be all smiley like it never even happened. It's so weird."

Mom doesn't say anything.

"He always wants to know where she is. He always wants her to be . . . available, I guess. He doesn't want her talking to me, or anyone else he doesn't like. Anyone who's just hers. He wants to be in charge of everything she does."

"Does he hit her?"

"No," I say as forcefully as I can. "It's not like that."

She nods. "That's good."

"But—" I take a breath. "She's scared of him. Sometimes. She worries he might hurt her. Even though he hasn't, yet."

Then it dawns on me, dark and sudden, like the sun burning out in the sky.

"And I think he *knows*. He *knows* she worries about what he might do, and I think . . . I think he likes that."

My heart feels like a black hole. No light. No life. Only endless darkness.

Mom shakes her head. "What a mess. Why hasn't she broken up with him?"

"It's . . . complicated. I think."

She laughs. "Sweetheart. I know you've never broken up with someone, but no. It is not complicated."

"She's tried. A couple times. But it never sticks."

"What do you mean?"

"He even broke up with *her* but then, like a week later, pretended he'd never even done it and made her feel like she was crazy. I don't know what to do." Shit. I went first person there. "I don't know how to help her," I add quickly.

"Oh, honey," Mom says gently, sadly. "You can't help her."

"Huh?"

"Isabel, I've had friends like this. There's nothing you can do to help people like that."

"Mom."

"You can't take this on yourself. I know she's your best friend, but you aren't responsible for someone else's bad choices."

I recoil. "Bad choices?"

"It's not her fault this boy is such a jerk," Mom concedes, "but the stakes are so low. She's not a single mom with three kids who's going to have to live in a shelter. The fact is, she could break up with this guy tomorrow and she isn't doing it. What does that say about her?"

"You're not being fair."

She looks at me sadly. "I get it. I get what's happened here. Frankly, Naomi can't be that popular with boys. So this guy got her convinced he was the only person who would ever really love her. And she thinks, well, maybe he's right."

He didn't have to convince me. I could see it for myself. I could see it in every canceled plan and all the weekends I spent alone and all the dinners where no one let me say a word.

"I like Naomi. You know I do. But she's not very . . . you know. Strong. Boys like that can see it. They can see the weakness. They prey on it."

She's right. She's right, even if she doesn't know who she's right about. If I was strong, none of this would be happening to me.

"And I'm sure it only makes it harder that Naomi doesn't have her mom around all the time," Mom says.

I think: *Naomi's not the only one*.

I think: *She's not the only one who doesn't have her mom.*

I say: Nothing.

"But maybe I should call her dad. If he doesn't know about this boy—"

"No," I blurt out. "He knows. Almost all of it, I think. He doesn't like her boyfriend, either."

"Ah, well," she relents. "I won't get in the middle of it, then."

Of course she won't get in the middle of it. She won't see what's happening right in front of her.

"All you can do is be there for her. Be a good friend. But you can't save her."

No one can save me. Of course they can't. I can't even save myself.

Mom stands up. She smiles at me. "I've got to tell you, Isabel, I'm just so grateful."

"For what?" I ask.

She cups my face in her hands, soft and sure. "You're too smart for anything like that."

It's just me and Mo tonight at the Forest, and based on how my set is going so far, I'm glad. At least only one of my friends has to see me crash and burn. There are some nights everything feels natural and right, like this stage is my home.

And some nights, I feel like I'm two seconds away from curling up in a fetal position and never saying another word.

"My brother and sister are way closer to my parents than I am," I say into the mic. "Or at least, they're way more similar to my parents, than I am. They're—um. I mean, I'm—"

I can't remember the next line. Has there has ever been a next line? All that's pounding in my head is *bringing this on yourself you're not that strong you're not that smart.*

I wipe a sweaty hand on the skirt of my gray dress. What does Mo always say? Stand-up means on your feet. So you have to think on your feet.

"I'm not like anybody in my family, but I used to think I was like my mom. We look alike. That's what everybody always said, you know, 'You look just like your mom.' But that doesn't mean we *are* alike."

The words are spilling out too fast for me to choose any with care. It's almost like I'm not choosing them at all. Like I'm possessed by Asrigoth, the Demon of Bad Stand-Up, and any second I'm going to start vomiting pea soup. Or trying prop comedy.

"My mom's a lawyer. Like a big-time, criminal defense lawyer. But not for the people who get busted with an ounce of
weed or something. She's only for people with a shit ton of money
who stole a shit ton of *other* people's money. You know how in
crime shows the police get this totally obvious serial killer in the
interrogation room, and he's *just* about to crack, and then the
lawyer waltzes in like, 'Don't say another word, Jeremy! They
can't prove you murdered the mayor's daughter who was also a
call girl!' That's my mom." Then I feel like I should clarify. "Not
the call girl. The lawyer. Except she doesn't defend murderers.
She defends white-collar con artists."

I call feel the room shift as everyone starts to realize this wasn't
supposed to be part of the set. No one stops me, though. The
floors might be sticky and the bar might be the site of several
health code violations, but there's a code. You can say what you
want up here. No matter what it is.

"Everyone likes to watch shows about serial killers, but trust
me when I say my mom's clients are just sociopaths with better
PR." I pause, to give the next part weight. "Oh, and they're all
guilty. Super guilty. Even if they *weren't* guilty of fraud or Ponzi
schemes or whatever, which they are, they'd be guilty of something else."

I take a step closer to the audience, like we're friends, like I'm
letting them in on some legit gossip. Which I guess I am. "My
mom has this one client, this guy whose been accused of defraud-
ing some of his investors, and my mom went to his house. She

told my dad he collects these little clown figurines. Just, like, dozens of tiny porcelain clowns all over his penthouse apartment."

That doesn't get a laugh, and why would it? It's just creepy. And, unfortunately, true.

"For real, that is a man just one bad night away from pushing tourists off Navy Pier. If there were any justice in the world, he'd be in prison for a few years. But there isn't any justice in the world, because even though he's totally guilty, my mom is going to get him off. Legally. Not sexually. And the worst part is, the worst part other than now I'm imagining my mom and fucking *Greg* having sex, is . . . she knows." I shake my head. "She knows he's guilty. She's said so. I've heard her. She knows he's a bad person and she's going to make sure he never faces any consequences."

And then I realize something. In the worst place to have one, I have the worst realization.

"No, you know what? That's not the most messed-up part. The really messed-up part is, she cares about him more than she cares about me. That fucking guy, who bankrupted a dozen people and just will *not* give up on his bad comb-over, that's her priority. Keeping him out of the prison he so clearly belongs in."

The weight of it sinks into my limbs, and I almost drop the mic. All the frustration, and rage, and pain bubble up in my throat, and my voice almost breaks.

"I mean, I'm just her *daughter*. Her only kid who still . . ." I swallow. "Her only kid who still needs her. But what's a daughter, when you've got clients?"

The red light flashes. That's okay. I'm done, anyway.

"Thank you," I say to the totally silent crowd. "I'm Izzy V." I clear my throat. "I kind of wish I wasn't right now, but . . . here we are." I put the mic back on the stand. "Hope you have a better night than I did."

There's some polite clapping, and what I'm guessing are less polite whispers. I walk like a horse with blinders back to the table.

"So . . . how do you think that went?" I ask Mo, and my voice is about an octave higher than usual.

She shakes her head. "Man, Izzy."

"That bad?"

"Worse."

"It would explain why no one laughed."

"Yeah," she says. "It's generally considered rude to laugh during a therapy session."

Ugh. I know it wasn't great, but that's melodramatic. "It wasn't a—"

"All it needed was a couch and a lady with long gray hair and statement jewelry asking how that made you *feel*."

"You don't get it."

"Like your mom doesn't get it?"

Silence.

"Talk to her about this, okay?" Mo lays a hand on my shoulder. "Not a bunch of dudes in a bar. Trust me, they will be of *zero* assistance."

"Okay."

"Great." She drags her bag up from the floor. "I'll see you later."

"You're not going to stay for a drink?"

"No, I'm going back to campus."

"Can I come with you?"

"I have a test tomorrow," Mo says.

"Please?" I ask. "I don't . . . want to go home. Right now."

Mo sighs, world-weary. "Okay. But you have to help me study."

"The Treaty of Troyes."

"Um . . ." Mo picks at her bedspread. "Agreement that Henry V would get the French crown when Charles died."

"Yeah." I put the flash card down. "Scottish rebel nobleman. Captured by Hotspur."

Mo looks unsure. "Archibald the Grim?"

"Right."

"Is it?" Mo grabs the card from me.

"Yeah."

"It's not." She sets it down. "It's his son. Archibald the Loser."

"Close enough," I say, suddenly feeling defensive.

Maybe Mo's feeling defensive, too, because she shoots back,

"Like what you did onstage tonight was close enough to stand-up?"

"Wow, straight for the jugular." I pick another flash card. "Chevauchée."

She pushes my hand down. "Forget the cards."

"You said you had to study."

"I do, but you're making it pretty hard," she says. "Tell me what's going on, because you clearly want to."

Why does everyone think they know what I want? They don't.

"You know, breakups can be really tough," she says. "I get it."

I shuffle the flash cards around, avoiding her eyes. "Uh—my boyfriend and I—we, um, got back together."

She shifts on the bed. "Oh."

"It was a misunderstanding," I try to explain, but she looks unmoved. "I thought he broke up with me, but I misunderstood him, so everything's good now."

"Is it?"

"Why wouldn't it be?"

Mo pauses. "I've noticed he . . . texts you. A lot."

I feel myself bristling. This is Naomi all over again. "You text me a lot, too."

She's slow to speak, careful with each syllable. "He wants to know where you are, a lot."

"Yeah." I look away, pick at the threads in her bedspread.

"He's got a lot of opinions about what you wear."

I feel like I'm being trapped. "Yeah."

"And he's never come to see you perform." She pauses. "I don't think he even knows you *do* perform."

"He wouldn't like it," I jump in. "It's better this way."

"Putting all of it together . . ." She hesitates again. "He seems kind of controlling."

She's just another person who's going to judge me. Just another person who looks at the mess I've gotten myself into and thinks there must be a reason for it. *She'd* never let herself be treated this way, so there *must* be something wrong with me.

"Yeah," I say, nodding sagely. "And you don't even know about how he locks me in a storm cellar and feeds on my blood like a vampire."

She closes her eyes. "Izzy—"

"What? Vampires make great boyfriends. They'll even watch you sleep."

She shakes her head. "I'm being serious."

"Anything can be funny. That's what you said. So why can't that be funny?"

"You're changing the subject," she says accusingly. And correctly. But I'm not defending this to her.

"Didn't you say that?" I ask. "That anything can be funny?"

"Yeah, but it matters how you tell it."

I have a flash of terrible inspiration. She thinks she knows everything, but she doesn't.

"Anything can be funny?" I say. "You just have to tell it right?"

"I think so."

Yeah. We'll see.

"I have a new bit." I lean forward, as if this is something big and exciting. "Can I try it on you?"

She looks skeptical. "A new bit? I think you should keep working on the material you have."

"It's rough. But just to try it out."

"Um. Okay." She gestures with an open hand. "Go for it."

"A priest, a rabbi, and a lemur walk into a bar," I start off, putting on my best hack comic voice, trying to sound like the most over-the-top, unfunniest jerk I've ever seen onstage. "Sorry, no, that's not right. A girl, her boyfriend, and whatever demon lives in his soul walk into a house party. It's October, and they haven't been dating that long, so this is the first party they've gone to together."

I don't know why I'm pretending this happened to someone else. I'm the girl. Or maybe I'm the demon. I like to keep my audience in suspense, you know?

"So we go into the party and I don't know anybody. Because they're all Alex's friends, and they're cool, and I'm just three raccoons in a trench coat." I pause. "And then this guy comes up to me. He's really nice, and super friendly, and cute in like the way Pomeranians are cute, you know? Nonthreatening. Basically a pillow with eyes. Like, you want to snuggle a pillow, but no one wants to fuck a pillow."

Any other time, that would get a laugh. But Mo just shakes her head, flipping through her flash cards like I'm wasting her time.

"So Pomeranian Boy and I are talking, and definitely not, like, *flirting*, because he's a human cotton ball and I have a boyfriend. I'm just happy to have someone to talk to, you know? Then all of sudden, my arm gets yanked back. It's Alex, of course. The kid is instantly *gone*, and I don't blame him, because Alex is *furious*."

Mo's head jerks up, and I can see it in her eyes. She knows I'm not doing a bit. She knows I'm about to tell her something important. I swallow and keep going.

"And he's all like, 'Why the fuck were you talking to him? Why were you smiling like that? He's going to think you're a whore. You're dressed like a whore.' And I'm like, *whoa*. Because this is coming out of nowhere." I take a breath. "And Alex was the one who picked out that outfit! Men, am I right?"

I hold my hands out, as if inviting audience response. Mo says nothing.

"So he pulls me out of the party, out of the house, and all the way to the L station. The platform is totally empty and I'm standing right in the middle, which I always do, when they're elevated, because I really don't like heights. And this station, there isn't even a wall, there's just, like, a railing, so if you looked over, you could see all the traffic, the cars and stores and things, fifteen feet below."

Someone's breathing is getting quicker, heavier, and I can't tell if it's mine or Mo's, because I can't look at her. I know how this sounds. I know she's watching me, pitying me, realizing just what kind of person I am. I shouldn't be telling her, I don't understand why I'm doing this, except that if I don't tell *someone*, I might break into a thousand brittle, tiny pieces.

"I'm standing in the middle of the platform, and Alex is standing closer to the tracks," I tell her. "Ignoring me. And I don't want to make him mad, so I let him ignore me. We're going home way earlier than I told my mom, so I pull out my phone. Of course, that's the exact second he turns around, and he's furious all over again. "'Who are you texting? Is it that guy?' And I try to tell him it's not, but he's got it in his head now, so he walks over with his hand out, like he wants the phone. Like he's going to take it. He backs me all the way up against the railing." I gulp in air. "One of the bars is digging into my back and my legs and I'm curling my hands around two of the others so hard I feel like they'll break—"

Without meaning to, my hands are curling around empty air, like I'm still there, which I'm not, I'm *not*.

"My heart is beating so fast, I'm trying to breathe but my lungs won't work, I'm so scared, I'm *so scared*, and he doesn't notice at all."

My heart is pounding, and I can't tell if it's because I'm telling a story I've never told before or—it's strange. I know I'm here, in Mo's cozy, comfortable dorm room. I know I'm safe. But it's like I can feel the October wind in my hair, the cold metal bar in my hands, the vibrations from cars passing below me. I'm safe. It's over. I'm not there.

But it feels like I am.

"He knows I'm scared of heights. That's my single big fear." I dig my hands into the covers, just one more piece of evidence this is today, not That Night. "I'm not going to fall over, but it feels like I am. He's not going to push me, of course he'd never *push* me, he'd never hurt me."

But he knew it scared me.

He wouldn't hurt me. But he would scare me.

He *wanted* to scare me.

"All of sudden, *whoosh*." I slide my hand through the air, trying to capture the sound of the train, the sound of my own relief. "The train flies into the station and it's . . . over. We went back home on the train. He kissed me good night in the lobby of my building. And I didn't tell anyone."

That's the end, so I close my mouth, fold my hands, and wait for Mo to say something. But Mo just sits in horrified silence. Is she in shock? Or is she waiting for me to keep going?

"Thank you, you're too kind!" I say, as if basking in the nonexistent applause. "I'll be here all week. Tip your waitress, but don't try the veal, because veal is just a shorter word for 'tortured baby cow'!"

She's got to say something. I've said so much, too much, and my throat aches. My body feels tight and raw, like I've been sitting under a blazing sun with no shade. She's got to say something, or the silence is going to burn me from the inside out.

She loosens her hands, which I only just now see have curled into fists. She shuts her eyes tight, then opens them. She clears her throat.

"I can't make you break up with him," she says softly. "I won't give you an ultimatum, because I know that doesn't work. I know it'll only make you dig in harder."

She's so sure she understands everything about me, but she *doesn't*. She can't understand how this feels. "How would you know?"

Mo shakes her head at me. "Do you think you're the only person in the world who's been in a relationship like this?"

"Like what?"

"Controlling. Toxic. Abusive."

"That's so dramatic. It's not *abusive*."

"Yes, it is."

"He wasn't actually going to hurt me. I was just afraid—"

"That's dangerous!" she says. "Even if he never hits you once, him making you hate yourself, making you scared of him is dangerous. To you. To your soul."

Sometimes, I feel like I don't actually have a soul. If "soul" just means "self." Sometimes, I feel like a terrible Frankenstein monster of a doll, all my parts assembled by other people, glued

301

together into a horror show of things I never chose for myself.

"But whatever he's telling you about yourself, it isn't true," Mo says, and I wonder if that applies to what I tell myself, too. "Whatever he's made you believe you deserve . . ." She sighs. "God, Izzy. You deserve so much more."

Alex always told me no one could ever love me more than he did. And sometimes, that seemed so romantic. Like he loved me beyond anyone else's capabilities. But sometimes, it felt crushing. Like whatever he gave me, however bad it was—this was the best I could expect.

"I can't make you break up with him," Mo says again. "But I really, *really* hope you do."

CHAPTER 21

ANOTHER AFTERNOON IN the cafeteria, another plate of salad in
front of me, another lunchtime conversation I can't quite hear
buzzing around me. Not that I'd be listening anyway. All I can
think about is the All-College Showcase auditions tonight. I
wish I could lock myself in an empty classroom to practice, or
even go over my note cards, but Alex would notice. So all I can
do is sit here. On the outside, I'm sitting here perfectly still, a
blank smile on my face. Inside my own brain, my mind is going
eighty miles an hour, reciting and considering and tweaking my
set.

That is, until Margot catches my eye across the table. "Do—
have—for—?"

Eight words, or maybe seven. Definitely about me. Definitely
a question. But I can never understand people in places this loud.

"Sorry," I say, leaning closer. "What?"

She repeats it.

"I, um." I smile. "One more time."

Her forehead wrinkles. Margot looks over at Chloe, but she's texting, oblivious. Beside me, Alex is digging into his pants pocket, and I know why. He starts to type on his phone, to tell me what Margot said, but I put my hand on top of his. This whole time I thought he was helping me, but all it did was keep me more tethered to him.

"It's okay," I say to him. "I've got this."

He opens his mouth, but I turn back to Margot.

"I can't hear you," I tell her, pointing to my ear. "I have this auditory processing disorder that makes it hard for me to understand people in really loud places like this." I take out my own phone, swipe to the Notes app, and hold it out to her across the table. "It'll be easier for both of us if you type it."

Her eyebrows have just about disappeared under her carefully flat-ironed blond bangs, but she accepts the phone without question and types.

"You're making it weird," Alex whispers in my ear.

"I'm being honest," I say without looking at him. "Sometimes that's weird."

Margot hands me back the phone.

Do you have Mr. Sparr for Trig, yes/no?
If yes, did you get the answer for the problem with the flagpole?

"Oh." I nod. "Yeah. I think I got that one—I'm not sure if

it's right, but I tried to work it out."

I haul my bag from underneath the table, pull out my math notebook, and flip through, searching for the page.

Movement in the corner of the cafeteria catches my eye. When I turn, I see my old table, and Naomi, and—Jack. He's leaning over her, grinning, getting all in her space as he flicks the end of the ribbon she's woven into her braid. She's staring down at her food like she can't see him, but her knuckles are as white as the plastic fork she's gripping. He says something to her, and she stiffens even more. The closer I look, the more I see it—Naomi looks different today, with her hair, and she might even be wearing makeup, which she never does. I can't hear him, but I don't need to. I don't have to know what he's saying to know exactly what he's doing.

He raises his voice for the benefit of his friends, sitting at the table behind him. So loud even I can hear him.

"Aw," he says, faux hurt in his voice. "Don't be like that, Naomi. Come on, tell us."

I read on her face, rather than hear, Naomi ask: *Tell you what?*

And even louder this time: "What half-blind half dude did you get all dressed up for?"

There are some people you're wrong about. There are some people who are a wonderful surprise. And there are some people that the very first time you see them, they're playing keep-away with a shorter kid's backpack, then putting it on top of the lockers, out of reach, and laughing like it's the funniest thing in the world.

One moment, and you know exactly who they are.

"Here." I push the notebook across the table to Margot. "My handwriting sucks but—here."

I'm already standing before I can think better of it, climbing over the bench before Alex can stop me, and crossing the distance between my table and Naomi's before I know what I'll do when I reach her.

"Where are you going?" Alex calls after me.

I think: *I'm going to help my friend.*

I think: *I'm going to do my job.*

I say: Nothing. Not to him.

"Who is it?" Jack's still pressing her. "Is it that guy who got a nosebleed all over you at homecoming last year?" Naomi goes even redder, and I can feel heads turning to look at Jacob, the cause of the aforementioned nosebleed. "I saw you coming out of the tech lab last week. Maybe it's Mr. Sinclair. I bet his mustache could *do* some things for you."

Jack is nothing but a heckler. Maybe he's worse than a heckler, actually, because Naomi wasn't asking him to listen to her or pay a cover charge for the privilege. All she was doing was eating lunch, and Jack thought that entitled him to her attention and her humiliation. That's all hecklers want in the end. The attention. And the humiliation.

"No no no," Jack says. "I changed my mind. I bet he's like

306

ninety, falls asleep halfway through your blow job, and his internet ad said: 'desperate, seeking same.'"

He's nothing but a heckler, and I bet he can be cut down exactly like they can. Naomi's just never learned how. It's a skill, like baking or archery or murder for hire.

I step up to the table, placing myself right against the short edge, directly in between them. I stare at Jack, unblinking. Ready. Just waiting for my opening.

"What are you looking at?" Jack asks me, already turning away by the last word. Naomi is looking away from both of us, her face almost a darker red than her hair. She hunches forward, as if someone's driving Jack's lacrosse stick into her spine.

I turn so my back is facing Naomi. So it's crystal clear just who I'm talking to. "I don't know, but I guess it can talk."

Jack's mouth drops open.

"See, the reason that works is the element of surprise," I say. "Right? Because you asked me a rhetorical question designed to shut me up, and I responded with an unexpected answer that implies you're not really a human being." I pause. "Which isn't fair. You are a human being. You're a *bad* human being, but that doesn't mean you aren't one."

"Whoa," I hear one of Jack's friends say. Jack himself just stares at me.

"But let's try it another way and see if it works better. Ask me again."

Jack narrows his eyes, maybe sensing the trap.

"Go ahead," I encourage him. "Ask me what I'm looking at again."

He turns to one of his friends. "What the fuck—"

I'm impatient now. "Fine, I'll just—" I point at him. "You'd say: 'What are you looking at?' but you'd do it in your 'don't you know who my daddy is?' kind of voice and I can't really pull that off."

Behind me, I hear Naomi make a noise, somewhere between a snort and a cough.

"So anyway, you'd say, 'What are you looking at?' and then I'd say"—I put my hand on my chest and ice water in my voice—"'Oh, nothing special.'"

Jack's face has gone from bright white to bright red. I wait a beat.

"The reason that works is the double meaning, right? Like I'm answering the question but I'm also implying you aren't special, which is true. And the truest things are the funniest ones. That's why you saying Naomi's hooking up with old guys on the internet isn't funny, because it's obviously not true. It's just the thing you thought would humiliate her the most."

Jack looks back to Naomi, as if suddenly remembering this all started with her. He starts to open his mouth, so I jump in before he can start in on her again.

"Maybe that's wasted on you," I say. "The double meaning and all. Maybe that's a little over your head."

"Over my—" He gapes at me. "Screw you, bitch, I got into Cornell!"

"Oh, Jack," I say, the way you'd talk to a twelve-year-old who still believes in Santa. "You didn't get *into* Cornell. Your dad *bought* you Cornell."

Jack's face goes from bright red to nearly purple.

"Do you think anyone's going to be impressed when you show up in Ithaca next fall? Do you think they won't be able to see exactly who you are?"

"Who *I* am?" he asks, looking to his friends for support. "Who the fuck are *you*, Isabel? I get it, you let Alex Akavian finger you in exchange for some secondhand popularity, and thought it made you something, but you're *nobody*."

He turns away, already deciding he's won, and I know why. He only knows the girl I was, the one who would have burst into tears at what he said, would have let his words worm their way inside her soul and wilt her, from the inside out. But that girl was not nobody, and neither am I.

"Everyone is somebody," I tell Jack. "Even you."

He smirks. "Yeah? Who am I?"

Oh, Jack, I think. *Don't give me that big of an opening.*

"You're a jerk," I say. "You're a bully. You think tearing people down makes you funny, but it only makes you an asshole. You think you tell it like it is, but you only hurt people you don't think will fight back, and all *that* makes you is a coward."

309

The words are flooding my brain faster than my mouth can spit them out. "This isn't going to last, you know? Sometimes, I wonder if that's *why* you treat people like this, because you *do* know. You know it's all about to be over." I take one last breath. "You peaked before you were legal to drive, and from here on out, it's just a slow descent into mediocrity and male-pattern baldness."

"I—" He gapes at me. "Fuck you!"

"Oh, no thank you," I say. "I would rather fuck a cactus. But thank you."

Alex appears at my side just in time to hear that line. Which is not ideal.

"What?" he gasps at me, as if I've reached over and casually crushed his windpipe. The second he notices Alex, Jack's focus instantly switches.

"Hey," he snaps at Alex, but points at me, "you need to get her out of here."

"He's not in charge of me," I say.

"I'm really sorry, man," Alex says.

I whirl on him. "Why are you apologizing to him?"

"Because you're acting insane," Alex says.

"So you'll apologize for this, but not for pushing me to the edge of a train platform?"

Behind me, Naomi gasps, short and sharp.

Alex's face darkens. "That's not what happened."

"It is," I say. "Some things aren't debatable. The sky is blue, you terrorized me, and Jack has never had a single original thought pass through his tiny walnut brain."

"Would you shut her up?" Jack says to Alex.

"What the hell is wrong with you?" Alex whispers to me through gritted teeth.

"Nothing," I say. "Not a single thing."

He pulls on my shoulder. "Come on."

I shrug him off. "I'm almost finished."

I put Jack Brawer, red-faced and murder-minded, back in my crosshairs. All his friends have materialized around him. I'd say they look stunned, but they always look vaguely dazed.

"I know you think you're funny because they laugh at your jokes." I gesture at his friends. "But trust me, it only means you've managed to find six people as thoughtless and unkind as you are. And come on, man, this is prep school. It's not like they were hard to find."

I still remember my first day of high school, with a campus map clutched between my clammy hands, staring across the cafeteria with my ears ringing from the noise. *One day,* I thought, *one day this is all going to feel like home.* Three years later, and it still doesn't. Three years later, and I still don't feel like I belong here. But it does feel different. Now, when I look around at the cafeteria, at all the faces watching me with wide eyes, it all seems so small. And if I never feel at home here, if that never happens, then—well. That's okay. All the windows are open, and I can see the trees and the grass outside them, the gravel path to the gate unrolled before me.

"This place is tiny, and you think it's the whole universe," I say to Jack, a little softer now. "I mean, we all do. I'm not trying to single you out. But if you think you're a king here, I just feel like someone should tell you . . . you're the king of a sandbox. There's a way bigger world out there, and in that world"—I take a breath—"you're a total fucking hack."

I sigh then, in the silence, watching them watch me. Jack, Alex, and Naomi, three pairs of eyes pinpointed on me. And probably more, in the sea of faces at the tables around us, but they're blurry and out of focus. All eyes on me. Just like onstage. Mo said I get onstage because I want to be loved, but maybe all I really wanted was to be heard. And now I have been.

"Jesus Christ," Alex says, finally breaking the quiet. "Is it over now, Isabel? Are you done?"

"Yeah. I'm done." I shake my head. "I am . . . so done."

Done with lunch. Done with school for today. Done with him, too.

I'm the first one to turn around and leave, but it doesn't mean I blinked first, even if that's what Jack says later, to make himself feel better. It doesn't feel a thing like defeat, not when I cross the cafeteria, my eyes pinpointed on the bright green Exit sign. I don't need the hallway to be filled with applauding classmates for this to feel like a victory. If Jack tries to get me suspended for bullying, if Alex breaks up with me over text, if Naomi never talks to me again, it'll still feel that way.

I spent so much time wanting people to like me, I never

stopped to consider if *I* liked myself. As if I didn't matter at all, the actual me. Only the version of me someone else could see. Or not see, in the case of the front office receptionist, who doesn't even look up from lunch as I breeze past her window and to the front door.

I've never ditched school before. My heart is pounding and my thoughts are lurching back and forth, because I can't believe I'm about to just walk out, I can't believe I said all those things to Jack, I can't believe I told Alex I was *done*, I can't, I can't—

I can't name what I feel, because I'm feeling absolutely everything, all at once. I'm furious and anxious and victorious and searching so hard for a word that can include them all. The way a body can. And when I push open the front door and blink into a high noon, bright and warm, I think I've found it.

When I step into the light, I feel like new.

CHAPTER 22

THE WALK HOME does nothing to calm me down, despite how long it is. With every step, I try to shake out all the adrenaline coursing through my body, shake off the knots in my shoulders, the pounding in my chest, and the indescribable lightness in my brain. Like I could take on the entire world. Or pass out in the middle of Michigan Ave. It's a toss-up.

When I get back to my building, I go straight up to the apartment, ignoring Norman the Doorman's raised eyebrows. I'm not worried. He's not going to tell my parents I skipped. There's a doorman code of silence.

When I get into my quiet, empty apartment, I go straight to my room, green and brimming with life and exactly how I want it. I sit on my bed, facing away from the door and where I came. Then I pull out the yellow notebook, open to the next blank page, and start writing a brand-new set. One I'm going to come up with by myself and speak into a mic, without worrying if anyone will like it. New words, all my own.

I write until my hands cramp, barely noticing the sun dipping in the sky outside my window. I should be getting dressed for the audition tonight. I should be practicing the set I have, not writing an entirely new one I won't even perform today. But that doesn't matter, nothing matters except these new sentences, messy and weird and half crossed out, but all mine.

It seems like hours later—it *is* hours later—when the door flings open behind me. I scramble to my feet, racking my brain for some lie to tell Dad about where I'm going tonight, but when I turn around, it's not my dad. Or my mom.

It's Alex.

He's standing there, one hand on my doorknob, halfway into my room, and all the way furious.

"Who let you up here?" I ask, keeping the backs of my knees pressed into the side of the bed, shielding my notebook.

"Who do you think?" he asks, barreling all the way into the room now. "The doorman."

"He should have buzzed the apartment first."

"Why? He knows I'm your boyfriend."

I hate the way he says that word. *Boyfriend.* I used to love the way it sounded, especially when he said it. It felt like a real-life kind of word, an adult kind of word, like "promotion" or "home decor" or "investment banking." But now it feels like a threatening flood, or slowly tightening vines, or a Venus flytrap. The way he says it, it feels like a noose.

"Are you still?" I fold my arms across my chest. "You change your mind a lot lately."

He clenches his jaw. "I knew it. I knew that's what this was all about."

"What are you talking about?"

"What am I—" He looks around the room, as if searching for an audience to agree with him. "Today at lunch! Jack!"

I'd almost forgotten Alex was even there. "Oh."

"Oh," he repeats. "Yeah. What, did you do something else to embarrass me today?"

"That wasn't about you. He was making fun of Naomi."

"So? Everyone makes fun of Naomi."

"I don't think Jack will anymore."

"You've lost it," Alex declares. "You have lost your fucking mind."

"Yeah," I agree. "I thought so, too, but all the other cult members said I'm fine."

"What?"

"It's a joke."

"That's not funny."

"I'm not really looking for notes at this stage."

Alex shakes his head. "Do you get it at all?" he asks. "Do you get how that makes me look?"

"I don't know, Alex," I say. "You look about the same to me."

"Huh?"

"Again. It's a joke."

"Stop making jokes!" he shouts. "This is serious. Everyone heard you. Everyone's going to think I can't—"

"What?" I ask. "Control me?"

He doesn't say anything, but his expression answers for me. He turns away.

"Good," I say. "I hope that's exactly what they think. Because it's true. You can't."

That makes him spin around on me.

"We're going to find Jack," he declares. "And you're apologizing." He makes a grab for my arm, but I take a step back.

"Oh, *fuck* that."

"Excuse me?"

"Fuck that," I say again. "Two syllables. Pretty simple."

Alex stares at me.

"We're going," he says.

"You can go wherever the hell you want."

"Isabel."

"Including actual literal hell, if you're feeling that."

"Isabel!"

"Lots of cool people to hang out with there, like Hitler and Stalin and, in about sixty years, Jack—"

Then he really does grab me. "Come on."

"Let go," I order him. He doesn't. He pulls but with only half his strength, like he actually thinks I'll give in. I yank back, as hard as I can. "Alex. Let. *Go*."

"Fine!" He releases my arm and swings his own arms wide,

palms out, an exaggerated demonstration of not touching me. "You're being so ridiculous!" Another wide, heavy swing of his arms, and his right hand sweeps across my dresser, knocking to the floor makeup and earrings and—

My orchid.

It's like I watch it in slow motion as the whole thing, pot and flower, topples off the dresser and crashes to pieces on the hardwood. Forgetting all about Alex, and our fight, and the fact he just *grabbed* me like that, I rush right past him, over to the smashed pot and drop down to my knees. I can hear him, behind me, taking a few steps back.

"What's wrong with you?" I throw over my shoulder at him.

"It was an accident," he says. "God."

For a split second, I accept that. It was an accident, of course it was, he never pays attention to his surroundings when he's mad. He's broken things before, or almost has. Except—it's weird. The things he breaks and the things he doesn't. He threw my bag that day in his room, and he didn't care if anything in there was breakable. He tried to grab my phone, the night on the train platform, and he didn't care if he broke that, either. But then I think about how careful he is with his own things. The heavy-duty screen protector on his phone. All his favorite movies stored carefully in a leather DVD case.

He only ever broke the things that were mine.

"Look at what you did!" I gesture to the mess splayed out on the floor. "You ruined it. You ruin *everything*."

"It's just a stupid plant!"

"*You're just a stupid plant!*" I shout back, not caring it makes absolutely no sense.

He has the audacity to roll his eyes. "Isabel."

"We're done," I say, loud and solid, like I can make each word crash to the floor, the thud reverberating into his body. Something he can't ignore. Something he can't talk over. "I can't do this to myself anymore. I can't let you do this to me anymore. Get out."

"Because you knocked over a plant and had a meltdown?"

I think: *You knocked over the plant!*

I think: *Even now, even with the smallest thing, you're trying to make me doubt myself.*

He lied to me all the time. And that's the thing about a lie: the more times you hear it, the realer it seems. He lied to me about who I was, and he did it so often I thought it must be the truth. That's not something I did. That's something *he* did. I'm not responsible for someone else's lies. I'm only responsible for believing him. And I think I can forgive myself for that.

"Not because of the plant," I tell him. "Because you've tried to make my life smaller and smaller, until you were the only thing in it. Too bad. It didn't work. The world is giant and scary and amazing and—I don't want you in mine, anymore."

"You'll change your mind," he says. "Three days and you'll come crawling back—"

"I'm not you. When I say something, I actually mean it."

"Isabel—"

I push past him and stalk to the entryway. He follows on my heels, and when I stop right outside the door, he stops, too. I point to it.

"Get out," I order him. "Get out of my room, get out of my building, get out of my fucking life."

It sounds odd coming out of my mouth. Not quite real. Like something from a movie, though they never make this kind of movie. They skip all the messy parts in between, all the doubt and the mistakes and the return, another return, every terrible return. They sail right over it to the inevitable showdown, then skip ahead to show her happy and safe. As if that is the end.

"Or what?" He takes a step toward me. "Or what, Isabel?"

I don't move back. Don't concede ground. Instead, I reach my hand to my left, to the intercom, and hover a finger over one of the buttons. "Then I press the emergency call button and the security guy carries you out."

We don't have an emergency call button. Or a security guard. But from the way Alex blinks and stops in his tracks, he believes the bluff. Does it make me weak, needing the lie of someone stronger than I am to save me? Maybe it does. I don't think I care. I've spent so much time worrying about being weak. About people seeing that weakness. Well, what if it's true? What if it's true and *so what* if it's true?

No matter what choices I made, or didn't make, I never deserved what Alex put me through.

I wish I'd left earlier. I'm leaving now.

I might not be strong like my mom, or brave like Mo. But maybe there's more than one way to be strong. And maybe I'm brave like me.

I get to be brave and scared and wrong and right and a million other things, in a million different moments, because this is not a movie, so the story gets to go on. Complicated and messy and limitless as it is. As I am.

For a long and terrifying moment, Alex just stands there, and I have no idea what he'll do. But finally, self-preservation wins against pride. He spins on his heel and leaves, slamming the front door behind him. For once, I don't wince at the sound. I take a breath in, three seconds. I let it out, three seconds. Just like Mo taught me. Then I walk back to my room, sink down onto the carpet, and prepare myself for a mutilated plant.

My carefully chosen planting pot is broken and dirt is smeared deep into my pink rug from Alex's large, heavy footprints, which track all the way out the door. But now that I look closer, it doesn't look like the stems got snapped or the roots unlaced themselves.

I run into the kitchen and find the next closest thing in size, a green ceramic bowl my mom would usually use for cut watermelon in the summer. I scoop the whole mess into my arms—flower, pot, dirt, and all—and carefully deposit it in the bowl.

It's 4:15. I'm supposed to meet everyone at the Loyola campus to sign up for audition slots, but maybe I shouldn't go. There are endless gardening and horticulture blogs I could consult, message boards and internet groups I could lurk in, to make sure the orchid lives. Do I even want it to live? If it does, will it always remind me of the person who bought it, and broke it, and nearly broke me?

Maybe it isn't up to me, whether it lives or dies. The only life I'm in control of is mine. Right now, even as I'm covered in dirt, hot adrenaline still coursing through my arms and legs, I feel like it's true, finally. I have a life. A real one. And I'm allowed to live it. Just the way I want to.

This orchid will bloom, or it won't. It will live, or it won't. It might curl up and die. Or it might thrive.

I kick off my dirt-covered shoes for a cleaner pair, but I don't have time to change my outfit. It's fine. That stage has seen bigger disasters than me, by far. My coat on my back, my gloves in my pocket, and my hand on the door, I take one last look at the orchid on my desk. From a distance, it doesn't look like much.

But it seems like a survivor.

"Are there still slots?" I ask the girl at the audition check-in table. She raises her eyebrows, and I can imagine what I must look like. I tried the bus first, but traffic was so bad I got out halfway and ran the rest of the way here. I might have burst a lung, but I made it before the start time.

"A couple," she says, pushing the clipboard toward me.

I scribble down my name in the only blank slot I see.

"Um, you know we're starting in like two minutes—"

"Yeah, I know, thanks!" I wave to her and rush away before she can remember she was supposed to ask for my school ID.

"Wow, you cut it close," Will says when I find him in the mass of waiting auditionees. Jonah's next to him, flipping through his flash cards. Just seeing the two of them makes me relax, for the first time in an hour. I'm here; I'm signed up. I'm also panting, adrenaline-shocked, and sweating in places I did not know I could sweat.

"If they haven't started," I reply, "I'm not late."

"No, actually, both those things can be true," Jonah tells me as I strip off my coat and sweater. "Maybe save the striptease for the judges?"

I flash him a smile, then bend down to retie my unlaced boot. "Don't worry, Jonah, I'd never steal your act."

"Ha."

"Where's Mo?" I ask, but when I straighten back up, she's right in front of me. And my mouth drops open before I can stop myself, because she looks . . . *terrible*. Her eyes are red, her hair's a mess—even her bow tie is a little askew. She's clutching a tissue to her nose like it's the only thing keeping her brain from leaking out through her nostrils.

"Oh my God," I say to her. "Are you okay?"

"I hab a code," Mo says, still with the tissue to her nose.

"What?"

"She has a cold," Will translates. "A bad one."

I wince. "Oh, Mo, really?"

She removes the tissue. "No, I'm talking like this for fun."

"You sound like you're underwater," Jonah says. "Did you take anything for it?"

"I took the whole fucking pharmacy," she says. Then sneezes. Twice.

God, this just isn't fair. I can't believe this is happening to Mo right before the showcase auditions. Mom always told me there's no such thing as luck; you win when you work for it. But in stand-up, so much depends on chance. You could get a crowd that isn't on your side. You could tell the wrong joke to the wrong person. Or you could get horribly sick on the most important day of the year.

Jonah nudges me. "Izzy."

"What?"

"She's saying your name."

I turn in the direction he's looking and see the check-in girl walking through the crowd. "Izzy V.?" She catches my eye. "That's you, right?"

"Yeah," I say, my brain already spinning through fifteen different excuses for why I don't have a student ID.

But then all she says is: "Okay, come on. You're up."

I balk. "Wait. First?"

"Uh." She turns the clipboard around so I can see my name at the very top. "Yes?"

I whirl back around to Jonah and Will. "Switch with me," I

whisper desperately. "Someone switch with me. I didn't mean to choose first, it was the only slot—"

"Hell"—Mo blows her nose—"no."

"But I didn't mean to choose first. It just was the last slot—"

Jonah grabs my shoulders and spins me back around. "Well then, the last shall be the first, Izzy. Break a leg."

The door is heavy, and it slams behind me when I enter the room. It's tiny—just a meeting room, or maybe someplace you can reserve for your study group. The whole thing is a nightmare of beige, from the carpet to the walls to the long table the three judges are sitting behind. Staring at me. Waiting.

"Hi," I say, looking from male face to male face and wondering if they chose men who looked so much alike on purpose. Like they pumped them out of a Middle-Aged Comedy Man factory with brown hair, glasses, and plaid button-downs so I wouldn't get distracted.

"Hey," the guy in the center chair says. "First up. Welcome. So, what's your name?"

I take another couple steps into the room. "Izzy V."

Two of them write that down in the notebooks in front of them, but the one on the end quips, "Just the initial? Did they give you that in kindergarten and you stuck with it?"

I don't know if this is part of the audition, but if it's a challenge, I'll take it. "No, actually, the US Marshals did. Witness protection. Can't be too careful."

No one laughs, but the one in the center smiles. He gestures to the empty space right in front of him, and I go to stand in it.

"Whenever you're ready," he says.

So I start. And it's weird. This room is so bright and quiet, completely different from the noisy bars and dark clubs I'm used to. But then, I think, maybe that's the beauty of this. No matter how many times I get up with this set, every time will be different. Same words. Half the time, on the same stage. But it will never be exactly the same, not once.

When I pictured this moment in my head, I thought it would feel . . . bigger. More momentous. The top of the mountain, the end of the finish line, the stirring swell of music at the end of a movie. But it's just a little conference room, with three men in chairs, and me. When I woke up this morning, I was so sure this would be the most important thing to happen to me today. I couldn't have pictured myself in the cafeteria, telling Jack he was the king of a sandbox. I couldn't have imagined myself ordering Alex out of my home.

Shakespeare said that life was a tangled yarn, both good and bad together. And I think it's true. But I also think life is moments. Big moments and little moments, and sometimes, they're not the ones you thought they would be.

All these thoughts should be distracting me. This should be making me stutter or drop a line. And if the judges are laughing, I can't hear it over the sound of my own voice. But I can hear myself, my own words, and I can tell that this is working, this is good. Sometimes, getting onstage feels like drowning on dry land. And sometimes, it feels like the universe is perfectly aligned.

I want to grab on to this little moment with both hands and hold tight. This perfect set, in this tiny room, with this small, quiet audience. But—no. This moment is meant to just be a moment. It's meant to change, because everything is. Even the words I'm saying right now will change, too, sentence by sentence and bit by bit. They're familiar, and comfortable, but that doesn't mean they're set in stone. Every stage, every show, every set, is a chance for them to change. For me to change.

And I am changed.

CHAPTER 23

I WAIT IN the hallway as Mo, Will, and Jonah each take their turn. We'd planned to go out afterward, but Mo says she feels like a walking germ factory, Jonah has a stats test tomorrow, and after everything's that happened today, I just want to put on sweatpants and fall asleep watching something mindless.

But the second I walk in the door, I know something's wrong. For one thing, all the lights are on, so somebody must be home. As I pass through the kitchen into the living room, I see both of my parents' coats thrown across the couch, which only makes me feel more uneasy—they weren't supposed to be home this early, and if they are, why is it so *quiet*? The only noise other than my shoes on the floor is what sounds like a TV. And it's coming from Mom's office.

That's where they are, both of them. Mom in her chair, Dad half crouched beside her, their eyes glued to whatever's on her computer.

"Hi," I say from the doorway, and they spin around to me so fast, so furiously, I drop my bag.

"Where have you been?" Mom demands.

"Um—"

"I called you"—she grabs her own phone to check—"eight times."

Oh, shit. I switched it to Do Not Disturb before going into the audition, and I must have forgotten to switch it back. "It was off. I'm—"

"Come in here," she says. "Now."

I edge into the room, to my usual spot on top of the cabinet. But when I see what's on the computer screen, I nearly fall off, because it almost looks like—

It almost looks like *me*.

I point at the screen. "What is that?"

Dad sighs. "What does it look like?"

It looks like a video. It looks like a grainy home video of a girl wearing a gray dress with a mic in her hands, and she almost looks like me. But she *isn't* me, she *can't* be me, because that would mean my parents know everything and I should offer final words before my untimely death.

It can't be me.

It is.

"When did you—"

"Today," Mom says.

I hold up both hands. "Wait, before you watch it—"

329

"We already watched it," Mom snaps.

"Twice," Dad adds.

I'm dead.

"I know, okay?" I say, words spilling out before I can choose them as carefully as I should. "I know it looks like I'm in a bar, and that's because I am in a bar—was in a bar—but not to drink, I was there to do stand-up—I mean, obviously you know about the stand-up. You already watched it. And I know I didn't tell you about it, exactly. Or at all. Semantics." I pause. "That's a joke. Not a good joke. Mine are usually better."

If it's possible, they only look angrier now.

"Mom, Dad, come on, it's not like you found all the corpses in my closet." They stare at me wordlessly. "That's also a joke! And that's all they are, okay? Whatever you saw, they're all just jokes."

"Just jokes?" Mom says, dangerously quiet. "These are *jokes* to you?"

She's a tougher critic than Cargo Shorts Braden. "Yes?"

"You know, Isabel, it's funny," she says. Having carefully analyzed what makes things funny, I disagree with this, but choose not to say so. "I can't tell if you don't remember trying to tank my career, or if you just don't care you did."

I recoil. "What are you talking about?"

Mom and Dad look at each other.

"Isabel." Dad shakes his head. "Do you *know* what's in this video?"

Of course I do. I'm on a stage and they're furious, so it has to be my set. Right? I step a little closer. The stage is the Forest, that's for sure. I try to remember the last time I wore that gray dress. Not for a while. I had to hand-wash it after I spilled soda on it at Mo's dorm when I helped her study, right after—

Oh my God.

My terrible set.

About my mom.

With a mixture of horror and dread, I step over to the computer, lean across them, and press play. When the sound comes on, it's not nearly as loud as my heartbeat.

"The really messed-up part is," the girl on-screen says, "she cares about him more than she cares about me. That fucking guy, who bankrupted a dozen people and just will *not* give up on his bad comb-over, that's her priority."

I'm dead and buried and the graveyard's on fire.

"I didn't know," I say, more to myself than them. "I didn't know anyone was filming."

"That's all you have to say for yourself?" Mom snaps back, turning the video off. "Not 'I'm sorry'?"

"You weren't supposed to hear that."

"Clearly."

"I'm sorry," I say to her. "I didn't think—I'd just had a really bad day and—"

"Decided to ruin my case?"

"Your case?"

"Yes, Isabel. *My* case, with Greg Shea, the man I love more than you apparently!"

"Mom, I don't—" I rub at my eyes. "I didn't say his full name. Or your name. I didn't even say my name!" I protest. "Not one time. I never—"

"I heard. Izzy V." When Mom smiles, it looks closer to a grimace. "Not much of a stretch."

"I could be anybody!"

"But you aren't. You're Isabel Vance, and you're my daughter."

"Who even gave you this?"

"A bartender," she says. "He said he films most of the open mics there."

Oh my God. Sean. The bartender at the Forest with the video camera. What a dick.

"But why would he—"

"I guess he thought I'd want to know my daughter was talking about my high-profile criminal cases on a public stage."

"He *knew* I was talking about Greg Shea?"

"Apparently."

"What is he, a cop?"

"Crime buff," Dad says.

"Complete and total nut job," Mom says at the same time.

I bury my head in my hands. I would, of course. I *would* have a meltdown in front of the only person outside Illinois federal court who knew what I was rambling about.

"It seems like the detail about the clown figurines tipped him off," Mom says.

"Lucky us," Dad mutters.

"But how did he know who you were?" I ask Mom. Her client, I get. He's rich and famous and a criminal. That's newsworthy. But my mom is just my mom.

"I'm the lead counsel on this case," she says, and it's amazing how I can still hear the pride in her words, even as she's furious about this and furious at me. And that makes me feel even worse. "I give statements. To the press. I'm not hard to find, if someone's looking."

I didn't know that. I didn't know my mom talked to reporters, I didn't know Sean held on to people's recordings if they didn't want to buy them, I didn't even know he was filming that night. I'm beginning to suspect I don't know anything at all.

"I don't understand," I say. "Why would he give it to you? Just to get me in trouble?"

"Frankly, you were not the focus of this."

"It's a video *of me!*"

"It's a video of what you said," she corrects me. "About *me.* About my *client.*"

"So he wanted *you* to get in trouble?"

"He wanted something better than that." When I just stare at her, she sighs. "I'll give you a hint, Isabel. It's green and rectangular and you clearly don't appreciate its value."

My heart drops into my stomach. "He asked you for money."

"He did."

"But that's blackmail!"

"It's extortion," Dad says.

"Jesus Christ, it's neither," Mom says to both of us, "because he didn't demand money for his silence. He sold us a product."

"A product?"

"The video of you. We could buy the footage . . . or someone else could."

"For how much?"

Mom and Dad glance at each other. "Does it matter?" she asks.

She wouldn't say that if it was twenty bucks. "And you paid him?"

"Yes."

"Why?"

"Are you kidding me?"

I try for a smile. "Not at the moment."

"This isn't funny," she snaps, and I shrink back. "This isn't a joke. Do you understand what would happen if that video made it onto YouTube?"

It would get a depressingly low number of views, that's what. "Mom, no one would watch it."

"They could. The point is, they could. If it got even a single view, you would have tanked my entire case."

"I don't—how—?"

"I shared the facts of the case with you," she says. "Well, with Dad, but with you there."

"Are you not allowed to do that?"

"No. Absolutely everyone does, but no." She huffs. "And you heard me say it. That I thought he was guilty."

"But you *are* allowed to think someone is guilty and still represent them. Aren't you?"

"I'm a trial attorney," she says. "It's the jury that matters, not me. If *they* think *I* think he's guilty—"

"But none of them are ever going to watch this—"

"It could poison the jury!" she shouts at me, and the force of it knocks me back. "It could jeopardize a case I've been working on for a *year*. It could ruin the relationship I have with my client; it could severely impact the way I'm seen at work. I would be a *joke*, Isabel. You could have made me a joke."

I feel guilty, and terrible, and they're looking at me like I don't feel guilty and terrible enough for their liking, and I don't know what else they want. This is my fault, but it's not *all* my fault; they're looking at me like they haven't done anything wrong and they *have*.

"You know what's a joke?" I say to them. "You thinking you can tell me shit, at this point."

They share a glance, then focus back on me.

"We're your parents," Mom says. As if I don't know. As if that isn't the whole problem. "That's what we're supposed to do."

"Yeah, that is what you're supposed to do, Mom," I snap back at her. "That's why it's so *weird* you haven't done it for *years*."

"That's totally uncalled for," Dad says.

"Oh, please. *You* haven't had a real conversation with me since I got my period," I tell him.

Mom screws her eyes shut. "Isabel."

Dad just looks lost. "I—come on, you know I don't know about girl things."

"Dan, oh my God, do not engage with that—" Mom says.

"No, seriously, as soon as I hit puberty, you started acting like I was some kind of alien creature," I say to Dad. "What do you think I'm going to do, maul you with a hidden set of teeth?"

Dad turns to Mom. "Teeth? What is she talking about, *teeth*?"

"Stop it," Mom orders me. "This is not about your dad."

"You're right," I reply. "It isn't just Dad that doesn't give a shit about me; it's you, too."

Emotional neglect is a gender-nonspecific opportunity. Like intramural soccer.

"How can you say that?" Mom gasps.

"How can *I* say it?" I balk. "*You* said it! You're not even mad I lied; you're mad it affected your *real* life."

"What do you mean, my real life?"

"Your job, Mom," I say, furious I have to spell it out for her. Like she doesn't know. "That's your real life. Not me."

Mom's eyes flash for a moment. Then they sink into something sadder. "I don't understand. I just don't understand why you're trying to hurt us like this."

"The twins are gone and you guys are done. Well, fine." I blink back tears that would indicate it is *not* fine. "But that means I get to be done, too."

"With what?" Mom throws up her hands. "Telling the truth?"

"You gave up on parenting me," I say. "Fine. I gave up on being parented."

"We didn't give up!" Dad protests.

"That's not fair," Mom says.

"It's not fair," I agree. "It's *not* fair for you to leave me at home all day and most nights, most weekends; it's not fair for you to treat me like an adult when it makes your lives easier and then treat me like a kid the one time I make your life harder."

Dad buries his head in his hands. "Oh my God."

"I'm sorry someone filmed me without my permission. I'm sorry you had to buy the tape."

"But not sorry you said it?" Mom asks.

And then, silence. She wants me to tell the truth, she says. But she doesn't want to hear the truthful answer.

"I'm sorry," I say, quieter, more evenly, "that for once I caused a problem you had to deal with. I'm sorry for once, *just once*, I didn't do my job."

"We never asked you for that!"

"You never had to ask!" I shout. "I knew what you wanted. 'Oh, Isabel is our easy kid. She's so good, we never have to worry. We just water her and turn her toward the sun!'"

"That is extremely dramatic," Dad says.

"No, don't forget, Dan," Mom says, "we're not even her real family. We're dogs and she's a cat."

"A miniature pig!" I yell. "It's like you didn't even pay attention to the set!"

"I guess I was more focused on you singlehandedly destroying my career!" Mom yells back.

"Yeah, well—" I try to shout louder than her, but my voice cracks. "What else is new?"

Mom's eyebrows scrunch together. "What?"

"That's all I've ever done, isn't it? That's how you feel, right?" I fold my arms across my chest and look down at my shoes. "I destroyed your career the moment you peed on a stick and found out I even existed."

Silence.

"I think Mom found out from a blood test," Dad says to me. He turns to Mom. "Wasn't it a blood test, with Isabel?"

"Dan," Mom says very quietly. "Stop."

Dad stops. Then Mom, who hasn't taken her eyes off me, leans forward. "What," she says, even more quietly, "are you *talking* about?"

My eyes sting. "Charlotte told me."

"What did Charlotte tell you?"

"That you didn't mean to have me. You only meant to have them. The twins."

Dad sighs. "Isabel, older siblings are basically sociopaths to their little sisters until adulthood."

Mom closes her eyes. "Dan."

"I'm the oldest in my family," he continues. "So I know."

"You have got to be kidding me," Mom says to me, shaking her head. "Charlotte told you? Charlotte also told you there was a monster in your closet. Do you still believe that, too?"

"But I heard you!" I say. "I heard you *myself.*"

"When?" she asks. "When could I possibly have—"

"You guys were having a dinner party, and all the boys were with Peter and all the girls were in Charlotte's room but she locked me out. So I started to go into the living room, but then I heard you talking about me. And how your maternity leave with me completely ruined your career and put you on the 'mommy path.'"

"The mommy track," she says, barely above a whisper.

"Yeah." I swipe at my eye. "And I knew it was true, what Charlotte always said, that I wasn't supposed to happen, I just did. I know you never wanted a third kid at all, and I get why. And then Ms. Gibson said to you—"

"Claire Gibson?" Mom looks to Dad. "She hasn't come to the apartment in years." She turns back to me. "When was this?"

I have to think about it for a moment. "Sixth grade."

"Sixth . . ." Her mouth drops. "You've felt this way for five years? You've thought we didn't *want* you for *five years*?"

I nod. But then I feel like I need to clarify. "I know you love me, I know you wanted me, but . . . you wanted other things, too, and having me meant you didn't get them."

339

"Isabel—" she starts to say, but I'm not through.

"I'm sorry I said all the stuff about your client, because it wasn't funny and all I did was mess things up more. But the lying, or whatever, the not telling you about things, acting like everything was normal, I did all of it for you, okay?" Mom just stares. "I made myself the way I was *for you.*"

A tight knot of anger is planted directly on my chest, dense and heavy and so hard to breathe through.

"You needed me to be fine," I choke out. "You always counted on me being fine. How could I ever tell you I wasn't?"

"You could have told me," Mom says. "You can tell me anything. Don't you know that?"

The knot of anger bursts open, sprouting weeds that snake up through my throat, strangling my vocal cords and all the things I want to scream at her. I can tell her anything? Doesn't that sound *so nice.* And isn't that such *total bullshit.*

"That's not true." I swallow. "You would have thought I was weak and stupid. You would have thought it was my fault—"

"What?" She looks alarmed.

"You said so yourself."

"I would *never* say—"

"No, Mom." I look her in the eyes. "You *said so yourself.* You've had friends like me. And there's nothing you can do to help *people like that.*"

She gasps.

"It wasn't Naomi?"

340

"It wasn't Naomi."

"Alex?"

"Alex."

"Isabel," she breathes out. "Honey, oh my God."

"Will someone," my dad says, "please clue me in, here?"

I stand. "Mom will."

Mom stands, too. "Wait," she says, reaching for me. "We need to talk about this."

I step out of range. "I'm tired."

"We still need to talk about it."

"I don't want to."

"If he—if Alex hurt you—"

That makes my dad's head snap up. "What?"

"It doesn't matter anymore," I say to Mom. "I took care of it. It's over."

"Oh." The relief on her face only makes me angrier.

"You were right. You couldn't help me, and you didn't need to," I say as I walk out through the door. "I didn't need you at all."

CHAPTER 24

BY THE TIME I wake up the next morning, both of my parents have left for work. No notes from my mom. No leftover breakfast waiting for me. It's like I don't exist, and I don't know why I feel hurt. I already knew that, didn't I? Why am I upset by them accepting what I already knew was true?

By the time I get to school, I've missed first period, and the rest of the day passes by in a blur. *This is how it's going to be forever,* I think. Classes where I don't talk to anyone. Hiding out in the study hall room or Ms. Waldman's classroom during lunch. More classes. More silence, at home and school and everywhere else, for the rest of the one and half years I have to be here. The eighteen months before I get to leave and start my real life.

I'm relieved when the final bell rings, but that doesn't last long. Because the moment I step outside the front doors, my heart drops into my uniform shoes.

Mo is waiting for me by the gate.

"Holy shit," she says, her eyes scanning from the headband in my hair, to the blazer with my school crest, all the way down to the hem of my gray pleated skirt. "It's true. It's actually true."

"Mo—"

"I didn't believe them, at first," she says, her eyes still on my clothes, my knee socks, the backpack over my shoulder. Anywhere but my face. "Jonah always said something was up, but Will and I told him he was paranoid. Turns out he was right. Do you know how insufferable Jonah is when he's right?"

I open my mouth, but she makes a slicing motion across her neck to cut me off. "Rhetorical question. So once we knew your actual name, Will found all your social media profiles, and I found a picture of you on this place's website"—she glances up at the school—"which looks like it should have fucking gargoyles, by the way—and here you are."

That's when she looks in my eyes, full-on, and I see all the hurt and confusion and anger, all bubbling under the surface.

"Please," I say, hands out, heart dropping. "Let me explain this."

I don't know what I *could* actually explain, if she let me. It's not a misunderstanding. I lied, and she knows, and I'm screwed.

"What's to explain?" Mo says, as if reading my mind. "You're a kid."

"I'm not a kid."

She nods at my uniform. "Either you're on your way to film some super-gross schoolgirl porn, or you're a kid."

343

I cross my arms over my blazer. "I'm seventeen. In three months."

"Too bad," she says. "I was pulling for the porn explanation."

"Are you mad at me?"

"Are you serious?"

I wince. "So I guess Sean told you?"

"What, no apology?"

"No, I'm sorry, of course I'm sorry." I rush the words out. "I only wondered if—"

"Sean didn't tell me. Not me specifically." She huffs. "He started bragging to people about this payout he got from some high school girl's rich parents."

Great. Not only did he destroy my relationship with my parents, he just had to destroy all my friendships, too.

"I didn't mean to hurt you."

She laughs, and it sounds horrible and wounded. "Oh my God, you really are a child."

I wish she'd stop saying that. I'm the same person I was when she thought I was twenty. She can't retrofit who I am just because I lied about something. A few things.

"Why are you laughing at me?" I demand. "Because I said I was sorry?"

"Because you think it's just me who needs the apology."

"But you just said—"

"I mean, yeah, I'm pretty pissed you lied to me from the moment we met, Izzy," she says. "That sucks. But this isn't some

344

petty high school drama. I'm not weeping in the girls' bathroom because you hurt my feelings. If you're going to apologize to someone, try Colin, who could have lost his liquor license serving you."

"You knew I wasn't twenty-one!"

"I didn't know you were in high school!" she shouts back. "There's a difference! A big one."

There would be a big difference if I was *six*, but not six*teen*, I want to tell her. But she doesn't want to hear it.

So I bite my lip and ask: "Are Will and Jonah mad at me, too?"

"God, why do you care?" Mo spits out. "Why is that all you want to know, whether people are mad at you? I don't know how to explain to you that this isn't about *your feelings*."

"I just wanted to know whether—"

"You know what your problem is, Izzy?" Mo says. "You are so fundamentally selfish."

I open my mouth, but Mo isn't done.

"All of us went out of our way to support you, to help you. We walked you through your set step-by-step, we taught you everything we knew, we gave you feedback every time, and you never once returned the favor."

"I didn't think you needed my help."

"That isn't the point." She grits her teeth. "You think you're the only actual person in the world, don't you?"

"Mo—"

"Did you ever see us as real people? Not just *tools* to get whatever you wanted? That alone should have clued me in. Kids can't see past themselves."

"That's such bullshit."

She narrows her eyes. "Oh, really?"

"If you're mad at me, just be mad at me, but don't pretend it's all justified because I'm sixteen."

"I walked you through every little thing in your life. And it wasn't even your real life! You just took and took and you didn't care enough to give us anything back." She throws her hands up. "You didn't care enough to give us the truth."

I stare at the ground and say nothing. Mo sighs.

"It would have changed things," she admits, "but you still should have told us the truth."

"I know."

"There were so many times you could have told us," she says. Her voice wavers. "Or me. Just me."

"I didn't want you to be mad."

"Well, I'm mad now!"

"I know it wasn't a good idea," I tell her. "I didn't know it then, but I know it now. And I'm sorry."

She shakes her head. "I know you're a kid and that means you're still learning this basic shit, but—"

"Would you stop calling me a kid?" I cut in.

"You *are* a kid!"

"I don't want to be!" Tears are filling up my eyes, which I

346

know only makes me look younger. "Okay? I don't want to be sixteen. I'm sick of it. I'm sick of being stuck at this school, I'm sick of not having any real choices, I'm sick of waiting for my actual life to start. Because this isn't it. God, this *can't* be it."

I might be imagining it, but Mo's face seems to soften. Her tight jaw loosens. Just a notch.

"But I didn't feel that way when I was with you," I say, rushing to keep her here, in this moment, where she might hate me just a little bit less. "And Will, and Jonah. I felt older, sure, but I also felt young. I know that doesn't make sense, but for the first time in my life, I actually felt *young*."

I'm half talking, half crying now, unable to stop the flood of words or the flood of tears. I feel ridiculous and hysterical and the most honest I've ever been, all at once. I'm feeling all the things I haven't wanted to, and a few I didn't know I needed, all at once. Everything all at once, in a single excruciating, liberating moment.

"I want that all the time," I say, and I don't know if I mean feeling young or feeling *this*, whatever it is. Maybe they're the same, somehow. "I want to feel that way every single second. I want to live in a dorm with a roommate I'll probably hate, I want to choose my own meals in a dining hall, I want to choose my own classes. I want to start being in charge of my own future.

"I want to make friends with people I didn't grow up with, who lived different kinds of lives from me, I want to stay awake with them on a Tuesday night talking about Shakespeare or philosophy or nothing at all until the sun comes up. I want all of it. And I don't want to wait."

I heave a giant breath in, feeling suddenly rubber-legged and light-headed, like I've run a marathon without any training. Mo stares at me, unblinking. She slowly unfolds her arms.

"I don't know what eighties movies you've been watching, but the truth is, lots of people don't like being sixteen," Mo says. "Lots of people think high school is a gigantic waste of their time. Lots of people can't wait to turn eighteen and get the fuck out of whatever shitty town or shitty family or shitty circumstances they were born into."

Mo looks away from me, into the crowd of my classmates, with their uniforms and backpacks.

"But not everybody gets this, you know? Some people have to grow up fast," she says. "I don't get why you want to give it up so badly."

When her eyes meet mine again, they're brimming. So are mine. She shakes it off.

"But you know, what? Fine. Pretend all you want, I guess. We're not going to rat you out to Loyola."

Loyola? "What do you—"

"We're going to be there, but it's to support the rest of them. Not you. Just so you know."

"Mo, what are you talking about?"

She blinks in surprise. "Have you not looked at your email?"

My school one, yeah, but not the separate one I set up for

348

Izzy. I start to dig my phone out of my bag, but maybe Mo wants one last knife turn, because she spoils it. "You're in the All-College Showcase," she says. "The only one of us who is."

My hands are shaking as I pull up the email, and my heart jumps into my throat when I see my name under *Performers*. Or . . . someone's name. Izzy V.

And all the way at the end, under *Alternates*, is Mo.

"Congrats, Izzy," she says. "I hope it was worth it."

And then she leaves, without looking back.

CHAPTER 25

I DON'T CARE how many times my alarm goes off. I don't care if I get kicked out of school for truancy, if I have to eat all my plants for sustenance, if I literally congeal into my bed. I'm never leaving my room again.

Not for a fire, not for a flood. Not even to let my mom in when she knocks, even though it's the first time she's spoken to me in two days. So she lets herself in, and I regret not shoving my desk chair up against the doorknob when I had the chance.

"Hi there," she says. Just because she's in here doesn't mean we have to talk. I pull the covers over my head, so whatever she says next is all muffled. Her fingers dig into the fabric and drag, ruining my cocoon.

"Come on," she says briskly. "We need to talk."

"I don't want to."

"Isabel, sweetheart"—she throws the covers back—"I gave you space. I gave you time. But we need to talk, even if you don't want to. This is happening."

When she uses that tone of voice, I know resistance is useless. One time, when Peter's seventh-grade teacher told him he was stupid in front of the whole class, my mom went down to the school and stood outside the principal's office—*stood*—until he agreed to reassign Peter to a new teacher.

I sit up, fold my arms across my chest, and wait for her to say something.

"What happened?" she asks.

"I kind of think we covered that," I say. "I got up and did a real bad set—"

"I mean," she interrupts, "what happened to *us*?"

That's a way more complicated answer.

"Start from the beginning," she says. "Tell me how we got here."

I tell her the shortest version I can, but it still ends up being pretty long. From the moment I hid from Alex and stumbled my way into stand-up comedy. I try to keep it linear, but it seems like every story requires another story to explain it. She listens to every word, without interrupting to ask questions, even when I can tell she has them. When I tell her about That Night on the train platform, she grabs my hand and holds it tight.

I finish up with Mo blowing up at me yesterday.

"Do you think she's right?" I ask Mom. "That I'm selfish?"

"You're a teenager. You aren't anything yet."

"Of course I *am* things. I'm a teenager, not a . . . toaster."

"I don't mean it negatively. But there's a reason we don't classify people as sociopaths until they're adults."

God, yeah, how could I possibly interpret *that* negatively? I stare at her. She laughs, seeming to realize how bad it sounded. "I only mean, you aren't anything for certain yet."

"So you *do* think I'm selfish," I say.

"I think you're self-centered."

"That's the same thing!"

"'Selfish' implies you don't care about other people, and I think you do," she says. "But I also think you put yourself in the center of the universe too often, and there's no one that hurts more than you."

How many times has Mo told me that? *That's not your job.*

It wasn't my job to make sure that heckler had a good time. It was okay if he didn't like me.

It wasn't my job to anticipate or somehow prevent what Mitch did. He was responsible for his own actions.

It wasn't my job to take care of Alex or manage his feelings. He was responsible for his own actions, too.

And for my mom—

"You are not to blame for me getting put on the mommy track," she says.

I want to believe that, but I'm not sure it's true. "If you hadn't had me—"

"Could I have gone further, without a second maternity leave in two years? Maybe. Who knows? Even if it's true, you aren't

352

to blame. I'm sorry you've carried guilt for that, because you shouldn't. I love you, Isabel. More than you can possibly imagine." She hesitates. "But you aren't the center of my universe."

I try to glance away, my eyes stinging, but Mom shifts so I'm still looking at her.

"I know that makes you feel bad. Sometimes it makes me feel bad, too." Her eyes well up. "When you're pregnant, everyone says, 'Oh, your kids will be your whole life. Being a mother is the most important job in the world. You'll never want to leave them.'" She swallows. "I loved all three of you. Unimaginably. But there was still a world outside you."

I'm not the center of my dad's universe, and that's always seemed—not fine, exactly, but unremarkable. I've asked so much more of my mother than my father. And that's not fair.

"What is the center of your universe?" I ask her. "If it's not us. Is it Dad? Is it work?"

"My universe doesn't look like that. It's not like the real universe, with the sun in the center and everything revolving around it. It's like—I've got all these things that matter to me. You kids. Dad. My job, my friends, my family, my . . . *self*, too. They're all important. I wouldn't be me without all of them. They're not planets. They're all part of a whole. They're like—" She struggles for it. "Like—"

"Flower petals."

"Yes," she says. "Like flower petals."

It feels so good, to give someone words for what they feel.

Maybe that's why I like comedy. Because someone can get up on stage and give you words for things you didn't even know you felt, and make you laugh until you cry.

"But something is wrong, here," Mom continues. "Something terrible was happening in your life, and you didn't think you could talk to me about it. Not only that, but I didn't notice it was happening."

"You're not a mind reader."

Her face crumples. "I'm your *mother.*"

"It's okay."

"It's not okay. I'm so sorry about what I said about Naomi. Not Naomi. You."

"Mom, it's okay."

"Jesus, Isabel!" The fierceness catches me off guard. "No. It's not okay, all right? It's not okay!"

"But I—" I falter. "I don't want you to feel bad."

"Not everything has to be okay all the time. And you need to stop pretending things are fine when they aren't." She lists examples off on her fingers. "You didn't want me to feel bad, so you didn't tell me about Alex. And you didn't tell me about stand-up. And most of all, you didn't tell me how neglected and unwanted you felt. You thought you were doing me a favor."

"Yeah."

She shakes her head. "You know what I kept thinking the other night? When I couldn't sleep?"

I fell asleep instantly, like the fight had sapped all my energy.

I feel awful now, thinking of her lying awake all night.

"This is you and the splinters, all over again."

"What?" I ask.

"When you were younger. You used to get all these splinters, from trees in the park. Do you remember that?"

Now that she says it, yeah. Almost every afternoon, after school, the twins and I would go to the park with our rotating cast of college-girl babysitters. The twins liked the sandbox and the swings, but I loved the trees. I wasn't supposed to climb them, but I did—or at least tried—at every opportunity.

I'd never do that now. I was so much braver then.

Maybe I can be again.

"I'd come home after work to find you in the corner of your room, fending off Ava or Caitlin and the tweezers. I tried to tell you the splinter had to come out. Even though it hurt. If we didn't yank it out fresh, it would just dig deeper and deeper into your body until it festered." She sighs. "It was going to hurt no matter what. You never wanted to hear that."

"It doesn't sound like I was very smart."

"You were only trying to protect yourself." She smiles, a bit sadly. "The splinter always came out, in the end. A real fight and some tears later, but we got it out. You and me."

You and me. I haven't felt like my mom and I were that for such a long time. Like—

"A pair," I say out loud, without quite meaning to.

She frowns. "What?"

"You and me," I repeat. "A pair. Sometimes I think about our family as two pairs. You and Dad together, and the twins together."

"And you?" she asks softly.

"The remainder."

Mom looks away. "We—" She clears her throat. "We've got to fix that."

I nod.

"I can't send you off into the world feeling like a remainder," she says, and breathes out heavily. "I only have a little more time, before you go."

"I'm sorry," I tell her. "For all the things I said the other night, about . . . us. I'm sorry I made you feel—"

"I'm sorry you felt like your job in this family was to be easy. I'm sorry you felt like you had a job at all."

I hurt myself in a thousand ways, and no one wanted it. It's both freeing and crushing to realize so many of the boxes I've contorted myself to fit inside . . . I built them.

"Work your hardest in school, but other than that—" When Mom looks at me, it seems like she's trying to keep from crying. "I just want you to be happy, in these last two years you have here. And if that involves some friends I wouldn't pick, some hobbies I wouldn't choose . . . so be it. The consequences will never be lighter than they are now. It's a good time to get into a little trouble."

"Thank you."

She straightens up, suddenly all business. "It doesn't mean there aren't consequences, though."

"What do you mean?"

"I mean you're grounded."

"But—I've never been grounded."

"Don't worry," she says, fighting a smile. "It does not have a steep learning curve."

"Mom!"

"Yes?"

"Nothing."

"That's what I thought." She kisses me on the forehead. "I've got to get to work. I'll see you tonight for dinner."

She shuts the door after her. I just sit there for a couple minutes, trying to figure out what you're supposed to *do* when you're grounded. She didn't say anything about my computer and didn't take my phone, either. Sort of an oversight, but hey. This is new for both of us.

When I grab my phone off my dresser, the calendar reminder automatically pops up:

ALL-COLLEGE SHOWCASE: TODAY 3 PM

An hour from now.

I put the phone down. I already decided I wasn't going. It never crossed my mind I was actually going to win a spot in the first place. Maybe if Sean the Bartender hadn't blown my cover, maybe if I still had my friends to help me through it, this would be a possibility. But now that they all know who I really am—

357

It isn't enough to stay home, I realize. *That isn't enough.*

For so long, I was so certain Isabel and Izzy were different people. That Isabel was who I used to be, and Izzy was who I truly am. I thought it was a transformation. But it wasn't, not exactly. Being Izzy was my real life, but so was being Isabel. The only parts that weren't real were the lies.

There are the lies I told myself, that I could never be strong, never be heard, never really matter. I know those things aren't true now.

There are the lies other people told me, that I was unlovable, I was nobody, I was small and should make myself even smaller for their benefit. I don't believe them anymore.

There are the lies I told other people, to get what I wanted. I haven't accounted for those yet. And I need to. I want to.

If the Showcase organizers know I'm not coming, someone else can go up in my place. It won't be a loss, that way. If I come clean now, if I tell the truth, I can still make things right.

There's a contact number in the email I got, but when I call, it goes straight to a full voice-mail box. Maybe I could text, or send an email, but there's no guarantee they'll see it in time. I call again. No answer.

My feet are on the floor, my hands are grabbing whatever shoes are closest, and my mind is racing into overdrive, because I know what I have to do. It would be too easy to stay home, curl up into my bed, and forget what was happening all around me. It would be easy, but it wouldn't be right.

I have choices, but they're mine to make. I have a voice, but it's up to me to use it. I have a chance to make things right, but I have to take it.

And it has to be today.

The auditorium is packed when I get there, and I'm surprised by how many people I recognize. There's Dave in one of the audience seats, scarfing chips and chatting up a beleaguered-looking girl next to him, one of the Aidans taking a selfie by the *All-College Showcase* banner, and so many faces I can pair with sets, and bits, and fist bumps after shows. So many people who said "Good set" to me after I went up, even if it wasn't true. And I realize— this is what I always wanted school to be like, but it never was. A community. A family. A home.

Even if my friends never forgive me for all the lies, even if I never get to go up again, I don't regret it. I can't. I found myself here.

It takes me forever to find Mo, and I almost cry with relief when I finally see her in the crowd. She isn't nearly as happy to see me. The second she spots me approaching, she holds up one hand, like she's a crossing guard and I'm a garbage truck waiting to run some ducklings over.

"Hi," I say, about to ask if she's seen whoever's in charge. But Mo has always been quicker than me.

"I don't want to talk."

"You don't have to talk."

359

"And I don't want to listen to *you* talk, either, okay?"

"That's not why I'm here," I say, trying not to show my impatience. "I—"

Just then, I catch sight of the same girl who ran the auditions and abandon Mo midsentence.

The girl seems even more frazzled this time, with a clipboard in her hands, two different pens lodged in her messy ponytail, and an expression that is half-panicked and half-homicidal.

"Hi," I say to her. "You're in charge, right?"

"Is it you?" she says, with so much hope in her voice I half expect her to hug me and say we're long-lost sisters. "Are you the last one?"

"I'm Izzy V.," I tell her, and she sighs with relief. "I'm one of the performers."

She crosses something off on her clipboard. "Yeah, and your call time was a half hour ago."

"I tried to call, but—"

"It doesn't matter." She waves me off. "Let's just get you signed in and we can get this thing started."

"Small problem," I say.

She throws a hand up impatiently. "Yeah? What?"

I clear my throat. "I can't perform."

"Of course you can," she says. "You're here."

"Yeah," I agree. "But I'm also sixteen."

She stares at me. Then says, loud enough for half the room to hear: "You're *what?*"

"I know," I say, leaning in closer, hoping she'll lower her voice a little. "I'm sorry, that's why I'm—"

"What the hell are you telling me right now?" the girl shouts, even louder.

That gets everyone's attention—including Mo's. She's beside us in a flash, angling herself so she's right between me and the girl in charge. I don't understand why until she says: "What's going on?" And then turns to me to ask: "Are you okay?"

Mo doesn't want to talk to me, or listen to me, or maybe ever forgive me, but she still wants to protect me. Like she always has.

"Yeah, I'm fine," I promise. "I was just explaining—"

"No *way*," the girl in charge shakes her head in clear disbelief. "No way you're sixteen."

It's actually impressive how many emotions Mo cycles through in the next half second. First confusion. Then realization at what I must have done. And finally, total shock I've done it. She stares at me and—maybe for the first time—has nothing to say.

"Go ahead." I shrug at Mo, then gesture at the girl in charge. "Tell her."

Mo's eyes might be stuck that wide forever, but she manages to say: "Yep. She . . . is sixteen."

"I wouldn't have registered anyone with a high school ID," the girl says.

"You didn't ask for my ID. I was very late for the audition, too."

There's a flicker of recognition across her face. She closes her eyes and groans for a full three seconds.

"Why," she says, almost begging, "would you audition for this?"

Good question. Difficult to explain in thirty seconds. I try anyway.

"So you know the Hydra in Greek mythology, where you cut off one head but then like eight heads grow from the stump? It turns out lies are a lot like Hydras—not that they're snakes, but—" I look to Mo. "Is it a snake, or is it more like a big lizard?"

"Stop," the girl orders me.

I nod. "Okay."

"What am I supposed to do?" she says, but it's less to me, more to the universe that has betrayed her. "There's supposed to be ten of you. What am I supposed to tell the judges, I let a kid sign up?"

"You could, um." I steal a quick glance at Mo, then look down at my shoes. "You could ask one of the alternates."

I feel Mo's head snap around to stare at me, but I don't look back at her.

I think: *You should have this, if you want it.*

I think: *If you want this, I want it for you.*

I say: Nothing. Not because I can't, but because I shouldn't.

It doesn't matter how much I want her up on the stage. It's not my decision. It's not my job to choose that for her, and it shouldn't be. My only job was to tell the truth.

What comes next is up to Mo.

"It's two minutes before the show!" the girl snaps at me. "I don't even know if any alternates are *here*. What do you expect me to—"

Mo clears her throat. The girl stops short. Mo raises her hand.

"I'm here," she says.

It takes a moment for the girl to get it. "You're an alternate?" she asks. Mo nods. The girl takes the pen from her ponytail and the clipboard from under her arm. "Which one are you?"

"Last name Irani," Mo says, "First name Mo."

The girl circles something, then makes a few notations on the sheet in front of her. When she shrugs, it's like her whole body is waving a white flag. "Okay."

Mo and I look at each other. We're both thinking the same things—it couldn't be this easy, right? No pushback, no debate, no need for an impassioned speech?

"What do you mean 'okay'?" Mo asks.

"I mean okay." The girl sticks the clipboard back under her arm. "You're in the lineup. You get three minutes, don't go over your time, and if you have to pee or throw up or whatever, do it now."

"Wait." Mo holds up both hands, like she's reconsidering. "There were three alternates. Shouldn't we see if the other two—"

"Nope," the girl says, glancing down at the clipboard again. "You're first on the list; you're the first alternate I would have called." She looks back up at me. "If I'd had more than *two minutes' notice.*"

"I tried calling!" I protest. Both of them ignore me.

"Any questions?" the girl asks. Mo shakes her head. "Okay. Well, Mo, you're going up first, so . . . hope you're prepared."

Mo blanches at that news, but her voice doesn't waver. "Yeah, I'm—it's all good."

"Go wait over there." The girl jerks her head at the small group of performers waiting by the stage. One boy is shaking both hands like they're covered with bees. Another is chugging from a water bottle like he just got airlifted out of the Sahara. I can practically hear Mo's heart trying to launch itself out of her chest, so she'll fit in just fine.

"Thank you," Mo says to her, and this time, her voice does shake. Just a little.

"Yeah, please don't." The girl gestures again to the waiting performers and then stalks away.

Mo turns to me. "I don't understand why you did this."

"You deserve it," I say. "It should have been you all along. I'm just . . . fixing a mistake."

"You winning wasn't a mistake."

"That's not the one I mean."

Mo looks over at the boys gathered by the stage. I know what she's feeling, at least some of it, I think. The nerves and the adrenaline and the desperate need to hear your own voice in the silence.

So when she asks me, "Are you going to stay?" I know why. As mad as she is with me, she wants me here. She wants me to hear her.

I smile. "They'd have to drag me out."

A few days ago, Mo would have hugged me. Squeezed my hand. Said something sweet and funny and charming I'd think about all day. But today, she smiles back, then leaves me where I'm standing.

The judges are taking their seats at the table, and for a moment, I have second thoughts. Maybe something could have come of this. They liked me enough to give me a slot, and if they ever see me again, at an open mic or a club, will they remember who I am? I'm throwing away not just this opportunity, but future ones, too. But when I look at Mo, now standing with the other performers, I'm certain, all over again.

I'm not throwing anything away. I'm setting things right, making this moment the way it should be. And maybe—I hope against hope—I'm starting to piece something broken back together.

I take the long way around the chairs set up for the audience. If Will and Jonah see me, they don't call me over. But I don't look for them, either. Instead, I find a spot in the very back, by the doors. And I wait, for something I've seen so many times before, but I might never get to see again.

And then there she is, clambering up the steps in her giant boots, waving to an audience who already loves her, because how could you not? She adjusts her bow tie—a sure tell that she's nervous—but the way she plucks the mic from its stand, you'd never know it.

"Hi," she says, standing onstage, in the spotlight, like she was born for it. "My name's Mo Irani, and I can't tell you how happy I am to be here."

CHAPTER 26

MY MOM SEES her world like flower petals, each part necessary to create something beautiful. For a long time, I assumed mine was like a solar system, where I was at the center—or should be. But now I think it's more like an endless hallway of doors—some that you can choose to open yourself, and some that other people have to open for you.

One by one, they open their doors, and let me back in.

Naomi is first. We get to choose our own seats in AP US History, and I used to choose a seat in the back corner, where it was easier for me to hide. But lately, I've been sitting in the front row, where it's easier for me to hear. I couldn't hide now, even if I wanted to. Having a very loud, very public fight in the cafeteria ended that.

Naomi always sat in the back, too. But in the opposite corner, as far away from me as possible. And then one day, she slides into the seat next to me. She doesn't talk. Neither do I. But I feel her there, and the distance between us.

We sit side by side for two days before she says finally: "I didn't expect that. For you to . . . be funny. Like that," she adds, and we both know she means more than she's saying.

"Thanks."

"But—" She wrinkles her nose. "You've kind of screwed yourself, right? With your new friends."

"They weren't ever my friends," I tell her. "Not really."

"And your boyfriend?"

"I don't have a boyfriend."

She doesn't look as surprised as I expected. Maybe she already knew.

"Where do you go for lunch?" she asks. "You don't come to the cafeteria."

My breath catches at that—she has been looking for me.

"The library. Or Ms. Waldman's room."

"Jack keeps telling people you're too scared to show your face."

I snort. *I'm* scared? "Let him, I guess."

She nods. But then, after a beat, she shakes her head. "No. Don't."

"Huh?"

"Show everyone he's wrong." She goes back to her notes. "We'll—" Her eyes stay on her paper, but I can see the hesitation, the uncertainty, and the decisiveness on her face. All of it, all at once. "I'll save you a seat."

Will is next. He invites me out the following week, to an open mic in a coffee shop, clearly picking a day Mo and Jonah were both busy.

"They know," he assures me. "They're cool with it. They're just not—"

"Ready?" I ask. "To see me?"

"For things to go back to normal," he says. "It's going to take a little time."

For Jonah, it takes another week. He surprises me one night, showing up halfway through my set. It takes me a moment to place his voice. And then when I do, it might be the first time a comic teared up at a heckle.

But Mo stays away, week after week. Will tries to make me feel better, saying she's really busy with school stuff. Or spending time with her girlfriend. Or in California for a long weekend, celebrating the Persian New Year with her parents. I believe him, but there are nights I know they must all be out together, without me. I don't blame her. I don't blame them, either. But it slices my heart all the same.

Will lets me vent about it nearly every time we see each other, because he's nice like that. And he always tries to get me to see it from Mo's perspective, because he's fair like that.

"She thought you two were so close," Will explains as we sit at our usual sticky table in the Forest. "That's why it hurt so much. When she figured out how little she actually knew you."

But when he goes to the bar to get another round, I grab my

opportunity to talk with Jonah alone.

"You're all going out without me, right?" I blurt out. Jonah slowly puts down his water but says nothing. "I only see you guys every couple weeks now and I know it must be because you're going out with Mo."

Jonah shakes his head. "If you know, then what do you want me to say?"

I start to say *I don't know*, but that isn't the truth. The truth is more difficult, but it's more important, too. "I want you to say . . ." I gulp. "That it won't be like this forever."

He's quiet for a while, and the silence nearly swallows me alive. "You're waiting for things to go back to the way they were."

I nod. "Yeah."

"Well, stop waiting," he tells me. "It's not going to happen."

How can he be so sure? It feels almost the same with Will now. "But—"

Jonah cuts me off with a gesture. "No, Izzy. You lied to us. For months."

"I know, and I'm so sorry, I've said I'm sorry a million times—"

"Yeah, okay," Jonah says. "But apologies aren't magic."

I almost tear up, because apologies are all I have, and if apologies aren't enough, then nothing is going to be enough. I almost ask him: *What else can I do?* But then I realize—that's his point. I've done everything that I could to fix my mistakes, but that doesn't mean they disappeared. I hurt my friends. And hurt lingers.

"Also," he continues, "it's kind of weird for adults to hang out with a high school girl all the time. Things are different not just because you lied, but what you lied about."

I didn't tell them who I was because I thought they'd treat me differently, and I didn't think that was fair. I didn't really consider what was fair to *them*.

"We've got to set boundaries." Jonah leans back in his chair. "And you've got to accept them."

I nod. We're quiet for a while, but this time, the silence doesn't drown me. He doesn't have anything more to say. And I have to accept that.

"You don't have to invite me out," I say finally. "Anymore. If it's too hard for you guys."

His response is an eye roll. "So dramatic. Will and I aren't abandoning you." He looks over my shoulder and waves. "And not to steal the moment, but neither is Mo."

I spin around in my seat. There, standing in the door, is Mo. I get to my feet, but then don't know what to do next.

"You guys take your time, okay? We'll give you space." Jonah pushes himself up from the table and heads to the bar.

Mo crosses the distance between us slowly, hesitantly. We stand an awkward distance apart, not quite knowing whether to be within arm's length of each other.

"I know I lied to you," I say. "Like . . . a lot."

She nods.

"And if you can't forgive me, I get it," I say.

She nods.

"And I'm sorry. I know I said it before, and I know it isn't magic, but I'll keep saying it for the next fifty years anyway."

"That's optimistic," she says.

"Assuming we'll still talk in fifty years?"

"Assuming the world will still exist in fifty years."

Touché. She cracks a smile, and so do I. Then she steps forward to close the gap, and I rush to meet her.

"I'm really glad you picked tonight," I tell her when we break from our hug. "To come."

She raises an eyebrow. "Why?"

I flash her my bundle of brightly colored note cards. "I'm trying out something new."

"Catcalling is the weirdest thing," I say into the mic, under the light, before all my friends. "Don't you guys think?" I pause. "And by 'guys,' I mostly mean 'girls.'"

"Woooo!" Mo cheers from the audience. Another girl who went up before me claps, too.

"See?" I point them out. "The exactly two women in this bar know what I'm talking about. I always wonder—what do these guys think is going to happen? Do they think some girl is going to swoon at their feet, like"—I take on the voice of a Disney princess—"'At long last! For six long years, I have waited at this accursed intersection, pining for the day a brave knight with a vape pen would ask to motorboat me from the back of his friend's Kia Sorento!'"

Who would have ever known the things I used to hide inside my head could make people laugh like that? It still doesn't seem quite real. But I soak up the laughter, without worrying why it's coming.

"It's taken me a long time to realize there are some men for whom the world is made *entirely* out of stuff to masturbate to. Seventh-grade style. Like they grew out of the wispy little mustaches and basketball shorts as formal wear, but not the constant, inexplicable boners." I take a step away from the mic stand and try to set the stage for an anecdote. "I used to go to this sleepaway camp, and one time, this boy got a boner at breakfast because of the Mrs. Butterworth syrup bottle on the table." I smile as I'm saying it, because it really was ridiculous. "I know. But can you blame him? She's a very proportional condiment. Girls would kill for that waist-to-hip ratio." I wait a beat. "If Mrs. Butterworth suddenly came to life, she'd be an Instagram influencer selling diet teas that light your intestines on fire.

"But I think the worst part about getting catcalled is when someone apologizes. Because it's never to you, right?" I nod, as if I can tell the audience is agreeing with me. "No guy on a street corner has ever been like, 'You know, after a little self-reflection, I've realized that asking you to sit on my face is probably inappropriate stranger-to-stranger interaction.'" As I talk, I walk over to the other side of the stage.

"One time, a guy said something gross to me," I say, "but

then he realized my boyfriend was next to me and instantly, just like, fell all over himself." I put on a dude-bro voice. "'Oh, I'm so sorry, man, I didn't realize.' He apologized to *him*. Not to me! And my boyfriend was like"—no one here will appreciate my excellent Alex impression, but I do it anyway—"'Oh, it's cool, no worries.'" I slip back into my own voice. "They were so polite to each other, so *sweet*, it was like watching the first five minutes of a rom-com."

That gets a laugh.

"So . . . I broke up with him. Because who was I to get in the way of their happiness?"

And so does that.

By the time the set is done (fifteen laughs over five minutes, not too bad for all-new jokes) my mouth is bone-dry. Instead of going back to my table, I head straight to the bar.

"Hey, Colin," I say, sidling up to the counter.

"Hey yourself," he replies. "What can I get you?"

I point at the tripod and camera set up on the bar, angled toward the stage. "Was that on, during my set?"

The first time I came back to the Forest, I wondered if Colin would have me kicked out, since he knew how old I actually was. But instead, he laid out his terms: I'm still allowed to watch my friends or perform, as long as:

1. It's during the week.
2. I'm chaperoned by someone he trusts.
3. I maintain a blood alcohol level of 0.000.

I instantly agreed, and we shook on it. But this is the first time I've performed since the fallout, so it's the first time I know I'm being taped.

"Oh, yeah," he says, sounding apologetic. "I took over doing it after Sean left." He shakes his head. "I'm real sorry he did that to you, you know? Doesn't matter how old you are."

"It's not your fault. Not at all."

"Still sorry about it," He reaches toward the camera. "You're young. Maybe you can show me how to delete your part from the tape."

"No!" I say, with so much force we're both a little surprised. "I mean, no, please don't delete it. I want it."

"You want it?" He sounds as unsure as I feel, but I nod.

"Yeah. I want to be able to put it out there," I explain. "But on my own terms. You know?"

"Well, okay, but I can't promise on the quality."

"As long as you can hear my voice," I tell him, "I'll be happy."

It takes Colin twelve hours to send me the video. It takes me fifteen minutes to set up a brand-new YouTube account, three minutes to upload the clip, and thirty seconds to post the link on every social media account I have.

It takes one weekend for the entire school to see it.

When I show up on Monday morning, I can feel the eyes on my back, even if I can't make out the whispers. It's okay. I've got a video with more views than my school has people, a comments

375

section with equal parts praise and horrific ridicule, and a phone in my pocket with a text from a freshman girl I've never met, who says she wants to be just like me.

I want to be the kind of person who deserves that. Today, and tomorrow, and forever.

Not everyone liked the set, and that's okay. Not everybody at this school likes *me*, and that's okay, too. I have the people I need. Naomi, who meets me by the door of Ms. Waldman's classroom every day before lunch, so I won't have to walk alone. Ms. Waldman, whose door is always open. And new people, too—like Ms. Tayhoe, the school counselor. I'd never met her before, but Mom wanted me to talk with her, so I did. I thought it would be too weird to talk about personal things with a stranger, but it wasn't. She doesn't judge me; she only listens. And there's nothing as nice as being heard.

It doesn't matter to me that, on Monday, Jack watches the video with his friends at lunch, whispering about how bad I am and how weird I look onstage. Because when he notices me watching him, he looks back at me with a healthy amount of fear in his eyes, and quickly shuts it off.

And then I see Alex.

He hasn't tried to talk to me, or convince me I made a mistake, or grab me in the hall, like I worried he might. I think my mom and Ms. Tayhoe had something to do with it. "The counselor knows how to handle it. She said it happens a lot, unfortunately," Mom told me. And then her face crumpled. "I'm sorry, Isabel.

I didn't know how much it happened."

Alex is at his usual table, in his usual spot, with a new empty place next to him. He stares at me, long and hard. He doesn't say anything, not that I could ever hear him in a place like this. He doesn't have to. I got so good at reading his moods, reading his face.

How could you do this? his tightly clenched jaw says to me. *How could you talk about me like that?*

He was never as good at figuring me out— or maybe he never really tried. But I try to tell him, without words, with all this distance between us:

There are so many things I could have said about you.

There are so many worse things I could tell the world about you.

I could tell everyone how he isolated me from my best friend. How he demanded all my time, all my attention, all of me. How he scared me, on purpose, and liked doing it. How he lied to me, made me think I was crazy and unlovable and needed him.

That's the worst part. He made me believe I needed him to love me, because no one else would. And he never even loved me at all.

I know what love looks like, *real* love, the kind my mom shows me, even if she isn't perfect. The kind my friends have for me, even when I make mistakes. That unshakable, ever-fixed mark. But I'm not sure Alex has ever seen what it looks like. He's responsible for what he did to me. That's a fact. He was damaged long before he met me. That's a fact, too.

So I try, in this wordless way, to tell him:

I hope you treat the next girl better than you treated me.

I hope you figure out how to care about someone, better than your parents ever cared about you.

I hope one day you know what it feels like, too.

We share one last, long look. One last moment of quiet between two people who know each other so well and not at all.

Then I turn around.

CHAPTER 27

FLOWERS BLOOM ALL year round. In every corner of the earth, in the harshest of climates and most temperate paradises, in the coldest winter snap and hottest dog days of summer, there is always something showing its face to the sun. And something still underground, too, waiting for its chance.

In the Arctic, cotton grass springs up by the rivers and wetlands, soft and white, like the snow that came before them. In Death Valley, wildflowers carpet the desert deep purple and gold, thriving where so little does and scattering their seeds for the life that's still to come.

But here, in June—it's like the universe unfurls itself. First, so slowly you barely notice it happening, and suddenly, you're surrounded by summer. Here, in the only home I've ever known, daylilies and lavender and roses finally emerge from their buds, with white ash trees green and leafy, and dogwoods in full flower.

And maybe, so late in the season it seems impossible, a single white orchid, too.

Not every day in June is beautiful, but Mo and all the other graduates got lucky, because this one is spectacular. The sky is clear and an almost unearthly blue above the University of Chicago's main quad. Next to me in the guest seating, a family wearing matching pins that say *Congrats, Josh* slather on sunscreen. I should probably ask for some. There's no shade here, and I could burn. But the way the sun wraps its warmth around me like a blanket, I can't imagine putting anything between us.

I still can't believe I'm here—I thought you'd need tickets or something for a college graduation. It feels so important, and it looks that way, too, with all the giant maroon banners flapping in the breeze, all the graduates in their caps and gowns, the deans and provosts and other titles I don't know with honest-to-God *robes*.

I went to Charlotte and Peter's high school graduation, but nothing about that—the scratchy microfiber seats in our school's stuffy auditorium, the orchestra's unenthusiastic rendition of "Pomp and Circumstance," the brag-filled speech by the valedictorian, aka Charlotte's archenemy—none of that was like this. If that graduation felt like an inevitability, this one feels like a celebration.

Outside, under the blue sky, with wind whipping around the graduates' tassels and birds singing in the trees nearby, I'm sitting on my own, but I'm surrounded by hundreds of other people who only want the same thing I do: to see the people we love cross the stage in front of us, and walk out into a brand-new life.

Jonah is first, and his gigantic family nearly breaks the sound barrier when his name is read. He eats up every second. I try to match their energy when Mo walks next, cheering so loudly the nice family next to me jumps. The way she smiles out into the crowd, I think she can hear me. I do the same for Will and then again at the end of the ceremony.

How amazing, I think, that this is the way they get to leave. That this is the day, and the place, and the moment they get to say goodbye to a part of their lives. Four years. That's an entire quarter of my entire life. It's easy to imagine leaving high school behind, but it's harder to imagine this. If high school feels like preparation for college, then college feels like preparation for . . . life. Real life. And how do you start your real life?

While the closing anthem plays, and the new graduates stand to file away, I try to capture this moment in my brain. Every sight, and sound, and scent, and lock it safely inside myself.

Songbirds in the trees, the sun on my face, the grass brushing up against my bare ankles, and the good in everything.

The aftermath of the graduation is controlled chaos. All the grads are dressed the same, which makes it almost impossible to find anyone. But I do, in the end.

I get a hug from Jonah, who takes a moment of relief away from the approximately eighty-seven members of his family who showed up. Then Will finds us both, flanked by his parents and two siblings.

"This is a zoo," Will says. "We're going to book it out of here."

"Yeah, I know. Maybe we can hang next week, though?" Jonah looks to both of us. Will nods, and so do I. Nothing could make me happier than the two of them deciding to stay in Chicago after graduation.

Except maybe if Mo had.

I find her last, after the boys have long since disappeared into the crowds. Her parents were seated in the accessibility section, way up front and way on the far side of the quad, so it takes us a while to spot each other.

"Congratulations." I hug her as tightly as I can. "I'm so happy for you."

"Yeah," she says, and her voice is strained, higher than normal. With my hands still on her shoulders, I take a step back so I can see her face.

"Are you okay?" Her eyes are too bright and her muscles under my fingers too tense for the answer to be yes. "What's wrong?"

"Nothing." She looks away. "I'm being so stupid. I'm fine—"

"Mo." I don't let go. "Tell me."

She stares past me, and I know what she's seeing. All the classmates she might never see again, under the banners of the school she chose, on the campus that's been her home for so long.

"I don't think I can do this," she admits.

"What?" I ask. "Graduate?" I reach out and shift her tassel around to the correct side. "I think you just did."

She bites her lip so hard it goes white. "No. I don't know if—you know."

"I don't, Mo," I admit. "I'm not really there yet."

"Move on." She shrugs helplessly. "Grow up."

They've always seemed so grown up to me. With apartments, and opinions, effortless abilities to navigate the world. But here is Mo, close to tears, and she doesn't feel grown up at all. I've always imagined it as something that just *happens*, at the preordained time. You hit eighteen, and the world makes sense. You make it to twenty-one, and there's no question about who you are in it. Maybe that isn't true. Maybe Shakespeare was wrong, and people aren't like plants, growing all for one short moment to blossom in the world.

Maybe we're perennials, who survive year after year, with moments we bloom and moments we die back. We return to our rootstock, to what's underground and unseen. When the earth gets cold and hard around us, we go back to that small seed. The core of who we are. And when we're ready, when we're stronger and older and better for the time we spent below, we raise ourselves above the ground.

And then we bloom all over again.

"I thought I knew what I wanted, but maybe I don't," Mo says, her words spilling out fast and raw. "Maybe I shouldn't move to New York. I'm not good enough to compete with comics out there—*real* comics, *real* people. I'm not ready to be on my own, without you and Will and—" She squeezes my arm. "Everything's changing. And I'm not ready."

I squeeze back. "You're never going to be ready," I say, and I can hear her, all those months ago, sitting with me in the Forest, teaching me how to write a joke. I wonder if she can hear herself, too. "You have to try it anyway. It's the only way you're going to learn."

She must remember, because she smiles. Then she lets go of my arm so she can wipe at her eyes.

"You're going to be fine," I promise her. "You're going to be great."

"Thanks," she says. Then her face nearly crumples again. "I'm really going to miss you."

"I'll come visit. On school breaks."

The gulf between us hasn't ever felt bigger, as I say that. Next year, I'll still have winter breaks, and the SATs, and a curfew. Mo and the boys will have jobs, and taxes, and an unknown future stretched out in front of them. It seems so exciting, all those possibilities. Everything their lives could be. And it seems scary, too, and overwhelming, and so . . . unknowable.

My world might be smaller, with fewer choices, but it has more handholds, too. I can see what's ahead of me, and I'm going to try to enjoy all the moments, simple and safe as they are, for as long as they last.

"Hey, so. We're going to get lunch." Mo turns to wave down her parents, who are still waiting in the accessibility section, talking with her girlfriend. "Do you want to come?"

I almost say yes, because it's an hour with Mo, and I don't have many of those left. But then I see her parents. Her dad, tall and with her exact same nose, pushing the wheelchair where her mom sits, looking at Mo with such overwhelming pride. Mo and I are family, with Will and Jonah. But this was her family first. This is a moment they deserve to share together.

"You guys go ahead." I hug her one more time. "I have somewhere I've got to be."

I double-check the address on my phone, then against the plain brick building in front of me. Triple-check. I have to actively resist a fourth time.

This isn't my first time, but it is my first time going alone. I could have picked a place I knew, somewhere that didn't scare me, somewhere I was known. But sometimes, what you really need is a brand-new stage. So this is the place I chose: the Robin. There's no sign, but it's the right address.

It's at a theater, not a bar, and it's all ages—I called and checked. It's an annoying thing to have to do, especially when so many of them are eighteen and older, unless you've got an adult with you. But it's also the right thing to do. Mom said she'd be my date to the places I needed a chaperone for, as long as I gave her enough time to block her calendar and didn't do material about her. It's a fair trade.

I don't know what's wrong with me, why I'm hesitating this way. I've been here before. Not to this door, but to this moment: standing at a threshold, with everything familiar at my back, and something unknown on the other side. It's hard to think of myself as the same girl who stumbled into her first open mic in January, but I am. Even if I've been engrafted new, she's not gone. Not entirely. She's in my roots, and nothing can bloom without its roots.

When I put my hand on the door, it feels heavy, like it might be locked, but all it takes is one gentle push, and it swings open.

ACKNOWLEDGMENTS

Comedy depends on the rule of threes. But since I figure you've read enough jokes at this point, I'll present you with three facts, instead.

Fact #1: I love stand-up comedy, and I love books.

Fact #2: Combining the two was much, much harder than I expected.

Fact #3: This book would not have been possible without the hard work and support of many people, all of whom have my eternal thanks.

My editor, Ben Rosenthal, whose insight, enthusiasm, and expert guidance helped me find the heart of this story. Thank you for believing in my ideas, despite the fact that they never have good comp titles, and for so rarely vetoing my jokes, even when you probably should.

My agents, both former and current: Sarah LaPolla, who was Izzy's first champion, and Natalie Lakosil, who helped me bring her into the world.

The entire team at Katherine Tegen Books, who made this book a reality.

My writer's group—Brian, Emily, Michelle, and Siena—who give the best feedback and bring the best snacks.

Leah, who was always the greatest test audience for my childhood comedy routines and is still my favorite critic two decades later.

My mother, who always made sure to tell me when I had "a good line" that deserved to be written down somewhere.

My father, who introduced me to *Saturday Night Live*, Monty Python, and Mel Brooks by the time I was ten and dutifully explained each and every inappropriate joke.

And most of all, Rob, who likes to say, "one day you'll appreciate my jokes," as if he isn't already the funniest person I know.

Thank you. Thank you. Thank you.

TURN THE PAGE TO START READING

GIDEON GREEN IN BLACK AND WHITE

CHAPTER 1

THE THIRD-GREATEST TRAGEDY of my life is that I don't live in a film noir.

The second-greatest tragedy of my life is that it's 498 days until my eighteenth birthday, which means 498 days until I get to leave San Miguel, California, more specifically, Presidio High School, and more broadly, my holding pattern of a life here.

Don't worry about the first-greatest tragedy, because it happened a long time ago and isn't interesting or special at all. It happens to lots of people, and I prefer to focus on the ways I'm not like most people.

Here are two examples:

Everyone else at lunch is wearing shorts and T-shirts, and I am wearing a trench coat.

Everyone else is eating lunch together, and I am eating alone.

Which is fine. It's good, actually, because it gives me space to think about things.

Like how nobody would ever eat a brown-bagged lunch in film noir. I can't think of any noir I've seen where the private investigator eats a chicken focaccia sandwich, and I've seen pretty much every movie in the genre. Nobody goes to high school in film noir, either, but no matter how many times I ask, Dad won't let me drop out. So here I am.

You're probably picturing me in a school cafeteria with a lunch line and tables fiercely guarded by rival cliques, but you shouldn't. That's a trope. Every kind of movie has its tropes—the things you know you're going to see, the things you start to expect—and is there a bigger one for teen dramas than cafeteria cliques?

Maybe there is. I don't watch a lot of them.

But this is Southern California. Nothing is indoors if it doesn't have to be, so benches and metal tables are scattered across the open-air campus. Everything here is sprawl, from freeways to lunch spots. And the only person who seems particularly attached to any given table is me.

Someone clears their throat. And when I look up, there's a whole crowd of someones gathered around my table.

Like I said, high school cliques are a trope, not reality, but if I had to sum this particular group up, I'd label them the Future Ivy Leaguer Overachievers. Perfect GPAs. Lots of extracurriculars. Would murder you with their bare hands if it meant moving one spot up on the class rank. Maybe that's not fair, I think, when I see Lily hovering in the back, looking uncomfortable. But after what she did to me . . . maybe it is.

And standing in front—so close her legs are touching my table, clearly in charge, clearly the one who cleared her throat— is Mia. I'm not sure exactly where it falls on my list, but the existence of Mia McElroy is definitely some type of tragedy.

If my life were a noir, Mia would be described in the script like this:

```
MIA MCELORY (F, 16): a real knockout dame with
legs that go all the way up to her pelvis
(because that's how legs work) and a slash of
red lipstick two shades darker than her hair.
```

But this is just high school, and Mia's just a girl with the personality of a piranha.

"Hi," Mia says, drawing out the word over five seconds so I can better hear the *go fuck yourself* subtext underneath. "We're going to need the table."

You're probably imagining her in a cheerleader uniform, but you shouldn't. That's another trope.

She clears her throat again. "Did you hear me?"

"Yes."

"So . . . ?"

"So, I don't agree." I take a bite of my sandwich. "You don't need the table."

"We do need the table, actually."

"Shelter is a need. Food is a need. Are you going to eat the table?"

"Oh my God," Mia mutters.

"Mia," I hear Lily say, but I refuse to look at her. "Maybe we could—"

"We need the table because unlike you, we have actual things to accomplish this lunch period," Mia says. "We're planning the Key Club's community food drive, which I know you couldn't possibly care about, because you don't care about helping the community, or like, anyone besides yourself."

I point at the lumbering guy at her shoulder—her boyfriend, I can't remember his name—who's texting on his phone, oblivious. "Really? *He's* helping with the food drive?"

Mia looks behind her. When she swats at her boyfriend's arm, he jumps out of his skin. "Could you get off your phone and do something about him?"

Mia's boyfriend shoves his phone in his pocket so fast you'd think it was on fire. He looks at me, then back to her. "But . . . he's just sitting there."

"Yeah, exactly," I say. "Thank you, Hired Goon."

"What?" he says.

Lily leans closer to Mia. "We could go on the lawn. If Gideon doesn't want to move—"

That's the first time I've heard Lily say my name in five years. Which wouldn't be remarkable, except she used to say it every day, when we were still best friends.

"No." Mia folds her arms. "We need a hard surface, and we need the space. He doesn't. There are plenty of other tables he could use—"

"But this is my table," I say.

"Smaller tables, more appropriate tables for one person—"

"I always sit at this table."

"—that would work just fine if *Gideon* would stop being so *selfish*."

I don't know what else to say to her. I chose this table in my second week of freshman year and I've sat here every single day since and so I have to sit here now. It makes perfect sense in my head, but I can tell from the way they're all staring at me it makes no sense to them.

"Why are you being so weird about this?" Mia snaps. "Just pick a different table."

"I'm not being weird."

"Of course you are," she says, then gestures at . . . well, all of me. "Who the hell wears a jacket when it's eighty degrees?"

"It's a trench coat. I always wear a trench coat." This gets no reaction. "People used to wear stuff like this all the time. And fedoras. And shoes that weren't made of plastic." I can tell I'm not helping my case, but I can't stop. "If someone from the 1930s or the '40s saw the way *you* dressed, they'd think *you* were the weird one. Not me."

"Wow. So you're really still doing it." When she smiles, it's toothless. "You're still playing detective."

I didn't play a detective, I was one. Was.

"I'm not a detective."

"It's almost cute," she continues, "how committed you are. Almost."

"You know, Mia, why don't you ask somebody else for their table?"

"Because you're the one eating alone."

"I always eat alone."

"Yeah. You do." Mia locks her sharp eyes on mine. "Have you ever wondered *why*?"

Maybe I could have left it there, if she hadn't said that. Or if it was someone else saying it. But after what they all put me through—Mia included, Mia *especially*—it's out of my mouth before I can stop myself.

"Your boyfriend is cheating on you."

Mia's eyes bug out. The aforementioned boyfriend's mouth drops open.

"*Excuse* me?" she says.

"Oh." I blink at her. "That means he's seeing somebody else."

She puts both hands on my table. "What the Jesus *fuck* is your problem, Gideon?"

"It's not my problem," I say. "It's your problem. Yours and—" I turn to her boyfriend, who still hasn't closed his mouth. "I'm sorry. I can't remember your name. Colton, Ashton, Braxton . . ."

"Matt," he says.

Okay, so I'm not batting a thousand.

"Matt," I repeat, "I'm sorry to be doing this to you, Matt—well, not that sorry, you *are* cheating on her." I take a breath and focus back on Mia. "Did you see how panicked he got, when you interrupted him before? I bet that's been happening a lot, lately. Right, Mia? He's all jumpy?"

Matt's phone rings in his pocket. Just once, a high, musical alert. He ignores it. "And see, *that's* interesting," I say. "That text alert, it's not the default tone. And no offense, Matt, but you seem like a default kind of guy."

"Dude," he says. "Don't do this."

Mia whirls around on him. "Don't do *what*, Matt?"

"I'm betting he programmed a special tone for one contact," I say. "A very special contact."

"Give me your phone," Mia says. "I want to see your phone."

"What? No!" Matt's hand rests protectively over his pocket.

"I just want to see your phone," she repeats, deadly calm. "Why can't I see your phone?"

"You don't need his phone," I assure her. "There are other clues."

Matt throws up his hands. "Clues? Nothing is happening!"

I point at Matt's face. "He's trying to grow a beard, too. Can you see that? I mean, it's not working, but—" I shrug. "Do you *like* beards, Mia? I bet you don't. So who's *that* for, do you think?"

"Shaving was irritating my skin!" Matt protests.

"His clothes are new, too, like he's trying to impress

somebody." I gesture at his pants. "Forgot to take the size sticker off."

Matt looks down at his jeans, swears, and rips off the sticker.

"What the hell is going on?" Mia yells at him, though she's pointing at me. "Is that little asshole right?"

Five feet six is exactly average height for a sixteen-year-old American male, but I don't think she's in the correct mental state to hear that right now.

"Babe, of course not," Matt pleads with her.

"It's Ava Clark, isn't it."

"Does Ava Clark wear pink lip gloss?" They stop and turn to stare at me. "Like sort of a peachy color, kind of neutral, little bit of glitter?"

"Why?" Mia, vibrating with rage, bites off the word. *"Why, Gideon?"*

"Oh, no reason." I point to my own shirt collar. "Just the stain on his jacket."

Mia looks for it. Finds it. And that's when she really explodes, a volcanic ball of righteous fury erupting in the middle of the open-air quad.

"What is that, Matt?" she demands. *"Whose* is that?" She gestures to her red lips. "Because it's definitely not mine!"

"Mia," he says, eyes shifting around the crowd that's started to gather around us. "I can explain." She waits. He flounders. Then— "Did you know humans were never meant to be monogamous?"

Swing and a miss, Hired Goon.

"I can't believe you!" she shouts at him. "You are, you're cheating on me!"

"Yeah. He is." I lean forward and smile at her. "Have you ever wondered *why*?"

For a second, Mia almost looks like she's going to slap me.

Then she does slap me.

CHAPTER 2

MR. WALLACE WOULD be a terrible detective.

He chose to be a high school principal, so it doesn't matter, but detectives have to be organized. They can't have papers covering every inch of their desk or folders piled up to the windows. How can you find clues if you can't even find a pen?

Another reason he wouldn't be a good detective: he doesn't have any clue how to lead an interrogation. He hasn't asked me a single question yet, and this chair is very comfortable. There's even a cushion. It's like he doesn't know the basics.

Maybe it's not an interrogation. It shouldn't be. It wasn't my fault.

Mr. Wallace types for a moment on his computer, then cranes his head around the screen to look at me.

"Gideon . . . ?"

"Green."

He types some more. Then stops. Then rolls his wheelie chair away from the computer, so that he and I are eye to eye.

"Have I seen you before?" he asks.

Here's something I like about noir movies: they don't blur the background. In most classic cinema, the camera focuses only on the person in the foreground and whatever they're saying and doing and feeling. And whoever's in the background . . . they're a washed-out blur. In film noir, the people in the background stay in focus. They still matter.

Lots of movies still blur out anyone in the background. Lots of people do, too.

"Have I?" Mr. Wallace prompts me. "Seen you in my office?"

I shake my head.

"Your name sounds so familiar," he says. "Gideon Green."

I shrug. He folds his hands on his desk.

"All right. Can you tell me what happened at lunch?"

"I told Mia her boyfriend was cheating on her. And then she hit me." I pause. "And then her boyfriend pulled her off and she started yelling at him—I mean, she was already yelling, but she yelled louder. And then he started yelling back at her, and then Mia called Ava Clark a home-wrecking trash bag, which isn't accurate because Mia doesn't have a home."

"Okay. Well—"

"Obviously she has a *home*, but not one with her boyfriend. Ex-boyfriend. So how could Ava Clark be a home-wrecker, is what I'm saying."

He stares at me, unblinking, so I must have missed a step.

"Lunch ended," I add. "And then I went to chemistry. And then your receptionist came and got me and then it's right now."

"Do you . . ." He scans my face, looking for something and not finding it. "Do you have any thoughts about what happened today?"

"The average person has about forty-nine thoughts every minute," I say. "But I'm pretty sure I have more than that, so . . ."

He does another scan. "I mean, do you feel responsible at all, for what happened at lunch?"

I scoff. "I'm not the one who cheated on her."

"Don't you feel like it was cruel," he asks, "to tell Mia something like that? To embarrass her like that, in front of everybody?"

I wonder if he even considered *she* might have been cruel. A person can be class president and in the running for valedictorian and still be hell on wheels, too.

But he knows Mia. He likes her. And he's never seen me before.

"You know," I say, "*she's* the one who hit *me*."

From the look he gives me, it's clear he thinks I deserved it. And maybe I did. But only for the last thing I said. Not for the other stuff, not for telling Mia the truth. That's a detective's job. Telling the world what's real, even if people don't want to hear it.

I'm not a detective anymore, but I still care about the truth.

"Mia was . . . remorseful," he says. "About that."

Please. The only way *remorseful* is in Mia McElroy's vocabulary is as an SAT word.

"But she did seem concerned this was part of a pattern, for you."

"Pattern?"

"She said—" He checks his notes. "'Gideon thinks he's like Sherlock Holmes, but the only way he's like Sherlock Holmes is being a high-functioning sociopath.'"

I didn't want to get into this, but of course Mia would make sure I had no choice. "She means my detective work."

That sends his eyebrows sky-high. "I'm sorry, you're . . . a detective?"

He's using the wrong tense. Just like Mia.

"I *was* a detective. Not anymore." I cross my arms. "I retired."

It was called Green Private Investigations and I founded it in the summer after fourth grade. I had a sign and an office and everything. I'd wanted to get a real business license, too, like Dad had with his restaurants—his first one was just going up, then—but he said the county clerk's office would never do it.

I charged clients a dollar a day and commission if I recovered something valuable. I usually didn't. It was all sentimental stuff, and it's not like Jennie Burke's mangy stuffed rabbit was insured. But I can still remember the way she flung her arms around my waist when I got it back for her.

I found a lot of lost toys. Recovered missing bikes and stolen game controllers and things like that. Figured out who was stuffing mean notes in desks or who told on somebody for flooding the bathroom sink at school or whether someone was cheating at heads up, seven up. And then—

"Wait," Mr. Wallace says, and it dawns on his face. "I remember you."

All the tendons in my body tense at once. He doesn't remember *me*. He remembers one single thing I did when I was ten, and that's if I'm lucky.

"Gideon Green, I knew I remembered that name," he says slowly, like it's coming back to him in pieces. "You were on the local news. Five years ago, something like that? Someone's necklace had gone missing, and you led the cops right to it. That was you?"

"It was actually a necklace and earring set."

"And they did a little mock ceremony for you, right? Gave you a medal, the police chief shook your hand, they put you on the local news. My wife taped the segment, she thought it was so cute."

Yeah, just what every detective wants. To be adorable.

Then he stops. Frowns. "Or . . . were you on the news twice? Once with the medal, and another time later—"

"Nope," I interrupt. "Just once."

You can find yourself on the other side of adorable in a flat second.

He nods, though, so I guess he believes me. One more reason

Mr. Wallace would be a bad detective: his memory sucks. I wish everyone's did.

"When did you retire?" he asks.

I take a deep breath before answering. "Middle school."

I never saw it coming. I should have, when the whole summer between sixth and seventh grades passed with no customers. Just me and Lily in my dad's garage, boiling in the heat until Lily would force me to go back to her house, which at least had AC.

What's going on? I remember asking her. *Why aren't they coming back?*

I don't know, Gideon, she said. But she knew.

Here's what happened: puberty had hit everyone else like a freight train, and I didn't even notice. When Lily started updating me with who had kissed who and who had broken up, I didn't hear her. Or I didn't understand what it meant, I guess.

That August, Lily went to sleepaway camp. We'd spent every whole summer together since we were seven, but all the other girls were going. When she came back, she had different clothes and stiff shoulders and a look in her eyes that was far away.

She also had a lot of excuses, mostly for why she couldn't come over. And when seventh grade started—a blur of new buildings and new teachers and triple the kids of our elementary school—she started avoiding my eyes and practically hurtling herself out of earshot whenever the bell rang. By the time I got out to the quad, she'd already be at a table with a bunch of girls who stared daggers whenever I got too close.

Finally, Mia took it upon herself to deal with me. And being Mia, she did it with all the subtlety and compassion of a hand grenade.

Don't you get it? Mia snapped at me after she'd cornered me by my locker. *She doesn't want to hang out with you. So stop coming over, already.*

She's my best friend, I protested. *Why doesn't she want to—*

Mia flicked her eyes from my thrift-store fedora to the Dashiell Hammett paperbacks spilling out of my locker. *Yeah. It's a real mystery.*

I didn't talk to Lily again.

This isn't the first-greatest tragedy of my life. Tragedies are bad things that happen without anybody clear to blame, which is what makes them tragic.

This was a straight-up betrayal.

Mr. Wallace shuffles papers around on his desk, watching me out of the corner of his eye. I think I was quiet for too long. I think I was supposed to say something, even though I didn't have anything to say.

"Well. Obviously, the events of today were . . . unfortunate," Mr. Wallace says.

"I'm sorry," I say. It's a little bit true. "I didn't know Mia was going to flip out like that." That's all the way true.

"Maybe you two could talk it through," he says, sounding hopeful. "We could set you and Mia up for peer counseling."

"Wouldn't we have to be peers, first?"

He closes his eyes. Sighs. Opens them again. "Just . . . please keep your deductions to yourself in the future."

I nod. "Okay."

He gets up, leads me to the door, and gestures out into the empty hallway. "I sincerely hope I don't see you here again."

He won't. I know what I am. Just a blur in the background.